CW00670019

RACING TIDES

First Published in Great Britain 2024 by Mirador Publishing

Copyright © 2024 by John Stephenson

All rights reserved. No part of this publication may be reproduced or transmitted, in any form or by any means, without permission of the publishers or author. Excepting brief quotes used in reviews.

First edition: 2024

Any reference to real names and places are purely fictional and are constructs of the author. Any offence the references produce is unintentional and in no way reflects the reality of any locations or people involved.

ISBN: 978-1-917411-14-1

Racing Tides

A naval action thriller

John Stephenson

Also by the Author
The Peak Line
Grod's Secret War

Chapter 1

The Straits of Hormuz

THE OFFICER OF THE WATCH felt the sweat trickle down his back as he scanned the horizon with field glasses. His clothes were sticking to him like glue as the temperature soared to more than fifty degrees in the midday heat with the sun high overhead. To the west was the coast of the Sultanate of Oman and the desert. Searching to the east the topography of Iran was clearly visible through the shimmering heat haze. One deck below in the Operations Room the people manning the plot were keeping a watchful eye on all shipping transiting the Straits. Leading Seaman Roy Stringer, an experienced radar operator, drew everyone's attention to a number of small, fast-moving vessels speeding away from the Iranian coast.

'They look to be approaching that tanker heading north about ten miles ahead of us,' observed the young Sub-Lieutenant, James Gartmore.

'That'll be the *American Eagle*,' responded Lieutenant Simon Barrington. 'She's American owned and registered. A quarter of a million tons. A big one.'

'Sir, there's a signal from the *USS Addison Burke*,' reported Yeoman Catherine Murray. 'They say the Iranians are threatening the *American Eagle*, but they are thirty miles to the north and too far away to intervene immediately. They ask us to give the tanker urgent assistance.'

Lieutenant Barrington passed the signal to the Officer of the Watch, Lieutenant Guy Hanson.

'Captain to the bridge,' called Hanson over the Tannoy system.

The captain appeared looking rather bleary-eyed and suffering from the heat. Hanson immediately passed him the signal. The captain, Lieutenant Commander Edmund Charles Carlisle, instantly forgot about his headache just as another signal arrived, this time from the *American Eagle* herself. It read,

"Am being attacked by vessels of the Iranian Revolutionary Guards. Shots have been fired at us and they are ordering us to stop."

'Send this in reply,' ordered Carlisle. 'Do not... repeat... do not stop. We are coming to your aid at best speed. Hold them off until we arrive.'

'There's another signal from the tanker, sir,' reported Yeoman Murray. 'They say they have taken casualties. Two crewmen dead and three wounded.'

'Okay, let's take the gloves off,' announced Carlisle as the klaxons began blaring out. 'Crew to Action Stations! Crew to Action Stations! Gun crews close up. Engine room give me maximum revolutions.'

Carlisle felt the deck sway as his command, the 6,000-ton frigate Aurora, powered quickly to full speed. The acceleration felt like that of a powerful car.

'Get ready to launch the chopper,' ordered Carlisle. 'We'll need it in the air without delay... and make sure it's fully armed.'

All across the ship the crew were running to their Action Stations, donning body armour and anti-flash gear. Many were carrying belts of ammunition and loading automatic weapons. Simon Barrington stood out on the starboard bridge wing and observed the gunners loading the twin 30mm. Standing just a few feet away from him was 22-year-old Able Seaman Ruth Goldman from North London assisting Geoff Watkins, another Londoner, as they prepared their Browning 50 calibre heavy machine gun sited in its protected sand-bagged emplacement. Prior to joining the Navy Ruth had worked for a well-known newsagents' chain while Geoff had been a delivery driver.

Carlisle was scanning the northern horizon with powerful field glasses when another signal came through from the *American Eagle* that the Iranians were firing rockets, and the tanker had been hit causing more casualties amongst her crew and starting fires. Carlisle hurried to the Operations Room and joined the people manning the plot. Roy Stringer pointed out the small, fast-moving objects which were the Iranian attack boats.

'Can we take them out at this range?' Carlisle asked of the Chief Weapons Officer, Lieutenant Mark Openshaw.

'We can use the 5-inch, sir,' replied Openshaw. 'There is also our Wildcat. They're about to get airborne. Then there are the drones, but we should wait for the range to close before launching them.'

'Very good,' acknowledged Carlisle. 'Open fire with the 5-inch as quickly as you can.'

Out on the foredeck the Mk42 5-inch gun began shooting under radar direction. Carlisle was under no illusions that the small, fast craft used by the Iranians made difficult targets.

'They keep disappearing behind the tanker,' observed Roy Stringer. 'They're using her as a gigantic shield.'

Finally, the flight deck crew got the Wildcat airborne, the fast machine passing down the starboard side of the *Aurora* loaded with rockets.

'I'd like to get the Vampire drone into the air as well,' said Carlisle to Lieutenant Openshaw. 'Ensure that it is sent out with a full armament as soon as possible.'

Then Roy Stringer was pointing to the radar plot and drew everyone's attention to more small vessels approaching at speed from the Iranian coast.

'This time they're coming for us,' responded the captain. 'Shift priority targets to this new threat. Helmsman, alter course twenty degrees to port.'

'Aye aye, sir… twenty degrees to port,' acknowledged the wily Master at Arms, George McGlashan from Clydebank. George was able to claim that he'd served in the Royal Navy for over thirty years.

Out on the starboard bridge wing Lieutenant Barrington was quick to spot the leading boats of the Revolutionary Guard powering towards the *Aurora* at close to fifty knots. The 5-inch was blasting defiance and creating a pall of drifting cordite smoke, but the Iranian boats were small and difficult targets, and they were still powering ahead and drove through the barrage. The stench of cordite stung everyone's nostrils. Suddenly Ruth Goldman on the starboard bridge wing was shouting,

'Torpedoes! Incoming torpedoes from starboard!'

The information was passed immediately to the captain in the Operations Room.

'Helmsman… hard a starboard… steer green nine zero,' ordered Carlisle.

McGlashan responded immediately and the helm was swung hard over, the *Aurora* responding quickly as torpedoes passed either side of the ship. Lookouts were then reporting sightings of more of these lethal weapons approaching. Carlisle was issuing orders to McGlashan, and the frigate was swinging and lurching first to port and then to starboard. It was their combined skill and experience which saved them from destruction and being blown out of the water. The Iranian vessels were still closing in at high speed and once in range the *Aurora* began shooting with her automatic guns, first the twin 30mm and then the 20mm machine guns. Three of the Iranian boats passed ahead of the *Aurora* at high-speed firing their own automatic guns and scoring hits. The frigate's bridge was raked with bullets and small shells. Able Seaman Gillian MacCreadie, was hit by flying glass and wounded while everyone was diving for cover, but her moans of pain quickly drew the attention of other crewmen to her plight. Geoff Watkins and Ruth Goldman were firing their Browning heavy machine gun continuously and both observed hits on one of the Iranian boats which began to slow down to a crawl whereupon it was blown to pieces by a direct hit from the *Aurora's* 5-inch. The starboard twin 30mm mounting was also in constant action and building up piles of spent shell cases. Another of the Iranian boats was disabled and left in a sinking condition. Crewmen were seen scrambling over the side into the warm waters of the Straits. The remaining Iranian boats then sped off northwards towards the tanker.

'Sir, Lieutenant Griffiths signals from the Wildcat that he is engaging the vessels of the Revolutionary Guards with missiles and has scored hits. Two of them are hit and on fire,' reported Simon Barrington to the captain. 'But he adds that men from surviving boats are attempting to board the tanker.'

'Signal him to continue his attacks on the Iranians with whatever weaponry he still has available,' ordered Carlisle. 'We must stop them seizing that tanker whatever it takes.'

On the *Aurora's* flight deck men were working feverishly to prepare the Vampire drone for launching with its complement of four Sea Venom missiles. Sub-Lieutenant Brooks in charge of maintaining the drone breathed a sigh of relief when the unmanned vehicle became airborne and flew off northwards in pursuit of the Iranian Revolutionary Guards. In the meantime, Carlisle was ordering the Engine room to give him everything.

'We're making 37 knots,' responded Lieutenant Commander Moirag MacLean, the Chief Engineering Officer. 'I think that's the fastest the *Aurora's* ever managed. We can't keep it up for long. Something will give.'

'Sir, Lieutenant Griffiths reports that personnel from the Iranian vessels have now boarded the tanker. He is engaging them with automatic fire and one man was seen to fall overboard but he is concerned about causing damage to the ship and casualties to the crew of the tanker. He says the Iranians are now trying to make for the bridge and the ship's control centres.'

Carlisle took over voice communications and spoke directly to Lieutenant Griffiths.

'You must stop the Iranians seizing the tanker. Do whatever it takes. We'll be with you in a few minutes.'

'We have the Iranians under constant fire,' replied Griffiths. 'Hawkins is engaging them right now with the 50-calibre in the door mounting. There go two of the Iranians... one of them has fallen down a stairway. I don't think he will get up... The problem is that they can probably get to the control centres from within the ship... out of our sight.'

'If they take control of the ship, we may well have to disable it,' warned Carlisle.

Running flat out the *Aurora* was now closing the range but Griffiths was reporting that the Iranians were seizing control of the huge vessel.

'She's altering course to starboard, sir,' reported Roy Stringer from the radar plot.

'It looks like the Iranians have taken control,' replied Carlisle. 'Helmsman... alter course twenty degrees to starboard.'

'Aye aye, sir... twenty degrees starboard,' acknowledged George McGlashan.

Carlisle was now wanting to place his ship between the tanker and the

Iranian coast. The tanker was moving at around 12 knots and *Aurora* was catching up fast despite the Chief Engineering Officer's protestations.

'Sir... I can see that the Iranians have taken over the *American Eagle*,' reported Lieutenant Griffiths. 'I don't know what they have done with her crew... perhaps taken them below and locked them up... If they're lucky.'

'Can you see into the tanker's bridge?' enquired Carlisle. 'Can you see anything of what's going on there?'

'It's difficult to see, sir. We're reluctant to get too close... the Iranians have small arms and automatic weapons. We have a few more ventilation holes in the cockpit which we didn't have when we took off.'

'We have the Vampire drone, sir,' proffered Sub-Lieutenant Brooks. 'She's approaching the tanker and sending us some pretty clear pictures. We've set up the video link. You may wish to take a look.'

In the Operations Room Carlisle and other personnel closely observed the pictures being transmitted across by the Vampire. Sub-Lieutenant Brooks was steering the drone right up to the huge vessel and the video footage was crystal clear.

'There's no sign of any of the crew,' commented Lieutenant Hanson. 'Only Revolutionary Guards.'

'We've got to get a team aboard her. It's the only way,' responded Carlisle. 'Marine Lieutenant Cavanagh to the bridge. Let's get a boarding party together. Lieutenant Griffiths... return to the *Aurora* immediately to await further orders.'

Lieutenant John Cavanagh RM duly arrived on the bridge and Carlisle explained that he wanted him to get his men together to board the tanker and seize control back from the Revolutionary Guards.

'You can choose your men... and women,' Carlisle informed him. 'There's just one caveat... I shall be leading the boarding party. Hanson, as First Officer you will be in command of the *Aurora* while I am otherwise engaged and indeed if I should become a casualty... You know what to do.'

'Aye aye, sir,' acknowledged First Lieutenant Hanson.

The Wildcat was now in the process of landing back on the frigate's modest flight deck while Cavanagh gathered his marines. In record time they had loaded the helicopter with their L119A assault rifles and an M2 Browning heavy machine gun. Carlisle hurried to his cabin and grabbed from its wall mounting his antique Royal Navy cutlass which had been used against the Dutch at Camperdown in 1797. Then, also armed with a 9mm pistol, he was clambering aboard the Wildcat in company with the frigate's contingent of marines, and the helicopter, although overloaded, was soon airborne and approaching the tanker from astern under Lieutenant Griffiths' skilful control. The helicopter also had a video link with the Vampire drone which was constantly providing valuable information both as to the layout of the tanker and the enemy dispositions. Griffiths approached at low altitude skimming the surface of the sea. Upon Carlisle's order Brooks fired two Sea Venom missiles into the superstructure at the stern of the tanker where a group of Revolutionary Guards were setting up a defensive position with automatic weapons and rocket launchers. Griffiths then briefly landed the Wildcat on the flat top of the tanker's bridge structure staying just long enough to unload the marines and their kit. A Revolutionary Guard who attempted to fire on the helicopter was quickly cut down by a burst of automatic fire from the marines. Carlisle then led his men down to the bridge which had been badly damaged by one of their own missiles with some electrical equipment still burning and creating a fire hazard.

Carlisle was first hit by the infernal heat of the early afternoon and the sickly odour of leaking oil. Wielding his 18th century cutlass, he was briefly surprised by a Revolutionary Guard who sprang out from the shadows behind an open doorway. The Iranian was carrying an automatic rifle, but Carlisle slashed at him before he had time to open fire. The man was struck several fearful blows to the head and upper body. Lieutenant Cavanagh completed the coup de grace with a burst of fire from his LA119. Carlisle then despatched four men led by Sergeant Campbell to search the Engine rooms and machinery spaces before proceeding to explore the upper decks of the huge ship. Several firefights then ensued with Iranians who were occupying the forward part of the tanker and two of the Revolutionary Guards were hit, one of them fatally. Sergeant Campbell then radioed that he had found twelve members of the crew including the captain, locked up in an empty oil tank.

'Release them and send them back to their posts,' ordered Carlisle. 'We'll need them to get this monster back on the right course as soon as possible.'

Meanwhile Lance Corporal Wayne Addleshaw and Marine Gaz Markham were pursuing two Iranians who were trying to run away through the labyrinth of hatchways and steel ladders down into the bowels of the ship. It was a very dangerous situation since there were many dark corners and shadows. From time to time the Iranians would turn and open fire and several times the marines had to dive for cover as bullets sprayed and ricocheted all around. Eventually Addleshaw spotted the two men crouched in a stairwell about thirty feet below and dropped a grenade which exploded among them with devastating effect.

The super tanker's captain, Sam McClusky, together with several other officers, including the First Mate, Puerto Rican Juan Valdez, returned to what was left of their bridge. They found that the steering had been damaged, and communications equipment had been destroyed by fire. Once the Royal Navy boarding party had satisfied themselves that the Iranians had been neutralised Carlisle returned to the *Aurora* and a number of members of his crew with expertise in engineering and communications were transferred across to the *American Eagle* to help get the super tanker back on course. Everything appeared to be going well until Roy Stringer called out from the radar plot,

'Enemy boats... six of them approaching fast from starboard... fifteen thousand yards.'

'Hell, that's all we need right now,' responded Carlisle as he joined Stringer at the radar plot.

'It's possible they could be armed with torpedoes like some of the others which attacked us earlier,' warned Guy Hanson.

'The tanker will be a sitting duck,' considered Carlisle as he sought to position his frigate between the super tanker and the incoming threat.

Out on the *Aurora's* foredeck the 5-inch recommenced shooting and the leading Iranian boat was hit by a lucky shot and disintegrated. Lieutenant Griffiths was still busily engaged in transferring personnel. Sub-Lieutenant Brooks reported that the Vampire drone had landed safely back on board the *Aurora* and was now being refuelled and re-armed, but it would take a while.

Carlisle was wondering what to do next when Petty Officer Danielle Sheldon, a communications specialist, reported,

'The RAF are sending us air cover from Al Duqum. I'm in radio contact with the airbase and with the planes. They're already airborne… should be with us in a few minutes.'

'Tell them to slam their gas levers into the firewall and get here urgently,' ordered Carlisle. 'The Iranians are about to sink us… and our tanker.'

'Aye aye, sir,' acknowledged Danielle as Carlisle ordered a course alteration to starboard with the powerful Iranian boats closing the range rapidly.

'Incoming torpedoes from starboard!' yelled Able Seaman Tam Yeobright who was positioned high up in the mast. 'Torpedoes!'

'Hard a starboard,' called Carlisle to George McGlashan.

The *Aurora* quickly answered the helm, leaning to port as she made her tight turn just in time as two torpedoes passed down the starboard side with two more to port. Personnel who were standing were flung off balance by the violent manoeuvres, some crew members being thrown to the deck. Able Seaman Emily Keenan struck her head on the corner of a generator and required medical treatment.

'Four more Iranian boats approaching fast from the southeast,' called Roy Stringer. 'Looks like they're intending to come round to attack from our portside.'

'We can't be in two places at once,' complained Carlisle. 'Where are those planes?'

The starboard 30mm automatic guns opened fire as the surviving five boats of the first attack group came within range. Several of the boats carried rocket launchers and the *Aurora* was faced with volleys of machine gun fire and salvoes of missiles. The forward part of the frigate was struck heavily by incoming ordnance and Leading Seaman Duncan Lennox manning a machine gun on the upper deck was hit by flying shrapnel and badly wounded. Only his body armour saved him from death. The Iranian boats were clearly intent on getting between the frigate and the tanker and crossed at speed ahead of the *Aurora*. Able Seaman Dave Finney manning a mini gun reported that at least two of the craft were carrying torpedoes.

'They're going after the tanker,' observed Roy Stringer.

'Alter course twenty degrees to port,' ordered Carlisle. He knew that he was in the process of being outmanoeuvred.

'Aye aye, sir. Twenty degrees to port,' acknowledged George McGlashan.

Aurora answered the helm, but the Iranian boats were faster and were now about to launch their torpedoes. Carlisle felt the sweat pouring off him in rivulets as he contemplated the destruction of the *American Eagle* not to mention his reputation and career prospects.

'What's going on down there?' he called to the engineering department. 'We've got an emergency up here. We need full power... urgently.'

'We're going at full revolutions,' reported Petty Officer Gary Southwark from Engineering. 'That's as fast we can go.'

At that moment there came a tremendous roar followed by a series of explosions and detonations.

'Is that the tanker going up?' enquired Carlisle with resignation from the Operations Room.

'No, sir,' replied Simon Barrington. 'The RAF have just arrived overhead... They've taken out most of the Iranian boats... There goes another one... direct hit from a smart bomb... Rats in a barrel.'

'Signal from the *USS Addison Burke*,' reported Yeoman Catherine Murray. 'They say they hope to be with us in less than thirty minutes. They're sorry for the delay but they're bringing two large salvage tugs to help get the *American Eagle* into port.'

'Signal them in reply... Sorry you missed all the action,' acknowledged Carlisle. 'Trust the Yanks to be late to the show,' he quipped to Guy Hanson.

'Never mind, sir,' replied Hanson. 'You'll be able to take all the glory. I can see the banner headlines... British Naval Captain armed with 18th century cutlass last used in 1797 beats off Iranian revolutionary attacks. The Press will love it.'

'It'll certainly give ammunition to criticise the Government,' replied Carlisle. 'British forces resort to use of 18th century weaponry.'

Chapter 2

AT THE BEGINNING OF JULY, *Aurora* finally arrived in the Frigate refit complex at Devonport. At Al Duqum they had patched up many of the holes, but the verdict of the technicians and dockyard repair specialists was that *Aurora* was in need of an overhaul. The opportunity would also be taken to enhance her radar fit with a new Type 1255 3D set. Her generator capacity was to be significantly increased and there was talk of fitting launchers for the new Anglo American Warhawk cruise missile. After his very recent experience in the Straits of Hormuz Carlisle was more concerned with an augmentation of the ship's close-range armament and he made this very clear to those in charge of the refit.

'We could try fitting a pair of Vulcan Phallanx CIWS,' suggested Clive Robinson from Babrock Engineering, the company overseeing the refit, 'but they're heavy installations and they could make the vessel top heavy. I'd recommend Sea Urchin... a new multi barrel close range gun system just being brought into service by the Japanese. It's got a rate of fire of 4000 rpm and a decent effective range. Their destroyer, *Yahagi*, is equipped with the system and she's here on a visit to Plymouth right now. I'll see about arranging to take you to have a look at it. I must say I was impressed.'

The following day Carlisle received an invite from the Japanese captain, Lieutenant Commander Chuichi Takahashi, to join him for dinner and to be given a guided tour of his ship. Carlisle was himself impressed by what he observed both in terms of the vessel itself and the smartness and professionalism of the Japanese crew. Discipline was tight and the men were quite obviously highly motivated and dedicated to the service of their nation.

'Sooner or later, we will all be put to the test,' warned Takahashi over dinner that evening. 'We face more than one potential enemy. There are the North Koreans. Every so often they fire ballistic missiles over our heads and into the sea on the far side. North Korea is a very unstable country. Who knows what they will do next.'

'I hear it was the North Koreans who supplied the torpedo boats to the Iranians who attacked my ship just last month,' acknowledged Carlisle.

'Then you will understand what I am saying,' replied Takahashi as the huge portrait of his hero the famous Japanese Admiral Isoroku Yamamoto stared down sternly upon them from the wall opposite.

'I fully understand,' agreed Carlisle.

'Then there is China... an emerging giant of the East,' observed Takahashi. 'China is our traditional enemy historically. But I am not talking about history. China is a growing threat to the whole world... to Japan, to Taiwan, Malaysia... everywhere. Sooner or later there is bound to be conflict.'

'It is certainly an unnerving prospect,' acknowledged Carlisle.

'When that happens, I hope you and your country will be on our side,' said Takahashi.

'I'm sure that we will be,' smiled Carlisle diplomatically...

'Kusawa! Bring us the next course,' ordered Takahashi.

His steward promptly appeared looking very smartly attired and bowed to both officers.

'Sir, may I present to you the next course.... Octopus,' announced Kusawa.

'Very good, Kusawa,' acknowledged Takahashi. 'You have done well.'

Kusawa bowed once again and left the officers to enjoy their meal.

'I am sorry if the cuisine may appear unfamiliar,' apologised Takahashi.

'No... I have some friends in London who run a Japanese restaurant. I was there the last time I was on leave,' replied Carlisle. 'Also, I have always lived near the sea, and I particularly enjoy visiting fish restaurants.'

'I can see that you and I are kindred spirits,' observed Takahashi.

'Tomorrow we are due to test our weaponry on your firing ranges off… how do you say in English… Lulworth Cove? I would be pleased for you to accompany us on board my ship.'

'Yes, I would be honoured.'

The following day Carlisle was welcomed aboard the *Yahagi* once again and introduced to several members of the crew including First Officer Raizo Yasuda and the Chief Weapons Officer, Lieutenant Kumagasa. It was a fine summer morning with a light southerly breeze as the *Yahagi* set out from Devonport initially escorted by the tug, *Irishman*. Carlisle stood out on the starboard bridge wing with Lieutenant Commander Takahashi and the Officer of the Watch, Lieutenant Sendai, who was scanning the horizon through powerful field glasses.

'I am not sure who will 'attack' first,' explained Takahashi, 'but the potential threat could come from the air or surface or sub-surface… just like a real-life scenario. We will just have to keep on our toes as you say here in England.'

It was not long before the alarm sounded, and the crew were being called to Action Stations as a pair of Hawk jets from the Fleet Requirements Unit screamed overhead at masthead height. The 5-inch on the foredeck was banging away noisily when Carlisle's mobile phone rang.

'Hello! Who's that?' he called. With all the commotion it was almost impossible to hear.

'It's your wife,' replied the voice. 'You know… that woman you haven't seen since not long after Christmas. Where the hell are you… and what's that dreadful racket at your end?'

'Sorry… I'm observing an exercise,' apologised Carlisle. 'I'm a guest on a Japanese destroyer somewhere off Lulworth Cove.'

'But you've been back in England for more than a week,' complained his wife, Alex. 'You've hardly bust a gut to get over to see me and the farm. I'm beginning to think you're not interested.'

'Don't be like that, Alex,' replied Carlisle. 'There have been some important things to sort out with the *Aurora*. I'll make sure to be on my way home as quickly as I can. I'll give you a call this evening.'

At that point, the *Yahagi* was 'attacked' by a formation of remotely controlled craft which approached at high speed. The scenario reminded him very much of his recent experience in the Straits of Hormuz. The Japanese vessel was blasting away with her 5-inch supported by automatic weapons and machine guns, but Carlisle was particularly interested in the new Sea Urchin system and observed its performance from the bridge wings. He was quickly impressed by its high rate of fire and then by its accuracy. Several of the target craft were hit and left dead in the water or sunk.

'A satisfactory performance, would you not say, Lieutenant Commander Carlisle?' remarked Takahashi. 'Well done, Kumagasa. We fought them off successfully.'

Kumagasa bowed in acknowledgement of his captain's praise.

'I will make sure that those people in charge of weapons procurement for our Navy are made aware of the effectiveness of Sea Urchin,' responded Carlisle.

Later in the day Carlisle returned to the *Aurora* and spoke to Clive Robinson of Babrock Engineering.

'So how was your day out with the Japanese Navy?' asked Clive. 'Did you see the Sea Urchin system?'

'Yes,' replied Carlisle. 'I was suitably impressed. I think we should order it to equip our own fleet.'

'Good,' said Clive. 'That's what I wanted to hear. We're working with Yokohama Instruments who manufacture Sea Urchin. If all goes to plan, we will be given the task at Babrock of helping to market the weapon with European and Commonwealth Navies.

Before dinner Carlisle spoke to his personal steward, David Warwick, and asked him to find out about train times from Plymouth.

'My wife is urging me to hurry up and take some leave. I must say, the prospect is appealing,' explained Carlisle.

'I'd recommend travelling during the working week, if possible, sir,' recommended David. 'Thursday might be a good day. Friday gets rather busy.'

Thursday morning found Carlisle taking the train first to London where he made his way to Liverpool Street. During the course of the journey, he exchanged texts with Alex.

'I've invited Jerome and Lucy round this weekend. Or rather they invited themselves,' texted Alex.

'I was hoping for some quality time to ourselves,' complained Carlisle. 'After all, you've been protesting about the lack of it.'

'Stop being so grumpy and try to be more sociable,' responded Alex. 'Oh, by the way my parents are coming round on Sunday.'

Carlisle boarded the train for Norwich and soon he was heading away from the bustle of the metropolis and into the more familiar East Anglian countryside.

'I should be arriving in Norwich around 6-30pm,' he informed Alex.

'I'll be waiting for you in the car. My white Alfa Romeo Spider. Gary has just been tuning her up. She goes like a bomb,' texted Alex.

'Sounds impressive,' acknowledged Carlisle. 'Off with your knickers as soon as we're home.'

'As you know I'm not much into knickers so that should not be an issue,' responded Alex. 'You might like to know I've picked up an interesting copy of the Kama Sutra in an antiquarian bookshop in Norwich. We can try out the positions. I've been practising standing on my head.'

'Wow,' acknowledged Carlisle.

The train arrived in Norwich ten minutes early, but Alex was waiting for him as promised and helped him load his heavy baggage into her car. It was a fine warm evening and the hood was down. They could hear several wolf whistles as they hugged and kissed.

'Good to have you home again, Eddie,' said Alex. 'Let's get on our way.'

Alex drove at high speed out of Norwich and into the Norfolk countryside. The Alfa Romeo was getting on in years but was maintained in excellent condition. It had originally belonged to Alex's Italian Aunt Isabella, Countess of Cavoura, who lived in a large villa on the shores of Lake Como in northern Italy. This explained why the car was left-hand drive. As they headed for home with the breeze running through their hair Alex turned on the radio where the DJ was playing 'Run Run Run' by Jo Jo Gunn. Both Alex and

Carlisle joined in singing the lyrics. For Carlisle it was good to be back. Things might well have turned out very differently and Alex was aware of this. Then Alex began to unbutton the white shirt she was wearing. It was one of Carlisle's shirts and apart from shades and a pair of black high heels appeared to be the sum total of her attire. Before they arrived in Wroxham, Alex had taken off the shirt, swung it around her head and let it go in the slipstream of the fast-moving sports car.

'Hey… that was one of mine!' protested Carlisle.

A few minutes later they were driving through Wroxham still with the top down. In the middle of the small town there were traffic lights and occasions when they had to slow down or even stop.

'Oh, look… There's Mrs Flowerdew,' called Alex to a lady aged about sixty-five with greying hair. 'Hi, Veronica. I'll be over to the WI meeting next week to give that talk on keeping poultry.'

Mrs Flowerdew approached the car as Alex waited for the lights to change.

'Oh, good gracious! She's got nothing on!' exclaimed Mrs Flowerdew in horror.

Other bystanders and motorists quickly began to notice the nude lady in the white sports car. Carlisle hurriedly searched around for anything to hand which might help to cover his wife's modesty.

'Here,' he said grabbing a dog towel from behind his passenger seat. 'At least put this across your doo dah.'

'We don't need that,' replied Alex dismissively and cast it aside.

To Carlisle's immense relief the lights turned green, and Alex was once again speeding away and heading for home overtaking any vehicles which got in her way.

'You crazy idiot. You'll get us both arrested,' remarked Carlisle.

'I had thought of meeting you naked at Norwich but then I thought better of it,' replied Alex. 'But this is the next best thing.'

Fortunately, they were soon turning into the lane which led to their farmhouse. Everything looked at its best in the early evening sunshine. Jack Blofield and his sons had been mowing the lawns and trimming the hedges. There was Flash the horse in his paddock and a gaggle of geese honking noisily as the car scrunched to a halt on the broad gravel forecourt. Their property was called Longfleet Farm and was centred around a large half-timbered house with a thatched roof. It had five decent sized bedrooms as well as four reception rooms and a library, so it was a fairly substantial structure. Outside it had several acres of gardens and lawns which sloped slightly downwards towards a lake with a body of water about fifteen acres in extent known as Longfleet Broad. This area of water was part of the acreage of the farm and kept private so there were no pleasure craft or holidaymakers to disturb the tranquillity of the place. A rather narrow dyke partly overgrown with trees and reedbeds meandered north-eastwards for a mile or two towards the southwest side of Barton Broad. The nearest villages were Neatishead and Barton Turf. Once indoors Carlisle was greeted by an array of family pets including Labradors, Elsa, Zara and Barley and cats, Bella, Carmen and Consuela. Still naked, Alex helped her husband to bring in his heavy baggage and suitcase. She disappeared briefly to fill the bowls of the multitude of creatures. Carlisle flopped down on their bed feeling somewhat exhausted after his long journey. He was beginning to doze when Alex leapt on top of him naked and began kissing him lasciviously and tugging at his clothing.

'My God... I thought for a moment it was the Revolutionary Guards!' exclaimed Carlisle.

'Come on, sleepy head,' exhorted Alex. 'Take all your clothes off... immediately.'

Within little more than an instant she had unzipped and pulled off his trousers. Then Carlisle felt her pushing down on him and smothering him with kisses. Alex was a beautiful brunette aged 33 with a perfectly formed body. In her younger days after leaving school, she had spent a year or two as a model in Paris and Milan. In this endeavour she had received some assistance from her Italian relatives, the Count and Countess of Cavoura. Subsequently Alex had got back together with her school friend, Lucinda, known as Lucy and the two of them had joined a commune somewhere on the French Mediterranean coast. Carlisle tended to perceive Lucinda as being not the best influence on his wife. In more recent times Lucinda, now married to Lord Jerome Banham-Hamilton, had bought a country house just a few miles away near How Hill on the other side of the River Ant. This meant, of course, that Alex and Lucinda were once again able to see a lot more of each other notwithstanding that Jerome still spent much of the time in London at their town house in Belsize Park. Carlisle had visited them a number of times at their London address which was an impressive property and contained amongst other things a wine tasting room. He recalled attending several wild parties here where people were taking all sorts of substances. The coke flowed freely and not just the fizzy pop.

'I think it's time I went on my back,' suggested Alex as they rolled over. Carlisle thought Alex's long legs were divine as she drew them back so far that her ankles were almost behind her ears.

Later that evening Alex demonstrated how she was able to stand on her head.

Early in the morning Carlisle began to surface with the sun shining in through the gap in the curtains. He was aware that several other creatures were occupying the bed apart from Alex and a warm wet muzzle was impatiently pushing against his face. His eyelids flickered, disturbed by the intrusion into his unconsciousness. Initially he could not decide what it was or where he was. He had recently been at sea so long he thought he was still aboard the *Aurora*. Then he discerned two eyes staring at him from very close quarters. A damp canine scent assailed his nostrils prompting a sudden flash of recognition. It was his rescue dog, Sam, a canine of rather dubious parentage although there was some lurcher in there for sure as well as some Staffordshire bull terrier and Labrador too.

'Alright, Sam. It must soon be time for you to go out,' murmured Carlisle.

Out? How could a dog go out on board a ship? More to the point what was Sam doing on the *Aurora*? Then he slowly collected his thoughts, getting his bearings and remembering that he was no longer at sea. Time and space stood still for a moment, but he glanced at his watch and saw that it was just after 6am. Still befuddled he slowly emerged from under the bedclothes and began searching for his slippers. They were not there. Alex was still fast asleep. Sam jumped up on the bed scattering the array of felines who had already gathered there.

'Careful… You're like a buffalo,' whispered Carlisle. 'You don't need to wake Alex.'

Carlisle reached for his dressing gown and headed for the kitchen with Sam and an entourage of various other creatures following at his heels. As he reached the last step he stumbled and almost fell headlong as an object blocked his footfall. It hissed angrily and shot away. Down the long passage leading to the kitchen with its stone flagged floor Carlisle was assailed by more cold wet noses.

'Elsa… Barley,' he murmured in recognition, 'and who are you?'

The raggy looking canine put its head appealingly on one side. It had a slight bald patch which appeared to have been 'painted' with some substance, most likely a mange cream. Carlisle opened the back door and released the various dogs who ran out into the fresh air on this fine summer morning. He knew it was safe to let them out since the farm contained plenty of open spaces and there were no main roads nearby. Then he glanced to the floor and observed the array of messy bowls and wondered how many more creatures Alex had acquired in the few months since he had last been home. Stubbing his toe on the kitchen table leg he put on the kettle and sat down in a rocking chair next to a window which had good views across the garden and the open water beyond. Almost absent-mindedly he began to finger the rather substantial heap of post which sat in an untidy mound on the working surface. Most of the letters were unopened even though some of them bore postmarks which indicated they had been here some time. The first letter simply contained a letter from his tailors in Norwich giving details of their new lines in clothing for this year's season. The second letter was more troubling. It was from the electricity company and was a final demand. The third letter was a bill for over £400 from a local animal feed supplier with a letter threatening legal proceedings if the account was not brought up to date within fourteen days. He glanced at the postmark on this letter and saw that it had been sent out three weeks ago. With mounting concern Carlisle opened another letter which was a final demand in respect of the telephone account. There was a threat that the phone would be cut off in a few days if the account was not settled immediately. At that point, the kettle began whistling and Carlisle poured himself a mug of strong black coffee. A footfall in the hallway caused Carlisle to glance up and see Alex framed naked in the kitchen doorway. In a sleepy voice she enquired,

'Eddie darling. Are you alright? I was worried just now when I woke up and you were not there.'

'No worries,' replied Carlisle. 'The dogs got me up and I've just put on the kettle. Would you like to join me?'

Alex moved across to where her husband was sitting and began massaging his shoulders.

'I gather things were very dangerous out there in the Gulf,' commented Alex. 'I do understand, you know. When they announced on TV that there had been a serious incident involving *Aurora* I was practically fainting with worry. I was on the phone to Mum and to Lucy. I didn't know what to do. It was such a relief when you phoned me and said you were okay. It was even better when you said you were coming home.'

'It certainly was rather hairy at times,' admitted Carlisle. 'But nothing we couldn't take care of.'

He omitted to mention that they were very nearly torpedoed and blown out of the water.

'There are just one or two things I've just noticed here,' he added, pointing to the heap of mail.

'I do understand if you've been very busy these last few weeks and months, but we need to do something about it. Leave these things to me. I'll try and get them sorted out as quickly as I can. But we need to ensure that there's not such a problem in the future otherwise we'll find ourselves being sued and the phone and the mains services will get disconnected.'

'I'm sorry,' apologised Alex. 'What with one thing and another there never seems to have been time to deal with the admin lately what with Flash's hooves and that agricultural course I'm doing at the Wensum Norwich University. I've just being doing the summer term exams. It's important to me that I pass.'

'I expect you'll gain some useful knowledge,' said Carlisle, 'but it's still essential that our bills are paid. You may need some assistance with these things. I'll have a word with our accountant, Mark Grenfell, in Norwich. He'll probably be able to send over a member of his staff regularly to help with the bookkeeping and keep up to date with correspondence… all that sort of thing.'

'Thank you, darling, that will be very much appreciated,' replied Alex. 'Come on now, it's still very early. Let's go back to bed.'

Carlisle slept soundly for a couple of hours. Then it was Alex who was prodding him and encouraging him to wake up.

'This is the copy of the Kama Sutra I picked up the other day,' she informed him. 'Isn't it fascinating. We've done that one… and that one just last night. Oh… and here's sixty-nine… Why don't we do that?'

Carlisle raised no objection and observed as Alex knelt astride him facing towards his feet. Then she was edging carefully backwards looking rather anxiously over her shoulder.

'You look just as though you were reversing your Alfa Romeo,' he remarked. 'Pause there one moment. There… a kiss for the left cheek… and one for the right cheek.'

Alex giggled excitedly like a schoolgirl and for a while Carlisle forgot about Iranian torpedo boats and threatening letters from the electricity company.

The following morning was Saturday, and a layer of grey cloud soon cleared to reveal plenty of sunshine and blue skies. At about 8am the air was still sharp and crisp and there was a faint tang of the sea carried on the light easterly breeze. Carlisle considered that it was clearly a morning to enjoy out of doors before Jerome and Lucy descended for lunch. Alex was still in bed as Carlisle paid a visit to Flash the horse who was being attended to by Sandra, a daughter of Jack Blofield. Flash, a fine chestnut gelding, actually belonged to Jerome and Lucy but most of the work involved in looking after him fell to Sandra and to Alex. The same applied to the white mare, Starlight, who occupied the next stable and who also belonged to Jerome and Lucy.

'Morning, Sandra,' greeted Carlisle cheerfully. 'How are Flash's hooves?'

'Still giving some trouble,' replied Sandra. 'We might need to call the farrier out again if they don't improve in the next couple of days. I hope it's not laminitis.'

'No, we could do without that,' agreed Carlisle. 'Best to keep a close eye on things.'

Carlisle then continued on his way passing a paddock containing a small flock of Herdwick sheep who were busily consuming a bale of hay which Arthur Richardson, a neighbouring farmer had brought over for them on his tractor. He then paused at the pig paddock and handed a bagful of old apples to Peppa, Doreen and Dolores the sows who expressed their gratitude by grunting loudly. Carlisle noted that Gemma and Diane were still in their pig houses. Gemma was suckling a new litter of nine piglets while Diane was by all accounts about to give birth. Not far away was another separate paddock containing one very large solitary pig, a boar known as Boris who was responsible for the new arrivals. Boris approached Carlisle with optimism when the naval commander produced a couple of large swedes and some juicy beetroots. Carlisle's dog, Sam, now joined him as he headed for the boatsheds situated down at the edge of Longfleet Broad. He could see that Jack Blofield and his sons had been carrying out some very necessary repairs to the sheds and there was clearly some new timber and the holes in the thatch had been filled. As Carlisle approached there was suddenly a most furious barking, and a solid dark object collided with his legs and nearly knocked him flying. A set of sharp teeth embedded themselves in the thick rubber of his boots and there was a savage snarling and growling not to mention a pungent odour.

'Get off! Get off! Unsavoury mutt,' yelled Carlisle as he tried to shake his foot free from its assailant.

'Gordon Bennett, what've you done this time? You've only gone and savaged the captain,' called a familiar Norfolk voice. The dog duly backed away.

'Hello, Jack,' called Carlisle. 'I knew you were here as soon as I was attacked. How have you been getting on these past months?'

Jack beamed his broad grin but said little at first. He and Carlisle then began an inspection of the Norfolk Wherry, the *Lord Rodney*, and then sat together on a rickety bench next to the slipway. Jack Blofield then offered Carlisle, 'Just a little snifter,' from his pocket flask.

'Ya know,' said Jack, 'I was copsing that wood like we agreed, and I came up towards the house to get my tools from the barn. Well, Gordon Bennett, as you know, he's a champion ratter an' 'e only went an' caught the biggest goddam rat I ever did see round your barn. Well, of course, 'e went straight to your kitchen. I expect 'e thought you'd be there and give him some kind of reward. But you weren't there so 'e takes this great big rat to your missus an' I was following behind. Well… Gordon Bennett... he drops this rat right on the kitchen floor in front of your missus. But it wasn't quite dead, so I gave it a clout with't shovel to finish the job. You never heard such a scream let out… but it wasn't from yon rat… it was your missus.'

Jack laughed, his well suntanned face grinning from ear to ear.

'Well, that's a funny tale, Jack,' smiled Carlisle. 'I can see you've made good progress with *Lord Rodney*.'

Together they clambered aboard the traditional Norfolk trading vessel with the dogs following at their heels.

'She's as good as ready to go back in the water,' advised Jack. 'I'd say she's as good today as she was a hundred and fifty years ago when she were new.'

Carlisle entered the tiny aft cabin and stooped through the short narrow passage to the cargo hold. They had restored the vessel as closely as possible to her original condition.

'She's superb, Jack. You and your people have done an excellent job. We should get her back in the water as soon as possible,' praised Carlisle.

'I've got my pal, Claspy, standing by to help with the re-launch,' replied Jack. 'He's got a crane. I was really just waiting for you to come home again so that you could give us the all-clear to go ahead.'

Carlisle was now itching to get the *Lord Rodney* afloat but for now he had to be content with his traditional Norfolk sailing yacht, the *Moonbreeze*, a thirty-footer built in the early twentieth century. Like the *Lord Rodney*, the *Moonbreeze* was a wooden hulled sailing vessel which they had restored from a hulk. Carlisle and Jack scrambled aboard, followed enthusiastically by the dogs, and unfurled the awning. Eventually they were in a position to set sail and cast off the mooring lines, gliding silently across the tranquil waters of

Longfleet Broad. Sam stood in the bows and sniffed the breezes. Overhead a flock of geese flew in formation honking to each other while mallards and crested grebes sat on the surface. Carlisle watched as a heron launched himself impressively from the branches of an Alder tree at the water's edge. Cautiously Jack handed the tiller to Carlisle and stepped along the side deck with a quant pole to sound the depth of water as they approached the narrow dyke which twisted and turned its way towards Barton Broad. At the entrance to the channel the *Moonbreeze* grounded in the shallow silted water and Gordon Bennett barked loudly as his master heaved with all his strength and finally pushed the vessel clear. The narrow waterway appeared even more overgrown than ever being full of half-submerged fallen trees and was particularly difficult to navigate.

'We'll have to do something about improving this dyke,' commented Carlisle to Jack. 'If we're going to invite the public to come sailing it won't look good if they're always running aground and getting stuck.'

'I'll have a word with my mate, Claspy,' replied Jack. 'He'll be able to do something about it… at a price.'

Nevertheless, the peaceful scene in the overgrown waterway seemed to Carlisle to be what the best of Broadland was about. It had a wild and timeless feel to it. Eventually they reached the mouth of the dyke as it met the western extremities of Barton Broad and they sailed out into open water. The easterly breezes helped them to gather speed with the wind in their sails. Carlisle was aware of the recent efforts which had gone into improving the Broad both in terms of the clarity of the water and from dredging and opening up previously silted areas. He was enjoying the peace and the freedom when his mobile phone rang.

'Where the hell are you?' demanded the voice on the other end. 'Have you completely forgotten we've got guests arriving for lunch in twenty minutes? Lucy and Jerome say they're on their way already.'

'Sorry, Alex,' apologised Carlisle. 'We were just checking out the *Moonbreeze*. I'll be back shortly.'

When Carlisle arrived back at the farm Jerome and Lucy were already there together with their two children, Anton aged 7 and Jocasta aged 10.

'What sort of time do you call this?' Alex admonished him. 'Your guests have been here half an hour. You've held everyone up.'

'Court martial offence, eh?' laughed Jerome. 'Put him in the brig. Mind you he's the captain... Do they still shoot them on their own quarter deck in the Royal Navy?'

'Actually, we've only just got here,' conceded Lucy. 'There was a hold up at Ludham Bridge. They were carrying out some repairs. We've been to check on Starlight and Flash. Starlight is fine. Flash is still having some trouble with his hooves.'

'Yes, I know,' replied Carlisle. 'I was talking to Sandra earlier this morning after the farrier had been. We're all hoping it's not laminitis...'

'We can do without that,' commented Jerome.

Soon they were sitting round the dinner table with views out across the lawns towards the Broad.

'Can I ride Starlight later?' asked Jocasta.

'Hopefully,' replied Lucy. 'But she's quite a big horse. You'll need a grown-up on hand.'

'Definitely,' added Jerome. 'The last thing we need is you taking a nasty tumble, young lady.'

'Did we tell you that Jocasta's got a place at Rovingdean?' added Lucy. 'We received a letter last Friday. It's such good news.'

'Taking after Mum, eh Jocasta?' said Alex. 'I expect you're looking forward to going there, aren't you? It's something special to go to Rovingdean. I went there as well.'

'Yes... sort of...' conceded Jocasta rather hesitantly. 'But I'm not sure how much I'll like it at boarding school.'

'Oh, you'll love it when you get there,' replied Alex. 'Your mum and I had loads of fun. We got up to all sorts of pranks. When we were a bit older, we were always getting into hot water. I lost count of the number of times I was sent to the headmistress.'

'And how's the world of banking at the moment?' Carlisle asked of Jerome.

'Well... as you know this business in the Middle East is upsetting the markets and currencies are taking a tumble,' replied Jerome. 'It was a particularly bad day on the money markets after your incident in the Persian Gulf. Investors didn't like it at all.'

'No, I expect not,' acknowledged Carlisle. 'I reckon things will get worse before they get better. I'd say there is another Middle East war brewing. You wait and see.'

'Oh, I hope not,' sighed Jerome. 'It's the last thing we want right now… or at any time.'

'Changing the subject and thinking of much pleasanter things,' chipped in Lucy, 'we're planning another of our parties at Belsize Park. You're both invited. Hopefully, it should be a good bash. Anyone who is anybody will be there so make sure you come.'

'Oh, I'd love to,' responded Alex. 'You can count us both in.'

After lunch Alex and Lucy accompanied Jocasta while she trotted gently around the farm on Starlight. Carlisle took Jerome and Anton sailing in *Moonbreeze*. They kept to Longfleet Broad and Carlisle felt it wiser not to venture down the dyke in its present condition. It was a very warm July afternoon, and Jocasta was sent to pat the farm animals while Alex and Lucy went skinny dipping in the Broad.

'The water feels lovely,' enthused Lucy. 'The best way to cool off on a hot summer afternoon. We don't yet have a swimming pool at our country retreat, but we'll rectify that soon enough. We've just had a big new indoor pool installed in the basement of our house in London… and a gymnasium too. You know this place would make an excellent venue for partying. Have you thought of that?'

'I'm sure it would,' agreed Alex, 'but Eddie is away so much. It's all I can do to try and hold the line. There are so many things I'd love to do but life seems to just revolve around work. In some ways it's getting a bit too much and then there's my university course as well.'

'I'm sure it's not half as bad as you make out,' replied Lucy. 'It seems pretty idyllic here… a paradise… a lovely place, the archetypal thatched house with roses in the front garden.'

'That may be how it appears at first sight,' cautioned Alex, 'but there are some fundamental things which are not right. For a start Eddie is away so much of the time I often feel I'm single. It wouldn't surprise me if I ended up a widow sooner rather than later. That business with the Iranians really shook me up.'

'Yes, I know,' said Lucy. 'But you've got Eddie back now. He's safe. Look… there they go in that yacht of his.'

'Before long he'll have to return to his ship and they'll send him off to another trouble spot,' bemoaned Alex. 'And another thing… time seems to be passing me by but nothing's happening as John Lennon used to say. You have two lovely children. I have none.'

'You're only how old… 33?' retorted Lucy. 'There's plenty of time to produce a family. Come on now… I'll have a quiet word with Eddie when the opportunity arises. You both need to let your hair down a bit… have some fun. Get yourself a boyfriend on the side.'

'Actually,' whispered Alex, 'there's a very nice young man I've become quite friendly with at uni.'

'Hey! Tell me more,' exclaimed Lucy.

'Keep your voice down,' urged Alex. 'He's 25 and his parents own a farm up in Lincolnshire… more than a thousand acres so it's a decent size. He's on the course so that he can get his qualifications in agriculture and eventually take over the running of the farming business.'

'That sounds really good,' enthused Lucy. 'Just 25 you say. Have you? …you know…?'

Alex nodded affirmatively and smiled sheepishly.

'Well done, Alex!' exclaimed Lucy. 'Now you're making me feel jealous. What's his name?'

'It's Andrew,' whispered Alex. 'Andrew Gibson… and he's six foot tall and good looking.'

'And is he… well-endowed in the down below?' giggled Lucy.

'Yes, he's well hung,' admitted Alex. 'We got talking together because we both like cars. He took a shine to my Alfa Romeo, and I liked his MG.'

'Has he been over to the farm here?' enquired Lucy.

'Yes,' replied Alex. 'More than once. I've been getting lonely with Eddie being away for months on end.'

There was a sound of voices coming from the direction of the boat sheds.

'Watch out... the men are coming,' whispered Alex. 'Not a word to anyone, Lucy, not even Jerome. Eddie would be very upset if he found out.'

'Yes, I do understand,' replied Lucy. 'Mum's the word.'

Sunday morning dawned wet and miserable with a steady drizzle off the North Sea. Carlisle stirred but then reminded himself that the in-laws were coming round today and went back to sleep for a while. Eventually he was woken properly by various canines and felines. Alex was up and about.

'You haven't forgotten Mum and Dad are visiting us today?' she reminded him. 'They're bringing Uncle Giovanni and Auntie Isabella as well... they're on holiday here for a couple of weeks. It's good of them to take the trouble to see us.'

Carlisle headed for the kitchen followed closely by all creatures great and small. On Sunday mornings he looked forward to a decent cooked breakfast, but he guessed that Alex would be too busy to provide such a thing right now. Heading out of doors he bumped into Sandra who told him she had fed all the farm animals this morning, but she had some gripes about Myrtle, the donkey. Perhaps rather surprisingly Sandra did not get on too well with Myrtle.

'She's been braying and making a fuss,' complained Sandra. 'It's every time I see to the horses, or someone takes them out for a ride. Myrtle thinks she should have all the attention.'

Carlisle headed for Myrtle's paddock and slipped the donkey a couple of juicy carrots and a sugar lump. After that Myrtle appeared to be satiated, at least for the time being.

Jack Blofield was in the boatshed with his son, Wade, and his friend, Claspy. They were discussing the practicalities of launching the *Lord Rodney*. It was quite a large, heavy vessel, more than sixty-five feet long, and Claspy was talking of bringing up a crane or even a pair of cranes so that the wherry would be supported at either end.

'The ground is none too firm here,' said Claspy thoughtfully. 'I reckon we should draw the craft out into the open first. We can put a crane here... where that area of concrete is. The second crane we can keep further back. It's got a decent jib. We can swing it out and we'll have the *Lord Rodney* in the water.'

'Aye… for the first time in goodness knows how many years,' added Jack. 'Do ya know… we discovered it submerged in Barton Broad when they was doing clearing and dredging.'

'It's amazing how it's survived,' agreed Carlisle. 'I can't wait to see it sailing out across Barton Broad. It'll be a phoenix rising from the ashes.'

At that moment, his mobile phone rang.

'Where are you?' demanded Alex. 'You know we've got family coming from Italy and I'm not going to be just left to do all the work. Fortunately, Sandra's kindly giving me a hand.'

'Yes, dear. I'll be over right away,' conceded Carlisle. 'Sorry, chaps. Duty calls.'

The men smiled and Jack gave a chuckle.

'See you later,' they called.

Alex's parents arrived early and Carlisle was reminded of the joke made by Jasper Carrott that he did not know much about Einstein's Theory of Relativity but the in-laws always seemed to turn up at the speed of light. Alex's relatives seemed to talk incessantly save for her father, Kenneth, who soon sat himself in an armchair in the corner of the living room and disappeared behind a copy of the Sunday newspaper. Carlisle mused that the poor fellow had worked out a long time ago that discretion was the better side of valour.

'Still you have a no bambinos!' exclaimed Auntie Isabella. 'No bambinos! What have you been doing all this time? How long have you been married?'

'Seven years,' admitted Alex sheepishly.

'Seven years!' exclaimed Auntie Isabella. 'It is a disgrace. What would the holy pontiff say if he knew?'

'Service life has an effect upon married life,' responded Carlisle. 'At least we find it does.'

'Eddie has to be away from home so much,' added Alex supportively.

'These are just excuses I am hearing,' criticised Auntie Isabella. 'In our country it does not mean that if a man is a serving member of the armed forces, he cannot have children. Please… I do not want to be angry. I am sure you have all sorts of difficulties to contend with… but Giovanni and I are wanting to set up family trusts. You are important to us, and we want to benefit you and your successors in a significant way. We are getting old now. Your uncle here, he is Count Giovanni di Cavoura. We have lots of money, but we need to have people… family… to pass it on to.'

'Isabella and Giovanni want to help you both,' added Alex's mother, Sophia. 'They want to be generous. They are very good people.'

'We never doubted that for a moment,' responded Carlisle. 'I know Alex has always been very fond of her aunt and uncle here.'

'We would like you to come and stay with us in Italy… for a holiday,' offered Uncle Giovanni. 'At Lago di Como.'

'Oh, yes. It's lovely where you live,' enthused Alex. 'Lake Como is so beautiful and all the countryside around it.'

'Perhaps later in the year,' hesitated Carlisle. 'Although I'm on leave right now I'm likely to be called back at any time. It was just that my ship needed some urgent repairs, and it was an opportunity for me to spend some time at home with Alex at the farm.'

'Ha… you are married to your navy. I can see,' grumbled Isabella.

'No, it's not like that at all,' retorted Alex. 'Eddie works very hard. He is doing very well and when he is promoted that helps us greatly. This big place is expensive to maintain.'

'And we are wishing to help you to keep it,' said Giovanni.

Later in the day the relatives departed back to Alex's parents' old vicarage near Beccles in Suffolk. Alex's father was a retired clergyman, and her mother was a schoolteacher although she was soon due to retire herself.

'Well, thank God that's over,' sighed Carlisle as they cleared up after the family visit. 'I feel I should have been wearing my body armour.'

'Don't be silly,' replied Alex. 'Giovanni and Isabella are my favourite aunt and uncle. They always have been. They have always been generous to me, and they want to benefit you as well. You should be more grateful.'

At around 8pm Alex checked on the farm animals and made sure they had plenty of food and hay. Jack Blofield and his sons were down at the boatshed putting the finishing touches to *Lord Rodney*.

'I don't think we need an evening meal,' remarked Alex as she returned to the farmhouse. 'I'm FTB. How about you, Eddie?'

'Me too,' agreed Carlisle as he put down the Sunday newspaper.

'Early night and off to bed,' proposed Alex picking up the copy of the Kama Sutra.

'I'm game,' replied her husband.

Monday morning appeared to start off alright with the sun shining and the prospect of a fine summer's day. Carlisle had helped Alex feed the growing collection of household pets but at around 9am there was a knock on the front door. Carlisle opened it and was greeted by the postman. Eric.

'One to sign for, sir,' announced Eric who handed Carlisle a cream-coloured envelope which had been franked with the logo 'Burnham Winterlees & Co. Solicitors'.

Carlisle opened the envelope hurriedly and was horrified to read a solicitors' letter threatening the issue of a writ for damages as a result of alleged flooding to a neighbouring farm caused by a blocked dyke. The solicitors were referring to damages in excess of £15,000. To add to his misery there was also a brown envelope which he opened and was mortified to find a county court summons claiming £4,000 through Norwich County Court. The claimant was Waxhams, the animal feed suppliers. To add to his woes the paperwork ominously referred to the fact that if matters were not dealt with in fourteen days there would be a court judgement entered against Alex and himself. Carlisle was initially at a loss as to what to do.

'Alex!' he yelled. 'What on earth is all this? We appear to be up to our necks in do do.'

His wife entered the kitchen and Carlisle thrust the documentation in front of her nose.

'How the blazes has this happened?' he shouted. 'Not good enough, Alex. If the worst comes to the worst, we shall… have to sell up this place and get rid of all the animals.'

'I'm sorry,' apologised Alex. It was certainly not the first time since Carlisle had been home on leave that Alex had accepted responsibility for failing to deal with bills and suchlike. 'Things have been getting on top of me lately.'

Carlisle continued to rant and swear while Alex burst into tears.

'Come here. Dry your eyes and give your nose a blow… It's really all my fault,' accepted Carlisle. 'This is a big place, and you certainly need more help in keeping it together. Let's keep our heads cool and think about how to tackle these problems. Your wealthy aunt and uncle from Italy were here only yesterday wanting to help us financially. Well, here's their opportunity. I suggest you give them a ring at your parents. Catch them while they're still here in England. In the meantime, I'll call my brother, Guy, and seek his legal advice.'

So Alex spoke on the phone that morning to her Uncle Giovanni while Carlisle spoke to his brother, a respected local lawyer with Messrs Kingham Kirkconnel & Carlisle, Solicitors of Norwich. Uncle Giovanni expressed his wish to be ready and willing to help with the settlement of the outstanding bills. Guy was a little surprised to hear from his brother with these financial problems, but he said he was agreeable to acting on Carlisle's behalf and they fixed up a lunch appointment for the following day at a local riverside pub, the Strumpshaw Fox. Both Carlisle and Alex, although unsettled by the situation, were reassured in part that something was being done to alleviate this crisis.

In the afternoon Carlisle and Alex were on hand to watch the relaunching of the *Lord Rodney* into Longfleet Broad. The process of getting the large and heavy vessel back into the water was not without its problems. At the first attempt one of Claspy's cranes very nearly overbalanced and the driver had to lower the bows of the wherry rather hurriedly before everything toppled over. The second attempt also had to be deferred when it was clear that the same thing was going to happen. Claspy and Jack together with assistance from his sons brought up large lifting jacks and baulks of timber. In the evening at around 8pm a third attempt was made and this time the *Lord Rodney* was carefully lowered into the water and floated proudly for the first time in more than one hundred and fifty years.

The following day Carlisle met his brother Guy at the Strumpshaw Fox, an attractive hostelry full of traditional Norfolk charm situated by the River Yare. They met in the pub car park and studied the menu before venturing inside where they were greeted by the landlord, a man aged about sixty or so with slightly greying hair.

'I'd like the sirloin steak,' requested Carlisle. 'Ah yes. And a pint of locally brewed ale.'

'Ay?' queried the landlord.

'Ah yes… and the Ploughman's Lunch for me, please,' said Guy.

'What?' questioned the landlord.

Sometimes Carlisle felt that Norfolk was almost a foreign land but through a process of sign language and speaking loudly and clearly, he and his brother made themselves understood at least sufficiently to receive their meals and their drinks.

'As far as the debt to the animal feed suppliers is concerned, I don't think there's any defence,' advised Guy as they sat down at a table in the pub garden.

'No. We'll just have to settle that,' agreed Carlisle. 'It's really just a matter of acting fast and doing what's necessary to stop them entering a judgment. We've got the money in the bank. To be honest I think Alex just overlooked things. I think she's finding the admin rather a burden.'

'As for the flooding of the neighbouring farmland we need to take the necessary steps to protect your position and then put in a defence,' advised Guy. 'You need to bear in mind that the neighbour's claims may be over-inflated or that the flooding was due to some problem on his own land not of your making. I'd like to make a site visit as soon as possible. Are you happy for me to speak to the other side to try to arrange something?'

'Er… yes. That's fine,' replied Carlisle.

They finished their lunch and the landlord's assistant, a lady aged in her sixties with greying hair came to take away the empty plates.

'That was very good. Most enjoyable,' Guy thanked her.

'Ay,' replied the lady.

Guy returned to his office and Carlisle went home to Longfleet Farm where Jack and his sons were getting the *Lord Rodney* ready and the single big black sail was in the process of being fitted. Alex and Lucy came over to the boathouses to admire the newly restored vessel.

'You're invited to our party in London… Saturday week,' proffered Lucy. 'I hope it will be a good bash. We've got Prince Faisal Al Raman coming… and Lord John Ravenmoor, quite a few city bankers and hedge fund managers as well as titled people and a sprinkling of people from the film industry and rock and pop.'

'I've already accepted on behalf of the two of us,' added Alex.

Carlisle recalled from previous parties he had attended at Belsize Park at the home of Lord and Lady Banham-Hamilton had ended with most of the guests high on cocaine or marijuana but there had usually been a pleasing number of pretty ladies with whom he could converse, and the food and drink were good so he smiled politely and said he would be glad to come.

'That's excellent,' said Lucy. 'So, I can count you in?'

The following week Carlisle accompanied Guy on a site visit to the neighbouring property, Low Marsh Farm owned by Robert Knighton. Carlisle and Robert Knighton did not get on all that well and there had been previous disputes. Furthermore, although Carlisle and Alex had lived at Longfleet Farm since they were married Knighton and his wife tended to regard them as newcomers, even strangers. Knighton met them at his front gate and introduced his solicitor, Mr George Cohen of Messrs Simons, Cohen & Partners of Norwich. They were then guided to the land running gently down towards the Broad. They then made their way along a path through somewhat boggy ground towards the dyke which led to Barton Broad. Carlisle was aware that this dyke was currently not in the best condition, and he had already planned to improve its condition as soon as time and money permitted.

'This is the problem area,' pointed out Robert Knighton. 'The flooding's tended to recede somewhat in the last few days but recently it's been so bad this meadow here has been like an extension to the broad and I've been unable to use it to graze my cows.'

'I can see you're able to use the big adjoining field,' pointed out Guy. 'I can see the cows grazing there at the moment.'

'That's as may be,' retorted Knighton, 'but my cows can't graze this fertile area of meadowland here and that's a problem which is not of my making.'

'Who is legally responsible for maintaining the dyke?' enquired Guy.

'I'll need to check the deeds properly,' answered Carlisle, 'but I've always seen it as being my responsibility at least in part.'

'I'll certainly want to have a careful look at the deeds and that includes your clients' title as well, Mr Cohen,' said Guy firmly.

'I hope that perhaps we might be able to reach some sort of settlement,' suggested Carlisle.

'Ar… but any settlement is going to cost you a bob or two and that's for sure,' cautioned Robert Knighton.

By the end of the week Guy had obtained copies of the titles to both farms from the Land Registry and called Carlisle over to his office to have a look.

'It's not as straightforward as the other side make out,' advised Guy. 'Old Knighton bears a joint responsibility with yourself for maintaining the dyke. If he's been suffering flooding recently then he is partly to blame. Don't make any offers or admissions to him at the moment. Leave it to me. I'll get it sorted out.'

Carlisle left the meeting feeling much better than he had done of late.

Chapter 3

THE FOLLOWING DAY, BEING SATURDAY, Carlisle and Alex drove down to London in their dark green Range Rover. Carlisle felt it was an opportunity to relax and let his hair down a little for a change. It should also do Alex some good. However, the heavy London traffic did not assist Carlisle's temper and when they finally reached Belsize Park they drove round and round for what seemed an age trying to find somewhere to put the car. Eventually they found a spot tucked away in a Mews development, but it was not really convenient being about four streets away from the Banham-Hamilton's house. Alex was clad in a high-quality dress shirt which she had purchased from a fashionable London clothing store when on a shopping trip with Lucy earlier in the year. It was white but had gold coloured metal buttons and was embroidered down the front with blue and gold which Alex felt gave it a kind of naval image. The cuffs were delicately finished in white lace. At the back, the garment ended in two rather inadequate and brief shirt tails with a distinct gap in between. Apart from shades, worn mainly for effect, and a pair of stylish black high heels with gold buckles that was the sum of Alex's party attire. As the couple walked from the car the summer evening breezes tended to lift the delicate fabrics of the dress shirt attracting the attention of the occupants of a white builder's van passing by.

'Whey… look at that!' someone called from the vehicle. 'Lost yer strides, darling?'

Some people are so uncouth,' complained Carlisle.

He was relieved when they arrived at the Banham-Hamilton's house, a large Georgian property. Jerome explained that it actually comprised two houses which they had acquired and turned into one. He was also eager to show them the new facilities they had recently added including the large indoor swimming pool down in the basement and the double jacuzzies.

'I hope you'll get an opportunity to use them both later in the evening,' said Jerome.

Lucy was busy greeting the guests who included people arriving in large Mercedes cars and SUVs, ladies in smart evening dresses and some of the gentlemen in tuxedos and bow ties.

'Darling! How lovely to see you again,' Lucy greeted each of the guests and gave them a big hug and a kiss.

'Mwa! Mwa!' they exclaimed in the manner of many people meeting each other socially in some upmarket districts of London.

A man dressed in 18th century style clothing was standing near the front door announcing the names of people as they entered.

'Lord and Lady Julian Ravenmoor! Lieutenant Commander Edmund Carlisle and Mrs Alex Carlisle! His Royal Highness Prince Faisal Al Raman bin saud!'

Alex glanced round and saw a well-dressed man of relatively youthful appearance with a carefully trimmed beard enter the house.

'I see you've been graced with royalty,' Alex whispered to Lucy.

'Oh, yes,' replied Lucy in hushed tones. 'I'll introduce you to him shortly. Tamandra will fix you up with drinks and something to eat. The children are not here this evening. We've sent them to stay the night with their auntie in St John's Wood. You know how these parties get late on.'

'Yes, I know what you mean,' smiled Alex.

Not long afterwards Lucy introduced the Carlisles to Prince Faisal whom they found to be a well-educated and cultured man in his late twenties.

'I hope that one day I will become king of my country,' explained the prince. 'I have brothers, but I am still quite young, and I am in line to the throne… eventually.'

'I look forward to you being crowned king,' said Alex.

'And what are your interests, my dear?' asked Prince Faisal.

'Well,' considered Alex. 'I like animals and my husband and I have a farm in the part of England called Norfolk.'

'Ah, so you are farmers?' responded Faisal.

'Well, I am,' explained Alex, 'but my husband, Edmund here, is a lieutenant commander in the British Royal Navy. He is captain of a ship… the frigate, *Aurora*.'

'Ah, yes. He and his ship were in the news quite recently. Your husband is a brave man… a hero,' praised Prince Faisal. 'May I salute you, sir?' he said to Carlisle. 'You have my intense admiration.'

'Thank you, your royal highness,' acknowledged Carlisle and bowed appropriately.

In the middle of the spacious living room a group of people had gathered talking loudly and making plenty of guffaws. Carlisle recognised one as being Lord Ravenmoor who had arrived around the same time as Alex and himself.

'Anyone who is anybody nowadays works in the City,' said somebody.

'And has a title,' added Lord Ravenmoor.

There was more laughter and guffaws.

'Well, I don't have a title,' cut in a man whose name was Gary Sharpe… 'but I do manage sixty million pounds in funds. Last year my bonus was two million.'

'Mine was five million,' contributed Lord Ravenmoor. 'But I am a director of a merchant bank. I help to manage billions.'

'Ere!' called Gary Sharpe who appeared to be addressing Alex. 'I need my glass refilling. Gor any decent champagne in this place, luv?'

'Excuse me, but that's my wife you're talking to,' intervened Carlisle. 'She is not a member of staff.'

'Eh, toffee nose… who d'ya think you're talking to?' replied Sharpe. 'I want my glass re-filling... right now.'

'Go and get some more champagne for my friend,' ordered Lord Ravenmoor of Alex. 'And you… haven't we met before?' he enquired of Carlisle. 'You're that navy fellow… petty officer or something like that… and you have a farm out in the middle of nowhere. Why don't you go back and look after your goats or whatever it is you keep there? This party is for people of a much higher standing.'

At this point Prince Faisal intervened on behalf of the Carlisles.

'You are a very rude man,' said Faisal to Lord Ravenmoor.

'Do you know who I am?' retorted Ravenmoor.

'Perhaps you cannot remember who you are or have some kind of dementia or memory loss,' responded Faisal. 'I cannot tell you save that you are clearly a man of lowly status. I would never invite you to my palace or to any of my homes.'

Lord Ravenmoor was turning an unusual shade of puce.

'Ere… you can't talk to his lordship like that,' said Gary Sharpe. 'You're just a fuckin' towel 'ead.'

At this point Lord Ravenmoor picked up his jacket.

'Come on, Arabella,' he ordered. 'We're leaving.'

He and his wife swept out with Ravenmoor calling out,

'This is a pathetic little party… We're off to socialise with people of a higher standing.'

Gary Sharpe looked around him with an air of uncertainty and moved unsteadily for the front door and departed himself.

'What on earth happened?' asked Lucy. 'Why have they suddenly left?'

'Do not worry, my dear,' counselled Prince Faisal. 'They were people of lowly status who you can well do without.'

'You didn't say something to them, did you?' queried Lucy.

'I think it was more the other way round,' said Carlisle.

For a while, the atmosphere was sullied by the unpleasant incident, but fortunately more people were arriving at the party.

Dr Samantha Langley! Called the man in 18th century costume… Dr Arnold Duvall! Mrs Nicole Edenville!'

Carlisle found himself introduced perhaps rather unexpectedly to several people from the scientific world. Dr Duvall was a balding man aged in his forties with spectacles who said he was a director of a company called Darkforce which worked in the fields of cyber security and Artificial Intelligence. He introduced their Chief Strategist, Nicole Edenville, and fellow director, Dr Samantha Langley, a very attractive blonde aged perhaps in her late thirties. Samantha had clearly been briefed about Edmund Carlisle at least to a point since she was aware who he was and that he was the captain of a British warship which had recently been involved in an incident in the Persian Gulf region. Samantha explained to Carlisle about her company's fields of expertise.

'But we are wanting to expand into the defence industry in the context of high technology,' advised Samantha. 'This is a good opportunity for us to talk to you about our work. Nicole here is our Chief Strategist and in charge of company policy making. You have been in combat recently. We wish to hear from you as to what kind of developments you would like to see bearing in mind your own experiences.'

'Survivability is a fundamental objective,' considered Carlisle thoughtfully. 'It all depends on the situation and the kind of threat one is facing.'

'Take your recent combat experience in the Gulf region,' proposed Nicole Edenville. 'What developments would you like to see to help deal with such threats in the future?'

'We need more effective weaponry for dealing with swarm attacks from high-speed craft,' explained Carlisle. 'The standard 5-inch gun was rather heavy and slow firing. Then we had lighter automatic guns from 30mm down to 7.62mm but these tend to be short on range and hitting power. To be honest I would say our ship's armament was not the best configuration for defence against that kind of attack.'

'You managed to survive though,' mused Nicole. 'You're still here to talk to us and your ship is still largely in one piece.'

'It was a close-run thing,' responded Carlisle. 'Sometimes I wake up in the middle of the night in a cold sweat shouting helm orders to the coxon. In my nightmares we don't always dodge the torpedoes.'

'I can see this is an area we need to work on,' remarked Nicole. 'Samantha and Arnold will take full note of what Commander Carlisle has to say.'

'If your ship was sent into a situation which was manifestly dangerous,' considered Samantha, 'would it not assist you significantly if your enemy was unable to see you?'

'Indeed, it would,' replied Carlisle. 'To be invisible to one's opponent would clearly put one at a distinct advantage to say the least. Do you have in mind stealth technology?'

'Er, yes,' replied Samantha. 'But what we would like to achieve is to take such technology to a higher level. I cannot say more at this stage.'

In the same room Prince Faisal was standing with Alex and several other people including Jerome and two of his fellow directors from Beswick's merchant bank. Tamandra was pouring out glasses of champagne, but Prince Faisal politely declined.

'Come on, Faisal,' urged Nigel Harrison-Wright. 'Just a small glass. Don't let the side down. There's a good chap.'

'No! no!' responded Prince Faisal. 'It is against my religion. I cannot consume alcohol. I am a Muslim.'

'Come along, Your Majesty, let's go and have a look at Lucy and Jerome's new facilities,' suggested Alex and led Faisal away from the other partygoers.

'Some of them get rather overbearing,' Alex remarked to Faisal. 'Loads of money but no sense or insight.'

Alex gave the new wine tasting room a wide berth. It was full of people trying Jerome's latest vintages. By the sound of things many of them were already getting merry.

'This looks more interesting,' noted Alex. 'This is clearly the library. It's pretty well lined from floor to ceiling with books and bookcases. I know both Lucy and Jerome are into antiquarian publications,' she commented while thumbing through several volumes. Unlike the wine tasting room there was no one else in the library and Alex and Faisal were able to converse quietly without being disturbed.

'Look at this wonderful bound volume of the Arabian Nights,' exclaimed Faisal. 'See these beautiful illustrations. They are marvellous works of art. Let us sit here on this comfortable Chaise Longue and I will read to you the Tale of Queen Shahrazad.' Alex was eager to sit beside this Prince of Arabia while he read to her romantic stories.

'There lived long ago a king named Shahriyar. He was married to a beautiful queen who appeared to love him as dearly as he loved her,' began

Faisal. 'One day he discovered that, in spite of her sweet words and smiles, she had been for many months conspiring with his enemies to kill him and to marry someone else. Then King Shahriyar fell into such a terrible rage that he was almost mad and in his fury he killed his queen with his bare hands.'

'Are you married, Your Majesty?' enquired Alex.

'No,' smiled the prince, 'and you can call me Faisal from now on. My family would like to marry me off, but I prefer the freedom to live my life here in London and other places. I have a house in Eton Square and another one in Gloucestershire not far from Cheltenham racecourse with gorgeous views overlooking the Malvern Hills. I do not have as much time to visit my country retreat as I would like. I also have a house in California.'

'And what are your interests?' asked Alex. 'What do you enjoy doing?'

'In my own country I used to like camel racing but there is not much scope for that here in England,' laughed Faisal. 'But I like fast cars. I am building up a collection. I have an Aston Martin and a Lotus and several others.'

'I have a white Alfa Romeo Spider,' said Alex. 'It is my pride and joy.'

'That is wonderful,' exclaimed Faisal. 'I love Alfa Romeos. I must come and see your car and perhaps you can take me for a spin.'

'I'd love to,' replied Alex. 'Preferably when my husband is back at sea. I do not mean to be so forward, but I must admit I get lonely when he is away for months at a time. To be honest I am not happy being a navy wife. Do you have other interests besides fast cars?'

'I like horse racing... ah yes... and antiquarian books and antiques,' replied Faisal.

'Anything else?' asked Alex.

'To be honest I have a weakness for pretty ladies,' admitted Faisal noting the glint in her eye which turned into a broad smile. Then she was hugging him and kissing him lasciviously.

Meanwhile upstairs Carlisle was deep in conversation with the people from Darkforce Plc. Eventually Arnold Duvall made his apologies and said he needed to get back to his wife and children in Hertfordshire. Nicole Edenville stayed a while longer. Lucy and Tamandra topped up everyone's glasses with more champagne. The ladies in particular were starting to become a little giggly. Carlisle was impressed by Samantha's beauty with her blonde hair and piercing blue eyes which seemed to stare into his soul. She was wearing a smart black evening gown made of delicate material which had a transparency. Nicole, Carlisle guessed, was rather older than Samantha but was well made up with long auburn hair and a blue evening dress.

'Why don't you try our new indoor pool?' suggested Lucy. 'After all it cost us enough money. We ought to make some use of it.'

Carlisle glanced around but could see no sign of Alex as a gaggle of people was gently ushered downstairs to what had formerly been a basement area but was now largely occupied by a luxury pool. It certainly looked very inviting being surrounded by large potted palm trees and the walls were adorned with copies of Roman frescoes. Lucy explained that they were based on designs found in some of the excavated villas in Pompeii.

'Oh dear. I'm afraid I haven't brought any swimming gear,' apologised Nicole.

'Oh, don't worry about that,' replied Lucy dismissively. 'We just treat it as a glorified bath. No one wears any clothing in our pool. That would be so old fashioned. Just put your things in that room over there.'

The small gathering did as they were instructed. Nicole appeared slightly embarrassed but Samantha simply asked Carlisle to assist her in unzipping from the back her long, black gown which dropped casually to the floor. They were joined by Lucy's younger sister, Lady Emma Hamilton, whom Carlisle had met before on a number of occasions and knew fairly well. Then everyone was getting into the pool, some jumping in noisily whooping while others took to the water more cautiously. Lucy came in too and Carlisle joined a small group of people, including Samantha, who were gently treading water by the edge of the pool while Tamandra and another young woman brought round yet more champagne and rather more ominously some substance which took the form of a white powder. Carlisle had no doubts as to what it was and several of the guests began snorting up.

'Come on, Eddie,' urged Samantha. 'It reminds me of my time at university in California. We had some good parties then I can tell you.'

Carlisle politely declined the offer of cocaine. A subsequent drugs test could mean the end of his career in the Royal Navy.

'Tell me more about yourself,' replied Carlisle.

'My mother is American, and we used to live in Vermont at a town called Burlington,' explained Samantha. 'My father was originally from Sweden, but my parents divorced when I was about twelve and I haven't seen much of my father since then. At school I found I had a penchant for mathematics and sciences and when I was eighteen, I was offered a place at Cambridge University to study Biochemistry which I was glad to take up. I graduated with an upper second and then went on to get a Masters. Then I was offered an opportunity to study for a doctorate at the University of Berkley California studying particle physics.'

'You are clearly a person of very high intellect,' observed Carlisle.

'Thank you,' acknowledged Samantha. 'You mean I'm not a dumb blonde?'

'No way,' replied Carlisle.

'What do you know about Einstein's Theory of Relativity?' asked Samantha.

'Do you mean General Relativity or Special Relativity?' responded Carlisle.

'Both of them,' clarified Samantha. 'And what about Einstein's Unified Field Theory? What do you know about that?'

'I'm afraid you're getting a bit above my head,' apologised Carlisle. 'But tell me… are you married?'

'No,' replied Samantha. 'I've had one or two relationships over the years but that's as far as it goes. Then I went to work in Silicon Valley in California. I did several different jobs in the scientific world until I joined Darkforce a few years ago and climbed my way up the greasy pole to become a director. The company has been doing well and was floated on the stock market last year. It's listed on the London and the New York markets. We now want to expand the areas of work and expertise we cover. That's why I am very interested in what you have to say.'

At that point Lucy appeared again and was urging people to now move on to the new luxury jacuzzi which was situated up a flight of stairs to ground level at the back of the house.

'There's no need to take your things,' called Lucy. 'We don't wear swimming trunks for the Jacuzzi either.'

There were actually two Jacuzzies connected by a kind of walkway and between them they could accommodate quite a number of people. Carlisle noted that these structures were sited partly out of doors. It was a fine evening so the weather was not a problem but Carlisle observed that although there were high walls providing an element of privacy from immediate neighbours there were blocks of flats close by where residents could stand on the balconies of the upper floor apartments, as indeed some were doing, and watch the activities at the Banham-Hamilton residence. Nevertheless, Carlisle found the bubbling water warm and comfortable as he was joined by Samantha and Nicole and Lucy's sister, Emma. The four of them gathered closely together. Everyone had consumed plenty of champagne and some were high on cocaine. The ladies were giggly, and Carlisle felt female fingers touching places which were usually off limits. Then he was receiving kisses from each of them. Samantha Langley was particularly forward and pressed her body tightly to his so that he could feel her well-formed breasts compressed against his chest and the bush of dark hair in her groin brushing his manhood. Although they were surrounded by people Carlisle fell for Samantha's advances, the two of them becoming locked together in a tight embrace.

'Yes… Yes… give me more,' urged Samantha as Nicole and Emma observed this lovemaking with open mouths and wide eyes.

'Go on you two,' praised Lucy from the adjoining terrace. 'Save some for me, Eddie. I'll come and join you as soon as I can.'

Eventually Samantha began to sigh and then to moan with pleasure attracting further attention from the many people around until she cried out ecstatically. Then they were done, and everyone gave a round of applause. Carlisle realised that he and Samantha had become the focus of attention and suddenly felt a wave of embarrassment.

'Excuse me, I need to go to the john,' announced Samantha bringing the situation down to earth.

Nicole said it was getting late and she needed to get home to her apartment in Chelsea. Her husband would wonder where she had got to. Carlisle was left talking to Lucy's sister, Lady Emma Hamilton.

'So how are things at the Bar at the moment?' enquired Carlisle. 'Have you appeared in any interesting cases lately?'

'Well, actually yes,' replied Emma. 'Obviously, I can't divulge any names. That would be a breach of client confidentiality. But I was acting recently for a wife whose husband had made a great deal of money out of drug dealing and supply. He even had his own farms tucked away in remote corners of the country growing funny substances plants. The problem for us was that we could not realistically claim a share of his ill-gotten gains for our client... not from that source anyway. We had another not dissimilar case where the husband and wife had come from Columbia. The wife, our client, wanted to claim her share of the estates and businesses over there. Another tricky one as I'm sure you can imagine.'

Emma edged up close to Carlisle and the two began to embrace.

'I didn't like to see you showing off with that blonde woman,' said Emma. 'I thought it was most inappropriate behaviour.'

'I'm sorry,' apologised Carlisle. 'I succumbed to temptation and got carried away.'

'Well, it should have been me,' retorted Emma. 'I felt jealousy welling up watching the two of you doing that.'

Carlisle put his arms around Emma. She felt warm and soft with ample breasts and pleasingly broad hips. Once again Carlisle felt a bush of female pubic hair brushing his genitalia. Emma was kissing him fervently.

'Hold me tight,' pleaded Emma. 'My knees have turned to jelly, and I don't want to drown.'

Carlisle held her firmly.

'Have you got a boyfriend?' he asked. 'I don't mean to be intrusive.'

'No... not at the moment,' replied Emma. 'Some of the Counsel in our Chambers are dishy but I never seem to have time to cultivate a relationship. I'm going off to one court or another every day and in the evenings I have to prepare the cases for the following day. You can understand the difficulties. I have to make do with my dog and my two cats for companionship in my small house in Camden. I hope that one day I'll find myself a husband and we'll have children and a nice house in the country. I'm only 32. There's time.'

'Time indeed,' agreed Carlisle. 'I have a wife and a nice place in the countryside, but we don't have any children... just lots of animals... dogs... cats... pigs... you name it.'

'It sounds great,' enthused Emma. 'I'll have to come over to your place sometime.'

Carlisle felt Emma's groin push firmly against his manhood and they were enjoined. At some point he noticed that Samantha had returned to the jacuzzi and was observing them from close at hand. Finally, Emma began to moan softly and then more loudly until she cried out with pleasure. Samantha was the first person to offer applause.

'Bravo... well done,' she praised Carlisle. 'I don't know where you get the energy.'

The three of them cosied up together and Carlisle felt relaxed with an attractive lady on each arm. He looked around but there was still no sign of Alex. The DJ whom Lucy had hired in for the evening was getting into his stride and loudly playing sounds from the sixties.

'Pictures of Matchstick Men,' remarked Samantha. 'From Status Quo's psychedelic era around 1968. Very appropriate.'

The three of them began to join in with the music,

'Did you know that Francis Rossi wrote this song mainly sitting on the john,' Samantha informed them. 'It was apparently the only way he could escape from his wife and her mother.'

At that point Lucy reappeared, this time with Alex, and the two of them climbed into the jacuzzi.

'I think the party's been going well,' remarked Lucy. 'We've got some celebrities this evening. Have you seen... that's Brad Pitstone just over there. He's been over in London attending a film premier and having a short vacation. I'll introduce you to him in a while.'

A short while later Prince Faisal appeared and joined the gathering in the jacuzzi.

'Faisal is an important investor in our company,' explained Samantha. 'Most of our research has to be privately funded and when we are pushing out the boundaries of high technology it doesn't come cheap. What we hope is that we can make a breakthrough and obtain government funding for project development. Lucy's husband's merchant bank, Beswicks, is also a backer. They have been very helpful.'

Carlisle began to sense the existence of some form of alliance.

'Are you with us?' questioned Samantha.

'But what am I to be with?' asked Carlisle.

'Our vision for the future,' answered Samantha. 'Expanding the boundaries of science and technology at the highest levels. Developing Einstein's theories... unified fields... anti-gravity... magnetism... quantum mechanics. Developing technologies which will take humankind to the stars.'

'It all sounds fantastic stuff,' mused Carlisle. 'But I have taken an oath of allegiance to the queen. I am loyal to queen and country. It cannot be any other way.'

'Don't worry,' replied Samantha. 'We would not be requiring you to break your oath of allegiance. On the contrary we hope very strongly to be able to benefit our armed services.'

'How might you achieve that?' asked Carlisle.

'By various means,' replied Samantha. 'If your ship were to be made invisible... both to radar and to the naked eye would that not put you at a distinct advantage in a combat situation? If your ship was in one location and transported within seconds to a fresh location hundreds of miles away, would you not say that such an ability could be exceedingly useful?'

'It clearly would,' said Carlisle. 'But you are talking about science fiction. If you were to develop a more powerful radar or a more accurate missile that would probably be of more benefit. It would, I think, be more realistic.'

'I can see that you require further persuasion,' sighed Samantha. 'I'm feeling rather tired. It's getting very late, and I must be getting back to my apartment in Docklands.'

'Yes... I think we ought to turn in,' suggested Carlisle and Alex agreed.

In the morning neither of them were in any hurry to rise early and both

Carlisle and Alex were nursing sore heads. Eventually they shuffled down for breakfast after 10am still feeling somewhat woozy. Carlisle picked up a copy of the Sunday Times.

'My God!' he exclaimed. 'The Russians have occupied Estonia and Latvia is under threat. Four RAF Typhoon jets based in Estonia and their crews are currently missing. NATO forces have been engaged by the Russians with casualties sustained on both sides.

Carlisle fumbled in his jacket pocket and drew out his mobile phone which he hurriedly began to check for messages. There was one in particular which stood out as very significant. It read:

'To Lieutenant Commander E. Carlisle. You are hereby ordered to re-join HM Frigate *Aurora* immediately and be prepared to get underway within 24 hours. Await further orders which will be forthcoming.

Rear Admiral R D Leighton Commander of the 9th Frigate Squadron.'

Carlisle passed his phone to Alex and showed her the message.

'Oh, Eddie!' exclaimed Alex. 'What are we going to do now?'

Chapter 4

THURSDAY MORNING FOUND CARLISLE STANDING on the bridge of the *Aurora* as they sailed eastwards up the English Channel in bright sunshine and a southerly breeze. The party last Saturday in London seemed a world away. Now it was back to business in no uncertain terms. They had been ordered to put to sea forthwith, the ship only partway through repairs and a refit which had hardly begun. Indeed, they had set out in such a hurry that they still had civilian contractors on board. There were radar technicians from Babrock but not all the parts for the new Type 3150 3D set had yet been delivered. Six of the ship's eight Harpoon anti-ship missile launchers were now loaded with the ageing but still deadly weapons. An additional twin 30mm gun installation was still in the process of being fitted on top of the hangar roof. Additional machine guns of both 50 calibre and 7.62mm were being sited in suitable locations around the superstructure and protected by stacks of sandbags. The latest news was not encouraging. Having seized and occupied the small Baltic state of Estonia last weekend the Russians were now poised to invade Latvia, taking advantage of the mounting trouble in the Middle East and Persian Gulf which had been occupying everyone's attention.

'Chinook helicopter from RAF Odiham approaching from astern, sir,' called Sub-Lieutenant Gartmore. 'She's loaded with stores and parts for the new radar. Oh yes… and there's a contingent of Special Forces soldiers arriving in a second helicopter.'

'Very good, Sub,' acknowledged Carlisle. 'Engine room… slow to six knots.'

The flight deck of the *Aurora* was only just capable of briefly accommodating the big twin rotar Chinook which paused just long enough to detach its underslung load. Then it was back in the air and flying off northwards.

'Second Chinook helicopter approaching from astern, sir,' reported Gartmore. 'It's carrying the contingent of SAS troops.'

'Make arrangements to put them in the spare accommodation next to the Marines,' ordered Carlisle. 'I expect they'll be working in close co-operation, so it makes sense to put them next door to each other.'

'Aye aye, sir,' acknowledged Gartmore.

The second Chinook duly touched down on *Aurora's* flight deck and its contingent of SAS men scrambled out unloading their weapons and their kit which included a number of large and heavy looking boxes. These turned out to be full of explosives and detonators. Then the second Chinook was airborne and flew away northwards while Carlisle ordered an increase in speed to 25 knots.

'Sir, there's a signal from HQ in Northwood,' reported Yeoman Catherine Murray. 'Here, sir. It says we are to proceed to Kiel in Germany to take on board additional electronic equipment and specialist civilian technicians.'

'Sounds interesting,' replied Carlisle. 'Navigator... set us a course for Kiel.'

'Aye aye, sir,' acknowledged Lieutenant Simon Barrington.

By late in the afternoon they were making good progress and well on their way through the Channel although speed had to be reduced because of the large amount of shipping of all kinds. The Straits of Dover required particular care with navigation and additional lookouts were posted around the ship. The *Aurora* then altered course a few degrees to port and skirted the peripheries of the Goodwin Sands.

'Two aircraft approaching at high speed from the northwest, sir,' announced Leading Seaman Roy Stringer from the radar plot. 'Identified as RAF Typhoons on forward deployment from Manston airfield in Kent.'

'Crew to Action Stations... Crew to Action Stations,' called Carlisle as the klaxons sounded. 'This is a drill. Keep weapons tight.'

The Typhoons swept in fast and low from astern making a thunderous noise.

'Hard a starboard,' ordered Carlisle as the two jets screamed overhead so low that they were almost skimming the surface of the sea.

Two civilian technicians who had been high up in the ship working on the radar set were almost blown away by the jet wash from the planes. For a while afterwards the air was blue from their curses. Then the scene settled down for a while and Carlisle invited the officer in charge of the SAS troop to join him for coffee and sandwiches in his cabin. A suntanned, fair-haired man, aged about 25 or 26 wearing Army uniform appeared in the doorway of the captain's cabin.

'I'm Lieutenant Dreis van Reibeck… 21st SAS Regiment,' announced the soldier in a distinct accent which Carlisle instantly recognised as South African.

'That's splendid,' greeted Carlisle. 'Do you take milk and sugar?'

'Yes, please… both,' replied van Reibeck as Carlisle invited him to take a seat in the rather cramped quarters and offered him a plate of bacon sandwiches.

'I must say your arrival is something of a surprise to me,' explained Carlisle. 'I had not known we would be accommodating special forces soldiers when we set sail last night.'

'I am sorry for the intrusion,' apologised van Reibeck. 'I can truthfully say that I do not yet know the purpose of my intended mission, but I am sure the powers that be will find a use for us. Our activities are, of course, highly secret but I believe our brief may possibly involve an attack upon installations in the Russian enclave at Kaliningrad.'

'That would make some sense,' acknowledged Carlisle. 'I expect NATO, and the Western governments would want to neutralise Kaliningrad as a base for the Russians to mount attacks.'

The two men discussed strategy for a while and then Carlisle asked van Reibeck about himself and how he came to be an officer in the British SAS.

'My family own a cattle farm out in Kwa Zulu Natal,' explained van Reibeck. 'It is fairly near a town called Weenen… Well it is not near anywhere really. Weenen means weeping in Afrikaans. It was the scene of a Zulu massacre of Trekkers way back in the 1830s. Our family owns about ten thousand acres... but the land is not of the highest quality. A lot of it is not really useable for anything.'

'So what made you come to England?' asked Carlisle.

'Well...' considered van Reibeck. 'Things have tended to go downhill in South Africa... since about 1994. It's not the same country as it used to be. Nowadays there is so much crime and corruption. The family on a neighbouring farm were all massacred. Some robbers attacked them one night in their farmstead... tied them up with barbed wire and then hacked them to bits with machetes. I did not wish to end up the same way. At least if I am a soldier I am given weapons... I can fight back. I did not wish to just get slaughtered like a farm animal.'

'I can understand that,' acknowledged Carlisle. 'But South Africa is a wonderful country. I have been there a few times on holidays and while serving in the Navy. I love the diversity of the people... I have friends there... and not just from the white communities...'

Then someone was calling him over the intercom. It was Roy Stringer from the radar plot.

'Four aircraft approaching fast from the west, sir,' called Stringer. 'Identified as F-15 Eagles from the Illinois Air National Guard on deployment to RAF Lakenheath in Suffolk.'

'Sorry but I'm needed in the Ops Room,' apologised Carlisle to van Reibeck. 'Crew to Action Stations... This is a drill. Keep weapons tight.'

The F15s approached in pairs thundering in at low level and streaming black jet trails as they practised anti shipping strikes. The powerful aircraft were using their afterburners which created a great roar as they screamed overhead.

'Hard a starboard,' ordered Carlisle as the *Aurora* lurched, throwing people off their feet.

At this moment Carlisle's mobile phone rang... It was Alex calling from Longfleet Farm.

'What's that dreadful noise?' questioned Alex. 'I can't hear you for all the racket at your end.'

'Is there some problem?' asked Carlisle. 'I'm in the middle of an exercise right now.'

'The pigs have got out again,' reported Alex. 'Sandra and I have been trying to get them back in their enclosures for the last four hours but it's no good. Boris is the main ringleader. Several of the sows are in heat.'

'Well… get Jack Blofield and his sons over,' advised Carlisle. 'Tell them to bring Dabble. He's a big chap. He should be able to deal with Boris.'

'We'll do our best,' replied Alex and hung up.

The *Aurora* reached the western entrance to the Kiel Canal early the following morning where the canal authorities provided a pilot and gave the ship priority over other traffic using the waterway. Carlisle remained on the bridge together with Lieutenant Barrington and Sub-Lieutenant Gartmore. The passage of the canal was largely uneventful but involved navigating their way through a number of locks and Carlisle was glad they had the professional expertise of the pilot, Hans Muller, to assist them. They finally reached Kiel dockyards around noon and, with the assistance of a tug, moored stern first to the quayside next to the German frigate, Karlsruhe. Within a short time, they were visited by Leutnant Shneider of the German Navy who promised to provide them with everything they needed. True to his word prominent red flags were flown as stocks of ammunition were loaded aboard including 5-inch shells and belts of ammunition for the automatic weapons. Dockyard staff also came aboard and assisted with the installation of the Type 3150 radar and the additional twin 30mm gun mounting on the hangar roof. The following day *Aurora* was moved to another berth where two further Harpoon missiles were loaded into the remaining empty launchers. The frigate now had her full complement of eight Harpoons. Further stocks of Aster 15 anti-aircraft missiles were also loaded. During the evening heavy lorries arrived under police and military escort and delivered what was described as additional electronic equipment. Civilian technicians came aboard with the necessary permits and security clearances and requested permission to survey parts of the ship with a view to installing the delivery which Carlisle noted included large coils of metal wire. Carlisle recognised Dr Arnold Duvall whom he had met just a few days ago in London. The situation was to say the least curious, but Dr Duvall explained to him that this was all part of Project Ultra and focussed around creating powerful electromagnetic fields. The project was at the extreme cutting edge of technology and secrecy was of the utmost importance.

'Once Ultra has been installed I would ask you to take the *Aurora* out to sea out of sight of land and the main shipping lanes,' explained Dr Duvall. 'We can then begin to test the system. I suggest we start with a low power setting and see what happens.'

Technicians and dockyard employees worked on the installation throughout the night. In the morning Carlisle was able to see that there were now two large metal boxes mounted within the superstructure of the *Aurora*, one behind the bridge and another one further aft near the hangar. In the Operations Room additional consoles had been fitted and amongst the familiar faces were several people whom he did not recognise. Carlisle was introduced to a Professor Robert Finch of Darkforce Plc. Like Dr Duvall he was a balding, bespectacled man in his forties but of slim build and about 5 feet 6 inches in height.

'I take it you're one of the boffins?' smiled Carlisle upon being introduced to Professor Finch.

'I'm sorry?' responded Finch with a Californian accent.

'A scientist,' added Carlisle.

'Yes, I am chief scientist at Darkforce,' explained Finch. 'I want us to be able to put to sea as soon as practicably possible to start carrying out testing but I think we'll need additional generator capacity. All this equipment will require a considerable amount of electrical power. The German authorities are being very helpful, and I am promised they will be providing the extra generators.'

'But what is the purpose of all this?' asked Carlisle.

'Let's learn to walk before we try to run,' replied Finch guardedly. 'Initially we want to ascertain whether our technology can render an object the size of a ship undetectable to radar. If we can achieve this objective, I'm sure the British Royal Navy would find it very useful to say the least. Would you not agree, Lieutenant Commander Carlisle?'

'Indeed, yes,' agreed Carlisle. 'I am very much in favour of Stealth technology, and I am interested in what you are developing.'

The following evening Carlisle was sitting in his cabin taking a short rest after speaking to Alex on his phone. There were still problems with pigs and the neighbouring farmer, Robert Knighton, was being difficult and trying to push forward with his claim. There was a knock on Carlisle's cabin door.

'Sorry to disturb you, sir,' apologised David Warwick, his personal steward, 'but there is a lady to see you. She says she is from Darkforce.'

Carlisle looked up and saw Dr Samantha Langley silhouetted in the doorway. Immediately he was captivated by her penetrating blue eyes and stunning figure.

'Lieutenant Commander Carlisle... how good to see you again,' Samantha greeted him and gave a salute.

'Samantha... come and take a seat. My steward, David, is just preparing dinner. Please come and join me.'

'Thank you, I'm pleased to accept your invite,' replied Samantha and sat down within the cramped confines of the cabin.

'That's absolutely splendid,' said Carlisle. 'So how are things in the world of science right now?'

'Oh, interesting,' replied Samantha. 'All these troubles in the world might have a silver lining somewhere. Who knows, governments might start to take an interest in our efforts... they might be persuaded to help fund our research.'

'My ship is suddenly full of scientific people so you may have a point,' replied Carlisle. 'I understand some testing is due to take place shortly? I'm keen to see the results... although currently I'm in the dark as to quite what is being tested. Everyone seems tight lipped.'

'Well... we are dealing with top secret technology,' advised Samantha. 'When we met in London just a few days ago I asked you if you knew about Einstein's Theories of Relativity and his Unified Field Theory... the link between electromagnetism and gravity.'

'Yes, I recall you did mention these things. I'm afraid they're a bit over my head,' admitted Carlisle. 'We didn't study them at Dartmouth Naval College. Physics seemed rather dull to be perfectly honest.'

'Well, the physics we are exploring is far from dull,' said Samantha. 'I'd like you to put to sea as soon as practicably possible so that we can begin to carry out some initial testing of the systems. Essentially it will involve the creation of powerful electromagnetic fields around your ship. Another naval vessel will be sailing with us. We have the full co-operation of the German Navy. All we want to achieve… at least to start with… is to render your ship difficult to detect by radar. Then we can see how things go. Nothing to be afraid of… eh.'

'No, I'm sure there isn't,' acknowledged Carlisle. 'I'm keen to make a start.'

'There is one little thing,' added Samantha. 'When dealing with intense electromagnetic fields they can have… how would one put it...? adverse effects on some people so appropriate precautions should be taken. Let me explain… All human beings are born with something called a time reference point. Every individual has their own time reference point usually relating to when they were born. These time reference points are linked to planet Earth's electromagnetic fields. Essentially, we are anchored to the universe we inhabit and oriented… in tune you might say… to our own universe and the way it works. Very powerful electromagnetic fields can disrupt this link so that individuals affected by the fields become disoriented, both physically and mentally. In essence the link with our universe is severed and we are in the realm of parallel universes and that kind of thing. You get my drift?'

'You're blowing my mind,' admitted Carlisle. 'I'm not happy about finding myself in a parallel universe.'

'No, nor am I,' continued Samantha. 'So, what we have to do is to create a link artificially tying each individual concerned back to their point of origin. We artificially create a parallel universe identical to our own using computers and a link is created to tie the individual to their time reference point.'

'Well, I hope you people know what you're doing,' sighed Carlisle. 'If things work as they're supposed to then I can see the advantages. If not, it could be a bit of a disaster.'

'Don't you worry,' replied Samantha. 'Just put your trust in us. We know what we're doing.'

The following morning the news was not good. The Russians were building up their forces on the Latvian border and trying to cut off the ports and sea lanes. The Russian Navy was moving naval units from their Northern Fleet to the Kaliningrad enclave and squadrons of planes including Sukhoi Su-24 bombers were being moved to airbases there. A senior civil servant from the Defence Ministry in Whitehall in London who went by the name of John Lloyd Carswell came aboard the *Aurora* with his assistant, Timothy Cookson, and introduced themselves to Carlisle.

'I'm sure the people from Darkforce will already have given you as much information about Project Ultra as they are permitted to disclose at the moment,' said Lloyd Carswell. 'I'm wanting to make a start on testing the systems as soon as tomorrow. Things are becoming rather urgent, and we don't want to hang about. I'll be speaking to the people at the Kiel naval base today. Obviously, we need their full co-operation, and I'm pleased to say they're being very helpful and giving us all the assistance we need. We'll sail in company with two German frigates, the *Karlsruhe* and the *Mecklenburg-Pommern*. They also carry additional equipment to assist with the creation of the electromagnetic fields.'

Around noon a meeting was convened in the wardroom of the *Karlsruhe* which was attended by the captains of the two German frigates together with their executive officers, leading scientists from Darkforce as well as the civil servants from London. Carlisle brought with him his executive officer, Guy Hanson as well as his Chief Weapons Officer, Mark Openshaw, and navigating officer, Simon Barrington. The meeting was opened by Kapitan zur See Wolfgang Bremer, a heavily built man, aged in his forties who spoke quite passable English.

'I am pleased to welcome you aboard my ship,' began Bremer. 'You are all aware that these are difficult times, and we are having to... how you say in English? ... stick our necks out. In this instance we are taking part in experiments which would normally take many months or even years. Unfortunately, we do not have that luxury so we will put to sea tomorrow. The *Karlsruhe* and the *Aurora* are now fitted out with equipment to create powerful... how you say? ... electromagnetic fields. At a given signal once we are well clear of the coasts and the shipping avenues both ships will turn on their special systems. The *Mecklenburg-Pommern* will be following astern to observe what happens.'

'Excuse me, sir,' interrupted Carlisle, 'but what do we expect to happen?'

'I will hand you over to Professor Finch of Darkforce,' replied Bremer. 'He can explain.'

'We will begin the trials using relatively low voltage,' advised Professor Finch. 'At this stage we are wanting to ascertain the effect of the electromagnetic fields on radar transmissions. Hopefully, these will be disrupted by the fields to an extent that an enemy would have difficulty identifying the transmitting vessel. Either they would not know it was there at all or at least they would have difficulty pinpointing its location.'

'You say the trials will be started using low power voltage,' responded Carlisle, 'but assuming things go to plan what will be the next stage in the process?'

'We would then consider increasing the power output,' replied Finch. 'But we will proceed cautiously… step by step.'

'And when the power output is increased, what will happen then?' questioned Carlisle.

'We will have to watch what happens,' advised Finch. 'We are at the extreme edge of technology and scientific theory here.'

When the meeting concluded Carlisle felt he was none the wiser. The following morning the three vessels set out from Kiel with the Karlsruhe in the lead and once they were well out into the open sea and away from Captain Bremer's shipping avenues the flagship ordered speed to be reduced to ten knots. The *Karlsruhe* and the *Aurora* were now sailing in close company while the *Mecklenburg-Pommern* trailed a couple of miles behind with its radar operators tracking the two leading ships. Upon an order from Captain Bremer the generators were activated and instructions given as to the power output. After some minutes Carlisle, who was standing on the bridge of the *Aurora*, became aware of a greenish haze surrounding the *Karlsruhe*.

'Signal from the *Mecklenburg-Pommern*, sir,' reported Yeoman Catherine Murray. 'They say they are having difficulty maintaining radar contact.

Apparently, our position on their radar plot has become diffused and indistinct.'

'Very good,' acknowledged Carlisle.

'The new system seems to be doing its job, sir,' commented Guy Hanson who was standing with Carlisle on the bridge as Officer of the Watch.

'Sir, the *Karlsruhe* is ordering us to increase the power output of the generators,' reported Catherine Murray. 'Here are the details of the instructions.'

'Signal the *Karlsruhe* that we are complying with Captain Bremer's orders,' acknowledged Carlisle.

The generators were now creating significant noise and vibration and some members of the crew were reporting that they were feeling unwell with headaches and nausea.

'Look, sir,' pointed Guy Hanson. 'The *Karlsruhe* is disappearing into that green mist. She's vanishing.'

'All you can see is the imprint of the displacement of the ship in the water,' added Sub-Lieutenant Gartmore.

'Sir, the *Mecklenburg-Pommern* is reporting that she has lost both radar and visual contact with both ourselves, and the flagship,' advised Catherine Murray.

At that point, the noise and vibration from the generators suddenly stopped and everything went quiet save for the various departments aboard the *Aurora* who were reporting in.

'We appear to have lost all power,' reported Morag MacLean from Engineering. 'I'd say the main fuses have blown. We're in darkness down here and switching to emergency lighting.'

In the Operations Room, the officers and crew members there were reporting similar problems.

'All power has gone,' advised Mark Openshaw, the Chief Weapons Officer. 'We couldn't do so much as boil a kettle right now.'

The *Aurora* slowed to a standstill and called for assistance. The *Karlsruhe* reappeared out of its green fog and turned about to close the stricken frigate. Strenuous efforts were made during the next couple of hours to get some kind of power restored but the efforts of the crews of the two ships were in vain and the *Karlsruhe* had to attach hawsers and take the *Aurora* in tow. Carlisle was relieved that darkness had fallen by the time they reached Kiel, and the *Aurora* was manoeuvred into her berth with the aid of tugs.

'Do not worry, Kapitan,' joked a dockyard technician who came aboard to investigate the problem. 'We can provide you with a ship built in Germany now your English vessel is kaput.'

Carlisle had endured a difficult and frustrating day and merely scowled in response. Soon the *Aurora* was crawling with fitters and technicians. Later he had a meeting with Captain Bremer and Professor Finch.

'We have identified the electrical problem,' advised Finch. 'Essentially, we need to increase the generator capacity and adjust the circuit breakers accordingly. The dockyard people are working on things already.'

'How long do you think they'll need?' asked Carlisle.

'They'll be working flat out all night,' replied Finch. 'The dockyard manager says they hope to have the issues sorted within three days.'

In the morning there were news reports that Russian naval ships had been stopping sea traffic in the Baltic and several vessels who refused to comply had been attacked or fired upon. John Lloyd Carswell came aboard the *Aurora* and spoke to Carlisle and some of the dockyard staff.

'This technical glitch is very inconvenient,' remarked Lloyd Carswell. 'We really need the *Aurora* for operations without delay. Things are getting worse in the Baltic what with the Russians strengthening their forces there. The Latvian Government keeps clamouring for more help, but our ships are spread so thinly.'

'We're doing our best to get things fixed as quickly as possible,' responded Carlisle. 'This Project Ultra has been occupying our time and resources.'

'Yes, I'm well aware of that,' replied Lloyd Carswell. 'The thing is… you'll need the new technology for the kind of operations you're likely to be sent on. Commodore Vincent will be coming to brief you on forthcoming tasking.'

The following day Carlisle received a visit from Commodore Charles

Vincent, a tall man of over six feet in height and smartly turned out. He had a commanding air. He was accompanied by Lieutenant David Tregellis whose main function appeared to be to carry the commodore's bags and papers.

'I don't need to remind you that what we are discussing must be kept completely secret,' explained Commodore Vincent. 'We're walking something of a tightrope here so not a word to anyone else. The Russians are making full use of their bases in Kaliningrad. Tregellis, pass me my black briefcase. Let me show you these maps. This one here shows the location of the Russian enclave and its position in this south-easterly corner of the Baltic. Here is the port of Baltijsk. The Russians are constantly strengthening their forces there and have recently transferred many units from their Northern Fleet and from their Kronstadt naval base near St Petersburg. These include the nuclear-powered battlecruiser, Admiral Kuznetsov and the destroyer, Sovremmeny. In addition, the Russians have been transferring air assets to Kaliningrad bases including several squadrons of Sukhoi Su-24 bombers and Su-22s. These ships and planes have been threatening seaborne traffic in the Baltic and preventing NATO forces from going to the aid of Latvia and Estonia. We have to do something about it, but you are, of course, aware that Russia has powerful nuclear arsenals left over from the Cold War era. This makes her a highly dangerous opponent. We have to tread carefully because we do not have any wish to trigger nuclear attacks or World War 3. This is where you and your people come into the picture. I understand you have a small specialist SAS unit aboard the *Aurora*?'

'Yes, sir,' acknowledged Carlisle. 'They are currently out training along the Baltic coast somewhere to the east of us.'

'Well get them back aboard your ship as quickly as you can. They are required for operations. You will soon be receiving orders from Northwood. Here are some photographs of the port of Baltijsk. You will be employed as a taxi for the SAS unit. You will proceed first to the Polish port of Gdansk. The Polish Navy and Airforce will give you protection and the German Navy will also be involved in the operation. I understand you have already been training with them?'

'Yes, that's correct, sir,' responded Carlisle. 'They have been our partners in Project Ultra.'

'That's splendid,' continued Commodore Vincent. 'You will then steam across the Gulf of Gdansk to the northern tip of this rather strange looking spit of land here... such things are a feature of that part of the Baltic. This will be a dangerous place to be so you will need to make good use of the new Ultra technology, so you don't appear as a big blip on Russian radar sets.'

'I hope Ultra works better than it did the other day, sir,' commented Carlisle. 'We had a total electrical breakdown, and the ship just came to a standstill with nothing working. If we had been in a combat scenario it could have been a complete disaster.'

'Yes, I know, but let's put our trust in the boffins and hope they've got it right this time,' replied Vincent. 'Now look here, old chap. I know we're sending you into dangerous waters but that's how it is. Normally we would have sent a submarine for this job, but the truth is we just don't have any to spare. All our SSNs are fully occupied escorting the Trident SSBNs. So that's why we're sending your frigate and a small troop of SAS men. Any questions?'

Carlisle sighed, his forehead deeply furrowed.

'We will get on with the job in hand, sir,' he replied.

'Don't get too despondent,' advised Vincent. 'You know, apart from the electrical breakdown on the *Aurora* the other day the experiments went very well. The Germans report that for a short time the *Aurora* became invisible to both radar and the naked eye. It's quite incredible really.'

It took several days of hard work by everyone to get the *Aurora* back into an operational condition and to fully restore electrical power. Guided by the scientists the Germans installed the additional generators and made other modifications. With the contingent of SAS men back on board the *Aurora* set sail eastwards bound initially for Gdansk. The journey was largely uneventful and they were accompanied part of the way by the *Karlsruhe* and then provided with air cover by F16s of the Polish Airforce. Having reached Gdansk after dark the *Aurora* was manoeuvred into a secure berth with the assistance of tugs in a location which was surrounded on more than one side by buildings. It is unlikely that many people would have observed the arrival of this British frigate. During the day, the *Aurora* took on fuel and stores and then set sail north-eastwards in the late evening across the Gulf of Gdansk under cover of darkness. The shipping lanes were still busy, but the traffic was heading west towards Germany and beyond or northwards towards Sweden. Additional watch keepers were positioned around the ship which was sailing without lights and completely blacked out. On more than one occasion commercial ships came uncomfortably close and frequent alterations of course had to be made to avoid collisions in the darkness. Eventually they approached Russian territorial waters, and with the assistance of the scientists, the Project Ultra equipment was activated. Initially the power output was kept deliberately low with the intention of making the *Aurora* undetectable by radar. Nevertheless, a thin greenish mist began to envelop the ship. They were steaming cautiously at about sixteen knots when Roy Stringer reported,

'Vessel ahead, sir… bearing green zero-nine-zero… speed about twenty knots.'

'Can you identify it?' questioned Carlisle.

'Russian patrol vessel,' replied Roy Stringer. 'Range… seventeen thousand yards... I'm getting a second contact on the same bearing, sir. Another patrol vessel or possibly a corvette.'

'Some of these smaller Russian vessels carry missiles,' remarked Guy Hanson. 'The corvette could be a Nanuchka class. They're heavily armed.'

'Crew to Action Stations… Crew to Action Stations,' ordered Carlisle as the klaxons blared out. 'Maintain darkened ship. Cox'n… alter course thirty degrees to port.'

'Aye, aye, sir… port thirty,' acknowledged George McGlashan.

Carlisle stood over the radar plot in the Operations Room and watched the courses of the two Russian vessels. They were still closing the range but appeared to be steering towards the *Aurora's* previous bearing. Carlisle ordered a further course alteration away from the patrol vessels which were now heading south-west and appeared to have lost the British frigate in the darkness.

'I think Ultra is doing its job, sir,' said Guy Hanson to the captain as the range opened.

Carlisle now ordered a further course alteration to take them back on a bearing towards Baltijsk and the top end of the Vistula Spit. The SAS unit under Lieutenant Dreis van Reibeck were gathering together their kit which included three electric powered, small raiding craft which were almost completely silent when underway. As well as their automatic weapons they carried several large boxes marked 'Danger High Explosive'.

'Our orders are to damage and destroy the dockyard facilities,' explained van Reibeck. 'There is a large crane sited near the harbour entrance. If we can fell that into the main channel, we will go a long way towards blocking up the harbour entrance. The best option will be if we can succeed in sinking a ship in the harbour mouth.'

'I think you will find that difficult to achieve,' advised Carlisle. 'We will let you go ahead and plant the charges. Once they have detonated and the Russians are dazed and confused, we will move in and open fire on the shipping. Having done our work, we'll get out of the way pdq and meet you at this location here down the Vistula Spit near the lighthouse.'

Carlisle pointed to a map which was laid out on the chart table. He was well aware of the risks involved. The chances of failure and disaster were high.

'Three small vessels ahead... range ten thousand yards, sir,' advised Roy Stringer. 'Could be minesweepers... bearing green four-five. Speed twelve knots.'

Carlisle crouched over the radar plot. The impression he gained was that these vessels were looking for the *Aurora* but did not know where it was.

'Cox'n... alter course twenty degrees to port.'

'Aye, aye, sir... twenty of port,' acknowledged McGlashan from the helm.

The *Aurora* settled on her new bearing and Carlisle ordered an increase in speed to twenty-five knots. The Ultra equipment was still working with sufficient power to deflect radar waves. The Russians knew they were out there somewhere but so far had been unable to find them. Further small vessels were detected by *Aurora's* radar and suitable course adjustments were made. Eventually the glow of lights appeared on the horizon and Carlisle took the *Aurora* close into the Vistula Spit. The Chief Sonar Operator, Petty Officer Franklin Henry, was reading out regular soundings as the depth of water under their keel diminished. Carlisle took careful note of the Sonar Operator's reports. If they were to go aground in this place it would be a total disaster and no doubt a major diplomatic incident if they were just left stranded in full view of everybody. At more than one point the water was so shallow that the *Aurora* was brushing the fine silt beneath her, but she kept moving ahead and as they steamed towards Baltijsk everyone was relieved when Petty Officer Henry reported an increase in the depth of water. Carlisle now ordered a reduction in speed to ten knots as they searched for a suitable place to drop off the Special Forces soldiers and conferred with van Reibeck and his second-in-command, Sergeant Wayne Kirby. Then the *Aurora* was slowing to a standstill in this highly dangerous location and members of her crew were assisting in lowering the electric powered assault boats on to the darkened surface of the water. Fortunately, there was no moon, and the sea was as calm as a millpond. A thin veil of mist was beginning to develop to help their concealment. With some difficulty the heavy explosive charges were hoisted into the boats with the aid of ropes. Then the soldiers themselves climbed aboard with their weaponry and disappeared silently towards the coast. Now the only sound was the steady humming emanating from the Project Ultra generators. The crew of the *Aurora* sat and waited. Everyone was on edge and gunners crouched behind their automatic weapons peering into the darkness. Ruth Goldman pointed to some kind of activity close to the shore. Marine Gaz Markham scanned the area with powerful field glasses.

'Could be a fishing vessel,' he observed. 'It's difficult to see properly in this murk. We'd better let them know on the bridge.'

On the port side Able Seaman Dave Finney reported some kind of commercial vessel emerging from Baltijsk. Carlisle felt the urge to open fire and sink it in the harbour entrance but to do so would probably compromise the efforts of the SAS team, so he felt obliged to let it go. He hoped another opportunity would arise at the right moment. More time passed and still everyone waited. Carlisle glanced at his watch and saw that it was after 1am.

Finally at 2-13am a huge explosion lit up the night sky and sent shock waves thundering out to where the *Aurora* was stopped and waiting. While people were trying to get back on their feet a second detonation boomed out from amongst the dockyard facilities. Carlisle waited for a third explosion, but none came. Standing out on the bridge wing with Guy Hanson, Carlisle searched the harbour entrance through powerful night vision field glasses and saw that there were several fires amongst the dockyard installations and shipping in the harbour. Then came the sounds of further secondary explosions no doubt as munitions and flammable stores caught fire.

'There's a vessel emerging from the port, sir,' advised Ruth Goldman.

Carlisle peered intently through the night vision glasses and sure enough a ship did indeed appear to be trying to escape.

'I'd say it looks like a tanker trying to make a run for the open sea, sir,' advised Guy Hanson.

'That's what we want,' replied Carlisle and called to the Chief Weapons Officer over the intercom.

'Open fire on that vessel attempting to leave the harbour. We want to sink her in the channel.'

'Aye, aye, sir,' acknowledged Lieutenant Openshaw. He had been waiting for this opportunity and the 5-inch was quickly brought into action with the first shots striking the target and causing fires to break out.

Bearing in mind Nelson's order to engage the enemy more closely Carlisle ordered the Engineering department to get the *Aurora* underway and head towards the harbour mouth. The 5-inch was maintaining a steady rate of fire and Carlisle ordered the surface weapons department to prepare number one Harpoon for launching with numbers two and three standing by. Suddenly the tanker was lit up by a thunderous explosion as her fuel tanks caught fire.

'She's drifting out of control, sir,' observed Guy Hanson.

'There's a second vessel emerging from the harbour,' reported Ruth Goldman. 'It could be a naval vessel… corvette or similar.'

'Nanuchka class corvette approaching, sir,' called Roy Stringer. 'Range six thousand yards. Speed… sixteen knots and increasing. She's coming out of the port area.'

'Shift to the new target and engage with 5-inch and two Harpoon missiles,' ordered Carlisle.

'Aye, aye, sir,' acknowledged Lieutenant Openshaw who was already flushed with success from the destruction of the tanker which was now listing over to starboard in a sinking condition. 'Firing sequences activated and countdown running.'

Soon afterwards the night was illuminated once more as number one Harpoon anti-ship missile was fired from its launcher sited ahead of the bridge and began speeding on its pre-programmed flight path towards the Russian corvette.

'The second Harpoon is preparing for launch, sir,' advised Mark Openshaw.

'Very good,' acknowledged Carlisle. 'Fire the second Harpoon as soon as you are ready.'

Before the second missile had been fired the Nanuchka class corvette was torn apart by a large explosion and became enveloped in a sheet of flame which rose more than a hundred feet into the night sky.

'The naval corvette has been hit,' reported Roy Stringer.

'Advise we adjust the targeting of our second Harpoon to a different vessel,' called Mark Openshaw. 'There is a big destroyer in the port… Sovremmeny class. Should we take her out, Captain?'

'Go ahead,' ordered Carlisle. 'After we've fired the second missile, we should get the hell out of here. We need to pick up our fares from the SAS and then hurry for home.'

Soon Lieutenant Openshaw was reporting that the firing sequences had been activated for the second missile. The *Aurora* had closed to within four thousand yards of the harbour entrance and continued shooting with the 5-inch. Shipping and dockyard infrastructure were being constantly hit and there were many fires. Then the second Harpoon missile was speeding on its way and hit its target with a loud detonation.

'Target destroyer successfully engaged,' reported Roy Stringer from the radar plot.

'Well done, everybody,' called Carlisle. 'Cox'n steer green zero four five. Engine room increase to twenty knots.'

The *Aurora* left this scene of destruction and headed southwards skirting the Vistula Spit. The Ultra equipment was still operating on reduced power and hopefully distorting radar waves which would otherwise have given away the ship's position to the Russians. Nevertheless, it was not long before Roy Stringer was reporting contacts ahead and to starboard.

'Two contacts ahead… range six thousand yards… speed seven knots.'

Carlisle conferred with Lieutenant Openshaw and they both carefully examined the blips on the radar plot.

'They may just be fishing vessels,' suggested Openshaw. 'They're small, surface contacts and slow moving.'

'Tell everyone to maintain a sharp lookout,' ordered Carlisle. 'And what about that contact to starboard?'

'Two contacts to starboard, sir,' advised Stringer. 'They're vessels steaming together. Speed 13 knots. On their present course they may cross our path.'

'I'd guess they are Russian patrol vessels,' warned Carlisle. 'Just in the wrong place at the wrong time. There's the lighthouse. Engine room slow to twelve knots.'

He conferred with Guy Hanson and Mark Openshaw.

'We could increase the power on the Ultra generators,' suggested Guy Hanson. 'That could render us invisible to the naked eye.'

'But if we do that the SAS men will probably not be able to see us either,' cautioned Mark Openshaw.

The Cox'n, George McGlashan was now bringing the frigate cautiously inshore while Franklin Henry called out the depth under the keel. Once again *Aurora* was brushing the silt in the shallow waters of this corner of the Baltic. Then someone on the port bridge wing spotted a light flashing on and off at regular intervals which was not the illumination from the lighthouse. Carlisle ordered a further reduction in speed but dared not bring his vessel any closer to the shore.

'I think it's them, sir,' called Sub-Lieutenant Gartmore. 'I mean the SAS unit.'

'Very good, Sub,' acknowledged Carlisle. 'Let the flight deck party know that we're bringing the Special Forces team back on board.'

'Aye, aye, Sir,' acknowledged Gartmore as the *Aurora* slowed almost to a standstill.

The SAS men were assisted up on to the flight deck with the aid of scramble nets and their electric powered assault boats were also recovered. Away to the north the fires and explosions caused by the squad and by the *Aurora* were clearly visible and lighting up the night sky. Van Reibeck and Sergeant Kirby were keen to report the success of their mission to the captain.

'The Russians didn't know what hit them,' enthused van Reibeck. 'I think they still have no idea who did all that.'

'Too right,' acknowledged Carlisle. 'Well done, chaps. Let's get away from here. Lieutenant Barrington... set us a course for Kiel. Engine room give me revolutions for twenty-seven knots.'

A veil of natural mist and fog was developing and assisted their escape as the *Aurora* hurried away to the west... Roy Stringer was calling out regular contact reports, but the Russians were clearly having difficulty locating the frigate and the Ultra equipment was still performing its job effectively. Suddenly Franklin Henry was calling out a submarine contact.

'We're being trailed,' he reported. 'There's a submarine astern of us... moving fast. I'd say it's too fast for a Kilo Class diesel sub. It has to be a nuke.'

'Tell Lieutenant Griffiths to get his crew airborne at the double with a full armament of depth charges and Stingray torpedoes,' ordered Carlisle.

'The sub's using active sonar,' advised Franklin Henry. 'He means business and he's running at nearly thirty knots. He has to be a nuke.'

'Submarine contact identified as Russian Victor Class,' reported Leading Seaman Darren Livesey.

'I didn't expect them to have anything like that in the confined waters of the Baltic,' said Franklin Henry. 'The shallow waters are not really suitable for them.'

'You're right,' acknowledged Carlisle, 'but the Russians have been moving a lot of their stuff down from the Northern Fleet to strengthen their blockade of the Baltic States. They've also been putting older Cold War vessels back in commission that had previously been laid up for years.'

'Sir, Lieutenant Griffiths reports that he is preparing to take off,' called Sub-Lieutenant Gartmore. 'He confirms he is fully equipped to make an anti-submarine attack.'

Carlisle and Guy Hanson joined the sonar operators in the Operations Room and watched the developing action.

'That contact is Lieutenant Griffiths' Wildcat,' advised Darren Livesey. 'The nuke is eight thousand yards astern of us. He's probably manoeuvring into a firing position as he'll be within range with his torpedoes.'

'I expect the Ultra equipment is interfering with his sonar and hindering his working out a firing solution,' responded Carlisle. 'This is a good test of Ultra in an anti-submarine environment.'

'How does it feel to be guinea pigs in an experiment?' joked Guy Hanson.

'Torpedo contact… make that three torpedoes incoming from astern,' called out Franklin Henry.

'Professor Finch… can we increase the power of the electromagnetic field?' urged Carlisle as the fan shot of torpedoes sped towards the *Aurora*. 'We are under attack. This is an emergency.'

'I am increasing the power to 50,000 gauss,' acknowledged Professor Finch. 'That is a lot of energy. It may have side effects upon the crew.'

'The alternative is for us all to be blown to atoms,' retorted Carlisle. 'Go ahead, Professor.'

'Two of the torpedoes are homing in on us, sir!' called Franklin Henry. 'We're going to be hit.'

'Brace for torpedo impact!' Carlisle warned the crew over the internal Tannoy system. 'Brace!'

There was little he could do. The sonar screens showed clearly the torpedoes heading straight for the *Aurora's* stern. Even calls to the Engine room for maximum revolutions would not save the ship from destruction. The torpedoes were too fast to be outrun. Then just as everyone was throwing themselves to the deck and saying their final prayers the Ultra system emanated a tremendous deafening whining sound as the *Aurora* was enveloped in a massively powerful electromagnetic field. Carlisle found himself flung to the floor of the Operations Room and initially could not stand up. Other officers and crew members appeared to be similarly affected and a weird greenish light appeared to pervade the vessel.

'We're out of control,' someone called. 'The systems are going haywire.'

'I can't see anything,' yelled Roy Stringer. 'The radar plot has gone u/s.'

Carlisle felt that the whole ship and its crew were being flung through a hole in the very fabric of space-time. Then everything went dark as if in a tunnel. When Carlisle emerged, or appeared to have emerged, he was back on dry land in bright sunshine. The scenery looked familiar with the fields of golden corn stretching out towards the north Norfolk coastline and the white painted windmill with its sails turning gently in the light southerly breeze. There was the house where he had grown up with its Georgian architecture and landscaped gardens. Everything looked just as he had remembered it. There was even Sally the Labrador running to catch a ball which his father had just thrown. The scene appeared entirely perfect and normal save that Sally had passed away a long time ago and his father, Charles Carlisle, had dropped down dead from a sudden heart attack about three years back. Viewed in that context the picture exhibited anything but normality. Nevertheless, Carlisle walked ahead and greeted his father, patting Sally who came running up to him enthusiastically.

'Are you staying for dinner?' enquired Charles who was dressed in the same old casual tweeds which his son remembered him wearing when relaxing at home.

'Yes... if you'd like me to,' replied Eddie. 'Is Mum at home?'

'Of course,' replied Charles. 'She's busy preparing the Sunday roast and there's plenty for all of us. Your grandparents are here too. They'll be very glad to see you again. They haven't seen you for a while. Come to think of it, nor have I.'

Eddie sought to avoid the issue. He did not know how to deal with it and found the situation totally surreal. He and his father walked for a while and chatted as they used to do in times past.

'Look... I'm terribly sorry about Mum,' apologised Eddie suddenly. 'It's all my fault. I wasn't there to give her support when she most needed it.'

'What are you apologising for?' asked Charles. 'Your mother's fine. Let's go indoors now. She'll be over the moon to see you again.'

They walked indoors where Eddie's nostrils were assailed by the pleasing aromas of traditional cooking.

'And it's Mother's home-made apple dumplings for pudding,' enthused Charles. 'Your favourite as well as mine.'

They entered the living room where Eddie found both his grandparents, Thomas and Elizabeth Carlisle, who greeted him warmly and finally to the kitchen where his mother almost dropped the dish of vegetables she had been about to place in the oven.

'I knew you would come back to us one day,' she exclaimed and hugged him tightly. 'You are going to stay with us now... forever... aren't you?'

Carlisle was metaphorically knocked off balance by this line of questions and did not know how he should reply.

'I do not know why I am here,' he conceded. 'It is outside my control. Perhaps I am dead. We were about to be hit by torpedoes fired from a Russian submarine. Maybe we were blown out of the water or more likely it is an effect of the Project Ultra equipment generating super strength electromagnetic fields and distorting gravity and the fabric of reality.'

'Do not press him, Margaret,' cautioned Charles. 'Eddie needs a chance to unwind and readjust. Go and take a comfy armchair in the library, Eddie. It's nice and quiet in there.'

Carlisle accepted the advice and sat down in a dark green chair with a high back, trying to gather his thoughts. But as quickly as this alternative reality had materialised Carlisle found himself back in the Operations Room of the *Aurora*... There was pandemonium. People were shouting and claiming one piece of equipment, or another was malfunctioning. Several people had clearly been injured, either from falling or from the electromagnetic field and its side effects.

'Thank God you're with us again,' exclaimed Guy Hanson. 'All hell's been let loose with the ship's systems. All departments are reporting problems. Radar and sonar are down. We're in no state to fight an engagement.'

'What happened to that Victor class nuke?' enquired Carlisle.

'I really don't know,' replied Hanson. 'With the sonar out of action we're effectively blind.'

'We're trying to fix our current position,' advised Simon Barrington. 'The weird thing is… we seem to have somehow jumped more than fifty miles in a matter of seconds.'

'It's the effect of the electromagnetic field,' murmured Robert Finch who was rubbing his forehead and clearly not feeling his best. He was joined by Dr Langley who had been helping to operate the equipment installed by Darkforce.

'We have taken advantage of small ripples in the fabric of space-time,' explained Samantha Langley. 'The powerful forcefields have punched their way through one of these ripples and we have come out the other side. That's why we are now about seventy miles ahead of our position when the submarine fired its torpedoes at us. When we increased the power of the generators when we were attacked, I set the Ultra equipment to switch back to low power after two minutes otherwise we would have just torn away into some parallel world and not come back.'

'That's just completely mind-blowing stuff,' exclaimed Guy Hanson. 'I don't know what to make of it. Suddenly we're using technology so advanced… it's light years ahead.'

By dawn the *Aurora* was well to the west and planes from the Luftwaffe and the Marinefleiger appeared overhead to provide air cover while naval ships including the *Karlsruhe* came out from Kiel naval base to escort the British frigate safely into port. The crew of the *Aurora* had their radios tuned in to the international news networks. The Russians were claiming that NATO had launched an unprovoked attack upon civilian shipping in Baltijsk and that the vessel which carried out the attack had been pursued by the nuclear submarine, *Aleksandr Nevsky* of the Russian Navy and sunk. Russian vessels sent out to look for survivors had found no one. Ominously the Russian President, Konstantin Vatutin, was blaming leading NATO members including the United States and Britain for the attack on Baltijsk and was promising retribution.

Chapter 5

ALEX WAS WOKEN EARLY IN the morning by the sound of heavy rain and shuffled downstairs to feed the array of dogs and cats who shared the old farmhouse. Pulling on her wellingtons and donning an old coat which she retained for such inclement conditions she ventured out of doors with the next port of call being the horses who appeared disinclined to leave their warm, dry stables. Soon she was greeted by Sandra who appeared somewhat flustered and out of breath.

'Boris has got out again,' she announced. 'He's in Robert Knighton's cornfield. There's going to be all hell to pay. As if we didn't have enough trouble already.'

Alex followed Sandra outside and down to Boris' paddock where the recalcitrant porker could clearly be observed destroying the neighbouring farmer's crops.

'If only Boris had left it another couple of weeks or so Knighton would have gathered in his harvest,' complained Sandra.

The two women sought to cajole Boris back towards his own paddock, but he was a big heavy animal and Robert Knighton's crops were clearly far more desirable and tastier than the soggy pig feed which the humans were offering.

'It's no good,' sighed Sandra. 'I'll need to summon help. Leave it to me.'

Alex was left alone with the enormous pig and inevitably Robert Knighton appeared waving a stick.

'Get your fucking pig out of my wheat!' shouted Knighton and struck

Boris with the stick several times. Fortunately, Boris was unharmed, and the stick broke in two.

'I'm very sorry,' apologised Alex. 'We have strengthened his paddock again but he's so strong he can get through even the best stock-proof fencing.'

'If you can't look after your livestock properly you shouldn't be allowed to keep animals,' retorted Knighton. 'I'll sue you and your husband for every penny.'

Alex was relieved when Sandra reappeared with Jack Blofield and several of his sons and their friend, Dabble, who was about six feet two inches tall and was just about the only person who appeared to be capable of taking on Boris on anything like equal terms. Alex and her small army of helpers eventually managed to coax Boris back into his own field, but it had been an exhausting process for everyone. Makeshift repairs were hurriedly made to the damaged fencing and Robert Knighton informed them that he would be speaking to his solicitors with a view to obtaining compensation. Alex tried to contact her husband on his mobile phone, but it was switched off. She tried again later in the day but was still unable to gain a response. She felt increasingly aggrieved at being left alone to look after the farm and all its headaches single-handed. Some days later Alex received a call from Andrew Gibson, her friend on the university course. He was back in the area getting ready for the start of the new term. Apparently, he was having some difficulty with accommodation as his landlord had put different tenants in the flat he had been renting, no doubt at a much higher rent, and it was no longer available to him.

'Why not come and stay with me for a short while... just to give you time to get sorted out?' proposed Alex. 'My husband is away at sea at the moment, and I'm stuck here by myself. I won't charge you any rent provided you help me out with looking after the farm here and all the animals.'

'That sounds a good offer,' replied Andrew. 'I think I'll take you up on that.'

The following afternoon Alex was relieved to see Andrew's MG pull up on the forecourt at Longfleet Farm. Andrew appeared keen to assist with all manner of tasks including grooming the horses and hammering additional fence posts along the boundaries of Boris' pig paddock. In the early evening, upon Alex's suggestion, they drove out in the MG to a local hostelry, the Fox & Hounds, not far from Neatishead and with views across Barton Broad. The weather was still not at its best, so they sat indoors but Andrew approved of the good choice of beer and it was 'Steak Night', and he was able to order an enormous mixed grill. Alex enjoyed her plaice but as the evening drew on, she felt aware that she and Andrew were being observed by some of the locals.

'That's Eddie Carlisle's missus,' someone remarked audibly. 'Who's that young chap she's with?'

'Well, it's definitely not her husband,' replied Jack Woods from the boatyard.

'She's got a bit of a reputation,' added Jack's wife, Doreen. 'If you ask me, I'd say she was no better than she ought to be.'

Alex began to fidget in her chair and then asked Andrew to drive her home to the farm.

'I was enjoying the ambience,' commented Andrew as they left the establishment. 'Good food, good beer…'

'But tongues were starting to wag,' replied Alex. 'Didn't you hear them?'

'Oh, take no notice,' advised Andrew. 'We'll give them something to gossip about.'

Back at Longfleet they were greeted by all the dogs and cats and watched television briefly. Andrew put a protective arm around Alex as she regaled him with all her woes and how her husband did not understand how difficult it was to maintain the place.

'He just has no idea,' complained Alex. 'He spends all his time away being captain of that ship. He might be in the Middle East or on some exercise in the Atlantic while I'm hammering in big fence posts and rounding up enormous pigs.'

'That's just the way things are,' sighed Andrew. 'We all have our cross to bear.'

'Do you fancy an early night?' suggested Alex, her mood brightening.

'That sounds to me like it could be a very good proposal in the circumstances,' acknowledged Andrew as Alex led the way towards the stairs with an entourage of family pets following them at their feet. Fortunately, Andrew was fond of animals generally.

'If you've no objection I'd prefer to use the guest bedroom?' proposed Alex. 'You know how it is… feelings of guilt and that sort of thing.'

'No probs,' replied Andrew as they began to hurriedly undress with their clothes scattered haphazardly around the room.

Then Alex was reclining on her back, drawing back her fine legs. Although she was a few years older than Andrew, he found her stunningly attractive. One of his mates at university had described her as 'fit' while someone else had said she was a 'real cracker'. Andrew was inclined to agree with their assessments and considered himself fortunate to be invited into her bed or at least the spare bed. With enthusiasm he played his tongue amongst the folds between her thighs until Alex began to moan and then cried out with pleasure. Both of them ignoring the resultant damp patch on the bedsheets they wasted no time, indulging in vigorous intercourse while Andrew's loud grunting reminded Alex of Boris the boar. Nevertheless, she was greatly enjoying the experience and entwined her legs tightly around Andrew's back while several feline and canine faces looked on. At least one of the cats looked astonished.

The following morning Alex was up early and pressganged Andrew into assisting her in the tasks of mucking out the stables followed by more heavy work hammering in stout posts both around Boris' enclosure and the sows' paddocks. She found his efforts helped significantly around the farm and felt that at last she was not having to cope single-handed. In the early evening, she repaid his hard work by taking him out for a meal at a pub called the Rose & Crown near Stalham. It had views over the river and once again Andrew enjoyed the beer and was able to sample two of the guest ales. Being a little further from home Alex was not known to everyone at this particular hostelry and felt more relaxed. Once they had finished their meals they retired to a cosy lounge where there were no other guests, and they were able to indulge in some kisses and cuddles. Andrew ordered another pint before they headed home to be greeted by the menagerie. Alex wasted no time in leading Andrew upstairs to the spare bedroom where they hurriedly undressed.

'Do you like sixty-nine?' she asked.

'I certainly do,' replied Andrew.

Alex giggled excitedly as she knelt astride him and carefully reversed her bare behind towards him until his lips kissed her satin smooth cheeks.

'You have a superb arse,' praised Andrew. 'It should win prizes.'

'I used to be a model, you know,' Alex informed him. 'In Paris and Milan. That was quite a few years ago now, soon after I left school.'

'That is impressive,' replied Andrew. 'Tell me more.'

He had to wait until another time as Alex pressed herself tightly against him. Not long afterwards she was showing Andrew how she was able to stand on her head.

The following morning the news reports on the radio were full of the mounting problems in the Middle East and now troubles in the Baltic as well. There was no mention of the *Aurora*. The small country known as Estonia had been invaded and occupied by Russian forces and Latvia was being threatened. It did not immediately occur to Alex that these events would directly affect Eddie. After attending to the animals Alex took Andrew with her on a shopping trip to Norwich in the Range Rover. After buying groceries as well as fencing materials they had a bite to eat in a convenient café down by the River Wensum. It was a fine day, and they were able to sit outside in the sunshine. Afterwards they strolled along the riverbank and watched the wildfowl and the passing boats.

'I fancy we might hire a small cruiser or even a launch sometime,' suggested Andrew.

'That sounds a nice idea,' replied Alex. 'Lucy is coming over this weekend but maybe sometime soon. I like the prospect, Andrew. Just you and I together.'

They arrived back home during the afternoon and set about unloading the purchases. Sandra was conveniently on hand together with Gaz and Les so the task was made easier by many hands. Once everything had been put away Sandra indicated that she wished to borrow Andrew to help with the fencing of the new pig paddock, but Alex said she had one or two jobs for Andrew indoors and ushered him inside. Once out of sight of the helpers Alex and

Andrew were soon locked in a tight embrace and subsequently Andrew found himself lying on his back on the settee with Alex on top of him smothering him with lascivious kisses.

'I enjoyed having you with me on our trip to Norwich today, Andrew,' Alex informed him. 'So often it's been a case of either I go somewhere by myself or I stay at home but there must be so many things we can do together.'

'Like hiring the boat on the river?' replied Andrew.

'Yes… there's a boatyard near here at Barton,' suggested Alex. 'We ought to check it out. I know they hire out cruisers there. Do you think I should take off my bra?'

'Definitely… and everything else,' enthused Andrew as Alex knelt astride him, pulling off her striped T-Shirt and then unclipping her bra and casting it to the floor so that her lush, well-formed breasts swung freely.

Soon Andrew was feeling the generous matt of black hair in Alex's groin pressing against his genitalia and they were locked tightly together with Alex pushing down on him vigorously, her face contorted with pleasure. They ignored the cautious tap on the door as Sandra put her head round.

'Do you want us to go ahead with fixing the roof of the hen run…?'

Sandra stopped in her tracks and looked shocked. The couple glanced up at this intrusion on their lovemaking.

'Sorry, Sandra,' apologised Alex. 'We're just a bit busy right now. Give me half an hour or so.'

'My goodness I can see you're busy alright,' exclaimed Sandra as she retreated hurriedly from the living room.

Later in the afternoon Andrew assisted Alex with culinary preparations in the kitchen.

'I want to make you something good for dinner this evening,' announced Alex as she pulled on her T-shirt which was short and white with blue horizontal stripes and a had a gold anchor motif on the front giving it a nautical theme. That was the sum of her attire. 'I think it would be nice if we stayed in this evening, don't you?'

'Yes, of course,' agreed Andrew. 'Good idea, Alex. Let me know what I can do to assist.'

'I have in mind a beef stew. We'll have prawn avocado for starters and for pudding I'll make us a big fruit crumble with apples, pears and damsons from our own orchard. How does that sound?'

'That definitely appeals to me,' enthused Andrew. 'I'm feeling hungry already.'

'Go and get me that pack of diced beef,' instructed Alex. 'Ah, yes and some carrots and potatoes and a couple of sticks of broccoli.'

Andrew was soon back with the aforementioned ingredients. Alex was rummaging in cupboards beneath the kitchen sink searching for suitable pots and pans. They made loud clattering noises and Andrew gained the impression that Alex was somehow venting her frustrations loudly banging these metal cooking vessels against each other.

'Oh, bloody hell!' she exclaimed. 'Why does the one you want always turn out to be right at the bottom of all the others!'

At the same time Alex was providing Andrew with stunning views of parts of her anatomy which should not normally be on show save perhaps in a GP's surgery. He was tempted to touch these regions but felt it wiser not to do so just at this moment. There was more clanging and banging and finally the large cooking pot which Alex had been wanting was unceremoniously flung from the cupboard narrowly missing Bella the tabby cat. After that brief drama, the scene became more settled, and the ingredients were duly put together and placed in the Aga. Alex then set to work on the preparation of the fruit crumble.

'Go and get me sufficient fruit from the store,' she ordered Andrew.

Andrew selected sufficient apples and pears and damsons. He had very recently been helping Alex to pick these from the trees in the orchard and knew where they were kept. When he returned to the kitchen Alex was once again rummaging in lower cupboards.

'I've got the fruit,' he announced.

'I'm looking for the crumble mix,' replied Alex. 'What you need always seems to find its way right to the back.'

Finally, Alex found what she had been searching for and recruited Andrew to help her chop up the apples and pears and to prise the stones out of the damsons. Then the ingredients were placed in a large white metallic dish which Alex put in the Aga.

'I think that's everything sorted for the moment,' sighed Alex. 'Where were we?'

She gave Andrew a rearward glance before bending over to fill the pets' dishes. There seemed to be plenty of bowls to fill for the profusion of dogs and cats. Andrew observed the procedure with interest.

'So when were you a model, Alex?' he asked as he admired her perfectly shaped form.

'It was a while ago,' replied Alex. 'Actually, I ran away from school when I was 17. I was at Rovingdean... you know... the well-known girls' school near Brighton. I was a bit of a rebel. My father was a clergyman, and my mother made tea and cakes for the congregation after Sunday service. You know the kind of thing. But I wanted to get out and see the world. I managed to get on a plane and flew to northern Italy to stay with my aunt and uncle near Como. They were very helpful and sympathetic. Even though my parents and my school were naturally very concerned for my wellbeing my aunt and uncle introduced me to a modelling agency in Milan. It was very exciting, and I met some big names in the fashion world. I kept that up for a couple of years. Then I met up with my friend, Lucy Hamilton. You'll meet her this coming weekend. I was still very much a rebel and when Lucy suggested I come and join the commune where she was living on the French Mediterranean coast, I didn't need much persuading.'

'So, what was it like at this commune?' enquired Andrew.

'Well... the sun always seemed to be shining,' replied Alex. 'At least that's how I remember it. Everything was very free and easy. In the warm summer months, we spent much of the time naked. We didn't bother to get dressed in the mornings and nobody minded. We'd walk down to breakfast in the nude. That was how it was. It suited me well at the time and it was a world away from my stuffy parents and church services.'

'So, you're a rebellious vicar's daughter?' concluded Andrew. 'I expect you met a few guys?'

'Yes... plenty,' acknowledged Alex. 'There was Paul... and Raymond.

They were about the same age as me at the time. Then there was Jean-Francois... I particularly fancied him. There was a problem though.'

'What was that?' asked Andrew.

'That if I really fancied a guy and wanted him to be my steady boyfriend there were plenty of other girls and young women who were after the same chap. I found it well-nigh impossible to hold on to one boy for myself alone.'

'Unfortunately, that's so often a problem,' sighed Andrew. 'But have you considered taking up modelling as a career again?'

'What... in east Norfolk?' queried Alex. 'I could take up modelling the latest fashions in wellington boots... what to wear in the cowshed and the chicken run this season.'

'I can see the practical difficulties. It's a shame,' replied Andrew and put his arm around Alex's waist. 'I think you're tied to the farm... but there are plenty of far worse situations to be in...'

He began to sing a short song which went:

'Alex smell your toast a burning
Ah won't you let me in for tea
In my heart there is a yearning
Some toast for you ,a crust for me.'

The following morning was Saturday, but Alex was up quite early with Andrew in tow, grooming the horses and feeding the livestock. Sandra soon appeared. She seemed rather frosty and sent Andrew to help the men with the heavy task of clearing the dyke of fallen trees and branches and other obstructions.

'I'm sorry about yesterday afternoon,' apologised Alex, looking somewhat sheepish.

'It'll end in tears, you know,' cautioned Sandra. 'Tell the lad to hurry up and find a place of his own. You're making him too comfortable here... wining and dining him and cuddling him in bed. What's going to happen when Eddie comes home on leave? There's going to be a right old barney, make no mistake. Have you thought about that?'

'Sandra... it's up to me what I do in my own house. Andrew's been very helpful around the farm. I've felt much better about things since he's been staying here. After all, you've found him of valuable assistance with all sorts of tasks yourself. You've got to admit it.'

'Yes… I'm not saying an extra pair of hands hasn't been of help. But that should be as far as it goes. I'm not saying he shouldn't come to the farm. But speaking as a close friend of yours my advice is that at the very least you should kick him out of your bed. Enough of that, Alex.'

'No… not just now, Sandra,' replied Alex. 'Andrew is a good chap and I'm already very fond of him. Tomorrow, I want to introduce him to Lucy. I'm sure she'll be impressed. Next week we plan to hire a boat… just for a couple of nights or so. I might need you to help see to all the animals. It won't be for very long.'

'Oh, Alex!' sighed Sandra. 'The next thing you'll be telling us you love him. Then where will we all be? If you don't take a firm line with him, I shall have to say something to him myself… and you know I don't mince my words.'

'You'll do nothing of the sort,' retorted Alex. 'You've no right to interfere in my private life.'

On Sunday Lucy Banham-Hamilton called over accompanied by Jocasta and Anton. Jerome was apparently busy in a meeting with the troubles in the Middle East and now in the Baltic region as well causing panic in the markets. Both children were keen to reacquaint themselves with the animals. Jocasta was keen to ride Starlight and soon got her wish although she was accompanied by Sandra. Alex took Lucy and Anton down to the boatsheds where Andrew Gibson was helping Jack Blofield and his sons to hoist the big single black sail on the *Lord Rodney*.

'It's been a labour of love putting her back together again,' said Jack.

'Ah, she's given us a few headaches… make no mistake,' added his son, Gaz.

'Can we come aboard?' asked Lucy. 'I'm not dressed for sailing, but I'd love to have a look.'

'We'll take you out on Barton Broad if you like?' suggested Jack. 'We've got a couple of life jackets for you… but there's nowt to worry about. The most difficult part will be getting down that muddy dyke. We've spent a lot of time recently dragging out fallen trees and branches and all sorts. Claspy has been organising some dredging but the jobs far from finished I can tell you.'

The *Lord Rodney* was carefully quanted away from the boatsheds and out into the middle of Longfleet Broad. Alex had brought Elsa, Zara and Barley the family dogs while Jack was accompanied as always by his dog, Gordon Bennet. Gordon was not a particularly big dog. He was mainly black but with brown or tan coloured brindling giving him a sort of camouflaged appearance. He had a face like a bulldog, a stocky body, short stumpy, almost bandy, legs and a curly tail like that of a pig. Throughout east Norfolk and amongst the old Broadsmen Gordon had a reputation as a champion ratter. On the downside Gordon always smelled unsavoury. Jack explained that wherever Gordon Bennet found any piles of muck or garbage he would be rolling about in them. To Gordon rolling around in excrement of one sort or another was even more pleasurable than catching big rats and bringing them home still alive to run around Jack's cottage or even to other people's houses. Alex had suffered such experiences on more than one occasion and understandably Gordon Bennet was not her favourite dog, notwithstanding that she was usually fond of animals generally.

'Where did you come by him?' enquired Lucy as Gordon Bennet stood in the bows and sniffed the breezes.

'Well, I 'ad 'im as a little pup,' explained Jack. 'I'll say 'e was the ugliest little thing an' I wondered what to call 'im. Then 'e got into all manner of scrapes like the time 'e brought in a dead rat to the carol service down at Barton church one Christmas… just a few years back. You can imagine what a rumpus 'e caused. Then on top o' that he loves to roll in everything and pokes 'is nose everywhere 'e shouldn't an' every time I say "Gordon Bennet!" So that's 'ow the name kinda stuck.'

'So, there you have your answer, Lucy,' said Alex. 'Sandra's always offering to give him a bath, but he never seems to smell any better.'

The men had considerable difficulty navigating the *Lord Rodney* down the dyke with much use having to be made of the quant pole. There were still many obstructions, and the big wherry drew more water than the nimble

Moonbreeze. On a number of occasions Jack thought they would have to abandon today's outing but finally they reached Barton Turf and open water. Alex and Lucy sat outside at the stern. Fortunately, it had turned out a fine day and the air was fresh with a faint tang of salt off the sea. Andrew came to join them and talked about the university course and farming.

'So where is it that you come from?' Lucy asked him. 'Are you a local lad?'

'Not quite,' replied Andrew. 'I'm from Lincolnshire. We've got a farm in the Wolds not far from a place called Binbrook. My family has owned it for generations back. My father and my Uncle John are keen to expand and develop it. We took over a neighbouring farm with about six hundred acres a couple of years ago when the couple who ran it wanted to retire. We have our eye upon bigger fish in the locality.'

'Do you intend to stay in farming?' asked Lucy. 'Is it arable farming or livestock that you're into?'

'I want to run the farm myself when my father and my uncle are prepared to hand over the reins,' explained Andrew. 'We're mostly into arable but we keep livestock as well. We've got sheep grazing on the higher ground up on the Wolds and we keep pigs as well.'

'Do you have any cows? Do you do dairy farming?' asked Lucy.

'We used to have a herd,' replied Andrew. 'But it wasn't making money. The big supermarkets screwed us into the ground on milk prices so we sold off our herd. Pity really.'

'And how many acres do you have now?' questioned Lucy.

'More than three thousand,' responded Andrew. 'But we're hoping to merge with another neighbouring farm pretty soon… the Mason-Gardner family at White Lees Farm. Some of their land adjoins part of ours and they're mainly into arable as well so it will make sense. We've had our eye on their farm for quite a while. Now it seems we'll have our opportunity. They have more than two thousand acres of good quality arable land.'

Jack Blofield then appeared with several mugs of tea and some biscuits which were appreciated by everyone. The dogs were particularly keen on the biscuits, but Gordon Bennet was not so welcome. Once Andrew had finished his mug of tea, he went to join the crew and was handed the big wooden tiller.

'I like your boyfriend,' remarked Lucy to Alex once they had adjourned to the wherry's rather small kitchen and were out of earshot of the men. 'He looks hunky. Can I borrow him later?'

'Sandra says I should kick him out,' whispered Alex.

'Oh no!' exclaimed Lucy. 'You mustn't do that. What a waste. Talk about looking a gift horse. If you don't want him, I'll carry him off back home.'

After sailing on Barton Broad for a couple of hours they headed back to the farm and were pleased that the sun had come out and created a pleasantly warm afternoon. Alex and Lucy were able to go skinny dipping in Longfleet Broad and were joined by Andrew while Anton stayed to help the men working on the finishing touches with the restoration of the *Lord Rodney*.

'We hope to hire a boat for a couple of days next week,' remarked Alex to Lucy as they bathed in the peaty waters.

'That sounds a good idea, but I would say that I prefer to be in the water rather than on it,' replied Lucy. 'I'm not the world's best sailor.'

'It'll give us a chance to be alone together, just Andrew and me,' said Alex.

'Well, indeed why not,' responded Lucy. 'Have you heard from Eddie recently…? I don't mean to spoil things, but events seem to be hotting up in the world rather at the moment.'

'I did speak to him on the phone a couple of evenings ago, but he says he can't tell me much at the moment. They don't call the Royal Navy the Silent Service for nothing. I don't have much idea where he is or what he's doing. He could be out in the Atlantic or roasting somewhere in the Middle East. What do I know? I'm just his wife.'

'You really must come over and spend a little time with us at our country retreat near How Hill,' proposed Lucy. 'Do you think we're in any danger in this country? If people start dropping bombs or firing missiles, they're likely to hit London first, I expect.'

'Try not to think about it,' recommended Alex.

A moment later two military jets flew over Longfleet Broad at low level practising dogfighting tactics.

'I hope they don't frighten the horses,' exclaimed Alex as a further pair of aircraft screamed overhead.

'I tend to try to avoid the news programmes at the moment,' added Lucy. 'They just make me anxious.'

'Me too,' concurred Alex. 'Let's think about something else. Andrew, be an angel and go and get my suntan lotion from my bag in the kitchen.'

Andrew did as he was asked, and the women observed him as he strolled naked towards the farmhouse.

'Nice bum,' commented Lucy.

'Yes… but I hope he doesn't bump into Sandra while he's there,' replied Alex. 'She might have something to fuss about.'

The women laughed at the prospect and not long afterwards Andrew emerged from the house with the lotion. Wearing just their shades Alex and Lucy pretended not to stare as he approached.

'The good thing about wearing shades is that you can look at guys without them realising,' noted Lucy. 'He's well-endowed isn't he. You don't want to kick him out.'

'Hush,' whispered Alex as Andrew sat down with them. Lucy rolled onto her front.

'Be a darling and put some of that oil on my back, Andrew,' requested Lucy.

Andrew duly obliged but when he had finished oiling her back, he paused. Lucy slightly wiggled her bare rump.

'Come on, dear. You've not finished,' complained Lucy. 'Don't worry… you can touch my bum. I won't bite you.'

'He's a perfect gentleman,' said Alex. 'Go on, Andrew. It's alright. I won't mind.'

Andrew duly complied with the instructions but then Lucy rolled onto her back and stretched herself out.

'Please continue,' she requested while presenting Andrew with her soft breasts and her pink nipples.

Unable to resist such advances Andrew succumbed to Lucy's embrace and they began kissing lasciviously.

'Hey... stop that! Andrew... Lucy!' called out Alex. 'Stop that at once. Look... Anton's coming... with some of the men from the boatsheds.'

Lucy glanced up and saw that people were indeed coming in their direction. She hurriedly pushed Andrew away and reached for her clothing.

'They fired a missile at Liverpool,' called Jack Blofield. 'And another one at Newcastle. Done a lot of damage they have. We heard it on the radio just now.'

'Oh no!' exclaimed Lucy. 'Were they nuclear missiles?'

'Don't think so,' replied Jack. 'The one at Liverpool landed in the docks and set a ship on fire. Some people have lost their lives... poor bastards.'

'Well... that rather puts a damper on things,' remarked Lucy. 'I'd been having a nice day up till now. Alex dear, I must be on my way once I've rounded up my children... but you must come over and see us at Ludham Manor... that's our new place in the country. It really is very close and there's so much I want to show you... And, Andrew... make sure you come too otherwise I shall be very cross.'

That evening Alex and Andrew sat glumly watching the television news. It appeared that Russian submarines had been able to operate close enough to British shores to launch salvoes of cruise missiles. Fortunately, these had been armed with conventional explosive warheads, but they had caused a lot of destruction at several places. Clydeside had also been targeted and there was concern that next time the incoming missiles might have nuclear warheads.

Several days later on Wednesday morning Alex and Andrew hired a modest three berth cruiser from a boatyard at Stalham. In the circumstances it seemed the right thing to do to try to get away from all the troubles of the world if only for a couple of nights. Alex had made appropriate arrangements with Sandra for the farm and all its animals to be looked after during this short break. During a fine afternoon Alex and Andrew headed south down the River Ant and then up the River Bure to Wroxham Broad where they found a sheltered cove partly surrounded by reed beds and anchored by mud weight. Alex put the kettle on, and the inevitable gaggle of waterfowl came quacking and honking around the boat demanding to be fed. However, the nearest other humans were out of sight, and it was not long before Alex was lying naked on the bed with Andrew making love to her. Alex sought to clear her mind of cares and entwined her legs tightly around her young man.

'It's better to live each day for itself,' she murmured. 'Who knows what tomorrow may bring.'

'I guess you're right,' concurred Andrew.

In the morning, they cruised up the River Thurne and explored the great wilderness of Hickling before taking a slight detour to Horsey Mere where once again they found a sheltered cove away from everyone else. Some distance to the east was Horsey Mill and the fresh air held the salty tang of the sea which was not far off beyond the dunes. After making love they put on the kettle and Alex made a pot of tea and beans on toast for both of them. Andrew suggested they put on the radio to find out the latest news, but Alex said the radio was banned.

'It will spoil the peace of this place,' she said.

Andrew was inclined to agree and after they had finished their repast they continued with their love making.

At the weekend Andrew paid a visit back home as the new term was due to start at university and he said he wished to see his family and get sorted out. Alex managed to speak to Eddie on the phone several times while Andrew was away. As usual Eddie gave little information, and Alex still had no idea where he was. Some days later the new autumn term started. Andrew came back to the farm with Alex at the end of the day, but Alex thought he was rather quiet and not his usual self. They had dinner at home and fed the menagerie of creatures. Eventually Alex enquired,

'Is everything alright, Andrew. You seem to have something on your mind?'

'Well... there is something important,' replied Andrew. 'And it affects things between us.'

'You can tell me what it is... go on.'

'I've got engaged,' replied Andrew. 'To Philippa Mason-Gardner...'

'To Philippa who?' questioned Alex aghast.

'Philippa Mason-Gardner,' repeated Andrew. 'I've mentioned her family before. They're the people who own a farm adjoining ours in Lincolnshire. They're well to do and we hope to take over their business.'

'Oh, Andrew!' exclaimed Alex. 'You never mentioned to me before that you had someone else. How could you be so heartless?'

'I'm sorry,' apologised Andrew. 'Perhaps we should go upstairs now, and I can explain it to you.'

'What you can do is pack your bags and leave,' retorted Alex. 'As far as I am concerned our friendship is at an end.'

'But I don't really understand,' stammered Andrew. 'What were you looking for in our friendship?'

'I didn't expect to be cheated on,' replied Alex. 'You're a cheat just wanting to take advantage of people all the time.'

'But I'm not like that at all,' said Andrew. 'Can't we go upstairs just one more time. I'll give you the best screw you've ever had.'

'No!' exclaimed Alex. 'Just get out of here… now!'

Andrew ducked and headed for the door as Alex hurled a valuable decorated Delft plate in his direction. Another missile quickly followed while dogs yelped and cowered in the corner and cats dived for cover. As he hurriedly exited Longfleet Farm Andrew was reminded of his grandad's old adage,

'Hell hath no fury like a woman scorned.'

Then Andrew was gone never to return, and Alex heard the sound of his MG crunching the gravel in the courtyard and driving away. Suddenly Alex felt a profound emptiness. Dreams built on sand crumbled to dust as she flopped down in an armchair and burst into tears. Gradually the dogs returned to her side and rested their chins on her knees while the cats cautiously crept out of their hiding places and climbed on to her lap, purring gently.

In the morning Alex was still weepy as she attended to the farm animals and the horses. Sandra appeared as usual to assist with these tasks.

'Andrew's gone,' explained Alex while sniffing into her handkerchief. 'I told him to leave.'

'Well done, Alex,' praised Sandra. 'It's all for the best although it might not seem that way just now.'

'He suddenly told me he'd got engaged to some girl who comes from a neighbouring farm where his family live. I was absolutely furious. He was just making use of me as his bit on the side.'

'I told you it would all end in tears,' Sandra reminded her. 'And you have to look at it this way, Alex. What were your intentions with regard to him? Were you going to divorce Eddie with all the upheaval that would create? I don't think so.'

For the next few days Alex moped around at the farm tending to the animals but feeling constantly depressed. She now felt even more alone than before she first brought Andrew home. On the News and in the papers there was talk of evacuating school children out from the towns and cities into the countryside. She considered the prospect of offering billets to some of these people. There was plenty of room at the farm. Then she wondered what Eddie would say when he came home next on leave. She decided to let the matter rest. One wet Sunday morning she woke up feeling even more disconsolate than of late. She had not been able to get through to Eddie on his mobile phone for several days. Lucy had not been in touch since Alex told her she had given Andrew his marching orders. Alex got to work cleaning out the hens and then giving attention to Myrtle, the donkey. While she remained angry with Andrew she missed having his help around the farm. As the day wore on the rain got heavier and Alex hoped that it would not result in further flooding and more disputes with Robert Knighton. Then her mobile phone rang while she was up a ladder checking on the guttering which was leaking in a number of places,

'Hello,' called Alex. 'You're very faint… it's a bad line. I can't hear you properly. Are you trying to sell something?'

'Alex,' whispered a voice on the other end of the line. 'Is it okay to speak?'

'Who is this?' demanded Alex. 'I'm up a ladder at the moment in the pouring rain and I'm not very happy.'

'It is Faisal,' replied the voice. 'I hope I have not phoned at a bad moment?'

'Oh Faisal!' exclaimed Alex. 'I'm sorry. I couldn't hear you properly just now but it's really good to hear from you. I've been feeling a bit down just lately with one thing and another.'

'Oh yes,' said Faisal. 'There are a lot of dark clouds at the moment what with the Russians firing missiles and people losing their lives. I hope the politicians will be able to sort things out. But I rang to let you know that I am buying a place not far from you... Hickling Hall. I don't know if you know it, but it is 17th Century Jacobean with mullioned lattice windows and tall twisted chimneys. It is a very interesting property oozing with history and the estate includes part of Hickling Broad. I was influenced by the fact that Jerome and Lucinda live not far away but I also remember you said you live near their country retreat.'

'Yes, that's right,' acknowledged Alex. 'They have a property only a few miles from our place here. We're at Longfleet Farm near Neatishead.'

'Yes, I remember you saying,' replied Faisal. 'I was wondering if I might call on you during the next couple of weeks if you are not too busy and drive you over to show you the new... or should I say old place.'

'I'd love to see it,' enthused Alex. 'Just let me know a date and I'll do my best to work round it.'

They then discussed arrangements for visiting and following Faisal's unexpected call the rain stopped, and the sun shone. Alex instantly felt much brighter.

Chapter 6

AT KIEL NAVAL BASE IN northern Germany work proceeded in highly secret conditions on loading the Aurora with fresh stocks of ammunition including large numbers of 5-inch shells. More than a hundred rounds had been fired during the recent raid against Baltijsk. Information supplied by spy satellites and agents on the ground indicated that a lot of damage had been caused to the dockyard facilities there and several ships had been sunk in the harbour including a tanker and a Nanuchka class missile corvette. A Sovremenny class destroyer had been badly damaged and would not be likely to be in a fit state to put to sea for many months at the very least. Even more secretive was the Project Ultra system with which the scientists were preoccupied. Tarpaulins were put in place to cover up the large metal coils currently installed on the Aurora and the additional electronic equipment which had recently appeared on the upper works of the frigate. Professor Finch and Dr Langley were still of the opinion that more generator capacity was required, and arrangements were made with the assistance of the German military authorities. Since the Baltijsk operation many members of the Aurora's crew had complained of suffering side effects from the use of the very powerful electromagnetic fields.

'Thank God we did not lose anybody,' commented Samantha Langley. 'Fortunately, the efforts we have made so far to establish secure alternative time reference points for the crew have worked to the extent that we have not yet suffered fatalities. However, we need to strengthen these in view of the very strong electromagnetic fields we are having to generate in dangerous combat situations. What we experienced in the Baltic the other day is likely to be repeated if this vessel is sent out on future operations of that kind and I expect it will be.'

'So, what would you recommend?' asked Carlisle.

'Leave that to us scientists,' replied Samantha. 'We know what we are doing. There needs to be a programme to provide protection for all the crew and for all civilian contractors like Professor Finch and myself who sail with the ship on operations. I suggest we start the programme as quickly as possible.'

'Is it likely to have an adverse effect upon the crew?' enquired Carlisle.

'I cannot give any guarantees,' replied Samantha, 'but without the protection the effects could be catastrophic. We can continue with the programme from as soon as tomorrow.'

'Okay. Let's go ahead,' said Carlisle. 'We're not yet in a fit state to put to sea but the powers that be will soon be sending us our next orders.'

Later that day several members of the crew reported feeling unwell with maladies such as headaches and depression and anxiety. Carlisle considered that an effort should be made to boost the morale of the ship's complement, and he conferred with Guy Hanson and Simon Barrington.

'Perhaps we should throw some sort of concert or party,' suggested Guy Hanson.

'Franklin Henry is the chap to speak to,' recommended Simon Barrington. 'After all he is in charge of the Aurora's Reggae band. We might even invite crews from the Karlsruhe and the Mecklenburg-Pommern.'

'That sounds a good idea,' responded Carlisle. 'Have a word with Petty Officer Henry and see what he says. After what we've been through recently it would benefit the crew to have a chance to let their hair down a little.'

After further discussion Petty Officer Henry, the Aurora's Chief Sonar Operator, said he would be pleased to help organise a concert. Guy Hanson said he would speak to the commanding officers of the two German frigates. Arrangements were put in hand for the concert to take place on the forthcoming Friday evening. There would be live music and dancing. Petty Officer Henry would front the musical entertainment, but all members of the ship's crew and guests would be welcome to contribute. The concert would take place primarily in the Ratings' Mess as this had the most space available. Arrangements duly went ahead, and an invite was also given to the crew of the German submarine U-99 and the Polish submarine, Orzel, which had joined the Project Ultra team. The vessels were now known together as Task Force 79 and were designated for special operations in the Baltic. Carlisle believed the concert would be an excellent way of helping the crews of the ships and submarines to get to know each other.

By Friday afternoon the Aurora's Ratings Mess had been rearranged as the venue for the concert and Petty Officer Henry and his band were practising with their instruments and with the sound gear. He was ably assisted by Sub-Lieutenant Brooks, Lance Corporal Wayne Addleshaw RM and Gaz Markham RM, communications specialist Petty Officer Danielle Sheldon as well as Ralph Davies and Leroy Moore from Engineering. Subsequently they were joined by Gustav Landsberg from the Karlsruhe who was owner of a saxophone and demonstrated his ability to play the instrument well. At around 5pm Commodore Vincent appeared with a smiling face and shook Carlisle warmly by the hand.

'I am the bearer of good tidings for once,' announced the commodore. 'I am pleased to be able to inform you of your promotion to full Commander. How does that feel?'

'I am greatly honoured,' acknowledged Carlisle. 'And very grateful for their lordships' appreciation of our efforts here on the Aurora.'

'That's not all,' continued Commodore Vincent. 'Is your executive officer around?'

'Yes,' replied Carlisle. 'He's just over there assisting with setting up the sound systems for our concert. Would you care to join us, sir. You're invited.'

'I will be very glad to accept,' replied the commodore. 'I am aware you chaps… and chapesses…can put on a good show. Is that Lieutenant Commander Hanson?'

'Lieutenant Hanson, sir,' acknowledged the executive officer as he turned to speak to Commodore Vincent.

'Congratulations on your new promotion, Lieutenant Commander Hanson,' beamed the commodore. 'There'll be cause for celebration on the

Aurora this evening. I have similar good news for your Chief Weapons Officer. Be pleased to inform Lieutenant Commander Openshaw of his promotion....and your Chief Sonar Operator?'

'He's just here, sir, testing the microphones,' said Hanson and introduced the commodore to Franklin Henry.

'Congratulations Chief Petty Officer Henry!' exclaimed Commodore Vincent. 'Well done everybody. Do you think I should say a few words to the assembled officers and crew this evening? I've been put in overall command of Task Force 79. I ought to say something... give everyone a bit of a pep talk, and a general idea of what we're up to.'

'Yes, I think that would be a good idea, sir,' acknowledged Commander Carlisle. 'And congratulations on your new appointment, sir.'

At around 6pm people began arriving for the event with some taking seats and others standing. Roy Stringer assisted with the introductions. He was rather miffed that he had not been included in the list of promotions but did his best to disguise his disappointment.

'Have we got our captain...? Yes... I see him over there talking to Commodore Vincent and Lieutenant Commander Hanson. They've both just got promotion. Do we have Sub-Lieutenant Gartmore...? He's supposed to be playing in the band.'

'He's just gone for a piss,' someone called.

Soon afterwards a large contingent of sailors and their officers arrived from the German frigates followed by men from the U-99.

'Do we have the Polish contingent yet?' asked Roy Stringer.

'They've not arrived yet,' someone replied.

'I'd better go and look for them,' proposed Lieutenant Barrington.

In the meantime, Chief Petty Officer Franklin Henry took the opportunity to introduce himself and members of his band which called Aurora Borealis.

'On the saxophone here, we have Gustav Landsberg from the Karlsruhe. Give him a cheer everyone!'

A big round of applause was duly given particularly from the German crews.

'On the drums we have Ralph Davies,' announced Franklin. 'He's a good guy from Engineering and he comes from London…like me. On the Reggae Keyboard we have Leroy Moore. What would we do without Leroy? He's also in Engineering and he comes from Stockwell. All three of us are from families who originally came from Jamaica, and we still have people who live in the West Indies. On the Bass Organ we have Marine Gaz Markham with Lance Corporal Addleshaw on the trumpet. From the officers and NCOs may I introduce Sub-Lieutenant Brooks on the Bass Guitar…the good old Fender Jazz Bass… with Sub-Lieutenant Gartmore on the piano and Petty Officer Danielle Sheldon on the clarinet. Well done, Danielle.'

At that point, the Polish contingent from the submarine, Orzel, finally appeared and headed instinctively for the bar. Commodore Vincent decided it was a good opportunity to say a few words.

'Ladies and gentlemen, Damen und Herren, Panie I Panowie… I have the honour to address you as the newly appointed commander of Task Force 79 of which you now form part. Our mission is by its nature highly secret, but I can at least tell you that this task force is to be involved in special operations in the Baltic. You are, of course, already aware that Russian forces have invaded and occupied the small country, Estonia. I can also inform you that today Russian forces have entered Latvia and are heading towards Riga. You are aware that both Latvia and Estonia are NATO members and firmly part of the Western sphere, so we have an obligation to go to their assistance. Indeed, Russian units have already engaged NATO forces, so this is a very dangerous scenario but if we keep together we are strong… and more powerful than our opponents. I look forward to working with you all during the coming weeks and months and I am sure it will be a successful association.'

Commodore Vincent then repeated his speech in German and a Polish officer acted as interpreter and gave the wording in Polish.

'Jeszcze Polska nie Zginela!' shouted the Poles in unison when they had heard the speech translated.

'We cannot wait to get to grips with the Russians,' announced a Polish lieutenant. 'We will give them a beating for all those years they put us under their yoke and for their treachery in 1944.'

'What a splendid spirit,' praised Commodore Vincent. 'With chaps like these on our side we're bound to win!'

The commodore then handed the stage back to Franklin Henry and Roy Stringer who announced they were now starting the concert.

'Ladies and gentlemen, Damen und Herren, Panie I Panowie... we'd like to begin the concert with a selection of songs from our hero, Smokey Robinson...a great musician. We'll start off with a number you all know, *'Tears of a Clown.'*

The band completed the number to welcome applause and then followed up with further Smokey Robinson hits including 'Shop Around', 'I second that emotion,' 'Just to see her,' and 'Tracks of my Tears,' The band then moved on to playing songs from Bob Marley for which Chief Petty Officer Henry donned a large wig complete with long dreadlocks.

'Ladies and gentlemen... Damen und herren, panie I panowie...we would now like to play you a series of great songs from Bob Marley and the Wailers. We'll start with 'Exodus.' I'm sure you're all familiar with this song.'

'Exodus movement of jah people!

Oh oh oh, yea-eah!'

The band duly completed this song and then covered many well-known Bob Marley hits including 'Jamming,' 'Buffalo Soldier', 'Iron Lion Zion,' 'I shot the sheriff,' 'One Love,' and 'No Woman, No cry.'

Following these great hits Chief Petty Officer Henry then addressed the audience once again.

'Before I take a short break, we'd like to play you a song with a feel-good theme to help you stay happy in these rather difficult times. So, here's Bob Marley's 'Three Little Birds,'

'Don't worry about a thing,

Cause every little thing gonna be alright.....'

Having finished this number Chief Petty Officer Henry temporarily handed the stage to a member of the crew of one of the German vessels.

'May I introduce Petty Officer... that's Bootsmannobermaat Martin Siebel... from the engineering department on the U-99. He's the guy who looks after the sub's diesel engines, but he also does a brilliant impression of

Rod Stewart, and a few other artists mark my word. I believe he's going to start with 'Maggie Mae' so take it away, Martin!'

Martin Siebel duly accepted the microphone and, wearing s suitable wig, everyone agreed that he made a very passable Rod Stewart look alike. Without ado Martin went in with:

'Wake up Maggie, I think I got something to say to you,

It's late September and I really should be back at school....'

Martin Siebel finished the song which included kicking a football around the stage and then followed with further Rod Stewart hits including Young Turks, Sailing, The First Cut is the Deepest, the Killing of Georgie and Baby Jane. Franklin Henry then returned to the stage to introduce a German naval officer, Leutnant Peter Foehne, the navigating officer of the frigate, Mecklenburg Pommern. Peter Foehne sat at the piano and with his fair hair and large oversized glasses made a spitting image of Elton John as he sang Goodbye Yellow Brick Road, Candle in the Wind, Saturday Night's Alright and Crocodile Rock. He was then joined by Franklin Henry's band, Aurora Borealis, to play Philadelphia Freedom:

The band finished the song and continued with the hit, 'I'm Still Standing'. Lieutenant Commander Moirag MacLean from the Aurora's engineering department then joined Peter Foehne to sing 'Don't go Breaking my Heart' with Moirag doing a very good impression of Kikki Dee. After a very brief interlude Lieutenant Commander Carlisle himself appeared on stage and took over the microphone.

'Here's a feel-good song which I've always liked, and in these difficult times, I hope it will help to lift everyone's spirits. Here's *'Love Grows' by Eddison Lighthouse, '*

Carlisle completed the song to much applause and was joined on the stage by Dr Samantha Langley carrying a big guitar.

'Ladies and gentlemen, Damen und Herren, Panie I Panowie,' Samantha introduced herself. 'For my first number I'd like to sing something a little more up to date so here's *My Silver Lining by First Aid Kit,*

'I don't want to wait anymore I'm tired of looking for answers,

Take me some place where there's music and there's laughter...'

Having finished this song Samantha went on to sing Big Yellow Taxi by Joni Mitchell and Jolene by Dolly Parton and received standing ovations for her performances.

'Before the next number I just want to tell you a little about myself,' explained Samantha to her multinational audience. 'I originally came from a rather quiet town called Burlington in Vermont. That's in the part of the U.S. called New England... a very attractive part of the world and we lived in a house overlooking Lake Champlain. I remember going fishing with my mom and dad and my sister. I guess the main problem was that not much happened in Burlington. Life was pleasant enough, but my daddy was a clever scientist and he was looking for something more exciting. Suddenly when I was twelve years old my daddy took off for the Big Apple... that's New York... And didn't come back so my mom and me and my sister, Diane, and our dog, Blue, were just left to fend for ourselves. My Mom went back to teaching. When I was in my teens, I took up playing the guitar and played in the bars and clubs. I made enough money so that when I was eighteen, I was able to take up the place I was offered at Cambridge University in England. When I got my degree, I managed to take my studies further and obtained a doctorate from the University of Berkeley, California. After that I worked for several different technology companies in Silicon Valley and eventually I started working for Darkforce and worked my way up to become a director. So that's where I am today. When I sing my next song, you'll know that it strikes a chord with some of the experiences in my life so here's *Nothing Breaks Like a Heart by Mark Ronson.'*

'Wow... a cool American blonde with a big guitar,' remarked Guy Hanson to Mark Openshaw.

'She's a clever one too,' replied Mark. 'She clearly excels in different fields...and not just the electromagnetic type.'

'American is she?' asked an officer clad in an unfamiliar uniform. 'I am Komandor Porucznik Aleksandr Szymanski...the captain of the submarine, Orzel, of the Polish Navy. This is my executive officer, Komandor Podporucznik Franciszek Zielinski. We are very grateful to you for inviting us to your concert. Please accept this gift of a bottle of Polish vodka.'

'Thank you very much,' acknowledged Guy Hanson. 'It has a picture of a bison on the bottle. I did not think such creatures had a connection with Poland.'

'Oh yes,' replied Szymanski. 'Although the eagle... orzel... is our national symbol we do have bison in our country. They live in the great forests which stretch into Belarus and even into Ukraine. At one time they were extinct but then they were reintroduced. I think you English helped with that programme. The major difference between our bison and those in America is that ours live hidden away out of sight in the forests whereas those in America are beasts of the open plains.'

'Well, I never knew that,' replied Guy, 'but I'd like to try the vodka.'

'Me too, I'm game,' acknowledged Mark Openshaw.

Commander Szymanski duly poured out generous measures for each of them and handed them a glass each.

'That's good stuff,' exclaimed Guy Hanson.

'We have brought several cases aboard so there is plenty for everyone,' advised Commander Szymanski. 'By the way, this gentleman here is my torpedo officer, Parucznik Marynarki Jakub Kowalczyk. We are all...how you say in your country... champing at the bit. We want to get our own back on the Russians. This situation seems to provide such an opportunity.'

'Yes, I suppose it does,' replied Guy cautiously. 'I'd say it's certainly a very dangerous scenario. Russia is still a powerful country. Their trump card is that they still have a lot of nuclear weapons left over from the Cold War era. I'd say we need to tread carefully. The last thing we want is to find London or Warsaw on the receiving end of a nuclear missile.'

'The Russians would not do such a thing,' blustered Szymanski. 'They are afraid of what the Americans would do in retaliation... and you British have nuclear weapons too.'

'No one knows what the outcome will be,' cautioned Mark Openshaw. 'Konstantin Vatutin has made it his stated objective to restore the old Soviet empire. That is bound to involve armed conflict. I am concerned for what the future holds.'

Szymanski quietly refilled their glasses until first one bottle of vodka and then a second were soon emptied. To Guy Hanson and Mark Openshaw, the world began to seem a better place. Guy noticed that both the British and German ratings were also being supplied with free vodka and people were joining in with the singing on stage. As the hour grew late the concert started to become rowdy and Mark Openshaw was not greatly surprised when the first punches were thrown. Glasses were smashed and Lieutenant John Cavanagh with a small company of the Aurora's Royal Marine contingent quietly moved in to make arrests. The broken glasses were quickly swept away and Commander Carlisle appeared again on stage to address the audience,

'Ladies and gentlemen, damen und herren, Panie I panowia... I'd next like to sing you a very beautiful song originally sung by Andy Williams which contains lyrics which I hope will give some solace to everyone in these difficult times and set the right mood,

'A time for us, someday there'll be,
When chains are torn by courage born of a love that's free...'

At the end of the song everyone gave Carlisle a standing ovation and calls were made for an encore which he was pleased to give. He did notice, however, that the Master at Arms, George McGlashan, carried away first one rating and then another. There was still rowdiness and many of the sailors of the different nationalities had consumed too much alcohol and some of them were fighting drunk. Carlisle handed the stage back to Franklin Henry and his band and they performed a number of well-known reggae songs but the fighting resumed, and Carlisle decided it was time to bring the curtain down.

In the morning George McGlashan appeared on the bridge with a number of sailors who were clearly nursing hangovers.

'OFF CAPS!' bellowed the Master at Arms in a voice so loud that Commander Carlisle nearly jumped out of his skin. 'Here are today's defaulters, sir. Able Seamen Callum MacDonald, Jack Walker, Liam Turner, Daffyd Williams, Patrick Rafferty, Frank Kerry, Gary Tucker, Geoff Parkinson and Harry Kirby. All of these men, sir, are charged with being drunk and disorderly and causing an affray.'

'You have the choice of allowing me to deal with these matters here and now or for you to be dealt with by way of a court martial,' explained Carlisle to the men facing charges.

The men all acknowledged that they would prefer their captain to impose discipline.

'Let me make it clear that I am deeply disappointed with your behaviour last night,' Carlisle admonished them. 'I am having to write letters of apology to the captains of the German and Polish vessels. What I wanted was an opportunity for the crews of the vessels in our Task Group to get together socially and have a pleasant evening. Instead, we ended up with a drunken brawl. Several of the German sailors had to be taken to hospital….one with a broken arm. Another had half a beer glass embedded in his face. It is difficult enough having to engage in combat with the Russians without the crews of our own allies fighting each other. What have you got to say for yourselves?'

'They started it,' replied Able Seaman Gary Tucker.

'Yeah…They said our Navy was rubbish,' added Callum MacDonald. 'They said we no longer rule the waves. It was that guy from the Mecklenburg Pommern. I left him with a beer glass embedded in his clock. Serves the bastard right.'

'But this is absolutely dreadful,' complained Commander Carlisle. 'If you want the world to have a high opinion of our Navy you have to show a good example…not to rise to petty jibes and taunts. We have a great history and much to admire and look up to in our forebears. Instead of getting caught up in drunken brawls we should always pause and think… what would Nelson have done in this situation? Remember our heroes like Sir George Rodney and Samuel Hood. Men to admire and be proud of. No one can take our history away from us, but we have high standards to keep. Now I'm going to be lenient with you this time. I sentence you to get all this mess cleared up and your shore leave is cancelled for the next three weeks. That applies to each and every one of you. That's all.'

'CAPS ON!' boomed out George McGlashan. 'And you lads there… go and get a couple of brooms and buckets and start getting all this lot ship shape. At the double!'

The defaulters were duly sent on their way. Carlisle turned and saw several of the scientists were standing behind him.

'I thought you handled them very well,' complimented Dr Samantha Langley. 'And your Andy Williams yesterday evening was amazingly good. I saw him in concert you know, when I was much younger than I am today, and you were the spitting image of the great man. He does look like Andy Williams, doesn't he, Arnold?'

'Yes… I guess he does a little,' agreed Dr Arnold Duvall.

'Andy Williams was a very good-looking man in his heyday,' continued Samantha. 'But we mustn't go on too much or the captain will get swell headed.'

They were interrupted by Catherine Murray.

'Sorry to butt in, sir, but Commodore Vincent is here to see you.'

The scientists shuffled away, and Carlisle invited the commodore to his cabin where they were able to speak privately.

'I hear your concert went well last night,' remarked Commodore Vincent affably. 'I've already spoken to the German captains, and they all say you put on an excellent show.'

'It did appear to be going well, sir,' responded Carlisle, 'but a few troublemakers got out of hand towards the end when it was getting late. We tried to restrict the alcohol to reasonable quantities, but the Poles brought their own… and I think the Germans did too. Eventually one or two people ended up in hospital.'

'Well, don't let it bother you. It's good for the crews to let off steam a bit. If a few punches are thrown… well that's all in the tradition of the Service!' laughed Vincent. 'But I digress and come to the point. The Russian nuclear powered battlecruiser Pyotr Velyke is being moved down from the Russian Northern Fleet to Kaliningrad. Clearly the Russians are intending to base it there to seal off the entire eastern end of the Baltic. With its powerful batteries of long range hypersonic missiles it will be able to dominate huge areas and keep NATO out. Such a ship will make it very difficult for us to intervene to go to the help of our allies in the Baltic states. This is where you come in.'

''Would not air strikes be more appropriate for dealing with such a large vessel?' queried Carlisle. 'And where is it right now?'

'As I understand the Pyotr Velikye has already set sail from Murmansk with an escort of an Udaloy class cruiser and several smaller ships. They are being shadowed by aircraft from the Norwegian Airforce, but the Norwegians are reluctant to launch attacks for fear of retaliation. They share a border with Russia up in the far north in the Arctic, as you know, and they don't relish the prospect of being the next country on Vatutin's list for invasion. The Russian vessels will have to pass through the Skagerrak, but the Swedes and the Danes are similarly reluctant to take on Ivan in a shoot out. But I hasten to suggest this would be a good place to prepare an ambush. You are to put to sea after dark tomorrow. There are a number of islands around there and I suggest you find yourselves a suitable hiding place to lie in wait. The U-99 and the Orzel are due to leave port tonight in secrecy with similar orders. You will be accompanied by the Karlsruhe. The Mecklenburg Pommern and a squadron of Tornado bombers from the German Marineflieger will be kept back in reserve to make a follow up attack should this be necessary. Some of the scientists from Darkforce will be coming with you so the new technology will be available for you to utilise. Have you any questions?'

'Yes, sir,' acknowledged Carlisle. 'What is the main armament of the Pyotr Velikye?'

'The ship has just completed a major four-year refit which has included the fitting of the new Russian long range anti-ship missile known as Tsirkon. It travels at hypersonic speed and has a range of a thousand kilometres. That's about six hundred and twenty miles. American carrier battle groups are its main intended target. If you get hit by one of those things you are toast, so make sure to keep well concealed. These are our orders from Northwood.'

The following morning Carlisle noted that the berths previously occupied by the submarines were empty, but he made no mention of it to anybody. He did, however, call his more senior officers together in the wardroom to discuss the operation and to work out tactics. The captain of the Karlsruhe and several of his officers were also invited to attend the meeting. The Germans were familiar with the geography of the region and advised as to suitable locations to lie in wait.

'I recommend we proceed through the Kattegat during the hours of darkness,' proposed Wolfgang Bremer. 'Navigation is not so simple so you should follow us closely. When we proceed out into the Skagerrak, we should aim for this small group of islands... here... just off the Danish coast... known as the Alesund Islands.' Bremer pointed out the geographical features on the maps spread out on the wardroom table. 'They will give us some cover. There is a concealed cove... here. We should wait for the Russian ships to come well within range and then fire our Harpoon missiles in salvoes. Hopefully, the Pyotr Velikye will be hit and disabled before it has a chance to return fire.'

While the meeting in the boardroom was still in progress the officers were joined by John Lloyd Carswell and Timothy Cookson from the Ministry of Defence in London.

'I have some important instructions from Whitehall,' announced Carswell. 'Essentially the Swedes are being threatened by the Russians to the effect that if they engage Russian forces, they will risk facing nuclear retaliation or invasion, so they have declined to allow us to attack Russian vessels in their territorial waters. The Danes are facing similar threats, and they have requested that we seek to avoid action which would lead to civilian casualties.'

Commander Carlisle studied the maps carefully and was joined by Guy Hanson and Mark Openshaw.

'Those Alesund Islands are clearly within Danish territorial waters,' remarked Carlisle. 'Are they inhabited?'

'There is a weather station and a lighthouse,' replied Captain Bremer. 'I think a few fishermen may live there as well but the islands are isolated. We can keep to our plans.'

Later in the day Carlisle spoke to Alex on his mobile phone. She was still complaining about the pigs and how she had been left to look after the farm single handed. He was not permitted to give her any information as to where he was and the forthcoming operation to attack the Russian battlecruiser was top secret. When she asked as to a timescale for his next spell of leave, he could not say. Indeed, he wondered seriously as to whether he would still be alive in twenty-four hours. The odds were not good, and his mind was full of doubts. Eventually darkness began to fall, and Aurora was preparing to put to sea. Carlisle resolved that if this was it and he was never going to return to the farm or to Alex he would at least sell his life dearly.

Chapter 7

The Battle of the Kattegat

IT WAS CLOSE TO MIDNIGHT when the Aurora cast off her mooring lines and slipped silently out of the dockyard at Kiel assisted by a small tug, the *Dachshunde*. Aurora was blacked out and the watchkeepers had been doubled as the risk of collision in the darkness was considerable. The German Navy had also provided a pilot, Ludwig Grobe, to help guide them through the intricate network of channels and islands and also a liaison officer, Leutnant Anton Barkmann. Assisted by Ludwig Grobe, Carlisle was giving regular instructions to George McGlashan at the helm. Somewhere ahead of them the *Karlsruhe* was already at sea steaming slowly northwards.

'Engine room, give me revolutions for eight knots,' ordered Carlisle as *Aurora* cleared the harbour area and altered course to the north and into the Kattegat.

'Kattegat means Cat's throat,' explained Ludwig Grobe. 'We will take the westerly channel… but keep clear of that bulk ore carrier out to starboard. She is a lot bigger than us and I would not recommend trying to occupy the same space as her at the same time.'

Carlisle acknowledged the pilot's advice and ordered a reduction in speed as the big ore carrier loomed closer in the darkness. It was with some relief on the bridge as the Aurora tucked in behind the huge commercial vessel. On her stern they could just make out her name, '*Albin Hanssen*' Stockholm.

'She will be sailing from Lulea up at the north end of the Gulf of Bothnia,' explained Ludwig. 'She is loaded with iron ore and bound for the Far East.

Not long ago she would probably be setting course for a British port or Rotterdam, but the Russians will not permit that now.'

Carlisle ordered a further reduction in speed to just five knots to avoid the risk of running into the big Swedish ship from astern. David Warwick appeared on the bridge with mugs of hot black coffee and plates of sandwiches. In this situation it was very important for everyone to stay alert. Ludwig Grobe was pointing out the geographical features with the island of Funin to port and Sjaelland to starboard, but his guided tour was largely academic as it was still the middle of the night, and the great bulk of the Albin Hanssen blotted out much of the scene. Sub-Lieutenant Gartmore was Officer of the Watch and was regularly reporting details of other vessels navigating the channels. The Aurora continued to maintain her blackout and radio silence. Ludwig pointed out the small port of Nyborg over to the portside and the bridge crossing the expanse of water to provide connection with Sjaelland and the Danish capital, Copenhagen. A large tanker passed slowly in the opposite direction heading south.

'She will be bound for Gdansk,' advised Ludwig.

The first signs of dawn were appearing as they passed Arnhus somewhere over to the west. The lights of the city were clearly visible, and Carlisle was rather surprised that the Danish Government had not yet considered it prudent to impose blackout restrictions. He surmised that such a position would change following events which were about to unfold. The Kattegat was now broadening out and the Albin Hanssen increased speed to ten knots. Carlisle ordered a corresponding increase and maintained their station as close to the stern of the bulk carrier as he considered prudent without risk of collision. Catherine Murray then appeared on the bridge.

'Signal from Northwood, sir. The Pyotr Velikye battlegroup is now steaming south at 22 knots forty miles west of Bergen. It comprises the battlecruiser, Pyotr Velikye as well as a Slava class missile cruiser, an Udaloy class destroyer and three frigates, one of which may be armed with long range missiles. There are also two naval auxiliaries and an ocean-going salvage vessel.'

Carlisle was glad when Guy Hanson and Mark Openshaw came to the bridge and the officers were able to confer about the developing situation and how they should deal with it.

'If we attempt to confront the Russians out in the open sea they will be able to hit us long before we get within effective range,' advised Mark.

'So, we will not give them that opportunity,' responded Carlisle. 'We will make straight for the Alesunde Islands… here,' he added pointing to the maps set out on the chart table. 'The Karlsruhe is already on course there ahead of us. As you can see, there are two main islands with a sound running between them. There are also several bays and coves where we can take cover. I am not familiar with the geography of the islands, but Captain Bremer says there is some higher ground which we can shelter behind. It is our best chance. We will make for the islands at high speed and rendezvous with the Karlsruhe.'

Guy Hanson and Mark Openshaw nodded their approval of their captain's plan and Carlisle ordered an increase in speed to twenty-seven knots which involved overtaking the Albin Hanssen and forging ahead as dawn began to break and the sun appeared over the horizon. Carlisle and his senior officers took the opportunity to research the offensive potential of the approaching Russian ships using computer-based data and information together with publications such as Jane's Fighting Ships.

'The Slava class is configured for surface action,' advised Mark Openshaw. 'It has powerful batteries of SS-N-12 anti-ship missiles.'

'They may also have added Tsirkon hypersonic missiles to its arsenal,' added Guy Hanson. 'We should consider it a priority target.'

'Yes… it represents a serious danger,' acknowledged Carlisle. 'The Udaloy is primarily an anti-submarine platform, but we'll need to beware of the frigates particularly if any are armed with Tsirkon.'

'The latest report said at least one of the frigates is armed with long range missiles,' added Mark.

They were joined on the bridge by Lieutenant Mike Addison, the *Aurora's* new Principal Air Warfare officer who had only been aboard the ship for the last three days.

'Sorry to throw you in at the deep end, Mike,' apologised Carlisle, 'but that's how it is at the moment.'

'Don't worry about me, sir,' replied Addison. 'I've seen quite a bit of action already. You'd be surprised. The Russians were not at all happy when we sailed through waters off the Crimea last year which they considered to be their own. All hell was let loose. We were buzzed by squadrons of Russian jets... some of them flying below the height of our masts on the London. Then a Krivak class frigate came and did the bump and hustle dance routine. We ended up with quite a few holes and gashes in our hull plating.'

'It sounds quite hairy,' mused Guy Hanson.

'I'm afraid the real shooting is about to start,' cautioned Carlisle.

'Signal from Northwood, sir,' reported Roy Stringer from the Operations Room. 'There's a large Russian reconnaissance plane... a Tupolev 142 Bear approaching our sector from the northwest... range about forty-five miles... speed... three hundred knots.'

'They'll be casing the joint ahead of the Russian task group,' advised Mike Addison.

'Unfortunately, they've probably spotted us already and will be reporting our presence,' said Carlisle.

'What do we do now, sir?' asked Mark Openshaw.

'Carry on,' replied Carlisle. 'Keep aiming for our rendezvous with the *Karlsruhe*.'

He and the other senior officers made for the Operations Room and Carlisle discussed the air warfare and surface radar plots with Mike Addison and Roy Stringer. The Tupolev 142 was now showing on their air search radar and was clearly carrying out active radar sweeps of her own.

'Should we try to shoot it down, sir?' asked Mike Addison.

'No... not yet,' replied Carlisle. 'It would draw too much attention. For the time being we should try to maintain a low profile.

'Another signal just come in from Northwood, sir,' advised Roy Stringer. 'Two of the Russian frigates have detached from the main group and have increased speed to thirty-four knots. One of these frigates is reported to be armed with Tsirkon.

'They're going to attack,' exclaimed Mark Openshaw.

To starboard a large freighter was exiting the Swedish port of Goteborg at fifteen knots. Carlisle ordered a reduction in the Aurora's speed and tucked in behind the freighter whose name, Varberg, was painted in white lettering on her stern. Carlisle closed up as near as he dared to the Swedish ship without unduly risking a collision. Soon the skipper of the Varberg was making a twenty-degree course alteration to port to take her into the Skagerrak and Carlisle followed suit. The Varberg then steadied her course with the Aurora close on her tail. Carlisle found the slow speed of the big freighter frustrating, but she provided some form of cover, and he decided to take the opportunity to address the crew of his own ship over the Tannoy system.

'Good morning, everybody. I feel it appropriate at this point to brief all of you as to our current situation. We are on course to ambush a powerful task force of Russian ships led by the nuclear-powered battlecruiser, Peter the Great. Have no doubt that some of these vessels are strongly armed with batteries of long-range anti-ship missiles any one of which could blow us out of the water. They include the new hypersonic missile known as Tsirkon. However, these are weapons more suited for use in the open oceans and we are in the narrow, confined waters of the Kattegat and Skagerrak. We will rendezvous with the *Karlsruhe* in the Alesunde Islands which will provide us with a measure of cover. At the appropriate time we and the Karlsruhe will fire salvoes of our Harpoon missiles at the Russian ships as they pass us in our concealed locations. I am sure I do not need to emphasize to you the importance of our mission. Russian forces have, during the last twenty-four hours, seized the Latvian capital city of Riga and they are now poised to continue their advance westwards. Latvia is a member of NATO, and we are treaty bound to come to her assistance. I have full confidence in each and every one of you and I know that you will all do your utmost to achieve a successful outcome to the forthcoming battle. Remember that all of us are walking in the shadows of great men like Nelson, Drake, Rodney and Samuel Hood. May God be with you.'

'That was awesome,' praised Dr Samantha Langley from her dimly lit corner of the Operations Room. 'I feel I'm walking six feet off the ground.'

'Well... let's get on with the job,' added Professor Finch. 'Remember that we're here with our special technology, Captain. You may need it.'

'The Tupolev 142 is approaching,' warned Mike Addison from the air warfare plot. 'I'd say he intends to overfly us to take a close look.'

Carlisle leaned over the plot and watched the incoming course of the big Russian aircraft.

'Crew to Action Stations! Crew to Action Stations!' he called over the Tannoy system as the alarms sounded. 'But keep weapons tight until I give the order to shoot.'

The Tupolev flew overhead at around three hundred feet slowing to about two hundred and fifty knots.

'He's coming round again, sir,' warned Mike Addison. 'He's coming down to less than two hundred feet and as slow as he dares without stalling.'

To the people standing on the bridge or out on the decks the Tupolev made an amazing sight as the huge aircraft thundered overhead with its distinctive swept back wings and four big engines with their contra rotating propellors. As for Carlisle he was not interested in the impromptu air show and this situation was considerably unwelcome.

'Signal from Northwood, sir,' reported Catherine Murray. 'The two Russian frigates are now fifty miles to the northwest. We are ordered to make for the Alesunde Islands at maximum speed to rendezvous with the Karlsruhe.'

'Give me maximum revolutions,' Carlisle ordered the Engine room as the Aurora vibrated with the increase in power output. The Swedish freighter was quickly overtaken but the big Tupolev continued to circle around keeping the British warship under constant surveillance. In the Operations Room, the electronic warfare team under Lieutenant Nigel Morton were tuning in to the Russian radio transmissions and at the same time attempting to jam their signals and communications. The sounds of Russian voices were clearly audible, and the British team included Petty Officer Elena MacIntyre whose mother was Russian and spoke the language fluently. Elena proceeded to give a running commentary and translation of the Russian chatter.

It was early afternoon before Ludwig Grobe was pointing out the Alesunde Islands on the horizon and the Aurora approached the sound which lay between the two main islands. The main problem was still the Russian

Tupolev which continued to drone around in an anticlockwise pattern reporting the location of the frigate.

Carlisle and his officers were in heated discussion as to whether to shoot it down when Catherine Murray appeared again.

'Signal from Northwood, Captain. One of the Russian frigates has fired a long-range missile and its target is us.'

'Take out that Bear immediately!' ordered Carlisle.

Lieutenant Addison's finger had been itching over the missile firing button for some time and in seconds one of the silos on the foredeck sprung into life and an Aster 15 shot from its launcher and engaged the Bear which had just flown overhead at two hundred feet making its latest pass. The missile hit the Bear on the underside of the inboard starboard engine and started a large fire, but the plane continued to fly. The Aurora now engaged with 5-inch and automatic fire and the Bear was quickly hit again. The crew of the Bear desperately sought to steer the burning aircraft away from the Aurora, but it began losing height and broke up spectacularly upon hitting the water. It was not clear whether there were any survivors. In normal conditions Carlisle would have sent the Wildcat or a rigid inflatable to check out the wreckage but the Aurora herself was under attack and it was vital to seek the shelter of the higher ground of the nearest island which Ludwig Grobe informed everyone was called Grundvega. Meanwhile Roy Stringer had picked up the incoming missile on the radar plot and fired large quantities of chaff. Nigel Morton's team also attempted to jam the missile's guidance system as Carlisle and Simon Barrington carefully navigated the Aurora into the sound at fifteen knots. The Russian missile still kept coming and was travelling very fast.

'I'd say it's going at more than three times the speed of sound,' advised Roy Stringer.

Carlisle was about to order the command, Brace, over the Tannoy system when the missile veered away, possibly confused by the growing chaff cloud. Out in the open sea the Varberg was steaming at around sixteen knots on a north-westerly course and the missile locked on to this big new target. There was a brilliant flash, but the thunderous detonation and shock wave took about twenty seconds to reach the Aurora due to the fact that light travels much faster than sound. The Varberg proceeded to burst into flames with clouds of black choking smoke billowing literally hundreds of feet into the clear skies. Carlisle continued to maintain radio silence and ordered speed to be reduced to ten knots as the lookouts searched for any sign of the Karlsruhe. There was a large cove to starboard, but the Karlsruhe was not there.

'I have… what you call… a hunch,' said Ludwig Grobe. 'Keep on this heading, Captain.'

They passed a sheltered bay which might have provided a good hiding place but there was still no sign of the German ship. Eventually the lighthouse hove into view. There were also a few fishermen's houses and a handful of fishing boats tied up to a small jetty.

'There is another sheltered inlet coming up to starboard,' advised Ludwig.

'There!' called Leutnant Barkmann. 'There is the *Karlsruhe*. She is signalling to us using her light and with flags. She tells us to come alongside.'

Simon Barrington carefully manoeuvred the Aurora into the inlet and dropped anchor. Carlisle and a number of his senior officers together with Leutnant Barkmann came aboard the *Karlsruhe* and had a brief meeting with Captain Bremer.

'The leading two Russian frigates will be heading past these islands within the next fifty minutes or so,' advised Captain Bremer. 'But we have bigger fish to fry as you say in England. Our main targets are the Peter the Great and the Slava Class cruiser, Marshal Ustinov. We will attack them with our batteries of Harpoon missiles. The Mecklenburg Pommern is holding back astern near Arnhus, and her orders are to attack any remaining Russian ships with her Exocets. There are also our submarines, the U-99 and the Polish Orzel. They will be lying in wait in the confined waters of the Kattegat, and they also have orders to sink any Russian ships which have… how you say in English… got through the net. We will let the Russian frigates pass us unmolested unless, of course, they attack us first. We will then let the bigger Russian ships come well within range and open fire with our Harpoon batteries when we can see… how you put it… the whites in their eyes.'

'It all sounds very straightforward, sir,' responded Carlisle, 'but the Russians outnumber us and some of them are more heavily armed.'

'We will just have to do our best with the limited resources available to us,' replied Captain Bremer. 'What would Nelson be doing if he was in our boots?'

'Engaging the enemy more closely,' quipped Carlisle.

'Well… there you have it,' smiled Captain Bremer. 'The reality is that we find ourselves fighting a war with depleted peacetime navies… how you say… the victims of repeated budget cuts and financial stringencies.'

'Don't I know it,' replied Carlisle.

They were interrupted by a petty officer from the Operations Room of the *Karlsruhe* who appeared in the wardroom of the German frigate with an urgent message for the captain. The man was speaking in German, but Captain Bremer explained to the British officers.

'There is a Russian submarine reported to be operating in our sector… a Kilo class diesel powered vessel. It will complicate the situation for us.'

'I would have been surprised if the Russian Navy had not deployed submarines to this area,' replied Carlisle. 'Do we have any more information as to its location, Captain?'

'It is reported to be currently about forty miles to the south-east of our current position,' replied Bremer. 'But it is headed on course for these islands.'

'We'd better get the Wildcat airborne,' said Carlisle to Guy Hanson as they returned to the Aurora leaving Leutnant Barkmann and Sub-Lieutenant Gartmore aboard the Karlsruhe for the time being to relay messages from the flagship.

In the meantime, the Russian frigates were steaming south-eastwards. Captain Bremer's orders had been to let them pass and leave other vessels in Task Group 79 to deal with them. As they approached to within a few miles of the Alesunde Islands the two Russian frigates slowed down and one of them began heading directly towards the islands while the other one stood off about ten or twelve miles distant. The Russians sent up a Kamov KA 27 Helix helicopter to reconnoitre ahead and within a few minutes it was surveying the waters around the islands.

'Get the Vampire drone airborne,' ordered Carlisle. 'And make sure its fully armed with Sea Venoms.'

'Aye aye, sir,' acknowledged Sub-Lieutenant Brooks. Fortunately, he had anticipated the order, and the Vampire was soon launched with a full complement of missiles.

There then followed a game of cat and mouse with the drone shadowing the Kamov helicopter as it began to search the rocky outcrops of the islands. The drone had a wingspan of more than fifteen feet and had the appearance of a small aircraft, but Sub-Lieutenant Brooks was skilled at using whatever cover he could find. A video link was quickly established between the drone and the Aurora so that the Vampire was sending back a constant stream of pictures to the parent ship. Sub-Lieutenant Brooks was ably assisted by Petty Officer Geoff Aspinall and Leading Seaman Richard Trevelyan. Everyone was holding their breath when the Kamov approached the inlet where the Allied frigates were at anchor but something else must have attracted the attention of the Russian crew and the machine veered away apparently searching towards the west and the sound which lay between the two main islands. It turned out to be a Danish fishing vessel and the Kamov and its crew spent about ten or fifteen minutes overflying this craft and checking it out. In the meantime, the nearest Russian frigate was cautiously entering the sound from the north at about nine knots.

'We can't just sit here, sir,' protested Guy Hanson. 'They're bound to find us, and we'll be sitting ducks.'

Carlisle gave orders to the Engine room to make ready to move as soon as anchors were weighed.

'This inlet has a bend in it about four hundred yards to the east and there is a sheltered cove just beyond,' he remarked to Guy Hanson. 'The video from the Vampire clearly shows these features. Signal the Karlsruhe to the effect that we are moving to that position and recommend that they do the same. It will also place us closer to the open sea for when we want to exit.'

'Aye aye, sir,' acknowledged the executive officer.

Under the expert control of Sub-Lieutenant Brooks and Petty Officer Aspinall the Vampire was approaching the Kamov from behind a promontory while the helicopter was hovering above a small Danish cargo vessel which had entered the sound from the south. Once they were reasonably sure of scoring hits Brooks and Aspinall opened fire and were gratified to see several of the Sea Venom missiles strike their target. The Kamov quickly caught fire and force landed on the water alongside the Danish vessel whose crew hastened to pick up the survivors of the helicopter's crew. Carlisle now proceeded to move the Aurora along the inlet to the sheltered bay and Captain Bremer followed at slow speed and anchored slightly further up the channel. Carlisle figured that their most dangerous opponent was currently the nearest Russian frigate which Roy Stringer had identified as a ship of the Neustrashimy class named Pavel Batov and it was now very close. Accordingly, Carlisle manoeuvred the Aurora so that its main gun and the portside battery of Harpoon missiles could be brought to bear if the Pavel Batov should happen to nose its way into the inlet. Having despatched the Kamov helicopter Brooks and his team turned their attention to the Batov and although they had fired off their missiles they proceeded to shadow the Russian frigate from concealed positions. For a while, the crew of the Batov were engaged in searching the Danish cargo vessel and trying to recover their damaged Kamov helicopter which was badly damaged but still afloat. Catherine Murray was continuing to provide information as to the main body of the Russian task force as soon as she received the signals. The information came from a combination of reports from the Norwegian Airforce and Navy and from spy satellites via Northwood and this showed that the Russian group would soon be passing close. Carlisle was concerned that the Pavel Batov was to the rear of their position and sought permission from Captain Bremer to put the Russian frigate out of action. Bremer was reluctant to allow such a move at least until the Allied vessels had opened fire on the main Russian body.

'We have arrangements in place to deal with the Pavel Batov,' signalled Bremer.

Carlisle was not sure what this involved but the only two Allied warships in this locality were the Aurora and the Karlsruhe and he did not believe they had the firepower between them to effectively engage the main group and sink the Batov at the same time. It was late in the afternoon when Captain Bremer signalled by light that he was moving out of the inlet to be in a position to fire his Harpoons at the Peter the Great and the Marshall Ustinov and ordered the

Aurora to follow. The main group of Russian ships had by now been clearly visible on the radar plot for a while. Carlisle ordered Lieutenant Griffiths to bring the Wildcat back to the Aurora to refuel. So far, they had not found the Russian submarine which was clearly somewhere to the southeast. Once again, this displeased Carlisle. The Pavel Batov was now underway at slow speed and heading south along the sound. Suddenly Roy Stringer was calling from the radar plot in the Operations Room to warn that the main Russian task group had fired an anti-ship missile which was now headed at supersonic speed towards the Allied frigates. Simultaneously, the Krivak class frigate which had previously accompanied the Pavel Batov also fired a missile. Roy Stringer wasted no time in firing chaff and creating dense clouds of the light material in the clear late afternoon skies. At the same time Cambridge graduate Lieutenant Morton and his specialised electronic warfare team were seeking to jam the guidance systems of the incoming missiles. The Karlsruhe succeeded in firing a salvo of four Harpoon missiles towards the main Russian group and a fifth missile towards the Krivak before a Russian missile struck the German frigate with devastating effect. Carlisle was crouched over the plots in the Operations Room of the Aurora but Simon Barrington who was currently Officer of the Watch and standing on the bridge said it was terrible to see.

'The whole forward section of the Karlsruhe has been destroyed,' reported Lieutenant Barrington. 'I can't imagine anyone surviving in that carnage.'

As he spoke a further two Russian missiles smashed at very high speed into the Karlsruhe which began to burn fiercely. Carlisle cautiously edged the Aurora towards the narrow eastern mouth of the inlet until he was sure that the Peter the Great could be accurately targeted. Roy Stringer was reporting that one of the Karlsruhe's missiles had hit the Krivak and Simon Barrington called from the bridge to confirm his visual sighting that the Krivak had been struck and was now on fire.

'Shall we finish them off, sir,' enquired Mark Openshaw.

'No, not yet,' replied Carlisle. 'We have bigger fish to fry, as Captain Bremer would have said. Save our Harpoons for the Peter the Great and the Marshal Ustonov.'

Using the blazing wreck of the Karlsruhe as cover the Aurora edged out of the relative security of the inlet as the main Russian group came within visual range and fired a salvo of six Harpoons. Roy Stringer reported that two of the Harpoons fired by the Karlsruhe had hit the Peter the Great while another had struck the accompanying naval supply ship, Boris Kosakov, which was now burning and out of control. One of the Russian frigates in the main body had come to a standstill and may also have been hit. Roy Stringer then reported that three of the Aurora's Harpoons had hit the Peter the Great and this was confirmed by Lieutenant Barrington from the bridge.

'She's still steaming but she's on fire for'ard,' reported Barrington. 'That Slava Class cruiser…we've hit her as well. I think two Harpoons struck near her bridge and control centres. '

'She's slowing down and slewing round to starboard,' called Roy Stringer from the radar plot. 'I think she may have collided with the damaged supply ship.'

Carlisle conferred with Guy Hanson and Mark Openshaw. The Russian group was badly hit and in disarray.

'Should we pursue them south?' asked Mark. 'Samuel Hood would have done so, sir.'

'We need to bear in mind we've only got two remaining Harpoons,' warned Carlisle, 'And we're on our own now. Where is that frigate… the Pavel Batov?'

'She's to the south of us, sir,' answered Roy Stringer. 'I can't say more than that as the island is obscuring our radar image in that direction.'

'Tell Lieutenant Griffiths to get the Wildcat back in the air and find the Batov,' ordered Carlisle. 'In the meantime, let's finish off the Marshall Ustonov. She's a threat while she's still afloat.'

The Aurora fired one of her two remaining Harpoons which struck the crippled Slava Class missile cruiser and then opened fire with her 5-inch, hitting the Russian ship repeatedly and starting numerous fires. The Peter the Great was still steaming southeast at around 18 knots accompanied by an Udaloy Class destroyer and several other vessels.

'Shell splashes to starboard, sir,' called Lieutenant Barrington from the bridge. 'I think its gunfire from the Russian ships heading south.'

'Missile launch from Russian frigate!' called Roy Stringer. 'They've fired a Tsirkon.' Roy wasted no time firing chaff.

'Hard a starboard,' ordered Carlisle as he brought the Aurora round and ordered an increase in speed. 'BRACE! BRACE! BRACE!' he shouted over the Tannoy. The hypersonic Russian missile gave no more than seconds to take any kind of evasive action.

There was an explosion, and everyone believed they had been hit as fragments of debris showered down around the Aurora.

'It's the Wildcat,' reported Sub-Lieutenant Brooks from the flight deck. 'Poor Lieutenant Griffiths and his lads were hit by the missile as they took to the air. 'I'm afraid they're all dead and the chopper is gone.'

'Engage that Russian frigate,' ordered Carlisle. 'Mark... fire our last Harpoon.'

The Aurora's final anti-ship missile blasted away from its launcher sited ahead of the bridge and sped towards the target ship which was about twelve miles distant to the east. In the Operations Room of the British frigate anxious onlookers studied the course of their weapon. Suddenly Roy Stringer was calling from the radar plot,

'The Pavel Batov is approaching from the south. They have emerged into the open sea and are altering course towards us.'

'We don't have any Harpoons left, sir,' cautioned Mark Openshaw. 'We've just fired off the last one.'

Carlisle ordered an alteration of course to take the Aurora back to the inlet as Roy Stringer reported a hit on the Russian frigate they had engaged with their final Harpoon. On the horizon a pall of acrid black smoke rose high into the sky as the vessel began to burn. Closer to hand the Karlsruhe was still afloat but heavily on fire and members of the German frigate's crew could be seen jumping overboard into the sea trying to escape from the flames and the choking smoke. Simon Barrington observed men assisting wounded comrades and feared that some of them would inevitably be badly burned. As the Aurora re-entered the inlet Sub-Lieutenant Brooks called the captain to inform him that the Karlsruhe's Lynx helicopter, which had been engaged in missile guidance when its parent ship was hit, was requesting permission to land aboard the Aurora. Carlisle wasted no time in granting permission.

'Get them refuelled and back in the air as soon as possible,' he ordered, 'And make sure they are well armed with depth charges and homing torpedoes. That Kilo Class submarine is still out there.'

Carlisle proceeded to manoeuvre the Aurora so that its main gun would be able to engage any ship which entered the inlet from either direction.

'The Batov has a modest one-hundred-millimetre main gun,' advised Mark Openshaw. 'But she also carries a battery of SS-N-25 anti-ship missiles. We don't want to be on the receiving end of those.'

'In these very confined waters I don't think they'd be able to get a lock on us with their missiles,' replied Carlisle. 'The range would be too short for the system to operate. I think the main problem is that she's bottling us up here. We want to get out into the open sea and finish off those crippled Russian ships but if we did so the Batov would be able to engage us effectively and sink us.'

'I think we need to request assistance,' suggested Guy Hanson. 'Should we stick our necks out, sir, and break radio silence?'

'Get on to Frederickshavn and Aarnhus,' replied Carlisle after a moment's thought. 'Give them our position and say we are trapped by the Russian missile frigate, Pavel Batov. Ask them to send air and naval support... a squadron of F-16s with smart bombs would do the job.'

'Aye aye, sir,' acknowledged the executive officer.

Meanwhile the Vampire drone had landed back on board the Aurora and was being refuelled and rearmed ready for its next sortie. Once the German Navy Lynx had been sent back into the air to search for the submarine the flight deck crew worked feverishly to get the Vampire airborne as well. Sub-Lieutenant Brooks and his team soon had the drone operational once again and the first task was to relocate the Batov which was hugging the coast of the island, its position masked by higher ground.

'There it is,' called Leading Seaman Trevelyan who was keeping a close eagle eye on the video link and the footage relayed by the Vampire. 'She's only about three miles away.'

'She could be here in minutes,' cautioned Sub-Lieutenant Brooks.

Carlisle emphasized the urgency of contacting the Danish forces and gaining their assistance.

'I'm not getting any response at the moment. Something must be wrong,' reported Danielle Sheldon. 'I'll try contacting other bases.'

In the meantime, the Batov was getting ever closer and Carlisle felt cold sweat trickling down his back.

'We ought to move from this position, sir,' proposed Mark Openshaw. 'We can turn to port and head out into the sound.'

'But then if the Batov follows us he can get into a position to fire his SS-N-25s at us,' replied Carlisle.

'My suggestion is we should make for the sound and then for Frederickshavn,' put forward Guy Hanson. 'That's the Danes' main base. They have missile armed frigates and shore batteries of Harpoons. It's a better option than just sitting here like a rat in a trap.'

Carlisle was not entirely happy with the proposal, but he gave orders for the Aurora to get underway and leave the inlet to the west. Soon the British frigate was in the sound and heading south at twenty-five knots. All the time everyone was keeping a sharp lookout for the Pavel Batov and once the *Aurora* was out in the open sea, she would be a sitting target for the Russian ship's missiles. Leading Seaman Trevelyan reported that the Pavel Batov was still steaming slowly northwards searching the eastern coast of the Alesunde Islands. Before Carlisle recalled the Vampire drone Trevelyan was able to confirm that the Batov had now altered course to starboard and appeared to be heading towards the badly damaged Russian vessels out in the Kattegat no doubt to render assistance.

'Small naval vessel approaching fast from the west,' advised Roy Stringer.

'Is it Russian?' asked Lieutenant Mike Addison.

'I think it's Danish,' replied Stringer. 'She's using friendly IFF. She's on a bearing which indicates she's come from Frederickshavn.'

'I'm trying to make contact with it,' advised Danielle Sheldon, 'But someone appears to be jamming the transmissions.'

'I think we know who that will be,' joked Guy Hanson.

On the bridge Simon Barrington and Sub-Lieutenant Gartmore observed the approaching vessel intensely through powerful field glasses while gunners with fingers on triggers sat behind their automatic weapons. It was only when the vessel was a mere few hundred yards away off the Aurora's starboard side that Danielle Sheldon said she was finally in radio contact.

'This is Lieutenant Commander Jan Petersen, commanding officer of the Attack Craft, Skaden, of the Royal Danish Navy,' announced a crackling voice which was difficult to hear with any clarity.'

'We have been attempting to make radio contact with your base for some time,' replied Carlisle, 'But no one has responded... until now that is.'

'We are sorry,' replied Petersen, 'But we have been subjected to massive cyber-attacks on our communications and government. We fear the Russians are preparing for an invasion... They are landing amphibious forces and paratroops on the Danish island of Bornholm as well as the Swedish island called Gotland. We fear they are intending to seize the Kattegat to give them access between the Baltic and the North Sea.'

'The Russian ships we ambushed may well have been part of a force to capture the waterways and bases in that region,' considered Carlisle. 'I think that part of their plan may have gone slightly wrong.'

'Where are you based?' asked Petersen.

'Currently we are operating out of Kiel,' explained Carlisle.

'I understand Kiel has been bombed today by Russian jets and several cruise missiles have hit the dockyard,' advised Petersen. 'You are lucky to have been away from there. I suggest you come with us, and you will be able to speak with some of our senior officers including Rear Admiral Rasmussen.'

Carlisle accepted the invitation, and the Aurora obediently followed the Skaden. It was well into the evening by the time they reached the port of Frederickshavn and Aurora was given a berth near to the Danish frigate, Niels Juel. Everyone was anxious to know what was happening, but the Danes had little definite knowledge of the current situation. Lieutenant Commander Sven Anderssen, the captain of the Niels Juel came aboard the Aurora at around 11pm, bringing his executive officer, Lieutenant Larssen, and conferred with Carlisle in his cabin. Anderssen confirmed that Denmark had been the subject of major cyber-attacks during the past forty-eight hours and the two Danish officers were under no illusions as to where these emanated from.

'It is a prelude to a Russian invasion,' sighed Anderssen. 'We know they have already invaded Bornholm, but they will not stop there. They clearly wish to occupy the Kattegat and its islands and ports. We are a small country, and we cannot take on the might of Russia single handed.'

'The Russian Navy is weakened after we ambushed their task force today,' replied Carlisle. 'Sadly, we lost the German frigate, Karlsruhe. I understand Denmark and Sweden are sending ships and helicopters to rescue survivors.'

'I can confirm this,' acknowledged Anderssen. 'They may try to save the Karlsruhe if they can put the fires out.'

'I'm not sure that will be possible anytime soon,' cautioned Carlisle. 'The German ship was hit by three Russian anti-ship missiles including two Tsirkons. I fear it is a total loss.'

'The Danish rescue teams will do their best,' said Anderssen.

'The Karlsruhe hit the Peter the Great with more than one Harpoon missile. We hit it as well but it's a big ship and it carried on steaming,' explained Carlisle. 'We hit the Slava Class cruiser, Marshal Ustinov, as well. After we scored two hits with Harpoons it collided with one of their supply ships which had been hit by the Karlsruhe.'

'You clearly did well,' acknowledged Anderssen as Catherine Murray knocked on the cabin door.

'Sorry to disturb you, sir, but there is a Rear Admiral Rasmussen here to see you.'

'Ah, yes. He is our base commander and the senior officer here,' said Anderssen.

Rear Admiral Rasmussen was a smartly dressed man, quite heavily built, and aged perhaps in his late forties or early fifties. Carlisle figured that the Rear Admiral probably had significant Viking ancestry in his DNA. The two officers greeted each other, and Rasmussen said he was relieved to be hosting the British frigate.

'We are rather isolated up here in northern Denmark,' said the Rear Admiral. 'It does not help matters that we have been subject to large scale cyber-attacks for the past few days so communication has been badly affected and government has been dislocated. I have been unable to receive orders from the Commander in Chief or the Defence Ministry. We will have to make our own decisions.'

'What do you suggest we do now, sir?' asked Carlisle. 'I understand the Danish Government has been reluctant to engage Russian forces in combat or indeed even to permit NATO allies to engage such forces on its territory or in its waters.'

'That position may now have changed,' replied Rasmussen. 'I understand the Russians have landed troops on the Danish island called Bornholm and I am sure that is a prelude to further moves. I suggest we get underway at first light… say 0500 hours…and head south down the Kattegat. We can then try to find out what is happening. I am sorry I cannot be more specific. I will fly my flag in the frigate, Niels Juel. We will also have the frigate, Thetis, and several Attack Craft armed with Harpoon missiles. It will be quite a powerful force.'

'I'm afraid we used all our Harpoon missiles engaging the Russian task force,' cautioned Carlisle.

'We will do our best to provide you with further stocks of missiles as soon as we are able,' said Rasmussen. 'In the meantime, I take it that your 127mm main gun is operable, and you have anti-aircraft missiles and a helicopter?'

'That is correct, sir,' answered Carlisle.

'Very good,' replied Rasmussen as the two officers saluted. 'We will sail at 0500.'

Rasmussen and Anderssen duly departed, and Carlisle tried to snatch whatever sleep he could manage. This was not easy in the circumstances and was made more difficult by the noise of jets flying overhead. At about 2-30am he was woken by Mike Addison, the Principal Air Warfare officer.

'Sorry to wake you, sir, but radar indicates unidentified aircraft approaching from the southeast,' advised Addison.

Initially befuddled by sleep Carlisle put on his uniform and stumbled his way to the Operations Room where a number of people were crowded around the Air Warfare display.

'We thought it prudent to wake you, sir,' greeted Petty Officer Backshall. 'Radar is showing a strong force of aircraft heading this way. We believe they are hostile… probably Sukhoi 24s or even Backfires.'

'Okay,' acknowledged Carlisle. 'Let's call the crew to Action Stations. Do the Danes know about this?'

'I don't know, sir,' replied Backshall as the klaxons began blaring out and disturbing the slumber of many tired men and women.

'We'd better warn them,' said Carlisle. 'This is not the time to make assumptions.'

'I've sent them signals but I don't know whether they've received them,' advised Catherine Murray. 'The Russians are jamming everything.'

'Somebody needs to go and physically tell them,' replied Carlisle.

'I'll go, sir,' volunteered Able Seaman Dave Rigby and disappeared into the night.

Rigby had not been gone for long when a big explosion shook the dockyard, and several jets screamed overhead making a thunderous noise. Further detonations followed with each one appearing closer than the last.

'May I have permission to launch Asters?' requested Petty Officer Backshall.

'Permission granted,' acknowledged Carlisle. 'And get the 5-inch into action… and the automatic guns.'

The blaring of the klaxons was exacerbated by the banging of gunfire as another flight of aircraft flew low across the dockyard bombing the port facilities. One of the jets overflew the Aurora and came under concentrated automatic fire while a second aircraft was hit by an Aster 15 missile and blew apart in midair. However, the bombing attacks continued, and the Danes were so far only offering light resistance with a handful of people scrambling to man machine guns and light flak.'

'Sooner or later, we're going to be hit if we stay here,' warned Guy Hanson. 'I suggest, sir, that we leave the harbour and put to sea.'

Carlisle was in two minds as to what to do when a heavy bomb struck the Niels Juel which was moored close by and started a large fire with ammunition exploding.

'Prepare to get the ship underway,' ordered Carlisle. 'Cast off the mooring lines. Engine room give me revolutions for slow ahead at five knots. Guy… make sure we double up the watchkeepers and maintain our blackout.'

'Aye aye, sir,' acknowledged the executive officer.

'Simon… we'll head north initially,' Carlisle ordered the navigating officer, Simon Barrington. 'Then when we're clear of air attacks we'll cut across towards the Swedish coast. There are some islands… here,' he added, pointing to a large map set up on a computer screen. 'These should give us some cover and we can then turn southwards. I don't know what we'll find but it's better than just sitting at Frederickshavn waiting to be blown out of the water.'

'My thinking entirely, sir,' replied Simon as the Aurora slowly traversed the harbour area and headed for the open sea. It was still the middle of the night and to the north was darkness. The port and dockyard installations were lit up by exploding bombs and raging fires as the air strikes intensified.

On the bridge Sub-Lieutenant Gartmore saw the Niels Juel hit by a second bomb while further bombs hit the area around the quayside where the *Aurora* had so recently been moored. In the Operations Room Petty Officer Backshall set the Aster 15 silos to launch missiles automatically at any aircraft which approached the ship. This turned out to be prudent when a pair of Sukhois appeared on the air search radar heading for the *Aurora* at high speed and low altitude approaching from astern. Leading Seaman Glenn Johnson opened fire with the twin 30mm guns mounted on the hangar roof but the Russian jets, known to NATO as Fencers, pressed home their attack. Their first bomb landed in the water about fifty yards off the starboard quarter while a second bomb hit the sea just short of its target and bounced over the Aurora's flight deck, exploding in the sea just yards off the port side. As the Russian planes screamed overhead almost colliding with the frigate's mast the Aster missile system sprang into action sending two missiles shooting into the night sky. The second Sukhoi was blown apart in a spectacular fireball while the leading aircraft was chased by an Aster 15 and manoeuvred so violently that it crashed into the sea. Out in the open waters of the Kattegat Carlisle ordered an increase in speed although watchkeeping remained very tight both for enemy activity but also because of the ever-present danger of a collision in the darkness in a busy shipping route. Once they were nearing the Swedish coast Carlisle ordered course to be altered to starboard with the Aurora now heading south at eighteen knots. After they had been steaming for an hour or so Carlisle concluded that the Kattegat was quieter than he had expected, and the coastal areas appeared to be subject to a blackout.

''Vessel ahead, sir,' reported Roy Stringer from the radar plot. 'Fifteen thousand yards off our port quarter… speed fifteen knots.'

'What's her course?' asked Carlisle. 'Can you identify the ship?

'She's altering course, sir, and turning about,' advised Stringer. 'I'd guess she's picked us up on her own radar. She's now heading towards us.'

'What's her nationality?' queried the captain. 'Is she Russian?'

'I'm trying to make radio contact, sir,' advised Danielle Sheldon. 'I'm getting something although it's difficult to hear properly because of the jamming. 'I'm sure I picked up Swedish… yes… She says she is the Swedish frigate, Gotland.'

'Signal in reply and tell her who we are,' ordered Carlisle.

'Aye aye, sir,' acknowledged Danielle. As well as playing the clarinet Danielle spoke twelve foreign languages fluently, so her linguistic skills were often useful.

The two ships closed steadily in the darkened waters and once they were about two thousand yards apart communications became easier and they were able to maintain a dialogue. The Gotland's captain introduced himself as Lieutenant Commander Gustav Larssen. They were based at Karlskrona and were on patrol in the Kattegat, but a crisis had blown up overnight.

'The Russians have launched amphibious attacks against the Baltic islands,' explained Larssen. 'They are trying to seize the western entrance to the Baltic and deny its use to NATO and allied countries.'

'We are based at Kiel,' responded Carlisle. 'Do you know whether we can get back there. I understand Kiel has been bombed.'

'Yes… it has been attacked,' replied Larssen. 'I do not know whether it will be possible to get through. We are trying to reach Helsingborg and

Malmo, but they have also been bombed and there are reports of landings by Russian forces and parachutists.'

'We will come with you,' said Carlisle. 'Unfortunately, we have fired all our Harpoon anti-ship missiles, but we still have most of our stocks of anti-aircraft weapons and we have a Lynx helicopter.'

'That is good,' replied Larssen. 'We still have full stocks of RBS 15 anti-ship missiles, and we have an Agusta helicopter.'

The two ships sailed southwards in company passing Angelholm where they slowed to twelve knots to navigate the narrow waters with Helsinger to starboard where they were joined by two Danish Attack Craft who warned that there were powerful Russian forces in the area. The small force arrived at the Swedish port of Helsingborg which was blacked out but nevertheless illuminated by fires clearly resulting from enemy action. Two freighters moored in the harbour were ablaze and it was clear that the port infrastructure had been damaged by bombing. Larssen spoke to the harbour master who advised caution in attempting to reach Malmo where there were reports of heavy bombing and Russian amphibious forces landing on the southern tip of Sweden. The bridge from Copenhagen had been struck by bombs and by gunfire from Russian warships and the rail service had been suspended. Apparently, the bridge had been hit while a train was crossing and there had been heavy loss of life. The captains of the small group of Allied ships were all of the opinion that they needed to do something.

'We are a peace-loving country but our homelands are being pillaged,' exclaimed Larssen. 'We cannot just turn away and abandon our people to their fate.'

At 0600 hours the small force set sail from Helsingborg, being joined by the Swedish corvette, Stockholm. The sun was now rising, and a chill wind was blowing from the east. Carlisle conferred with his senior officers and with representatives from Darkforce.

'The Project Ultra equipment is operational,' advised Professor Finch. 'I recommend that we commence with a low power setting. We can then increase the power output should this become necessary.'

'Very good,' acknowledged Carlisle. 'I have a feeling we may need it.'

'Unidentified aircraft approaching from the south,' called Petty Officer Backshall from the air search radar plot.'

'How many planes?' questioned Carlisle.

'I count fifteen contacts,' responded Backshall. 'No IFF. I think they're Russian.'

'Crew to Action Stations! Crew to Action Stations!' called Carlisle over the Tannoy system. The klaxons were blaring out their cacophony of noise. 'Danielle... signal the other ships in our group that enemy aircraft are approaching.'

'Aye aye, sir,' acknowledged Danielle Sheldon. 'The Gotland is reporting that the Swedish town of Lund is under air attack and Russian forces are converging on Malmo.'

'The planes are splitting into two groups,' called Petty Officer Backshall. 'I'd say they plan to attack us from different directions.'

'Commence shooting with the 5-inch once they come within range,' ordered Carlisle.

'Range... eight thousand yards,' called Backshall. 'We've identified the planes as Fencers. The 5-inch is loaded and being prepared to shoot.'

There was a loud bang emanating from out on the foredeck as the Aurora's main gun opened fire on the fast-approaching Russian bombers. The Gotland quickly began shooting with her twin 57mm Bofors mounting and the skies above the waterway known as the Oresund became peppered with black puffs of smoke from exploding shells.

'Seven aircraft approaching from starboard,' reported Backshall. 'Height... eight hundred feet. Range two thousand yards and closing rapidly.'

Mike Addison hurriedly appeared in the Operations Room and took over the Air Warfare con.

'Eight aircraft attacking on the port side,' called the PWO (Air). 'The two Danish Attack Craft are engaging with 76mm.'

'Ensure our Aster launchers are programmed to fire automatically,' ordered Carlisle.

The Air Warfare department had already pre-empted this instruction and six anti-aircraft missiles burst skywards from the VLS silo ahead of the

Aurora's bridge. Sub-Lieutenant Gartmore, as Officer of the Watch, and personnel manning light automatic weapons saw four of the attacking aircraft blown out of the sky by Asters. Another Russian jet was hit by gunfire and crashed into the sea off the port side of the Gotland. Lieutenant Nigel Morton's electronic warfare team were tuned into the Russian radio frequencies and the chatter of the Russian aircrew could clearly be heard in the Aurora's Operations Room. As the planes attacked and were engaged by missiles and gunfire from the Allied warships the blood curdling screams of Russian pilots sent cold shivers down everyone's spines,

'Ya popal! Ya popal!' shouted one Sukhoi pilot. (I'm hit! I'm hit!)

'Formulirovka Dmitri umer,' reported one of his comrades (Dmitri is dead).

The Air Warfare team in Aurora's Operations Room had no time for sentimentality as the remaining aircraft pressed home their attacks from both port and starboard sides. The frigate's 30mm automatic guns were firing continuously and sending up arcs of coloured tracer. Roy Stringer and his team even fired chaff rockets in an effort to fill the sky with metal and put the Russian pilots off their aim.

'Hard a starboard,' ordered Carlisle as two jets came thundering in firing salvoes of rockets and opening fire with their 23mm guns. A third plane came in from astern flying fast and low and dropped a stick of four bombs which sent up great geysers of grey water around the after end of the Aurora, soaking the men and women who were out on deck. The captain's violent manoeuvring had saved the ship from serious damage but several members of the Aurora's crew were casualties including Leading Seaman Patrick McGill who had been manning a heavy machine gun on the port side and was badly wounded when a 23mm shell exploded on hitting the deck in front of him. Russian jets now attacked from starboard at low level quickly hitting the Swedish Corvette, 'Stockholm' with three bombs and bringing the ship to a standstill while fires raged and smoke billowed hundreds of feet into the skies. One of the Sukhois which hit the Stockholm was shot down by an Aster missile fired by the Aurora while another was brought down by the Gotland. Sub-Lieutenant Gartmore, who was standing out on the starboard bridge wing, saw a Russian jet cartwheeling into the sea and breaking up on impact with the water. Then all was quiet, and the surviving Russian aircraft disappeared presumably headed back to their airfields. The Gotland sent out a radio transmission seeking help for the stricken Stockholm and her crew but meanwhile the small ad hoc task group of Allied warships continued to press on. A pall of smoke rose high on the horizon. The Gotland reported that Malmo had been heavily bombed, and the Russians had surrounded the city. The only way of getting in or out of Malmo was by sea but Russian amphibious forces were now attacking the port.

'Unidentified vessels approaching from the south,' reported Roy Stringer.

'They're probably Russian, sir,' observed Mark Openshaw to the captain. 'We've no anti-ship missiles left, sir.'

'What about the Karlsruhe's Lynx?' enquired Carlisle.

'I'll enquire with the helicopter support team,' replied Mark, 'but it was engaged in missile targeting when its parent ship was destroyed.'

'Unidentified vessels now identified as two Nanuchka class missile corvettes,' called Roy Stringer.

'The Gotland says it is attempting to engage the Nanuchkas with RBS15 anti-ship missiles,' reported Danielle Sheldon, 'But there is a technical problem. The missiles won't fire, and they suspect the cabling for the launchers was damaged in the Russian strafing attacks. '

'Looks like we're up a gum tree,' mused Carlisle.

'The Danish Attack Craft are firing salvoes of Harpoons,' advised Danielle. 'Range to target…forty-six thousand meters.'

'The Nanuchkas are launching SS-N-9 anti-ship missiles,' reported Roy Stringer. 'Six missiles fired… no…make that twelve. I believe our task group is their target.'

Dr Langley said quietly in the captain's ear,

'The Ultra system is activated, Commander Carlisle. Request you give me authority to programme Project Ultra.'

'Permission granted,' replied Carlisle as Roy Stringer called out the rapidly closing range of the incoming missiles.

Aurora was firing large quantities of chaff while Lieutenant Nigel

Morton's electronic warfare team used all their technical skills to try to jam the guidance signals of the SS-N-9s. Once the missiles came within range the 5-inch main gun commenced shooting, but they were difficult targets. One of the SS-N-9s crashed into the sea but the remaining eleven missiles continued on their course towards the Allied vessels. The Gotland opened fire with her twin 57mm Bofors guns and the Danish craft were shooting with their 76mm weapons. Another Russian missile disappeared from the radar plot while the Aurora started to become enshrouded in a green haze and her crew became aware of a familiar whining or buzzing sound.

'Ensure the Asters are programmed to launch automatically,' ordered Carlisle.

'Aye aye, sir,' acknowledged Mike Addison as the first salvo of six missiles sped skywards from the silo on the Aurora's foredeck.

'Three incoming missiles destroyed, sir,' reported Addison.

'The Harpoons fired by the Danish craft have scored hits on the Nanuchkas,' called Roy Stringer. 'Five missiles hit their targets.'

Shortly afterwards the two Danish Attack Craft were both hit by Russian SS-N-9s, the Storen exploding and the Gribben being set ablaze and left in a sinking condition.

'Captain... the Gotland is signalling to us. They say they can no longer see us and are we okay,' advised Danielle Sheldon.

'Tell them we are alright,' ordered Carlisle as another salvo of Asters shot from the missile silo on Aurora's foredeck.

'Two more SS-N-9s taken out,' called Roy Stringer.

Unfortunately, two surviving Russian missiles hit the Gotland with brilliant orange flashes followed by a big column of fire and smoke which billowed hundreds of feet into the air. The Swedish frigate soon lost power and slowed to a standstill, a sitting target for Russian forces.

'The Gotland is radioing for assistance,' reported Danielle Sheldon. 'They say they have many badly wounded crew and need urgent help.'

'Substantial force of unidentified aircraft approaching from the south,' called Mike Addison. 'Upwards of fifteen aircraft. No IFF.'

'Clearly hostile,' responded Carlisle as Roy Stringer called out,

'Unidentified vessels approaching from the southern entrance to the Oresund. No IFF. Probably Russian light naval forces. Launching anti-ship missiles.'

'Two SS-N-9 missiles approaching on a bearing of Green four-five,' warned Mike Addison from the radar plot.

'Captain, I am increasing the power of the Ultra system,' advised Dr Langley calmly. 'I recommend you inform your crew as there are likely to be side effects.'

'Time to impact of Russian anti-ship missiles... twenty-eight seconds,' called Roy Stringer.

'BRACE! BRACE! BRACE!' shouted Carlisle over the Tannoy system.

Expecting to be blown out of existence in an instant the Aurora's crew felt the fabric of reality metamorph as what seemed like a huge tunnel opened up in the sea and swallowed the six-thousand-ton frigate in a gigantic tsunami. The Aurora appeared to be being swept underground and everything became dark save for a weird greenish haze. People tried to cover their ears in a vain effort to shut out the tremendous rushing noise. Carlisle felt he was about to lose consciousness when everything suddenly became quiet, and he found himself back in the library of his parental home in north Norfolk sitting in a comfortable antique Chippendale chair with Donna the black and white cat sitting on his lap purring contentedly. Carlisle sat in the chair for some time until his father poked his head round the door.

'Eddie... someone's just arrived who I think you'll be interested to meet,' announced Charles Carlisle. 'We're inviting him to stay for lunch. You'll be able to talk about naval matters with him although I think he'll have quite a lot of catching up to do!'

Eddie Carlisle was hardly feeling in a frame of mind for socialising. He did not know whether the Russian missiles had hit his ship, and this was the result but out of politeness he made the effort to leave the comfort of the chair and followed his father to the living room with its high Georgian ceiling. A man aged perhaps in his early fifties and wearing strange clothes of good quality but from an earlier age entirely, proffered his hand in greeting. These included a linen shirt with a high collar, a single-breasted tailcoat and a cravat wrapped up to his chin. He had long sideburns and short hair which was receding from the front. His breeches were of a tight fit and he wore leather riding boots. Carlisle guessed from these that the man had arrived on horseback.

'This is your Great Great, about twenty times, Uncle Samuel,' introduced Charles Carlisle. 'He was a naval officer like you and I… just in a different time.'

For once Eddie Carlisle was left speechless not knowing what to say. This whole experience was completely mind blowing and out of this world. Nevertheless, he shook his Great Uncle's hand, which felt surprisingly firm, and did his best to manage some sort of smile from a whitened visage.

'Do take a seat, both of you,' urged Charles Carlisle. 'Can I get you something to drink, Uncle Samuel?'

'A glass of port would be most welcome,' replied Uncle Samuel.

'And you, Eddie?' asked Charles.

'A cup of very strong black coffee, please,' sighed Eddie.

'Great Uncle Samuel fought at several famous battles, you know,' explained Charles. 'He has an illustrious history.'

'Yes… I was with Sir George Rodney and Samuel Hood at the Battle of the Saintes. Later on, I was at Camperdown… that was in '97. I kept the cutlass which I used when storming aboard the Dutch flagship. It was the same one I had used at the Battle of the Saintes in '82 when leading a boarding party on to the huge French flagship, the Ville de Paris. She was a 104-gun monster but we took her. I had some brave lads under my command.'

At that point Eddie's mother called to let everyone know that Sunday lunch was about to be served, and everyone should take their places in the dining room. Eddie was amused to observe that Donaldson, the cat, had already occupied his seat at the dinner table. He recalled how in days gone by Donaldson would take up his place for his favourite Sunday lunch usually a good two hours before it was served.

'You sit there, Eddie,' said Charles. 'Then you can be directly opposite Great Uncle Samuel, and he can tell you all about his exploits. Father, you sit next to me and Mum can sit next to you on the opposite side.'

Charles then sat at the head of the large antique dining table while Margaret, Eddie's mother, sat next to him and began serving the Sunday roast which today was beef with parsnips and carrots and roast potatoes and plenty of gravy and horseradish sauce. Great Uncle Samuel rubbed his hands together in pleasant anticipation of a good hearty meal.

'Do you have electricity on your ship?' asked Samuel of Eddie.

'Yes, Great Uncle,' replied Eddie as he took a helping of mustard. 'My ship would not be able to function without large voltages. We've had to have extra generators installed to provide the considerable power output we need.'

'It's a wonderful thing... electricity,' mused Samuel. 'Still, I expect you can resort to your sails if you get becalmed or you find yourself being chased by the French fleet?'

'We don't have any sails, Great Uncle,' replied Eddie. 'We have diesels for economic cruising and gas turbines for running at high speed.'

'What are these diseasles?' queried Samuel. 'I am not familiar with them at all.'

Eddie Carlisle attempted to explain to his Great Uncle the basic principles of the workings of diesel engines but he faced an uphill task and eventually he was rescued by his mother who intervened,

'This is all rather above our heads, Eddie. Great Uncle Samuel... why don't you tell us some of your seafaring stories. They're always very exciting. I like the one about how you helped save Jamaica from the French.'

'Oh yes! The Battle of the Saintes,' exclaimed Samuel. 'I had been starting to tell Charles and Eddie about what happened back in 1782. It was during the American Wars. The French and the Spanish had initially tried to take Gibraltar from us but we gave them bloody noses and so they tried a different tack. We were having a difficult time in the Americas. The Yankee rebels were supported by the French who were the strongest power in the world in those days. They had defeated our Army under General Cornwallis at Yorktown. The French were allied with the Spanish and not forgetting the Dutch... so you can see that everyone was ganging up on poor Albion. Between them all they drove us out of our American colonies and then our possessions in the West Indies were threatened as well. The French sent a big fleet under their Admiral Comte de Grasse, and they soon began seizing our island colonies. St Kitts was lost and others too. Then the Windward Islands and Jamaica itself were slated to be the next dominoes to fall. Jamaica was our most valuable territory in the Caribbean… because of the sugar, you see… even more valuable than our American colonies had been. The French and the Spaniards were well aware of this, and they knew that if they took Jamaica, it would be a great blow to our nation's economy. By dint of good fortune our Admiralty sent out a big fleet of our own under that brilliant tactician, Sir George Rodney. He flew his flag in HMS Formidable, with ninety-eight guns. His second-in-command was Samuel Hood flying his flag in HMS Barfleur. I was then a young lieutenant on the Barfleur… aged 23 as I recall…I think that's right. I was born in 1759.'

''Yes, dear, that would make you 23 at the time of the Battle of the Saintes,' agreed Margaret. 'Please tell us more.'

'The French flagship was a huge monster with one hundred and four guns,' continued Samuel. 'The Ville de Paris, it was called… enough to make a man foul his breeches.'

'Samuel, really. That's not appropriate at the dinner table,' Margaret castigated him.

'Anyway,' recounted Great Uncle Samuel, 'I recall it was just after 4 o'clock in the afternoon. I searched through my telescope. I was high up in the foretop at the time when I espied the French fleet. In the Barfleur we were right at the head of the British line, and I called down to Admiral Hood to tell him the Frenchies were in sight. Under Samuel Hood we chased after the French throughout the evening and into the night but in the early morning everyone was becalmed. Eventually we sailed into a gentle wind, and we continued our pursuit of the French but only eight other British ships were still with us. All the rest were still becalmed so we were out on a limb and very vulnerable at this time. The French Admiral Comte de Grasse was well aware of this and began preparing to attack us but by the grace of our good Lord the rest of our fleet managed to catch up. They were helped by the fact that the bottoms of our ships were now sheathed in copper which made them faster than the French and Spanish ships. The French were very surprised as to how fast our ships could sail. On the Barfleur we awaited the French attack, and we were also awaiting the signal from our Admiral Rodney in the Formidable. They were still six miles behind us but eventually we received a red signal telling us to engage the enemy even though the French still outnumbered us two to one. De Grasse realised we had a very strong fleet of ships behind us and broke off his attack and headed towards the Saintes Islands. We continued to pursue the French and were concerned that we might lose them but then two French ships collided and were damaged. By 12th April, our fleet had caught up properly with the French who were in some disarray having suffered another collision. Samuel Hood ordered his rear division to take the lead as they were fresh, and HMS Marlborough opened the battle and engaged the French. We exchanged broadsides and ships were damaged on both sides. Poor Captain Blair on the Anson was sliced in two by round shot. Captain Robert Manners of the Resolution… he was only 24 years old…was severely injured and died of his wounds. Finally, the Formidable approached the Ville de Paris which had already been damaged. Although it was a bright sunny day in the West Indies the fog of war was everywhere but to some extent it helped us as did the direction of the wind which then blew to the south causing the French line to separate and put them in an unfavourable position. We were then able to break their line by sending our ships through the gaps in their line of battle. In that situation our ships were able to fire their guns on both sides without the French being able to return fire. The French Glorieux which was astern of the Ville de Paris was blasted by our concentrated fire and completely dismasted. The French were getting a real pounding and suffering heavy casualties which they would throw overboard making a feast for the sharks. The French were cut off from their objective by our fleet and the Glorieux had no option but to surrender to us. The captain of the Glorieux was already dead. By 2pm the French were in full retreat with us in hot pursuit. The Cesar was totally dismasted and captured by the Centaur. Then the French also lost the Hector which was captured by HMS Alcide. By 5-30pm the Ville de Paris was isolated… cut off from her fleet… and we in the Barfleur were hot on her heels. HMS Russell under Captain Saumarez sailed along the stern of the Ville de Paris firing broadsides that blasted the

French flagship. Then HMS Russell moved to her leeward side to cut off her retreat while we in the Barfleur manoeuvred to the opposite side. By 6 o'clock with more than three hundred men dead and her masts and rudder shot away the Ville de Paris struck her colours. Admiral de Grasse had indicated he would prefer to surrender to Admiral Hood in our ship. I was one of the first of our men to board the French flagship and I was appalled by what we found. Nearly all the French officers had been either killed or wounded save for Admiral Comte de Grasse who did not have a scratch on him. Later Admiral Rodney also came aboard the Ville de Paris and Admiral Hood presented the French commander to him. It was a great day for us but a very bad day for the French. We had won a great victory and saved Jamaica from being lost to the French.'

'I expect you got some prize money,' interrupted Eddie, 'what with capturing the French flagship and their fleet commander?'

'Oh yes, I got some prize money alright,' replied Samuel. 'But it wasn't as much as I had hoped for. The Ville de Paris and other French ships we had captured sank in a great storm as they were being brought back to Blighty. But there were other ships which we had captured. After the actual Battle of the Saintes we pursued the French survivors, under the command of Admiral Hood, and captured the Jason and the Caton which were both 64-gun ships of the line and we took some smaller ships as well in the Battle of the Mona Passage. When we eventually got home, I was given more than a thousand pounds in prize money. That was a lot of money in 1782.'

'I'm sure it was,' replied Eddie. 'What did you do with it?'

'Ar, indeed,' considered Great Uncle Samuel. 'I purchased a property… White Hall Farm…near Melton Constable… not all that far from here… and married Charlotte Manningtree. She was the younger daughter of a local landowner and farmer, Sir Oliver Manningtree.'

Eddie was fascinated by this conversation but suddenly began to feel giddy and even nauseous. Making polite excuses he retired back to the library which strangely metamorphed into the Operations Room of the Aurora.

'The captain's regaining consciousness,' someone was saying. 'Hopefully he'll be alright now.'

'We've made it through the Kattegat, Captain,' said Dr Samantha Langley. 'Project Ultra worked again. We'll soon be entering Kiel dockyard. A tug is standing by to lead us in.'

Carlisle struggled to recover and restore his command of the situation and was soon giving orders once more. It was evening and the light was beginning to fail but everyone could see that the dockyard had been badly damaged, and several buildings were still on fire or smouldering. The wreck of a ship, with its masts and superstructure protruding above the relatively shallow water presented a hazardous and awkward obstruction as the Aurora slowly and cautiously manoeuvred towards her berth. No sooner had they tied up to the mooring bollards and made the ship secure than a leutnant from the German Navy came aboard together with a petty officer.

'They told us you had been sunk!' exclaimed the leutnant.

'Who did?' questioned Carlisle.

'Everyone,' replied the leutnant. 'The survivors of the Danish and Swedish ships you were with say you just vanished… presumed sunk with all hands. The Russians claim they sank you… and all the other vessels in your group.'

'Well… you can see for yourselves that we survived,' responded Carlisle.

'It is a miracle,' observed Petty Officer Bode of the German Navy.

'I believe we have Professor Finch and Dr Langley and their team from Darkforce to thank,' commented Guy Hanson.

'I'll second that,' agreed Carlisle as his eyes met the blue sapphires of Samantha Langley. 'This handful of people saved us from destruction.'

'Not for the first time,' Samantha Langley reminded him. 'I think you owe us a favour or two, Captain.' Her eyes opened wide as Carlisle kissed her on the lips. Guy Hanson smiled benignly. Carlisle felt Samantha squeeze his hand tightly giving him a secret signal. Then he remembered Alex.

Chapter 8

THE SOUND OF TYRES SCREECHING to a halt on the driveway made Alex's pulse quicken. She glanced out of the living room window and caught sight of the black Maserati.

'That's Faisal,' said Alex to the various cats and dogs. 'He's a prince, you know... Royalty... so you must all be on your best behaviour.'

Alex opened the front door and was soon exchanging greetings with the Saudi Prince she had met in London some weeks earlier.

'I hope I am not too early,' apologised Faisal. 'The drive did not take me as long as I expected. Isn't she a beauty?'

Faisal invited Alex to inspect his new car both inside and out. 'I bought it in London's Mayfair last Thursday. She's my latest toy and my pride and joy.'

'That's my car... the white Alfa Romeo Spider parked over there,' replied Alex. 'She goes like a bomb... even though she's no spring chicken.'

'What is spring chicken?' queried Faisal.

'Don't worry,' replied Alex. 'It's just one of those expressions we have in England. Come and have a look around the farm. I'll introduce you to Myrtle, the donkey, and the horses.'

Faisal was introduced to a number of different animals although Alex bore in mind that Faisal was, of course, a Muslim, and accordingly she sought to keep him well clear of the pigs.

'I am very anxious to show you round my new project,' enthused Faisal. 'If you have a few hours to spare I will drive you across there. It will only take a short while in the car.'

Alex spoke briefly to Sandra and said she would be out and about for part of the day and asked Sandra to keep an eye on the animals. Sandra confirmed she would be at the farm until the evening as she was assisting with fencing repairs. Alex then accompanied Faisal in his brand-new Maserati crossing the River Ant at Ludham Bridge and the Thurne at Potter Heigham. Soon they were taking a narrow lane which threaded its way across the open marshes until a large building hove into view, the only structure of any significance visible for miles.

'That is my latest investment,' explained Faisal. 'Old Hundred Hall. It dates from the 17th Century. That is… how you say… Jacobean. See the tall chimney stacks with the twisting design in the brickwork and the latticed mullioned windows. I only completed the purchase three weeks ago, but I have already engaged contractors to help with the restoration. You can see from the outside that they are making some progress. The previous owner made a start but did not have the resources to finish the task. At present I am making use of the West Wing as living quarters. The East and North Wings will have to wait their turn in the queue.'

Alex followed Faisal indoors where they met some of the contractors' workmen who were engaged in renovating the high ceiling of the main entrance hall and were also decorating the library and one of the sitting rooms. Faisal spoke to them briefly and discussed the intricacies of the restoration.

'You are doing a good job, Ashley,' praised Faisal. 'His team are successfully restoring the beautiful bonded wallpaper you see here. It was originally made in Holland in the early 17th Century.'

'It is all hand painted,' added Ashley. 'We are doing our best to copy the work of the original artist.'

Faisal then introduced Alex to a smartly dressed young man of possibly Asian or Middle Eastern origin whom Faisal called Mohammed.

'He is my gentleman's gentleman,' explained Faisal. 'He looks after my affairs on my behalf. Everything from ironing my shirts to booking restaurants and hotel rooms….and this is his assistant, Anwar Hussein.'

'Pleased to meet you both,' smiled Alex.

Faisal then took Alex on a guided tour of the rest of the house which included the first and second floors.

'Essentially we are seeking to restore the house from the ground floor upwards,' explained Faisal. 'This is the main bedroom here where I sleep. The four-poster bed you see there also dates from the 17th Century. It is rumoured that it was originally made for a mistress of King Charles II... I can't remember which one. I am not an expert in these things. See these intricate carvings in the woodwork... they do not make beds like this nowadays.'

'That boy at the foot of the post looks well endowed,' giggled Alex.

'I expect it is some kind of fertility symbol,' surmised Faisal. 'There are more embellishments like that one if you look carefully.'

Faisal then led Alex outside into the grounds where lawns sloped gently down towards the Broad where activity focussed upon clearing reeds and vegetation.

'That is Hickling,' advised Faisal. 'This part of the Broad is badly silted and overgrown, but we will get it sorted... like everything else. I hope to establish a marina for people to bring their boats. I can see it all in my mind's eye. You can see that it has wonderful views. There is nothing to spoil the wide panorama.'

Faisal then showed Alex back in doors but through a different entrance. Everywhere there was restoration work taking place as Faisal led Alex down a rather dimly lit corridor and entered a spacious room where there appeared to be no natural light.

'This is my home cinema,' enthused Faisal. 'Look at the size of the screen. It makes a big difference to just watching TV. Let me give you a demonstration. We'll start with a satellite news channel.'

Alex sat with Faisal as a TV presenter discussed the current political situation and the impending presidential elections in the United States on CBF News.

'This is history in the making,' stated Don Jackson, the presenter. 'Let's look at the latest opinion polls... These are right up to date...published only this morning. The latest poll puts Democrat nominee, Joe Valdez, on 59% of the vote while Republican nominee, Jack McConnell is trailing way behind. He's going to have a tough job on his hands if he wants to catch up with his

Democrat rival. Let's turn to our political commentator, Caroline Galford-Markland… Caroline… what do you make of this?'

'I think a great deal hinges on the two candidates' approaches to the current situation in Europe,' replied Caroline. 'Joe Valdez has a major power base amongst the Hispanic community in the United States, but he has a lot of support from Americans across the spectrum. The overriding reality is that the American people don't want to get dragged in to something that they see as happening literally thousands of miles away and which has nothing to do with them.'

'Can I just bring in Everleigh Maynard-Johnson here,' interjected Don Jackson…'Everleigh… you're an influential spokesperson for the Gay Community in San Francisco. How would you explain the apparent landslide developing in favour of Joe Valdez.'

'I would reiterate the point which Caroline has just made,' responded Everleigh. 'Joe Valdez is mounting his election campaign on a platform of keeping America out of foreign wars. Indeed, he states that no American life should be lost in the conflict in Europe and no drop of American blood should be spilled. He has the right feel for the way Americans are thinking right now. If Jack McConnell fails to change his policy on this issue pretty damn quick, he's heading for a big defeat.'

'Let me bring in Brad Whiteman,' interrupted Don Jackson. 'Brad… you're a supporter of Jack McConnell's campaign. How would you respond to the criticisms you've just heard of his policies?'

'I think we have to stand by our responsibilities to NATO and to our European allies,' replied Brad. 'Nobody wants to see American lives lost but we have obligations… we are treaty bound to Europe.'

Faisal and Alex's viewing was interrupted as Mohammed poked his head round the door.

'Sorry to disturb you, Your Highness, but the architect has just arrived and there are some aspects he wishes to discuss with you.'

Faisal gave a sigh but vacated his seat and asked Alex to follow him. The architect, a bespectacled man aged perhaps in his forties was waiting in the main entrance hall.

'I have the plans here for the new gymnasium and pool complex,' announced the architect whom Prince Faisal introduced to Alex as Julian Tattershall. The gymnasium will be situated next to the Home Cinema Room while the indoor swimming pool will be housed in this proposed new room which is currently partly occupied by an old conservatory which is in a derelict condition. The new pool will be heated and have large amounts of glazing giving views across the lawns to the open water beyond.'

'What do you think, Alex?' asked Faisal.

'We don't have an indoor pool at our farm,' replied Alex, 'But I remember the new pool which Lucy and her husband have created at their house in London. Theirs is situated below ground level... but they are actually short of space. You have plenty here, Faisal. Essentially you can make your proposed pool as big as you want. I suggest you also create an outdoor pool for use in warmer weather... surrounded by terraces and patios. I can see it in my mind's eye. It would be a great place for people to sit out in the summertime.'

'I can see that I should employ you as my consultant,' smiled Faisal. 'I am also wanting to create covered accommodation for my collection of cars. In due course I hope to establish a motor museum as well. It is just a matter of finding the time.'

'You certainly have your hands busy,' observed Alex.

Faisal spent more than an hour talking to the architect and discussing the plans which the architect had brought with him. Eventually Alex was somewhat relieved when Julian Tattershall went to another part of the grand house to speak to other people who were engaged on various aspects of the restoration work.

'I would like another look at that four poster you have up on the first floor,' mentioned Alex. 'I am fascinated by some of the ornate carvings in the woodwork. '

Faisal led the way upstairs and pointed out to Alex a room he had set aside for an art collection. In the main bedroom Alex was once again impressed by the size of the chamber and the views across the marshes from the latticed mullioned windows. In the middle distance the brick tower of an old windmill stood sentinel in the wild landscape, its once proud sails reduced to the basic stocks one of which was pointing skyward while another reached down almost to the ground.

'It is situated within the boundaries of my new estate here,' explained Faisal. 'I intend to restore it and turn it into a feature here.'

'I'm looking forward to that,' enthused Alex. 'Too many of the traditional Broadland windmills have been allowed to fall into dereliction and even to be totally lost. I see you have a collection of books here on this side of the room.'

'Yes,' replied Faisal. 'The main library is downstairs and being renovated but I wish to have a collection here in my own bedroom as well. The bookcases you see there are from Portland House in London. They date from the eighteenth century.'

Alex began thumbing through some of the books on the shelves. One particular volume drew her attention.

'I love Kipling,' she exclaimed. 'Particularly the "Just So Stories". My favourite of these is the "Butterfly that Stamped".'

'It is a favourite of mine too,' admitted Faisal. 'This volume here is a 1st edition from 1902. Look at the wonderful illustrations.'

Alex and Faisal sat down on the edge of the bed and Faisal began to read aloud from passages selected from the book.

'This, O my Best Beloved is a story- a new and wonderful story- a story quite different from the other stories- a story about The Most Wise Sovereign Suleiman- bin – Daoud- Solomon the Son of David.

There are three hundred and fifty-five stories about Suleiman- bin – Daoud; but this is not one of them. It is not the story of the Lapwing who found the water; or the Hoopoe who shaded Suleiman-bin-Daoud from the heat. It is not the story of the Glass Pavement, or the Ruby with the Crooked Hole, or the Gold Bats of Balkis. It is the story of the Butterfly that Stamped. Now attend all over again and listen! Suleiman-bin-Daoud was wise. He understood what the beasts said, what the birds said, what the fishes said, and what the insects said. He understood what the rocks said deep under the earth when they bowed in towards each other and groaned; and he understood what the trees said when they rustled in the middle of the morning. He understood everything, from the bishop on the bench to the hyssop on the wall; and

Balkis, his Head Queen, the Most Beautiful Queen Balkis, was nearly as wise as he was.'

Alex drew herself up against Faisal who placed a protective arm around her as though he was reading to a child.

Faisal are you going to rule wisely when you become king of your country?' enquired Alex.

'Yes. I shall rule wisely and fairly,' replied Faisal.

'Then may I be your Most Beautiful Queen Balkis... if only for an hour or a day?' asked Alex.

'Certainly, my queen,' smiled Faisal and continued reading,

'And yet Suleiman-bin-Daoud was not proud. He very seldom showed off, and when he did, he was sorry for it. Once he tried to feed all the animals in all the world in one day, but when the food was ready a huge animal came out of the deep sea and ate it all up in three mouthfuls. Suleiman-bin-Daoud was most surprised and said, 'O Animal, who are you?' And the Animal said 'O King, live for ever! My name is Small Porgies, and I am the smallest of thirty thousand brothers, and our home is at the bottom of the sea. We heard that you were going to feed all the animals in the world and my brothers asked me to go and find out when dinner would be ready.'

Faisal showed Alex the illustration of Small Porgies rising from the depths of the sea to eat all the food that had been arranged ostensibly to feed all the animals in the world. At that point, his mobile phone rang.

'Sorry to disturb Your Highness,' interjected Mohammed, 'but there is a Mr David Delaway here from Darkforce Plc. He says it is very urgent that he sees you immediately.'

'Sorry, Alex... my Queen Balkis,' apologised Faisal. 'It seems I am in demand today. Come with me.'

Alex followed Faisal downstairs where they met a bespectacled man in a grey suit aged about forty or so.

'I'm sorry to butt in on Your Highness like this,' apologised David Delaway, 'I know I was not due to meet you until tomorrow, but my phone has run out of charge, and I was unable to forewarn you that I was already on my way.'

Faisal ushered the man into the library and offered him a comfortable chair. Alex sat to one side behind Faisal while Delaway explained the purpose of his visit.

'Your Highness, you will be aware that at Darkforce we are engaged in a number of secret projects including Ultra which is already being tested experimentally by several governments including the British. I am pleased to confirm that the German and British governments are in the process of signing contracts with Darkforce for the delivery and installation of Ultra systems. Following on from research undertaken in connection with Ultra we have been developing a powerful quantum computer which is now ready for testing in operational conditions.'

'That sounds encouraging so what is the urgency of your visit here?' enquired Prince Faisal.

'Without beating about the bush,' replied Delaway, 'We need seventy million dollars to complete the development and get one of these quantum computers aboard a Royal Navy warship. This particular venture is called Schrodinger's Cat, but I have not told you this. The whole project is, of course, covered by the Official Secrets Act so not a word to anyone else about this, either of you.'

'You are wanting me to invest a great deal of my money into your project… but how do I know whether it is effective?' queried Faisal.

'There is to be a demonstration of Schrodinger's capabilities this coming weekend,' advised Delaway. 'It will take place in Liverpool, and you will be given instructions as to how to reach the venue. Rest assured that Schrodinger has a computational ability many thousands of times more powerful than the average human brain. The technology is based upon the use of information from the Multiverse… parallel worlds and all that kind of thing. Essentially once the computing power available from our world has been attained, we can use the power from the next parallel world and the next one and so on….and all at super-fast speed. You can understand that in a combat situation such technology will be war winning. '

'Yes, I can understand that,' acknowledged Prince Faisal. 'I will attend the demonstration as long as somebody gives me details of where it is to take place so that I can find it.'

After what seemed an age to Alex, Prince Faisal and David Delaway concluded their business for that day and David went on his way. Alex expressed to Faisal that she was wishing to hurry back upstairs to the four-poster without further delay. This time there were no interruptions. Later in the evening Faisal drove Alex back to Longfleet Farm and it was agreed that he would call again in two days' time. Alex also expressed a wish to accompany Faisal on his forthcoming visit to Liverpool which was a city she had not visited for some years.

The following day Lucy paid a call on Alex who told her about her new liaison with Prince Faisal.

'Well done, Alex!' praised Lucy. 'He's very rich you know and he's ultimately an heir to the throne of his country. '

'I am aware of that,' acknowledged Alex. 'He seems to be involved with all kinds of business ventures and projects. He's agreed to me coming with him to Liverpool on Saturday to attend a demonstration of some new computer technology which he's being asked to invest in.'

'Is that Darkforce?' asked Lucy.

'Yes,' replied Alex.

'Jerome's merchant bank is providing a lot of the finance for their new ventures. They have some brilliant positively mind-blowing ideas.'

The next day Alex called on Lucy at the house near How Hill as Lucy wished to show her the new manicure room which she had created.

'I seem to be spending a lot more time out here than in London these days,' explained Lucy, 'So I felt I ought to transfer some of the facilities here to Norfolk. I haven't yet been able to persuade the masseurs from London to come out this far but I'm working on that. In the meantime, I can provide services myself and I have a guy, Mustafa, who comes out from Norwich. Unfortunately, it's his day off but I'm happy to give you a massage myself.'

'Yes... I'd like that,' replied Alex. 'I could do with some relaxation and recuperation.'

'Couldn't we all,' agreed Lucy. 'Take off your things and make yourself comfy on the surface there. You've got nice views out across the countryside and the How Hill Estate. There's no one to bother us. The kids are at school and Jerome's at work in London, of course. I take it you haven't heard much from Eddie lately?'

'I did hear from him yesterday actually,' replied Alex, 'But he's still very buttoned up as to everything. I still have no idea where he is, and their missions are all highly secret so he's unable to tell me anything about what he's doing. I often feel I'm a single person.'

'So, tell me more about Prince Faisal,' probed Lucy. 'I know he's very rich... but what else. You will have done it, of course. Is he well hung?'

'Yes,' divulged Alex. 'He has a great big four poster bed with amazing intricate carvings in the woodwork and he says it was made in the 17th Century for a mistress of King Charles II.'

'Wow! That's absolutely wonderful!' enthused Lucy as she spread more massage oil across Alex's back and buttocks. 'When he screws you just imagine that he's the king and you're his mistress.'

'I do,' revealed Alex, 'Or more truthfully, I think of myself as his queen. Queen Balkis, to be precise.'

'Queen Porkies?' queried Lucy.

'No, Balkis,' Alex corrected her. 'They're a character from a Rudyard Kipling story... "The Butterfly that Stamped".'

'I was never really into Kipling,' conceded Lucy. 'Jerome likes Kipling. I'm more of a Jackie Collins reader. I like raunchy stuff... plenty of bonking and all that. Anyway, time to turn on your back, darling. Let's oil your tummy.'

Alex rolled over with her substantial breasts flopping freely and stretched her arms above her head while enjoying Lucy's massage.

'Did you say you were going off somewhere with Faisal this weekend?' asked Lucy.

'Yes, to Liverpool to look at some new military technology,' advised Alex.

'You'll need to be careful going there,' warned Lucy. 'They've had one or two Russian missile attacks recently. Do you think it's wise?'

'The way I see it, we're at risk wherever we are these days,' responded Alex. 'Besides it sounds rather exciting, venturing into dangerous territory with a prince of Arabia.'

'You're very brave,' praised Lucy. 'Talking of being brave I can give your legs a waxing. I'm sure Faisal will be impressed. You have very good legs to start with.'

'Thanks,' acknowledged Alex. 'Yes, I'll take up your offer.'

'I have a special piece of furniture here,' explained Lucy. 'I picked it up at an antique shop in London a few weeks ago. It's an 18th Century birthing chair. Come and try it out. It's an experience.'

Alex was slightly perplexed by the unusual chair but did as she was told and complied with Lucy's instruction to put her feet through the stirrups which Lucy then strapped tight. Alex's fine long legs were now fixed firmly in a raised position and well apart.

'In days long gone by women will have given birth in this chair,' commented Lucy.

'I would very much like to have children myself,' responded Alex, 'But not right now in your massage parlour, thank you.'

Lucy turned on the TV as a distraction and as background and neither of them paid the programmes much attention. There was an Australian soap followed by a programme about baking cakes. Alex did enjoy the documentary about East African wildlife as Lucy began to inflict pain tearing off the waxing strips. Alex was relieved when this process was finally concluded but Lucy had not quite finished.

'Let's tidy up your bush a little,' proposed Lucy. 'I can offer you several different styles. There's the Brazilian… that's nice and neat. It leaves just a narrow strip of pubic hair. Alternatively, I can shave off all your bush. That's very popular nowadays. I'm sure Faisal would like that.'

'No, I'm proud of my bush,' replied Alex. 'I don't want it shaved off.'

'Well, how about this one?' suggested Lucy as she showed Alex a glossy brochure with photos of different options. 'I'm sure Faisal would be impressed… and Eddie too when he eventually comes home.'

'Yes, I'll go for that one,' agreed Alex pointing to the photo of the lady with the bush shaped into a heart.

'A good choice,' concurred Lucy and set to work carefully trimming Alex's pubic hair accordingly.

When the task was nearly complete a TV announcer suddenly came on air with urgent news of an accident which had just befallen the President of the United States.

'We've received reports that the US President Holman. F. Landon, aged 79, has been admitted to the Bethesda Naval Hospital in Washington after suffering a fall at the White House this morning. Initial eyewitness accounts indicate that the President was accidentally knocked down by his rescue dog, Hustler, when the President got out of bed. The White House is denying reports that the 79-year-old President is in a serious condition, some say unconscious, and that it is business as usual at the White House. Normally the role of the President would be taken on immediately by the Vice President but unfortunately Michelle Jackson-Franklin is currently being held hostage in Iran with no likelihood of an early release by her captors.'

The TV reporter handed over to the BBC current affairs specialist who speculated as to the possible implications of this unwelcome development.

'This certainly puts the U S Administration in a very difficult situation at this time of crisis when what is really needed is strong and determined leadership. Even before this latest incident Holman F. Landon was seen as a lame duck president rapidly approaching the end of his second term in the White House and therefore ineligible for re-election. We need to look ahead to the forthcoming U S Presidential Elections where Democrat nominee, Joe Valdez is now well ahead in the polls on 64% with his Republican rival, Jack MacConnell, trailing way behind. Joe Valdez is gaining strong support at home on an isolationist platform and a promise to keep America out of the war which has broken out in Europe so unfortunately the beleaguered European countries should not expect significant help from that quarter anytime soon. '

Lucy stood back briefly to admire her handiwork.

'That's very disappointing,' observed Alex.

'I thought I've done a good job,' retorted Lucy.

'No, not that,' corrected Alex. 'I mean the news… what's happened in America with the President being injured like that and the Americans not wanting to help us stop the Russians.'

'Oh, I wasn't really listening,' admitted Lucy. 'The news is always depressing. I think it's time to undo these stirrups and we can have a proper look at you.'

Alex was duly released and felt somewhat stiff and achy as she stood up, but Lucy was clearly pleased with the end result.

''That looks really impressive, even though I say it myself,' remarked Lucy. 'Your gentlemen in your life ought to be well turned on. By the way I'm planning another party for later this month. It'll be here, not in London. How does that sound?'

'Yes, great. I'd love to come,' accepted Alex.

On Saturday morning Alex heard the anticipated sound of tyres scrunching to a standstill on the gravel driveway at Longfleet Farm. She looked out of the living room window but instead of the expected Maserati there was a very large dark green saloon which she recognised as a Rolls Royce. A very smartly dressed chauffeur stepped out and began walking towards the house and knocked on the front door. Alex recognised the man as Anwar Hussein whom she had previously met at Old Hundred Hall.

'His Highness welcomes you to accompany him on today's business trip to Liverpool,' Anwar informed Alex.

'Thank you. I am very grateful to His Highness,' acknowledged Alex and followed Anwar to the impressive car where Anwar held open a rear passenger door. Once inside she was greeted by Faisal who introduced his Special Branch bodyguard, Detective Superintendent James Duggan, who was sitting in the front passenger seat.

'He is my personal protection officer,' advised Faisal. 'We will be safe with him... and this car, a modified Rolls Royce Silver Spur, is well armoured and bullet proof.'

'Just call me 'Jimmy'. I used to be with Strathclyde Police in Glasgow,' Duggan informed Alex. 'I've been in a few situations in my time... nothing worries me now.'

As the big car pulled steadily out of the driveway, with Anwar Hussein in the driving seat, Alex saw Sandra with her father, Jack Blofield and several of his sons peering from the open door of the stables. She wondered what they would think. She had told Sandra that she was going to Liverpool for the day with Prince Faisal and Sandra had made some quip about having to remember to curtsey to Alex now that she was the guest of royalty. Then the car was heading for the familiar city of Norwich with its cathedral and Faisal kept looking at his watch as they struggled through the Saturday shopping traffic. Finally, they were through and heading out to Peterborough and then up the A1 towards Newark. Alex found the ride both quiet and comfortable and reflected that she could get used to riding in style like this. Eventually they picked up the M62 and headed west at high speed over the Pennines. They were making much better progress until they approached the environs of Manchester and the traffic ground to a standstill at a Police road check. Jimmy Duggan was speaking to someone on his mobile phone. Faisal was fuming with frustration and constantly glancing at his watch. After some minutes a police vehicle appeared, and an officer beckoned them to follow along the hard shoulder. They proceeded at some pace with the Police vehicle using its siren and flashing blue lights. Alex began to feel self-important as many faces in stationary cars and lorries turned to see the big Rolls Royce hurry passed with its personal police escort. Jimmy Duggan was once again speaking on his mobile phone and even when they were through the check point they retained the escort and sped through the heavy traffic. Jimmy Duggan turned with a smile of satisfaction on his face,

'See... I've pulled a few strings for you,' he quipped. 'When these guys have to turn back we'll get a fresh escort from Merseyside Police who'll lead us all the way to Liverpool Docks.'

Jimmy Duggan was true to his word and the dark green Rolls hurried through the suburbs of Liverpool still with its escort. Alex was not very familiar with the city, but she recognised a thoroughfare called Brownlow Hill and then Lime Street. Then they were navigating their way through the city streets down towards the Docks and their destination at the International Cruise Terminal. Alex could see several very large and impressive ships moored at the quayside.

'That's the new aircraft carrier, Eagle,' pointed out Jimmy to Faisal and

Alex. 'The big ship to the right of her is the liner, Princess Royal. She's here being fitted out as a troopship. See… she's being painted battleship grey. Her cruising days to the Caribbean are over for the time being.'

'I have sailed in her more than once on cruises,' responded Faisal. 'It makes me sad to see her being prepared for war like that… going into harm's way.'

Heading into the dockyard areas there were further check points but on each occasion the Rolls Royce and its escort were ushered through without delay and Anwar Hussein parked the Rolls in a designated area. Then they were walking across a drafty quayside with the huge ships towering above them and blocking out the sun and ushered up a gangplank to a modern looking research vessel called the Ganymede.

'She looks to be privately owned, not a naval ship,' commented Jimmy Duggan. 'It says on her stern she's registered in the Bahamas.'

As they boarded the Ganymede several officials stopped and searched everyone with the exception of Prince Faisal. Alex presented no problem, but the officials were most concerned by Jimmy Duggan's Beretta pistol which he kept well out of sight inside his jacket of his suit.

'I'm afraid you will have to hand that over to us for safekeeping while you are aboard this vessel,' advised the official in charge. 'You can have it back when you leave the ship.'

'No one separates me from my Beretta,' retorted Jimmy. 'I'm Special Branch. His Highness Prince Faisal is my client and I'm primarily responsible for his personal protection and safety.' Jimmy waved his Special Branch card at the security men, but they were unbending.

'Look, pal. This is my personal firearm,' argued Jimmy and clutched the senior official by the lapels.

'Fetch the director,' someone called.

A bespectacled man aged about forty-five appeared with a female assistant and apologised to Prince Faisal.

'I'm very sorry for this misunderstanding, Your Highness,' apologised the director who introduced himself as Professor Carl Jaeger of Darkforce Plc. 'Of course, you can come through with your party and your personal protection officer can keep his weapon. You know how we have to be careful about such things. Let me show you through to the main Bar and I'll introduce you to some people you may wish to meet.'

Carl Jaeger was keen to introduce Faisal to the UK Government's Defence Procurement Minister, Geoff Hornby.

'We're very interested in Project Schrodinger,' explained Hornby. 'I understand Darkforce still need quite a lot of money to complete the set up but it's the kind of technology we need to keep ahead of the Russians… and the Chinese, of course.'

Professor Jaeger then introduced Prince Faisal to the Malaysian Navy Minister, Juhar Haji Mahirrattan.

'I gather from your name that you have made a pilgrimage to Mecca?' enquired Faisal.

'Yes, when I was a young man,' replied Juhar.

'That is good,' acknowledged Faisal. 'You are a Muslim brother. I can see that we have much in common. Here is my business card. We must meet up for dinner soon, perhaps in London while you are here in England.'

'I would be glad to accept your invitation,' thanked Juhar. 'As well as being Navy Minister for our country I am also governor of the Malaysian Province of Sabah on the northern side of the island of Borneo. That is where I come from. I used to say to people that I lived round the corner from the head-hunters. It is not far from the truth but nowadays we are more concerned about Chinese encroachment. They are trying to claim ownership of nearly all the South China Sea. Last month their planes and warships made no less than fifty-seven incursions into our sovereign territory. It is getting very bad. They are harassing our oil and gas installations out at sea. I am sure that shots will be fired before long.'

A young lady appeared with a tray carrying many glasses of white wine. Faisal politely refused.

'We are both Muslims,' he informed the young lady. 'Do you have coke or lemonade perhaps…or a nice cup of tea.'

'Certainly, sir,' replied the lady. 'Abigail here will take your orders.'

Faisal and Juhar were also introduced to the Pakistan Defence

Procurement Minister, Mohammed Khan ul Hak before everyone was invited to an exhibition area one deck below which was kitted out with a profusion of the most up to date technology. The area was dimly lit rather like the Operations Room of a warship and Professor Jaeger drew peoples' attention to a very large computer screen which showed a map of part of the west coast of Britain and the sea areas around it. Liverpool was clearly visible together with the ships occupying the port.

'This ship marked here is the aircraft carrier, Eagle, and this one the destroyer, Ardent,' advised Professor Jaeger. 'Let's take a look further out to the west. You can see a lot of commercial shipping going about its lawful business. Let's take a closer look at a sea area to the north-west of Ireland. The Schrodinger system is seeking to draw our attention to something out there. Jaeger was assisted by several operators and the exhibition area became coloured by a greenish haze and affected by a kind of strong draft such as one might experience standing on a station platform on the London Underground rail network.

'That's the Schrodinger system gathering information from the Multiverse,' explained Professor Jaeger. 'There's definitely something there. I believe it's sub-surface. The system is getting in closer and providing us with information. Here it comes... Russian Navy... Kilo Class diesel submarine... Admiral Ushakov... speed 18 knots. Depth... 33 metres... heading east. Course green zero four five. I'd say she's intent on attacking shipping leaving and entering the port of Liverpool and possibly the Clyde as well. Mark... Get on to Northwood. We'd better warn them there's a Russian submarine operating in that location.'

'But how does the system function?' asked Faisal. 'Does anyone else know this Russian submarine is out there?'

'The technology is highly classified,' advised Carl Jaeger, 'But the system is gathering in information at very high speed from a considerable multiplicity of sources. As far as we are aware we are the first vessel to spot the intruder. You can see from the radar plot that there are currently no NATO warships or aircraft heading for the position of the Admiral Ushakov. Hopefully thanks to Schrodinger that will be about to change.'

'That is very impressive,' commented Juhar Haji Mahirrattan. 'I will be presenting a very favourable report to my government.'

'What is your opinion, Your Highness?' Carl Jaeger asked of Faisal.

'I am similarly impressed,' replied Faisal. 'You are, of course, wanting me to confirm my financial commitment to the Project. I am prepared to invest £35 million in exchange for shares worth that amount and a permanent seat on the Board of Directors of Darkforce Plc. I understand you are asking me to provide a further £35 million. I am willing to provide this in return for the equivalent amount of debenture loan stock at a favourable rate of interest. I am sure my lawyers can work out the finer points of detail with Darkforce.'

'I am sure they can,' smiled Jaeger. 'I am very grateful to Your Highness for your very considerable support. I am confident of securing a contract to supply the system to the UK Ministry of Defence. As for the Americans we will have to await the outcome of their forthcoming elections.'

Mark was reporting from the plot that an RAF P-8 Poseidon aircraft was now heading towards the location of the Russian submarine contact. Shortly afterwards a draft of cold air blew through the exhibition area and the diffused greenish light reappeared.

'Schrodinger is wanting to tell us something,' announced Carl Jaeger. 'It is drawing our attention to a location further out in the Atlantic and several hundred miles north-west of the location of the Kilo Class.'

'It is sending us a message,' reported Mark. 'It's putting us on the alert… Warning… Delta IV Class Russian missile submarine manoeuvring towards a firing position.'

'The Delta IV is a rather elderly class of Russian ballistic missile submarines,' queried Geoff Hornby. 'I would not expect to find one near the British Isles. Are you sure Schrodinger has got its information correct?'

'Schrodinger is providing more details,' advised Mark. 'It says the submarine is the Dmitri Polzharsky and gives the course, speed and depth which we are passing immediately to Northwood. Apparently, this particular submarine has been modified to serve as a cruise missile carrying launch platform… an SSGN. It is a big nuke loaded with more than thirty SS-N-38 land attack cruise missiles. The SS-N-38 is an up-to-date missile capable of supersonic speed. It can be armed with either nuclear or conventional warheads. Schrodinger is warning us to take urgent action as the system says the submarine is close to being in a position to commence launching missiles.'

'Do we know who is the intended target?' asked Geoff Hornby. 'If the Delta IV is about to launch its missiles it may be too late for us to stop this process.'

'We are seeking this information as we speak,' replied Mark, 'But bearing in mind the location of the submarine I would suggest it is aiming for targets on or near the west coast of Britain.'

'Like... Liverpool?' queried Faisal.

'Let's hope not,' sighed Geoff Hornby.

'The P-8 Poseidon aircraft which had been tasked with finding the Kilo has been diverted to deal with the Delta IV,' advised Mark. 'Without Schrodinger no one would know there were Russian submarines out there until the missiles and torpedoes were fired.'

'Your Highness, would you care to come with me to my office on B deck,' proposed Carl Jaeger to Prince Faisal. 'You may bring your security team. I have communicated with my directors, and everyone is more than happy to accept your terms.'

The Prince and his small entourage duly accompanied Carl Jaegar down a steep flight of steel steps to B deck where they entered a room of modest size and were invited to take seats at a large table in the centre. Prince Faisal was handed a number of official looking documents which he began to read carefully. Carl Jaeger was applying some pressure for him to sign there and then but Faisal said cautiously,

'I understand my lawyer is on the way. Indeed, he should have been here already. I wish to have him present and to advise me that everything is in order before I place my signature on any legally binding documents.'

Faisal took out his mobile phone and began speaking to someone.

'Simon... where are you?' demanded the prince. 'You were supposed to be here for 1pm.'

'I'm dreadfully sorry, Your Highness,' apologised Simon, 'But I'm stuck in a big traffic jam on the outskirts of Liverpool. I hope to be with you in the next thirty minutes. I think it's all this extra security… it makes it difficult to move.'

'I understand the problem,' replied Faisal. 'Please speak with my Special Branch Security Officer, James Duggan. He will help you get through.'

Faisal duly passed his phone to Jimmy Duggan who had an animated conversation with the lawyer from London.

'Just leave it to me, pal,' Jimmy assured Simon. 'I'll get on to Merseyside Police for you right away.'

Jimmy Duggan was true to his word and the lawyer arrived, slightly dishevelled and out of breath, within twenty-five minutes. It then took some time for Simon and Prince Faisal to consider the documentation together. Eventually Faisal confirmed that he was happy but before he signed any documents he wished to check the position with the operators in the exhibition hall. They found the personnel in a state of some excitement.

'My name is Mark Overton,' said Mark, 'But we've just received information through Schrodinger from Mark Overston and Marc Overstrand from somewhere in the Multiverse. Jamie here has just had a similar experience. It seems we're receiving messages from ourselves or at least from people very similar to ourselves. It's absolutely mind blowing. How many copies of us are there?'

'It's all about parallel universes,' remarked Carl Jaeger. 'I'm sure there are thousands of worlds very similar to our own existing side by side… perhaps even occupying the same space. Just think how many versions of us there are out there.'

Prince Faisal confirmed that he was most impressed by Project Schrodinger and wished to sign up the relevant documentation. Carl Jaeger led the way back down to his office where they sat round the large table. The task of executing the formal paperwork took some time but eventually the task was completed. It was at that point that a member of the Darkforce staff hurried into the office and informed Carl Jaeger that he was required urgently in the exhibition hall. Apparently Schrodinger's Cat was warning that the

Russian Delta IV Class submarine was launching cruise missiles and the first of these was now on its way.

'They've just fired six SS-N-38s,' advised Mark Overton. 'I'm afraid these are headed for us… for Liverpool. We've only got a few minutes to warn everyone to take cover.'

'What the fuck!' exclaimed Carl Jaeger. 'Send an urgent message to Northwood immediately. We'd better warn the authorities here on Merseyside as well.'

'I'll see to it straightaway. Sir,' acknowledged Mark. 'I've already notified the police and the NHS and told them to expect casualties.'

'Good man,' replied Carl who then turned to Prince Faisal and his team. 'I'm terribly sorry but I think you people should get away from here as fast as you can. There's very little time and I expect the port here will be targeted.'

Faisal gathered his small team and hurriedly made their way to the exits and out on to the quayside. At this stage there was no panic but people were clearly concerned that there was some kind of emergency and were asking what was wrong. Alex was beginning to think she had made a mistake coming to Liverpool today. As they approached Faisal's Rolls Royce there was a roar like that of an express train and a brilliant flash of light followed immediately by a thunderous explosion. A large building situated prominently on the waterfront became quickly engulfed in smoke and flames and a series of further detonations followed in rapid succession. A liner moored along the quayside was hit and set on fire while another missile crashed into an area where soldiers were gathering ready to board their shipping. Alex turned her head away from the terrible carnage which ensued.

'Everyone into the car…! Hurry!' yelled Jimmy Duggan as Anwar Hussein jumped into the driving seat. As soon as the team were in the car Jimmy was exhorting him to 'Step on the gas, pal!'

Prince Faisal pulled Alex into the car as it sped away. At the exit from the port's parking area a barrier blocked their path, but Anwar drove straight through it at speed. The big, armoured Rolls Royce shrugged off the impact and when a small white car tried to occupy the same space it was unceremoniously smashed out of the way. Alex closed her eyes as Anwar drove at high speed along Parliament Street. A pedestrian who had unwisely stepped in front of the car was catapulted over the roof and Alex managed a glance out of the rear window catching a glimpse of a man collapsed in the roadway. She gave a shudder but then with a loud screeching of tyres, Anwar Hussein was turning into Great George Street only to be met by a tidal wave of humanity, men, women and children, running shouting and screaming towards them. Anwar had no option but to jam on the brakes and come to a halt. A police officer, his face covered in blood and his hair singed, only recognisable as such from his tattered and blood-stained uniform rushed up to the big Rolls Royce.

'Lime Street Station's been hit!' he yelled. 'Don't go up there... It's carnage... bodies everywhere. They've got the Liver Building as well. The whole place is on fire and going up in flames.'

'Anfield's been hit!' shouted a middle-aged woman. 'My husband was just telling me on his mobile phone. He says it's dreadful... hundreds have died. All they'd done was go to watch the football on a Saturday afternoon.'

Anwar wasted no time in turning right up a side street. There were still people running around in a terrified state and the sinister smell of burning managed to permeate inside the specially modified and bullet proof car. As they turned into Brownlow Hill the cacophony of sirens from emergency service vehicles rushing towards the city centre became deafening. Alex gave another rearward glance and could see several tall columns of dense black smoke rising into the otherwise clear skies. Faisal realised that he had become drenched with sweat. It had been a very frightening situation, but it had all happened so fast. As they joined the motorway network the vehicles from all three emergency services still kept coming and the traffic on the westbound carriageway soon ground to a standstill.

'It's all the work of that fucker, Vatutin,' commented Jimmy Duggan. 'I'll wager he has a submarine out at sea somewhere. Where's our Navy?'

Alex immediately thought of Eddie and wondered where he was. Regrettably, the conflict with the Russians was escalating rapidly and the chances of him coming home any time soon were receding. Eventually Anwar turned on the radio and found the channels full of news broadcasts and emergency announcements.

'We're getting reports that Liverpool has been hit by up to ten cruise missiles,' announced the presenter. 'Lime Street station was hit by two missiles as a train had just arrived at the station. Anfield football ground has also been targeted while a game with Leeds United was in progress.'

The presenter then gave details of emergency phone numbers for people to ring who were concerned about friends and relatives. All the indications were that casualties were heavy.

'We're lucky to have got out of that hell hole alive,' sighed Jimmy. 'At least we still have our skins.'

Later on, there were further reports indicating that both Southport and Blackpool had also been hit by missiles. The sea fronts at both towns had been struck again resulting in large numbers of casualties. Blackpool Tower had been damaged and was being evacuated as it was beginning to lean at a precarious angle. The radio presenter said that the Prime Minister, Robert Stewart, would be addressing the nation at 9pm that evening. Before Faisal and his travelling companions arrived home there were reports that the submarine building facility at Barrow in Furness had been badly damaged by cruise missiles fired from a Russian submarine. So far, the British Government was refusing to say whether any of the nuclear submarines being built there had been destroyed but commentators indicated that this was almost certain. Just as the big Rolls Royce was turning into the lane which led to Longfleet Farm there was one piece of welcome news which helped to raise everyone's flagging spirits.

'The Ministry of Defence has just confirmed that a large Russian submarine has been attacked in the Atlantic to the west of Scotland by an RAF P-8 Poseidon aircraft and by warships of the Royal Navy and the Royal Netherlands Navy. We understand that the submarine has been hit by a homing torpedo and brought to the surface where the crew are surrendering to NATO forces.'

'Well done, lads!' cheered Jimmy Duggan. 'Isn't that worth a wee dram in celebration?'

'Not at my house,' replied Prince Faisal. 'It would be against my religion.'

Sandra Blofield was outside the front door of the Farm anxiously awaiting their return.

'I was worried sick when I heard that Liverpool had been hit by those Russian missiles,' she exclaimed. 'I really thought I might never see you again, Alex.'

Alex moved to step out of the car, but her legs buckled and gave way so that she collapsed to the ground.

'Let's all help the lady,' said Jimmy. 'She's clearly suffering from shock. It's not surprising after what we've seen today.'

Jimmy briefly explained to Prince Faisal and Anwar Hussein the mode of carrying a person known as 'fireman's lift.' Between them they managed to assist Alex indoors and eased her down on to a comfy sofa in the living room. Alex began to shake uncontrollably.

'Do you think I should call an ambulance?' asked Sandra anxiously. 'She looks as white as a sheet.'

'No… give her a mug of strong tea wi' plenty of sugar,' advised Jimmy.

Sandra accepted the advice and various dogs and cats sat around Alex producing a calming therapeutic ambience.

'I'd better be on my way home,' said Faisal. 'I'm sorry that today turned out to be such an ordeal. I'll call you tomorrow.'

Bella and Carmen, the cats, curled up on Alex's lap while Elsa and Zara the Labradors rested their chins on her knees. Sandra had turned on the television which was full of breaking news. There was terrible footage of the results of the attack on Liverpool and other towns on the west coast of England. Many hundreds of people had died when missiles had struck Lime Street station and Anfield football ground. There was speculation that the death toll was as high as three thousand and many more people had been seriously injured. The presenter reported that the Russian submarine which fired the missiles had been caught as it was heading northwards probably to attack the Clyde shipyards. Later there was reference to the reaction in America to these extremely unwelcome developments. The up-to-date opinion polls were showing Joe Valdez with more than 65% of the vote with his promises to keep America out of the conflict in Europe. Even Jack McConnell was wavering in his support for America's European allies.

'It looks like we're on our own,' sighed Sandra as she covered Alex with a warm rug.

Alex had by now fallen asleep and Sandra concluded that was the best medicine.

Chapter 9

Bornholm

CARLISLE AND SEVERAL OF HIS officers carefully studied the charts of the surrounding seas and waterways and the inevitable conclusion was that they were trapped. With the Russians now in control of the Kattegat and a number of the Baltic islands as well there was nowhere for the Aurora to sail.

'We could just sit it out here at Kiel, sir,' suggested Simon Barrington. 'Sooner or later there's likely to be a settlement of the current conflict.'

'That hardly seems a satisfactory scenario,' replied Carlisle. 'There's no sign of a peace settlement anytime soon. On the contrary the situation gets worse by the day and this ship is desperately needed for operations.'

'The Kiel Canal is currently blocked, but the German authorities are trying to get it re-opened as quickly as possible,' added Guy Hanson. 'One of the sunken freighters should be re-floated by the end of the month.'

'That seems a long time to wait… and what about the other wrecks and obstructions?' queried Carlisle.

'We can get you out,' proposed Dr Langley from somewhere at the back of the gathering of officers. 'We got you safely into Kiel. Now we can extricate this ship and its crew.'

'It's worth a chance, sir,' responded Mark Openshaw. 'When it comes down to it we really have no other option.'

'How long would you need to get the Ultra system programmed?' Carlisle asked of Samantha Langley.

'I can have us out of here within the next five days,' responded Samantha.

'May be four,' cut in Professor Finch. 'I suggest we use the canal route. It's the quickest way back to the North Sea, of course. The Ultra system can circumnavigate all the obstructions.

As if to remind everyone of the great dangers they currently faced the decks of the Aurora shook as a Russian cruise missile exploded somewhere in the dockyard followed by several more detonations in rapid succession. Before nightfall the area was attacked by Russian Sukhoii aircraft which hit a German frigate and an ammunition storage facility which blew up in a massive series of explosions turning night into day. The Project Ultra team worked tirelessly to set up the system and by the following afternoon Professor Finch was confident to announce that they should be in a position to make a breakout within twenty-four hours… That was until Commodore Vincent appeared at the door of Carlisle's cabin bringing his fresh orders from Whitehall.

'I know you're anxious to get out of here as quickly as you can,' began the commodore, 'But our Government are under a lot of pressure from some of our European allies to do whatever we can to help them dislodge the Russians from the Kattegat and the Baltic islands. You know we're not getting much assistance from across the Pond at the moment what with them being in the middle of their election campaigning and the President still being in intensive care, poor old fellow.'

'So what is it we're being tasked to do, sir?' asked Carlisle.

'The Danish island of Bornholm,' continued Commodore Vincent. 'The Russians are already working hard to turn it into a military fortress with airfields and missile batteries. We need to do whatever we can to upset their efforts. You are to put to sea within the next forty-eight hours and using the Ultra stealth technology you are to land a contingent of SAS and Marines on Bornholm so that they can attack the new Russian installations and carry out sabotage. When they have done their work, you are to take them back aboard. Oh yes… and that Russian Slava Class missile cruiser…'

'What about it, sir?' asked Carlisle. 'You mean the Marshal Ustinov?'

'Yes… that one,' replied the commodore. 'You hit it with at least two Harpoon missiles recently during that skirmish in the Kattegat.'

'It was more than just a skirmish, sir,' corrected Carlisle.

'Well, whatever it was the cruiser was towed into the port of Roenne on Bornholm in a badly crippled state. All the reconnaissance reports indicate that it is still there. We want it sunk… so be a good chap and finish the job.'

'But we've no Harpoons left, sir,' complained Carlisle. 'We fired them all in that skirmish you mentioned.'

'Don't worry,' replied Commodore Vincent. 'We've arranged for you to take on a fresh stock. Make good use of those remaining forty-eight hours. You'll need to replenish with full bunkers of fuel and make sure your magazines are all restocked.'

Commodore Vincent was true to his word and well before dawn the German authorities were delivering fuel and ammunition including those vital Harpoon missiles. The following evening Professor Finch and Dr Langley were reporting that the Ultra system was operational.

'We're certainly going to need it,' cautioned Carlisle. 'The latest reports indicate the Russians have installed batteries of their latest SS-N-44 anti-ship missiles. Those things are hypersonic and have a range of more than three hundred miles. They can blow us out of the water long before we get anywhere near the island.'

'Put your faith in Ultra, Captain,' said Professor Finch reassuringly. 'The Russians could deploy missiles with a range of three thousand miles, but it won't help them if they can't see us,'

'And don't even know we're there,' added Samantha Langley.

The following morning the port of Kiel was shrouded in dense fog and Carlisle and his crew took the opportunity to slip their moorings and move silently out of the dockyard assisted by the tug, Seehunde. Once out in open water the tug's small crew wished the Aurora well and headed back to the port. In these conditions the use of radar was essential. The British frigate was crawling at six knots but the risk of collision or being run down by some giant tanker or bulk carrier was ever present. Sub-Lieutenant Gartmore was Officer of the Watch and was providing the Captain with regular reports of shipping movements in their vicinity. Eventually Carlisle felt it appropriate to invite the commanders of the Royal Marine and SAS contingents to join him for breakfast in his cabin. David Warwick brought in plates of sandwiches and mugs of hot black coffee.

'The government have another little job for us,' explained Carlisle to Dreis van Reibeck and John Cavanagh.' Here are your sealed orders. It goes without saying that this operation must take place under the cloak of utmost secrecy so not a word to anyone at this stage. I understand the Russians are turning the island of Bornholm… what was until recently a place where wealthier Danes owned second homes and went on their holidays…into a heavily militarised fortress.'

Carlisle produced a number of maps which Commodore Vincent had supplied and proceeded to study these in detail with his Marine and Special Forces commanders.

'The centre of the island is quite heavily wooded,' advised Carlisle. 'I understand this is the area where the Russians are siting long range missiles. Somehow, I have to get you SAS chaps ashore so you can make your way to that part of the island and take them out.'

'It all sounds so simple and straight forward,' replied van Reibeck. 'But first you have to get us there without us all being blown out of the water. Then we have to land on the island without being caught and assuming we get that far we have to somehow find these missile batteries. No doubt the Russians have placed them in the back garden of someone's luxury villa.'

'Probably behind the sauna,' joked John Cavanagh.

'I'll aim to drop you off in a remote spot on the south side of the island,' continued Carlisle. 'We'll use the electric boats and make use of the cover of darkness. All being well there might even be some mist and fog at this time of year.'

'Are there any friendly locals who might lend us a hand?' asked John Cavanagh.

'I was just coming to that,' replied Carlisle. 'We have an agent, Eilsa Svenssen, with whom you will aim to rendezvous. She is familiar with the island and knows her way around it.'

'Forgive me for interrupting, sir,' apologised van Reibeck, 'But could my sergeant join us for this briefing?'

'Yes, I think that would be appropriate,' agreed Carlisle.

Wayne Kirby was duly summoned to the captain's cabin over the intercom and invited to join the meeting.

'Captain to the bridge,' called the Officer of the Watch, Sub-Lieutenant Gartmore. 'Hostile vessels reported ahead.'

'Sorry chaps,' apologised Carlisle to the Marine lieutenant and special forces soldiers as the klaxons began to blare out.

'Crew to Action Stations! Crew to Action Stations!' ordered the captain. Everyone knew the drill and their allotted stations. Carlisle hurried to the Operations Room and joined Roy Stringer who was hunched over the surface radar plot.

'Two Russian patrol vessels ahead,' advised Roy. 'I'd say they've picked us up on radar. Tarantul class missile hydrofoils.'

'We should take them out without delay, sir,' advised Guy Hanson. 'They are likely to be armed with anti-ship missiles... possibly SS-N-9s or SS-N-22s.'

'But we need to conserve our battery of Harpoons,' replied Carlisle. 'Our mission would be a failure if we expended most or all of our missiles on a couple of small patrol vessels.'

Several miles over to starboard lay the German island of Lundberg with its lighthouse and a small harbour used mainly by fishing vessels.

'Starboard thirty, cox'n,' ordered the captain. 'Engine room give me revolutions for thirty-two knots.'

The Aurora leaned to port as she commenced her manoeuvre. The sun was beginning to rise but the conditions were still misty, and visibility was not good.

'The Russian vessels have launched missiles,' advised Roy Stringer. 'Range of enemy vessels... thirty-six thousand metres.'

'Mike... ensure the Asters are programmed to launch automatically,' ordered Carlisle.

'Aye, aye, sir,' acknowledged Lieutenant Addison.

'And commence shooting with the 5-inch as soon as the missiles come within range,' added the captain.

Meanwhile Aurora was firing large quantities of chaff creating clouds of the thin metal strips. Nigel Morton's electronic warfare team attempted to jam the guidance signals of the Russian missiles which were approaching at supersonic speed. Out on the foredeck of the *Aurora* the 5-inch main gun began blasting defiance while a salvo of six Aster 15s shot skywards from the silos to engage the incoming threat. Explosions in the sky to the north-east indicated that several of the Asters had found their targets while another Russian missile was hit by the radar directed 5-inch. Carlisle was now bringing the Aurora round the westerly coast of the island which was about six miles long and certainly helped to blanket the British frigate from the Russian vessels. Guy Hanson was keen to re-engage the enemy boats, but Carlisle was mindful of his orders and indeed was concerned that secrecy had already been compromised.

'The Ultra system is activated, Captain,' advised Dr Langley. 'I would recommend initial usage of moderate power output.'

'Very good, Dr Langley,' acknowledged Carlisle. 'Permission granted to activate the Ultra system on limited power sufficient to block out our radar image.'

Soon the Aurora had cleared the island called Lundberg, but the charts showed another island, Ostschwartzlund several miles to the south-east and Carlisle ordered a course correction to take them round the south shore of this feature. The Ultra system was by now creating its familiar buzzing sound and the greenish haze had begun to form around the ship.

'We'll soon be invisible to enemy radar,' advised Samantha Langley as Carlisle and George McGlashan carefully navigated the Aurora through the narrow channel between Ostschwartslund and a large sandbank off the north German coast.

'Reduce speed to fifteen knots,' ordered the Captain.

'Enemy aircraft to port, sir,' announced Lieutenant Addison from the Air Warfare plot. 'They're heading west at two thousand feet.'

'Let's hope they haven't spotted us,' acknowledged Carlisle.

Meanwhile Sub-Lieutenant Gartmore was scanning the route ahead with powerful field glasses.

'There's some kind of vessel coming out of that inlet over to port, sir,' warned Gartmore. 'Could be a Russian patrol vessel. She's gathering speed. I'd say she intends to take a look at us.'

Damn it, that's all we need right now,' cursed the captain. 'Cox'n, steer green four five.'

'Aye, aye, sir,' acknowledged George McGlashan.

'That patrol vessel is still heading our way, sir,' advised Gartmore. 'She's making a good rate of knots as well.'

'Four Russian planes approaching from the northeast,' warned Lieutenant Addison. 'Range... twenty thousand yards and closing rapidly.'

'Engage with Asters,' ordered Carlisle. 'Mark... open fire with the 5-inch on that Russian patrol vessel.'

The 5-inch swung round to port and fired six rounds in quick succession. The first shell fell beyond the target but the second and third shots hit their mark, and the enemy vessel caught fire and began to slow down whereupon it was hit again.

'Four Sukhoi-24 Fencers approaching on the port beam,' called Lieutenant Addison. 'Am engaging with Aster missiles.'

A salvo of five missiles blasted skywards from the silos on the Aurora's foredeck and Sub-Lieutenant Gartmore who was standing on the bridge wing with a large pair of field glasses observed the leading pair of Russian jets being blown apart. The third aircraft took violent evasive action and tore off a wing from excessive g forces beyond which the structure of the plane was capable of withstanding. The remaining fourth aircraft now peeled round and attacked from astern at high-speed skimming the surface of the sea.

'Hard a starboard,' called Carlisle as a bomb struck the Aurora's flight deck and smashed through the hangar destroying the German Lynx helicopter which was stowed there. Several of the fitters who were working on the machine at the time were killed and a fire broke out in the adjoining galleys causing further casualties.

'We have an unexploded bomb back here,' called Sub-Lieutenant Brookes over the Tannoy system.

Carlisle ordered a further reduction in speed as the damage control teams set to work attempting to put out the fires. He was particularly concerned that the pall of black smoke billowing from the after part of the ship would serve as a beacon for enemy forces. Indeed, Mark Openshaw and Roy Stringer were soon reporting new contacts.

'Two Russian vessels detected to the north-east,' called Stringer. 'One of them is identified as a Nanuchka class corvette armed with SS-N-9 anti-ship missiles. I believe the other is a Matka class. She may also be missile armed. Range... thirty-six thousand metres.'

'Take them out with Harpoon immediately,' ordered Carlisle. 'Engage with the 5-inch as soon as they come within range of the gun.'

'Aye aye, sir,' acknowledged Mark Openshaw.

'Count down running for salvo launch of three Harpoon missiles,' reported Roy Stringer.

'The Nanuchka has fired four SS-N-9 missiles,' warned Danielle Sheldon.

'PWO (Air)... engage those incoming missiles the instant they come within range of your Asters,' ordered the captain.

In the meantime, Nigel Morton's team were already firing clouds of chaff in an effort to create an alternative false target for the Russian SS-N-9s. Two of the weapons were successfully diverted away from the Aurora and the third and then a fourth missile were engaged by Asters and destroyed. Mark Openshaw was then able to report that they had fired three Harpoon anti-ship missiles at the Russian vessels which had also now come within range of the 5-inch. Searching with the aid of his powerful field glasses Sub-Lieutenant Gartmore was able to observe a series of hits on the Nanuchka by shellfire followed by a missile strike. The Russian vessel was duly set on fire and brought to a standstill in a crippled condition. Carlisle then ordered fire to be shifted to the Matka which took one of the Harpoons as well as gunfire and was quickly reduced to a blazing hulk.

Towards the after end of the Aurora the Master at Arms, George McGlashan, was leading the damage control parties and after an hour was able to report to the captain that the galley fires had been extinguished. This was of some relief to Carlisle but there were still serious issues.

'That bomb is stuck fast,' reported McGlashan. 'It's lodged between decks. We believe that to get it out we'll have to cut a big enough hole in the side of the ship and roll it out into the sea. There's no other way.'

'That's not good at all,' replied Carlisle. 'With an unexploded bomb on board we'll have to abort the mission.'

'They won't be too pleased to welcome us back in Kiel with a UXB on board, sir,' cautioned Guy Hanson. 'I suggest, sir, that we find a secluded location to work on defusing the bomb and making some emergency repairs to the ship.'

'A few miles further along the north German coast there's a sheltered bay, sir,' advised Simon Barrington. 'I recommend we aim for that area. Then we can drop anchor, and the damage control parties can work on getting rid of the bomb and shoring up the holes.'

'Yes, okay,' acknowledged Carlisle.

It did not take long for them to locate a quiet cove where pine woods grew down almost to the shoreline and afforded a measure of concealment. Lieutenant Van Reibeck approached the captain and introduced Corporal Henny Stein.

'My corporal has some experience in bomb disposal,' explained Van Reibeck. 'He has served in Afghanistan and Iraq. He certainly knows a thing or two about dealing with UXBs. '

'Well, that's good to hear,' responded Carlisle. 'How many bombs have you defused, Corporal?'

'More than I care to remember, sir,' replied Stein. 'In Afghanistan one of the main problems were improvised explosive devices. I have seen good people blown to bits by such things.'

'I'd prefer not to think about that right now,' responded Carlisle. 'Where did you say you come from?'

'Nottingham, sir,' replied Henny Stein.

'Oh, yes. I've got family there and old friends who went to the university,' said Carlisle.

'I'm not quite sure we're talking about the same place, sir,' cautioned Stein. 'I come from Nottingham in Kwa Zulu Natal. It's off the M2 main road from Durban to Pietermaritzburg. If you drive far enough you eventually come to Ladysmith and Rorkes Drift.'

'I should have gathered that from your South African accent,' smiled Carlisle. 'We'd better introduce you to the damage control party.'

Henny Stein was duly set to work and conferred with George McGlashan and John Cavanagh. Nobody was in any way pleased to be informed by Henny Stein that the bomb was dangerously unstable and could explode at any time. By early evening work was still proceeding slowly and everyone associated with the disposal of the bomb was exercising extreme caution. In the meantime, Danielle Sheldon reported to the captain that Kiel dockyard was coming under very heavy air and missile attack from Russian forces. Indeed, the Russians had now brought up long range mobile missile batteries to bombard Kiel and other places and installations and the Germans were saying that they would have to evacuate that area as operating from Kiel was now untenable.

'It sounds as though there would be no point in returning there, sir,' cautioned Guy Hanson despondently. 'I think it would just result in our being sunk.'

Carlisle conferred with Professor Finch and Dr Langley regarding Project Ultra and the use of the highly advanced technology to make an escape. The scientists recommended to the captain that once the bomb had been defused they should head back westwards as quickly as possible and Ultra would get them through enemy held territory to the Skaggerack. Professor Finch warned that this should be done without delay as Denmark was coming under very heavy pressure from Russian forces and there was now talk of the Danish Government being evacuated to London or Brussels. Southern Norway was also in grave danger of succumbing to Russian advances and southern Sweden had already been invaded. Carlisle was minded to accept the scientists' advice when a signal arrived from HQ in Northwood on the orders of no less a person than the Prime Minister, Robert Stewart.

'Imperative that you proceed to planned destination without further delay and destroy enemy forces there.'

Bornholm was not specifically referred to no doubt for fear of the communication being intercepted by the Russians, but Carlisle was well aware of what the orders meant and quite clearly he was being told to inflict as much damage upon the enemy as possible before retreating westward.

'Simon, set us a course for Bornholm,' ordered the captain. 'We have to get the job done. We'll approach once it begins to get dark and make use of the Ultra system,' he added, turning to Professor Finch and Dr Langley.

'The bomb is still there, sir,' reported George McGlashan from the remains of the hanger, 'Corporal Stein is working as fast as he can, but the thing is very unstable. It could detonate at any moment and blow us all to kingdom come.'

'Just take your time,' acknowledged Carlisle. 'I don't propose to move from here until after dark anyway.'

Nevertheless, he was well aware that time was passing quickly and at 20,00 hours he ordered that anchors be weighed and with the Ultra system functioning on relatively low power the Aurora moved slowly out of the protection of the cove while Simon Barrington navigated a somewhat sinuous course between a series of offshore islands. It was not long before radar was reporting the presence of unidentified vessels ahead and Carlisle ordered a course alteration to port to take the Aurora to the seaward north side of an offshore island called Hilvum, This feature was only about five miles long and as the Aurora passed the eastern end of Hilvum steaming at about sixteen knots with a layer of mist and fog beginning to form there was suddenly an almighty bang up for'ard and the frigate ground to an abrupt standstill. Everyone who was standing at the time was thrown off balance and crew members were even catapulted from their seats. Inevitably there were injuries, mostly cuts and bruises. Able Seamen Liam Turner and Frank Kerry who had been watch keeping in the foc'sle ran forward and caught a glimpse of the mast of a ship disappear under their bow. It was difficult to see anything in the murk and gloom but both men were able to discern a vessel, fortunately significantly smaller than their own, being run down by their own ship and bowled over on its beam ends. The mystery vessel then quickly disappeared being submerged by the dark waters of the Baltic. Several survivors appeared floundering in the water and scrambling nets were thrown down the starboard side of the Aurora to give those people some chance of being saved. Mark Openshaw reported that they had just collided with a Matka Class patrol vessel of the Russian Navy, and it was clear that the ship had sunk. George McGlashan reported from the hangar area that the impact had dislodged the unexploded bomb and recommended lowering it over the side without delay. A large hole had already been cut in the port side of the hangar to facilitate this operation. Carlisle immediately gave orders for the bomb to be carefully lifted and then slowly inched down into the water with the assistance of chains. He gave a sigh of relief when George McGlashan reported that the bomb had been removed and instructions were given to the Engine room to proceed slowly from the scene at five knots. Six members of the Matka class vessel's crew had been pulled out of the water while the bomb disposal was taking place. All the survivors were covered from head to toe in oil and had to be taken down to the sick bay for medical treatment. Carlisle's next concern was to ascertain whether his own ship had sustained significant damage in the collision and George McGlashan was sent for'ard with a party of men to investigate. The Aurora was fortunate in that three years ago it had undergone a refit to strengthen the hull for clandestine operations in Arctic waters which included having to navigate through ice fields. The ship's bows had been filled with concrete and other structural stiffening had been carried out at that time. Now George McGlashan was recommending to the captain that heavy shoring timbers be fitted in place in the fore part of the frigate.

'There are a few holes and leaks up at this end,' advised the Master at Arms. 'But nothing we can't take care of.'

'Very good, Chief,' acknowledged Carlisle. 'I'll leave the task in your very capable hands.'

The captain assessed that the ship was sufficiently sound for him to authorise a modest increase in speed to fifteen knots and relying largely upon radar to assist with navigation amongst the islands not to mention thick banks of fog the Aurora headed on a northerly course out into the open waters of the Baltic. Dr Langley came to the bridge and advised Carlisle that he should consider an increase in the power output of the Ultra system. Initially Carlisle was reluctant to sanction such an increase because of the effect this might have upon the crew. However, Roy Stringer and Mark Openshaw were soon reporting the presence of a Russian Gorshkov Class frigate approximately fifty miles to the north-east.

'We believe the Gorshkov may be armed with Tsirkon,' advised Mark.

'I'd say they're trying to secure a missile lock on us,' added Nigel Morton. 'Danielle is eaves dropping on their communications and they know we're here somewhere. They're just having difficulty pinpointing our exact position.'

Carlisle considered the situation and conferred with Guy Hanson and Mark Openshaw.

'Without Ultra we'd just be a sitting duck out in the open sea,' commented Guy Hanson. 'The Russians would be able to blow us out of the water from three hundred miles away.'

'Dr Langley… can you increase the power of Ultra without it blasting us into another dimension?' asked the captain.

'Yes, Captain,' acknowledged Professor Finch who had arrived on the bridge. 'We are now learning how to exercise enhanced control of the system. I can confirm that we can increase the power output of Ultra gradually so that we can largely avoid the unpleasant side effects we have sometimes experienced recently.'

'Well, we'll just have to take your word for it,' replied Carlisle. 'The important thing is that we're invisible to our opponent's radar.'

Carlisle gave orders to the Engine room for revolutions to make twenty-five knots. Mark Openshaw and Roy Stringer were continuing to provide information on the position of the Gorshkov class frigate.

'We'll approach Bornholm from the south-east,' the captain informed Simon Barrington. 'They're less likely to be expecting anyone hostile coming from that direction… we hope.'

'Enemy aircraft detected,' advised Mike Addison, 'Four SU-24s on a bearing of zero five zero… height… five hundred metres. I'd say they are looking for us.'

'Hopefully they won't be able to get a fix on us,' replied Carlisle. 'As long as Ultra does its job.'

'The Gorshkov is heading on a southerly course at twenty knots, sir,' reported Roy Stringer. 'She's been joined by a Nanuchka class corvette.'

'Helmsman, alter course twenty degrees to starboard,' ordered the captain.

'Aye aye, sir, twenty degrees starboard,' acknowledged George McGlashan.

'The SU-24s have altered course to the west,' advised Mike Addison. 'I'd say they've lost us,'

Carlisle continued to order regular course alterations. It would mean taking longer to reach Bornholm but hopefully the Russians would be confused.

'The Gorshkov is preparing to launch missiles,' warned Danielle Sheldon who was eavesdropping on the Russian transmissions.

'It doesn't make sense, Captain,' queried Samantha Langley. 'Perhaps there is another NATO ship in the area.'

'The Gorshkov has fired a Tsirkon anti-ship missile,' called Mark Openshaw.

'How far away is the Gorshkov?' asked Carlisle.

'Forty-two miles to the north, sir,' Mark informed him.

'The missile is headed towards us at hypersonic speed,' warned Mike Addison from the air warfare plot.

Carlisle hurriedly conferred with Guy Hanson and Mark Openshaw.

'If we try to shoot down the missile we'll give away our position to the enemy,' advised Guy.

'May be that's what they have in mind,' acknowledged the captain. 'Mark... keep weapons tight until I give the order to shoot.'

'The Tsirkon is still on course,' called Mike Addison. 'It's heading in our direction at more than three times the speed of sound.'

Carlisle ordered a further course alteration and an increase in speed to thirty-two knots. The Russian missile continued to home in and Mike Addison, the PWO (Air), was urging the captain to give him permission to open fire. Carlisle held firm as Simon Barrington joined Mike Addison in calling for him to shoot.

'If that thing hits us we're all toast,' exclaimed Simon.

'Time to impact... forty-five seconds,' advised Roy Stringer.

'We must engage the missile now,' implored Mike Addison as anxious faces turned towards the captain in the Operations Room.

'Time to impact... twenty-two seconds,' called Roy Stringer.

Carlisle was about to give the order for the crew to BRACE when the Tsirkon missile suddenly changed course apparently selecting a new target. Members of the crew hunched around the air warfare plot saw the Russian missile strike a large vessel, probably a tanker or bulk carrier. Soon Danielle Sheldon was reporting that she was picking up distress calls from a Polish collier, the Gdynia, which was stopped and on fire twenty miles to the east.

'She says she has casualties... dead and wounded,' reported Danielle.

'Should we go to their assistance, sir?' queried Simon Barrington.

'Perhaps that is what the Russians want us to do,' replied Carlisle. 'Helmsman... alter course thirty degrees to port.'

The new course took them away from the stricken collier and heading directly for Bornholm.

'I hope this fog keeps us invisible,' remarked Simon Barrington. 'I must admit I was genuinely scared by that Tsirkon missile. I thought it had our number on it.'

'You're not scared are you, Dr Langley?' asked Carlisle.

'Put your trust in Ultra,' replied Samantha. 'Darkforce has all the answers.'

'The Gorshkov is now at a range of fifteen miles,' advised Mark Openshaw. 'Do you want to sink it, sir?'

'I admire your aggressive spirit, Mark, but secrecy is all important,' replied Carlisle. 'Hold us on course, Simon.'

Enveloped in a thick fogbank the Aurora passed astern of the Russian frigate and Carlisle then ordered a course alteration to starboard to take them on a bearing parallel to the south coast of Bornholm.

'I've made contact with our Danish agent, sir,' advised Danielle Sheldon. 'She's sending us a signal to let us know where to land our special forces teams.'

'Very good, Danielle,' acknowledged Carlisle. Soon he was ordering a reduction in speed and the Aurora was feeling her way along making full use of radar while Roy Stringer called out reports of all shipping movements in the area.

'Agent V is telling us to bring the Aurora into a sheltered bay near the south-eastern tip of the island,' continued Danielle as she drew the captain's attention to a map on a computer display. 'She says it will protect us from the weather and the Russians should not see us unless they stumble right on top of us.'

The Aurora had by now slowed down to seven knots and began feeling her way inshore with the sonar team taking echo soundings of the depth of water under the keel.

'There's shallow water over to starboard,' advised Simon Barrington. 'Could be rocks so we'd better keep clear.'

'It wouldn't do to run aground and get stuck fast here,' acknowledged Carlisle.

'Agent V is guiding us in,' reported Danielle. 'I've got a clear signal.'

'Depth under keel… seven fathoms,' called Franklin Henry. 'There's a gentle shelving of the seabed towards the shoreline.'

'I think we're now in the bay which Agent V referred to,' said Simon Barrington. There is land to both port and starboard. I recommend we tuck ourselves as close inshore as we can without going aground.'

'There are some cliffs over to starboard about five hundred metres away,' advised Simon. 'I suggest we drop anchor in the lee of the high ground. It should give us some protection.'

Carlisle ordered speed reduced to three knots and carefully manoeuvred the Aurora into her temporary anchorage with the cliffs rising to around two hundred feet.

'Depth under the keel… six fathoms,' called Franklin Henry.

'Okay We'll drop anchor here,' ordered the captain. 'Stop engines.'

The SAS and Royal Marines wasted no time in lowering their electric boats into the still waters together with their weapons and kit. Carlisle wished them good luck with their mission. He was under no illusions as to the dangers they faced and wondered how many would return. Then the special forces teams were heading off towards the shore hopefully to make contact with Agent V. In the secluded bay all was quiet, the only sounds being from the wildlife and the background hum and buzzing of the Ultra system. Carlisle increased the number of lookouts and ensured that the personnel for these duties were changed with each watch. Ultra might be cloaking them in invisibility but they were well and truly within enemy held territory. Although it was late at night Carlisle found it difficult to sleep and conferred with Guy Hanson and Mark Openshaw who was currently Officer of the Watch.

'I'm itching to finish off that Russian cruiser,' remarked Carlisle. 'But we'll have to wait until our Marines and SAS teams are safely back on board. I'm afraid it could mean sitting around here for several days. The chances of us being spotted by the Russians… or at least by somebody… are very high.'

'Unfortunately, you're right, sir,' agreed Mark Openshaw. 'But I do think that if our position here is compromised we should attempt to sink the Marshal Ustinov before we head for home.'

'I am of the same view,' agreed Guy Hanson. 'It's expected of us… and it would be a big boost to morale in Europe. Let's face it… things have not been going too well recently.'

With the coming of dawn Carlisle was relieved that the fog remained persistent and showed no sign of clearing. They were now playing a waiting game and in many ways it made him and others feel more scared than they had been when locked in combat with enemy forces. Fortunately, the weather was helping to keep enemy air activity grounded but Roy Stringer reported Russian light naval forces patrolling off the coast. Carlisle was most concerned that they could be spotted from the shore. During the morning Ruth Goldman, who was on lookout duty, reported seeing a small boat approaching through a break in the fog and the crew were called to Action Stations. Fingers itched on triggers of automatic weapons and pulses beat faster as the small vessel approached the Aurora. Sub-Lieutenant Gartmore said he believed it was a Danish fishing vessel and Danielle Sheldon was ordered out on to the foc'sle and called to the men on board once they came within hailing distance. The crew of the boat appeared reluctant to approach the frigate too closely but eventually curiosity got the better of them and they drew alongside.

'Are you Russian?' someone asked.

'Don't reply to that,' cautioned the captain.

'Who are you?' enquired Danielle of the men in the small vessel.

'We are the Danish fishing boat, Thor,' someone called back.

'Then we would be obliged if you would keep away from our ship,' cautioned Danielle. 'We are the Russian destroyer, Sverdlov. We have orders to open fire on any vessel which comes within three hundred metres of our own ship.'

The Danes who had been out on deck hurried below and the small fishing vessel chugged away into the fog and disappeared.

'Should we move from here, sir?' Guy Hanson asked of the captain.

'That was good thinking of Danielle to say we are Russian,' replied Carlisle. 'Hopefully, they won't go spilling the beans to all and sundry that there's a British frigate anchored in the bay. We'll stay put for the time being.'

Fortunately, the fog persisted and if anything became more dense. The scientists were able to reduce the power output of the Ultra system which was of some relief to Carlisle as he anticipated that they would need the system again to save their skins sooner rather than later. Nevertheless, he remained concerned about the vulnerability of their location and lookouts were posted ashore to give warning of anyone approaching from the landward side. A headland not far away to starboard was chosen as a suitable vantage point for several sailors while two more ratings were sent off in the opposite direction to keep watch for any activity. Night fell once again, and the crew of the Aurora waited. Danielle Sheldon reported that the special forces teams had made contact with Agent V and the operation was going to plan although the missile sites were well guarded. Later in the night some members of the crew including people posted ashore reported a muffled explosion to the north-west followed by what sounded like a second detonation not long afterwards. It was early morning by the time Danielle was advising the captain that the SAS had signalled 'S' meaning operation successful. His elation was short lived as the fog began to lift with the result that the Aurora was now visible to anyone who might be present in the vicinity. It was not long before the ratings posted ashore were reporting that some of the locals were taking an interest in the British warship. Carlisle was feeling uneasy.

'I do think we ought to move from this place,' he remarked to Simon Barrington and Guy Hanson. 'I suggest we sail round to the eastern side of the island. There's an inlet here,' he pointed to a large map displayed on a computer screen.

It did not take long for the Aurora to weigh anchors and get underway keeping quite close to the shore. The Ultra system was set to generate sufficient power to mask their position to radar. The climatic conditions remained misty which helped when Roy Stringer called that a Russian Matka class patrol vessel was in the vicinity. Carlisle wished to avoid action at this stage as their mission was still far from completed. Mike Addison reported that a Russian Ilyushin reconnaissance aircraft was approaching from the east at a height of two thousand metres. Carlisle ordered an increase in speed to twenty knots as Danielle Sheldon advised him that the special forces teams were heading overland towards the coast and would aim to rendezvous with the Aurora at the inlet chosen by the captain. Franklin Henry was calling out the depth of water under the keel. The south side of the island had soft sandy beaches but as they steamed round to the eastern side the topography became more rocky and Carlisle was concerned that they might make contact with some underwater obstruction. The coastal area at this part of the island was quite heavily wooded and it was with a measure of relief that they found the inlet and inched their way in at five knots to drop anchor where stands of pines and other tree species extended down to the water's edge. By now it was early afternoon, and the sun was high in the sky. Soon Mike Addison and his air warfare team were calling out airborne contacts on the radar plot and a pair of Sukhois thundered overhead at about two hundred feet. Carlisle had his heart in his mouth wondering whether the Aurora had been spotted but a combination of the Ultra system and the cover from the trees appeared to have saved them on this occasion.

'The special forces teams say they should make it here this evening and intend to re-join us under cover of darkness,' Danielle advised the captain.

'I hope we can hold out that long,' replied Carlisle as another pair of

Russian jets roared overhead heading westwards. 'I'll wager they're looking for our SAS men and Marines.

Once again the captain posted a number of ratings ashore to keep watch and after an hour or so those near the shoreline were reporting Russian naval patrol boats passing close at hand not far from the entrance to the inlet. Soon afterwards Callum MacDonald and Andy Baxter who were occupying an outcrop of rocks about a mile to the north-west were signalling to the Aurora that they could observe Russian troop movements in the distance. As late afternoon turned to early evening Carlisle welcomed the return of mistiness and fog and figured that they might have at least some small chance of getting out of here in one piece. Danielle was keeping him regularly up to date with the locations of the SAS men, but he was still worried about those Russian ground forces. It seemed that the SAS would have to infiltrate through them to reach the Aurora. Indeed, it was not long before Callum MacDonald and Andy Baxter reported the sound of gunfire and shooting in the distance to the north. Carlisle lamented the earlier destruction of the Lynx helicopter and considered that it was a serious loss. Had they still got the use of that machine they would have been able to ferry the special forces soldiers back to the Aurora. It was after 20.00 hours when the first of the electric boats made their way silently back to the parent ship. Scramble nets were placed over the stern of the frigate and SAS troops were helped back on board. Dreis van Reibeck went to see the captain and reported the success of the mission.

'We destroyed all the missile batteries on our target list,' he enthused. 'It should help to increase our chances of engaging the Marshal Ustinov. The local knowledge is that she is still at Roenne being patched up presumably to enable her to reach Kaliningrad or Kronstadt.'

'Good man...You did well,' acknowledged the captain as John Cavanagh joined them on the bridge still covered in camouflage make up.

'We actually saw the Marshal Ustinov,' enthused Cavanagh. 'She looks a bit of a mess at the moment. Large areas of the ship look burnt out. I'd reckon they'll want to get her to a dry dock for major repairs... probably a thorough rebuild I should say.'

'I take it she would be unlikely to be in a position to return fire against us?' questioned Carlisle.

'Doubt it very much,' replied Cavanagh. 'I'd say her command-and-control centres are burnt out. She's really just a hulk at the moment. One thing I would caution though. We also saw several mobile anti-ship missile batteries being manoeuvred into position along the coast close to Roenne. We identified them as SS-N-40s. They will represent a threat to us. I did consider taking them out, but it would have blown our cover prematurely and the cruiser is, of course, our primary target.'

Carlisle appeared thoughtful. He did not welcome the presence of those missiles although it did not surprise him at all that the Russians had put them there. The Russians were clearly trying to turn the island into a fortress. With all the Marines and SAS soldiers safely back on board the Aurora set course up the east coast of Bornholm soon passing Nexo and then Arsdale and Listed during the hours of darkness. Professor Finch and Dr Langley were making good use of the Ultra system, which was humming loudly, and the now familiar greenish haze pervaded the ship. Roy Stringer was making regular reports of shipping movements in the area. Fortunately, the mist and fog appeared to have kept the Russian air force grounded at least for the moment. All appeared to be well until they approached Sanveg on the north-westerly promontory of the island, an area where there were rocky outcrops with cliffs and high ground. Roy called out,

'Someone's trying to get a fix on us. I hope the Ultra system is working well.'

'Don't worry,' said Samantha Langley to Carlisle. 'Ultra will keep us invisible to their radar.'

'Yes, but they clearly have at least a hunch that we're out here,' replied the captain. 'We'd better increase the power of the system.'

Professor Finch was reluctant to apply too much generating capacity but nevertheless this was increased as they rounded the promontory and headed south for Roenne at twenty-five knots. George McGlashan reported that the repairs to the bows were holding up reasonably well although he advised the captain not to exceed their present speed except in an emergency. He was glad when the captain ordered a reduction in speed as the Aurora closed in towards the coast and the surface warfare team began searching in earnest for their target ship. John Cavanagh was standing on the bridge with Carlisle and Mark Openshaw as dawn broke and the sun rose slowly above the cliffs. It was going to be a fine autumnal morning, and the mist and fog had cleared.

'The Marshal Ustinov will still be in the harbour at Roenne,' advised John. 'But I am worried about those mobile missile batteries. I know they exist. I've seen them with my own eyes.'

'Engine room reduce revolutions for eighteen knots,' ordered the captain.

'Depth under the keel reducing to twelve fathoms,' called Franklin Henry.

Carlisle noted that the coast line was quite well wooded providing cover for concealed shore defences and it was almost with relief when the topography changed, and beautiful sandy beaches extended right down to the shore.

'There's the headland,' called John Cavanagh. 'The harbour is just beyond it.'

Carlisle and Mark Openshaw hurried to the Operations Room where personnel were gathering around the surface warfare plot.

'Radar shows a large naval vessel… I'd say about twelve thousand tons… moored near the harbour mouth,' advised Roy Stringer. 'I'd reckon that part of the harbour would normally be occupied by car ferries and cruising ships. Now it's a base for the Russian Navy.'

'Depth under the keel reducing to nine fathoms,' called Franklin Henry from sonar.

Carlisle ordered a further reduction in speed to fifteen knots.

'Submerged obstruction to starboard,' warned Franklin. 'Could be a wreck or an outcrop of rocks. '

'Helmsman, alter course ten degrees to port,' ordered the captain.

'Ten degrees… port,' acknowledged the Master at Arms.

'There's a vessel exiting the harbour,' called Mark Openshaw from the surface warfare plot. It's not the Marshal Ustinov.'

'I'm identifying it as a Grisha class frigate,' advised Roy Stringer.

'Damn it,' cursed Carlisle. 'That's all we need right now... Surface Warfare Team prepare to engage with 5-inch. That's our cover blown. They'll know we're here.'

The Aurora's main gun swung round on a bearing to engage this new threat, and seven rounds were fired in quick succession. The first shot went over but the second and subsequent shells hit the Russian frigate. One round hit the vessel's bridge while another exploded in its boilers causing a dark cloud of oily black smoke and steam to billow high into the clear morning air. Aurora's Surface Warfare Team wasted no time in pumping further rounds of 127 millimetre into the wounded Russian vessel which soon slewed to a standstill on fire.

'We have a fix on the Marshal Ustinov,' reported Mark Openshaw from the surface warfare plot.

'Very good,' acknowledged Carlisle. 'Prepare to engage the cruiser with four Harpoons.'

'We have a firing solution, sir,' acknowledged Mark. 'Countdown running.'

Personnel on the Aurora's bridge and those manning automatic weapons or on watch duties had a grandstand view of the four anti-ship missiles blasting away from their launchers and curving round to home in on the big Russian cruiser. The Marshal Ustinov could now be seen from the Aurora moored next to what appeared to be a freighter or supply ship. Dockyard workers could be observed on the quayside with people belatedly running for cover as the Harpoons homed in at high speed followed by a succession of big explosions each one following rapidly after the other. The missiles were programmed to strike the Russian ship's command and control centres, and the cruiser's mid ships areas were soon ablaze. Determined to finish the job properly Carlisle ordered the surface warfare team to follow up the missile attack with gunfire from the 5-inch while the Aurora closed in towards the harbour area so that the British frigate's 30mm automatic guns were in range and opened fire. Suddenly a massive explosion tore upwards and outwards from the Marshal Ustinov with shock waves buffeting the *Aurora* out at sea. People on the quayside were blown away by the huge blast which was soon followed by a second explosion.

'Their ammunitions going up, sir,' reported Simon Barrington from the Aurora's bridge.

'We'd better get out of here as quickly as we can,' said Carlisle. 'We'll have stirred up a hornets' nest.'

The Aurora tuned about and headed due westwards at twenty-five knots. Fires and explosions could still be seen erupting from the port of Roenne even after the island disappeared over the horizon. Inevitably it was not long before Mike Addison was reporting,

'Enemy aircraft approaching at high speed from six o'clock... four MIG-29s... range twelve thousand metres and closing rapidly.'

Carlisle heard Dr Langley's calm voice beside him.

'With your permission, captain. I propose to increase the power output of the Ultra system.'

'Submarine contact ahead at sixteen thousand metres,' called Franklin Henry from sonar. 'Identified as Russian Kilo class...'

'Go ahead, Dr Langley,' responded Carlisle.

As the Russian jets screamed overhead firing their guns the six-thousand-ton bulk of the Aurora vanished into a wormhole in the fabric of space-time.

Chapter 10

ALEX WAS ASSISTING SANDRA WITH the task of grooming the horses when her mobile phone rang. It was Faisal.

'How is my little angel?' enquired the prince.

'Fine. Are you coming over tomorrow?' asked Alex. 'I've got a new outfit I'd like to show you. It's practically transparent.'

Sandra cast Alex a reproachful glance.

'Sorry, Alex. I've got to go to London for a directors' meeting of Darkforce,' replied Faisal. But you're welcome to come with me. I'm sure you'd find it interesting… and there'd be opportunities for you to go shopping and we can dine at a restaurant afterwards… perhaps Claridges or the Savoy. They're a couple of my favourites.'

Alex thought for a moment but remembered her experience accompanying Faisal to Liverpool. She was still shaken up and having nightmares.

'No, I think I'll stay at home at the farm this time. There's a lot to do… But you're still coming to Lucy's party over at Howe Hill on Saturday, aren't you?'

'I hope to do so,' responded Faisal a little hesitantly,' 'But I've got the architect coming over to Old Hundred Hall sometime over the weekend. I'm not sure what time he's going to turn up.'

After the call had ended Alex said to Sandra,

'Do you think he'll come?'

'Come where?' queried Sandra.

'To Lucy's party, of course,' replied Alex.

'You know, it would be a very good thing if he didn't come,' cautioned Sandra. 'Let him go to his business meeting or whatever it is he's doing. Your place is here at the farm looking after the horses and all the other creatures who live here.'

'I suppose you're right,' acknowledged Alex reluctantly, 'but everyone has to have a little spice in their lives.'

Indeed, Alex awaited the arrival of Saturday evening with some impatience. She drove herself over to Lucy's country retreat in the Alfa Romeo and was one of the first guests to arrive. Inevitably Lucy had a big hug and a kiss for everyone.

'Darling, how lovely to see you again,' she would greet each person.

Initially Faisal was not present, and Alex began glancing impatiently at her watch. Finally, at after 7pm he arrived driving his Maserati which drew favourable comments particularly from some of the male guests who crowded around the prestigious car. Faisal was keen to show off his steed and even let a few individuals sit themselves in the driver's seat. Alex felt excluded. Everyone was more interested in the car than in herself. Finally, the throng dispersed in search of sustenance and alcohol and at last Faisal acknowledged Alex's presence.

'I'm sorry I'm a little late, but the architect turned up at 3 o'clock and there was a lot to discuss,' apologised Faisal.

By now the weather was turning colder and a northerly breeze began to blow from off the sea. Alex was wearing her expensive new dress shirt made from an almost transparent material and agreed with Faisal when he said he was feeling the chill and proposed that they head indoors. Tamara met them at the front door and offered flutes of champagne which Faisal politely declined. He was pleased, however, to accept a plate of salmon pinwheels and subsequently they sat at a long table draped with a large white tablecloth in the dining room and made polite conversation with some of the other guests. Both Faisal and Alex enjoyed the fois gras and the caviar dishes but at some point after 9pm Faisal's mobile phone rang, and Alex discerned that the caller was the private secretary to the Minister of Defence who was referring to a forthcoming high level meeting early the next morning.

'But that's Sunday,' protested Alex.

Faisal tried to make some excuse to the caller that he had a prior engagement but not long afterwards his mobile phone rang again. This time it was from the office of the prime minister, Robert Stewart.

'The prime minister is holding an urgent meeting at Chequers tomorrow morning at 7am to discuss the dangerous situation in Europe,' the caller informed Faisal. 'Your Highness, he respectfully requests that you attend.'

Once again Faisal attempted to make excuses, but the caller was emphatic, and Faisal felt he had no alternative but to confirm he would be attending.

'I'm sorry, angel,' Faisal apologised to Alex. 'It seems as though our plans have been upturned once again.'

Faisal then proceeded to call Mohammed on his mobile phone to tell him of the situation and to prepare an overnight bag for him and make all necessary arrangements.

'I'm afraid I'll have to be on my way,' Faisal apologised to Alex and to his hosts. Then he was gone. Alex felt bitterly disappointed. Once again, she was the lonely captain's wife.

'You look as though you've lost a shilling and found sixpence,' remarked Lucy. 'Let's see if we can put things right. Come with me, Alex. There's an interesting person I'd like you to meet.'

Lucy led the way down a corridor squeezing past the crowds of guests who were still arriving at this hour. Then they came to a large Victorian style conservatory which Alex remembered as having quite panoramic views during the daytime. Now, of course, it was dark outside, but Lucy began speaking to a small gathering of people.

'This is Sir David Waldegrave,' announced Lucy. 'He's in the diplomatic service. This is his wife, Lady Edwina.'

Alex dutifully shook their hands as Lucy introduced a tall African young man aged perhaps in his mid or late twenties.

'This is Jean-Marc Moussavou,' announced Lucy. 'Remind me which country you are from, Jean-Marc.'

'I am from the Republic of Gabon,' responded Jean-Marc. 'It is a very beautiful place… in West Africa… a paradise… but I find that not many people in England have been there or know anything about it.'

Lucy ushered Alex into a convenient vacant chair next to Jean-Marc and then sat down herself.

'I think you said you are in the diplomatic service, Jean-Marc?' continued Lucy.

'Yes, my father is the Gabonese ambassador to Denmark but with the Russian invasion our embassy there has had to close, and we have moved to London while the emergency continues,' explained Jean-Marc. 'I myself am working my way up through our country's diplomatic service but for me it is… how you say in English… early days.'

'You still have a long way to climb up the ladder,' added Lucy.

'I am still learning the job,' admitted Jean-Marc. 'But I enjoy the work. After all I find myself here in England. It is a very beautiful place too, but very different from Gabon.'

'Excuse me but I must go and keep an eye on what's going on in the kitchen,' apologise Lucy and disappeared.

Alex found herself conversing with the young Gabonese gentleman and her morale began to slowly improve. Jean-Marc was smartly dressed in a dark suit of Saville-Row quality. He was clearly a tall man as well as being clean-shaven and his skin was an attractive shade of brown. Soon he was engrossed in conversation with Alex telling her all about his country and his family.

'I am not married,' explained Jean-Marc. 'I did have a young lady, but I believe she has now married someone else. It does not trouble me too much. For now, I am happy to be free to see the world.'

Alex proceeded to tell Jean-Marc about her own situation and how she had been left to run the family farm while her husband was away for long periods at sea. Before long they were exchanging phone numbers and e-mail addresses. Later in the evening Lucy was encouraging them to come and make use of the new indoor swimming pool which she and Jerome had recently completed. Alex noted that it was influenced by Roman baths she had seen in Italy with artwork on the walls which reminded her of a house she had explored in the ruins of Pompeii.

'There's an annexe over there where you can put your clothes while you're in the water,' Lucy informed them.

'I'm sorry but I did not think to bring any swimming things,' apologised Jean-Marc.

'Oh, don't worry about that,' replied Lucy. 'Everyone uses the pool au naturel.'

In the annexe Jean-Marc attracted many favourable glances from the female guests as he removed his clothing which Alex carefully folded and placed with her own attire. A middle-aged lady who stopped to admire his physique was duly admonished by her husband.

'What is the matter?' Jean-Marc asked of Alex.

'Don't worry,' Alex reassured him. 'The ladies fancy you, that's all.'

Soon they enjoyed the warm waters of the pool and Alex forgot about being lonely. She and Jean-Marc talked about their families and their aspirations. Jean-Marc enthused about Gabon and its wonderful scenery and wildlife.

'It is a really beautiful place yet few people to whom I have spoken in this country have even heard of it. I come from Libreville which is the capital, but a few hours' drive will take you to the Loango National Park,' explained Jean-Marc. 'It is a different world. There are herds of elephants and hippos. If you go down to the coast you are likely to see whales and dolphins.'

'It sounds wonderful,' replied Alex. 'Just my kind of place.'

'I would like to take you there,' smiled Jean-Marc. 'May be when I next get some leave from work… perhaps in a few weeks from now.'

Their conversation was interrupted by a blinding white flash followed by a rush of very warm air, almost like a tropical storm.

'What's going on?' asked a young man close by in the pool.

'Someone says a missile has crashed… over to the west,' replied the lady who had recently admired Jean-Marc's physique.

Moments later an American banker named Gary Lungstrom working in the City of London came running into the pool area from the gardens, clearly in a state of panic, his hair and clothing tattered and singed.

'My God… there's been a nuclear explosion!' he yelled. 'Everyone take cover… we're being zapped!'

Almost immediately there was another brilliant flash of light when everything seemed to turn white for a few seconds and once again everyone experienced another blast of heat followed by a thunderous trammel in the distance. People began running around like herds of terrified animals not knowing which way to turn. Men and women who had just been enjoying relaxation in the pool were now rushing naked in all directions. Everywhere there was pandemonium.

'Come on,' called Jean-Marc to Alex. 'Let's get out of here.'

Alex found herself out of doors and following Jean-Marc down some steps which led to a large and cavernous wine cellar. Then all the lights went out and they found themselves in almost total darkness.

'We'd better stay here for a while,' cautioned Jean-Marc. 'There may be more missiles heading this way.'

They did not have to wait long before there was another flash of light followed a while later by what was clearly an explosion.

'That one seemed further away,' said Jean-Marc but Alex could hear the screams of frightened people emanating from somewhere above them in the house and its grounds. There was clearly still panic and disorder all around.

Alex and Jean-Marc sat down on a wooden bench and huddled together. Alex realised she was shaking, the situation reminding her very much of her recent experience in Liverpool.

'We'll be alright,' Jean-Marc reassured her and placed a comforting arm around Alex.

They remained that way in the darkness for several hours until someone with a torch appeared at the top of the cellar steps and called down,

'Is anyone there?' It was Jerome.

'Yes… there's the two of us,' replied Jean-Marc. 'We're okay.'

'We're trying to get some sort of power restored as soon as we can,' advised Jerome. 'Brian's rigging up a couple of large generators in one of the outbuildings. Unfortunately, the Grid's been knocked out and we can't get any info from anyone at the electricity company.'

'What's happened?' asked Alex.' We've all been absolutely terrified. We heard several big explosions in the distance.'

'Ruskies seem to have been trying to hit our airbase at Marham,' replied Jerome. 'Other places have bought it too... Catterick and the RAF bases around Lincolnshire. Good job we've dispersed our assets otherwise we'd have lost everything.'

While they were still talking the lights came back on and Jerome persuaded Alex and Jean-Marc to come back to the house. Many of the people who had come to the party were still there and some were listening to the radio and trying to get information as to what was happening. With the coming of daylight Alex drove Jean-Marc over to Longfleet Farm where Sandra and others were doing their best to calm the horses and to reassure them that everything was alright now. Jean-Marc was initially anxious to get back to London by train, but enquiries indicated a temporary suspension of rail services and news reports warned of gridlocked traffic in and out of the capital. Eventually he managed to speak to his father on his mobile phone who was able to confirm that his family in the London area were safe and no one had been harmed.

'There... everything will be fine,' said Alex. 'You can stay with me at the farm for a while. Maybe you can help out with looking after the animals. There is always plenty of work to do.'

For the next few days, the situation began to settle down although there were reports of Russian missile attacks up in Scotland and the RAF base at Lossiemouth was hit. Jean-Marc was still anxious to get back to London to be with members of his family and to return to work. At the same time Alex was wishing him to stay with her and the two of them settled on a compromise that he would return to London but would then organise for them both to fly out to Gabon, perhaps for a couple of weeks.

'That way we can get away from all these troubles...at least for a short while,' proposed Jean-Marc. 'I don't think there will be many Russian missiles crashing in that part of West Africa. It will be a safe haven for us.'

The following day a large black Mercedez arrived at Longfleet Farm, sent by the Gabonese Embassy, and Jean-Marc was driven away. Initially Alex felt alone once more but her spirits were lifted again that evening when Jean-Marc rang her on his mobile phone to let her know he had arrived safely back at the

Embassy in London and also to let her know that he was making efforts to arrange flights for the two of them to Libreville.

'You will need to make suitable arrangements for people to look after the farm and your animals while you are away,' advised Jean-Marc.

Alex spoke to Sandra who was not at all happy about her flying off to West Africa at this critical time but Sandra was persuaded that it would give Alex a chance to recuperate after her recent experiences under fire from Mr Vatutin's rockets.

'I'll stay in the farmhouse while you're away,' responded Sandra. 'Les says he can come and join me for a few days, so I won't be on my own… and there are all the dogs and cats and horses.'

'They make good companions,' agreed Alex. 'You won't have time to be lonely.'

Two days later Jean-Marc was on the phone again.

'Can you get to Stanstead Airport tomorrow night?' he enquired of Alex. 'I've got clearance for you to accompany me on a flight arranged by the Gabonese Government. It helps with being in the country's diplomatic service. I was able to pull a few strings.'

Alex was both excited and apprehensive at the prospect, but she accepted the invitation and made suitable arrangements with Sandra. Time passed quickly and before she had time for second thoughts, she was meeting Jean-Marc at the airport and boarding a plane bound for Libreville. After a rather long flight the plane landed in Gabon during a thunderstorm, but the immigration formalities were surprisingly brief, and Alex was ushered into a large black Mercedes with tinted windows while Jean-Marc pointed out to her the local landmarks. Alex was tired after the overnight flight, but she observed a large modern city with plenty of high-rise buildings and skyscrapers. Eventually the car paused at an upmarket residential avenue with security gates and an attendant who acknowledged the driver and Jean-Marc and allowed them to enter. Then the car stopped outside a large modern house with palm trees swaying gently in the front grounds.

'Journey's end. This is my place,' announced Jean-Marc. They were greeted by an African lady who smiled and greeted them warmly.

'This is Claudette. She is my housekeeper here,' he added as he led the way to the front door.

'I have put out clean fresh towels for you both in the bathroom,' advised Claudette in French. 'I expect you will be tired after your journey, but I will have lunch ready for you when you feel up to it.'

Jean-Marc led Alex up to the first floor to a spacious bedroom at the rear of the house with spectacular views across the city with the sea forming a backdrop.

'You can see the Gabon estuary and the Gulf of Guinea out over there,' pointed out Jean-Marc.

Then he was testing the shower fitment in the en-suite and managed to get it to work after a fashion. Initially some rusty looking water and some dead beetles shot out of the nozzle but after a while it flowed cleanly, and Jean-Marc invited Alex to join him.

'I thought you'd never ask,' she laughed.

After showering they made use of the towels provided by Claudette and got dressed and went downstairs where Claudette was preparing lunch which included local seafood and fresh produce she told them she had bought that morning at the local market. Although she was still feeling weary Alex was glad of the sustenance. Later Jean-Marc took her for a leisurely stroll along the avenue and pointed out the residence of the country's agriculture minister. Then they met a middle-aged man whom Jean-Marc introduced as Claude Baptiste, the Minister of the Interior. To Alex the minister appeared surprisingly open and friendly and invited them to join him for drinks on the terrace at the rear of his mansion. As they sat under the palm trees which provided welcome shade from the afternoon sun and tropical birds came and sat on the small table next to her Alex felt the experience to be quite surreal and a world away from the problems and indeed severe dangers at home in Britain. Indeed, the minister was anxious to know as much as possible about the current situation in Europe and asked many questions of both Alex and Jean-Marc.

'One might say it is a paradise here,' considered Claude. 'But we are… how you say… out of the way on the peripheries?'

'Right now, I'd say that was the best place to be,' cautioned Alex. 'I have recently experienced missile attacks from Russia, and it was absolutely terrifying. You really do not want to have to face that kind of thing.'

After Claude had refilled their glasses several times Jean-Marc and Alex thanked him for his hospitality and returned home. It was too early for dinner, so they headed upstairs to Jean-Marc's room. Alex flopped on to his bed which was of a generous size and pulled off her attire. Then she was lying naked on her back with her fine long legs well apart and her ankles almost behind her ears. Jean-Marc leaned forward and divested himself of his clothing.

'You know, Jean-Marc, you really are very well endowed,' complimented Alex.

'I have not had any complaints,' responded Jean-Marc.

'Well, hurry up then,' urged Alex as Jean-Marc kissed the tangle of dark hair between her glistening thighs.

Jean-Marc eased his impressive manhood into Alex's dark chasm, gently at first.

'Come on,' said Alex impatiently, 'I like to have it all the way up. That's a bit better. Now I've got you;… you can't get away now.'

'I don't wish to cause you any pain or discomfort. Does that please, madam?' enquired Jean-Marc.

'Yes… I'm sorry… I'm a bit of a nymphomaniac,' apologised Alex. 'It doesn't help that my husband is away at sea most of the time. Nowadays I'm always dying for sex but I'm hardly getting any.'

'Well let's see what we can do to put matters right,' responded Jean-Marc as he began thrusting hard into Alex who moaned and sighed approvingly. Eventually Alex began to tremble and called out ecstatically. Then they paused for breath and changed positions with Alex kneeling on the bed with her impressive behind raised up, her buttocks starting to sway from side to side enticingly and then shaking.

'Hold your bottom still,' requested Jean-Marc.

'Sorry… I'm excited about being fucked by you,' giggled Alex as Jean-Marc reintroduced his very large phallus.

'You know…you have an excellent arse,' Jean-Marc complimented Alex. 'Tomorrow we shall go to the beach… It is a very quiet place away from the crowds. It will be a good place to relax. The day after we can go shopping.'

'That sounds good,' replied Alex.

'Then the day after that I shall take you to my other house in the Loango National Park,' Jean-Marc informed her. 'Then we can get right away from the cares of the world. You will be able to swim with the dolphins.'

'I'd really love that,' sighed Alex as Jean-Marc thrust hard into her yet again.

Their activities were finally interrupted by Claudette calling to them to say that she was shortly to serve dinner on the terrace.

The following day Alex was woken early by a pair of Ibis who came to drink at the pool in the grounds. The sun was already shining brightly, and Claudette had prepared breakfast.

'You're an early riser,' remarked Alex to Claudette.

'I am out at the market just after 6am,' replied Claudette. 'I am able to buy fresh fish direct from the fishermen and the best agricultural produce straight from the farmers.'

Alex enjoyed the food and then Jean-Marc was driving her down towards the coast in his Land Rover. On the way Alex spotted a market selling clothing and she persuaded Jean-Marc to stop while she examined the wares. One of her first priorities was swimwear as they were headed for the beach. Alex bought a black thong which was basically just a rather small triangle with a piece of thin string.

'But where is the top?' asked Jean-Marc.

'Oh, it doesn't have a top,' replied Alex. 'Look at this outfit here. Isn't it just amazing. I must have it.'

Alex was admiring a native style leopard skin garment which incorporated a very short skirt but was also topless although it had a kind of strap over the right shoulder.

'You must also have the spear to go with it,' proffered the stall holder in French.

'You will look like a girl from the jungle,' smiled Jean-Marc as Alex settled up for the thong and the native outfit.

Then they were on their way and Jean-Marc was driving through a less salubrious quarter with open sewers and piles of rubbish strewn everywhere. Alex was distressed to observe real squalor with people living in homes which were just made of refuse with a sheet of corrugated iron for a roof if they were lucky. Then Jean-Marc found an unmetalled trackway full of ruts and potholes and the Land Rover bumped and bounced uncomfortably along for what seemed some distance until finally the open sea suddenly appeared before them. Jean-Marc continued to drive along the edge of a long almost deserted beach with endless fine white sand stretching away into the distance. The landward side was fringed with rows of palm trees which swung lazily to and fro in the gentle breezes blowing off the Gulf of Guinea. Finally, they came to a halt and alighted from the vehicle.

'It's beautiful!' exclaimed Alex.

Jean-Marc glanced around. In the distance some boys or young men were playing football. A little closer at hand a young woman was sitting looking out to sea. Apart from those few people the place was deserted.

'We will stop here,' said Jean-Marc and produced a beach mat for them to sit on under the shade of some palm trees.

Alex was eager to divest herself of her clothing and pulled on the black thong which she had just bought at the market stall.

'It seems to serve little purpose,' observed Jean-Marc as Alex performed a brief pirouette and then ran down towards the cooling waves.

'Come on in,' she called to Jean-Marc. 'The water feels lovely.'

As the sun rose higher in the sky the temperature warmed up and Alex was glad to be able to cool off in the sea. Then the two of them retired to the beach mat under the shade of the palms. A handful more people appeared on the beach including a couple who discarded all their clothing and who appeared to be making love in the water.

'We can do better than they can,' remarked Alex to Jean-Marc and pulled off the black thong. Then she was leading Jean-Marc down to the sea. 'Come on, Jean-Marc… don't be shy.'

She and Jean-Marc embraced in the warm waters and Alex felt her friend's impressive manhood once again. Eventually they felt satiated and retired back to the beach mat. After a while, a group of African boys appeared and set themselves up just a short distance away.

'They will probably be from the shanty town we passed through on the way here,' commented Jean-Marc rather grumpily.

Alex felt her pulse rising as the boys who were aged perhaps about seventeen or eighteen proceeded to throw off their clothes and went running into the sea. After splashing about rather noisily in the water they emerged and started playing football au naturel on the beach close to Alex and Jean-Marc.

'They're actually rather good,' observed Alex. 'They play skilfully.'

'Well, I suppose it gives them something to do,' replied Jean-Marc who was feeling rather irritated by the intrusion of the young men.

Alex stood up naked and muttered,

'I'm turned on by all their dicks,' and advanced boldly to join the players.

At first the African boys were a little surprised by the intrusion of this European woman into their game, but Alex showed she had some skill herself.

'I used to play football at boarding school,' she informed them in perfect French, 'as well as Netball, La Crosse… basketball… you name it. We used to win a lot of our games.'

Jean-Marc's mood did not improve when Alex sat down and chatted with some of the young Africans.

'It is time we were making for home,' he called out to Alex. 'Claudette will wonder where we are.'

With some reluctance Alex was prised away from her new friends.

'Can we come to this spot again tomorrow?' asked Alex.' Xavier and Pierre say they come here nearly every day at around the same time.'

'Tomorrow we are going shopping,' retorted Jean-Marc as they climbed aboard the Land Rover and hurried away.

The following morning Jean-Marc was true to his word and took Alex to a number of good quality clothing stores where she made a number of purchases. Then he took her to an art exhibition in the city centre and introduced Alex to a number of African artists. Alex was most impressed by the paintings of Etienne Kasanga who was a wildlife artist.

'Look at this painting of a herd of elephants emerging from a forest,' exclaimed Alex. 'I would love to buy it and hang it above the mantelpiece in our living room at home in England,'

'Etienne is a very talented artist,' agreed Jean-marc. 'I have several of his paintings… a couple of them are in my house in the Loango National Park.'

Alex was duly introduced to Etienne, a fairly young man aged perhaps about twenty-nine or thirty.

'I am from Brazzaville in the Republic of the Congo,' explained Etienne. 'I painted the picture of the elephants about two years ago in a location bordering the Congo River. Unfortunately, the elephants have suffered very badly from the activities of poachers who make a lot of money from selling the ivory from their tusks. I am involved with protecting the wildlife in that region. The French Government have been very helpful. They have provided us with some soldiers and helicopters. It is a very difficult problem because often the poachers are themselves heavily armed with assault rifles and such like. Unfortunately, there have been many conflicts and civil wars affecting the Congo and weaponry is quite easy to obtain.'

'I would love to help in whatever way I can,' replied Alex as she settled up with Etienne to buy his painting.

'I am here until next Friday,' said Etienne. 'Then I return to Brazzaville. Perhaps Jean-Marc and yourself would like to join me for a few days and I can take you both for a trip of your lifetime up the jungle and see the elephants and other wildlife in their natural environment.'

Both Alex and Jean-Marc agreed that this would be a very exciting prospect and an opportunity which should not be turned down. Etienne said he would liaise with Jean-Marc to make appropriate travel and hotel arrangements for them.

The following day Alex was keen to return to the beach, but Jean-Marc had other plans.

'Today we shall drive down to my second home on the edge of the Loango

National Park. There are beautiful beaches there… you will be able to watch the whales and the dolphins. I guarantee it.'

Alex was duly coaxed into agreement with this plan and after packing up clothing and anything else which they might need they headed off south in Jean-Marc's Land Rover past high rise blocks and miserable shanty towns and found the open road. At one point Jean-Marc had to break sharply as a troupe of baboons suddenly emerged from the bush and ran across the highway. More than once lugubrious water buffalos stood in the middle of the road causing Jean-Marc to have to swerve sharply to avoid hitting them. The journey took quite a few hours and eventually the roadways became little more than rutted tracks but they finally arrived at some security gates where an African man acknowledged Jean-Marc and duly opened the gates to allow him entry. Then they were negotiating their way up a long driveway fringed by palms and other tree species native to the region until they arrived at a large villa with panoramic views over endless beaches with the now familiar fine white sands and with the ocean beyond.

'It's lovely!' exclaimed Alex as she clambered rather stiffly from the vehicle after the long journey in the heat of the West African afternoon.

They were greeted by a rather dusky but attractive lady of mixed race, aged perhaps in her mid-thirties, whom Jean-Marc introduced at his housekeeper, Renee.

'Welcome to Santa Rosa,' smiled Renee. 'It is very good to see you both. This is a wonderful place but it can get somewhat lonely and isolated out here. Let me help you with your things. '

As with Jean-Marc's house in Libreville Alex found herself shown to the first floor where Jean-Marc's bedroom was situated to the rear of the house with spectacular views out across the endless beaches and the Gulf of Guinea. After showering after their journey Jean-Marc took Alex for a gentle stroll in the grounds of the house. There was a path leading down to a causeway where Jean-Marc led the way to a small island comprised of sand on which was situated a rustic boat shed. Inside was a fishing cruiser where two men were carrying out maintenance. Alex understood from their conversation with Jean-Marc that they would have the boat ready for the next day. Then the two weary travellers retired back to the house where Renee had prepared dinner on the terrace. Alex was struck by the peace of this haven. The war in Europe seemed a very long way from here.

In the morning Renee called them down for breakfast and then Jean-Marc was taking Alex for a bracing stroll along the coast. There was mile upon mile of the beautiful white sands fringed by palm trees which swung gently in the cooling breezes blowing in from the sea. Then they headed back towards the causeway and the small island and Jean-Marc spoke to a man named Christophe who informed them in French that the cruiser would be ready in a couple of hours and he would take them out in the vessel to see if they could spot the abundant marine life.

'That sounds wonderful!' enthused Alex. 'I can't wait to get aboard.'

'We still have a couple of hours to kill,' replied Jean-Marc and led Alex back up to the house and his room where the two of them hurriedly threw off their clothes and made passionate love in Jean-Marc's generous sized but rather elderly bed with the springs creaking and groaning noisily. Eventually they were interrupted by Renee calling to them to say that Christophe had the boat ready. Alex was keen to be aboard and Christophe was soon casting off the mooring lines and then cautiously navigating the cruiser through some shallow water until they reached the open sea where he was able to push forward the throttle. Alex glanced back at the house and was impressed by its size. Apart from Santa Rosa there were no other buildings in sight, just endless beaches and forests. Ahead of them there was just the ocean and Christophe passed Alex a pair of powerful binoculars to assist her in searching for signs of marine life. It did not take long for a school of dolphins to join them, the playful creatures splashing and cavorting all around the vessel. Christophe eased the throttle slightly. Alex thought it was wonderful. Then Christophe was pointing to a waterspout in the far distance and altered course towards the sighting.

'They will most likely be Southern Right Whales,' advised Christophe in French. Christophe was a Gabonese man aged about forty, of medium build and average height. He wore a white shirt with one or two oil stains and a dark green baseball cap.

The dolphins kept company with them as more waterspouts appeared and then Alex was becoming increasingly excited as large marine creatures began showing themselves above water. Chistophe throttled back further, and Alex said she could make out at least five whales. Suddenly one of the big creatures leaped clean out of the water and then landed back in the sea with a huge splash.

'I can make out several males and a couple of females,' observed Jean-Marc. 'One of the females has a calf.'

Christophe manoeuvred the cruiser as close to the huge creatures as he dared so that Alex was able to see the barnacles attached to them as if they were ships. The whales then slowed down and blew more waterspouts. At one point a large whale was so close that it actually touched the hull of the cruiser causing Christophe to make an urgent course alteration to starboard. Fortunately, no harm was done but the mariners felt that discretion was the better side of valour and gave the whales a slightly wider berth. After some time, the whales dived well beneath the surface and eventually disappeared. The sun was now rising high into the afternoon sky and the ocean appeared empty. Alex took the opportunity to pull off her shirt and applied generous amounts of suntan oil before sunbathing naked on the roof of the vessel.

Back at Santa Rosa Alex was keen to tell Renee all about the exciting day they had spent whale watching. Jean-Marc said he would consider taking Alex in the boat, which was called La Croix du Sud, to take a look at some of the islands in the Gulf of Guinea including Sao Tome.

'Yes, I would love to do that,' enthused Alex.

'I will speak to Christophe and hopefully he can organise something for the next day or two,' acknowledged Jean-Marc.

Subsequently he conferred with Christophe and checked the weather forecasts for the region. He and Christophe took due note of the storms predicted for the next couple of days but then conditions were expected to settle down.

The following day conditions were rather unsettled and windy, but Jean-Marc took Alex for a drive into the rain forest in the Land Rover where they saw buffalos and wild pigs including a species known as Red River Hogs.

Then Jean-Marc drove along the coast where they spotted Hippos and Alex was excited to see a whale basking just offshore. Jean-Marc then drove deeper into the forest and parked the Land Rover under some trees while he led the way on foot urging Alex to make as little sound as possible. Their patience was eventually rewarded when Jean-Marc pointed out a feline of modest size, rather bigger than a domestic tabby, with a reddish-brown coat.

'It is a wild species called a Golden Cat,' advised Jean-Marc. They are one of my favourites although our wildlife is thankfully still plentiful in Gabon and there are many species to delight us. Come with me... on foot. I have a feeling we may be lucky.'

Jean-Marc hacked at the dense foliage with his machete and after walking some distance in the heat of the afternoon came across a pile of dung which had clearly been created by an animal of significant size. Jean-Marc then tracked the footprints and clods of dung until they came to a clearing in the forest where Alex was amazed to see a whole herd of elephants.

'We must keep down wind of them,' advised Jean-Marc in a hushed whisper. 'If we disturb or surprise them they will run away or worse than that, they might charge at us.'

Alex did as she was advised and counted upwards of twenty elephants. There was a bull tusker and several older females as well as a number of infants in varying stages of development. She and Jean-Marc observed the animals for some time until the huge creatures eventually lumbered away into the depths of the forest. Jean-Marc then drove further into the wilderness where he and Alex spotted several species of monkeys together with a troupe of Mandrills. Jean-Marc then mentioned to Alex that he thought he had caught a glimpse of an unusual animal and stopped the vehicle on the edge of the forest.

'There... look,' he whispered to Alex. 'A Bongo... We have been very fortunate today.'

It was dark by the time they arrived back at Santa Rosa but once again Alex was recounting with much enthusiasm the abundant wildlife which she had seen that day.

During the night there were thunderstorms and spectacular forked lightning which continued into the following morning. Jean-Marc kept his ear to the radio and was listening intently to the weather forecasts.

'Give it another forty-eight hours,' he said to Alex. 'Then this tropical storm should have passed over and we can see about taking La Croix du Sud to have a look at Sao Tome.'

Alex took the opportunity to put on the leopard skin native girl outfit she had bought at the market a few days earlier and was keen to show it off to anyone who happened to be around. Renee appeared suitably impressed as did Simone who assisted Renee in keeping the house in order. Alex was particularly glad about the reaction of Sebastien, the gardener, whose eyes nearly popped out of his head in amazement and the reaction of Paul, who was carrying out some repairs to the roof, was rather similar. Later Renee appeared wearing her own native girl outfit which consisted principally of a very short skirt made of plant-based materials and little else.

The following morning the weather was still somewhat unsettled with a swell on the ocean making conditions rough. Alex was not pleased when Jean-Marc told her he needed to hurry back to Libreville to get some provisions and some components for La Croix du Sud.

'It is better that you stay here,' he told her. 'Renee will look after you until I get back. I shall be as quick as I can.'

Once again Alex had the feeling that she was being side lined and slouched in a corner of the spacious living room pouting and looking generally fed up. She heard Jean-Marc drive away and felt she had been dumped in the back of beyond and wished she was back home at Longfleet Farm with Sandra and the animals.

'Attention, Alex!' called Renee. 'Today we will go for a ride in my Jeep and then we will find whatever we find.'

Alex felt slightly better as she climbed into Renee's vehicle, and they set off bouncing uncomfortably along a rough trackway which ran parallel to the beach but several hundred yards inland. The palm trees provided some cover from the windy conditions. It was not long before they were encountering monkeys and baboons and one or two species of antelope. Eventually they came to a rather muddy river and Renee drove cautiously along the north bank until she stopped and pointed out to Alex some large animals submerged in the green waters a couple of hundred yards away.

'Hippos!' announced Renee. 'And if I am not mistaken… that log over there near the riverbank is actually a crocodile.'

Suddenly Alex forgot about being abandoned and became engrossed in watching the abundant wildlife. Renee gave Alex plenty of time until one of the Hippos emerged from the river and began heading in their direction. Renee did not waste any time in turning the Jeep through one hundred and eighty degrees and beat a hasty retreat.

'They are potentially very dangerous creatures,' explained Renee. 'Last month a local boy who happened to have been riding his bicycle near this river was bitten clean in half by a bad-tempered Hippopotamus.'

'I wish you had not told me that,' replied Alex.

Now Renee was driving her Jeep across a rather rickety wooden trestle bridge. Alex was sure she spotted more than one crocodile lurking in the murky waters and hoped the old bridge would support their weight. Then Renee was heading in a southerly direction along an unmetalled road which led towards the beach. Ahead of them stretched mile upon mile of fine white sand with the Atlantic rollers breaking on the shore. Renee drove for several miles and then parked the Jeep in a comparatively sheltered spot under some palm trees.

'We will stop here for a while,' she announced and laid out a large beach mat. 'I have brought a small picnic… du pain, du beurre and… how you say in English… le salad?'

'I can see you have everything well arranged,' remarked Alex. 'It is what we call in England a crab salad. It looks very nice. I'm looking forward to tucking in.'

'What is… tucking in?' queried Renee.

'Don't worry,' replied Alex. 'It's just one of those figures of speech we have in Angleterre.'

Renee looked slightly perplexed. Alex looked about them. There was not another soul to be seen in any direction.

'Who lives down that way?' asked Alex while pointing towards the south.

'Nobody,' responded Renee. 'It is a National Park… an area reserved for wildlife and the natural world. There is no one but us for miles around.'

'Don't you get lonely living out this way?' asked Alex. 'There are a lot of people in Libreville but along the coast here it is empty.'

'What you say is true,' acknowledged Renee. 'But I have lived in big cities… London… Paris… Bordeaux to name a few. But big cities can be the loneliest places in the world. They have so many people but most of the people are strangers.'

'But what about relatives?' asked Alex. 'Do you have a husband or a boyfriend… parents… siblings?'

'Don't ask me,' replied Renee guardedly. 'The less I say the more my work gets done. I had a husband once… but he is gone. When people ask me, I say he's gone to Timbuktu. And what about you?'

'I have a husband, as you know,' replied Alex. 'A naval officer commanding a frigate. The trouble is that he's away most of the time nowadays. To be honest I don't like being a captain's wife. I feel that time is passing me by. At the very least I should have a couple of children. We have pets and we have a rather small farm with plenty of animals but there is definitely something missing in my life.'

'I understand what you mean,' responded Renee. 'It's getting warm. Let's go for a swim. The sea is calming down.'

The two women pulled off their clothing and ran naked down to the shore where the Atlantic rollers were now breaking more gently. Renee pointed to a large marine creature basking near the coast.

'A Humpback,' she called to Alex. 'Let's see if we can get a little closer.'

Both women were good swimmers and eventually managed to get within a few yards of the huge mammal before Renee advised Alex that they should take care and not get too close. Her advice was correct when the whale began to stir and then moved further out to sea to seek deeper water. Renee and Alex then returned to the beach. There was still not another soul in sight. The scene was one of complete tranquillity with the endless white sands stretching far into the distance.

'Let's take a walk,' suggested Renee. Alex nodded in agreement. 'We should make sure to keep within the shade of these trees. The sun can get rather hot in the afternoons even at this time of year,' cautioned Renee.

Alex was not sure how far they had walked or for how long but the war in Europe and the cares of the world seemed to have faded away and now there was peace. Renee gently held Alex's hand, and they continued walking together for some time.

'My mother is French, and my father is Gabonese,' explained Renee. 'My mother was a doctor, and my father is a businessman… He owns property and a night club in Libreville. They produced me but eventually they went their separate ways when I was in my early teens. For a while I lived in Paris with my mother but after some time, I felt homesick for Gabon. Then I assisted my father with his club and his various businesses in Libreville.

'Did you not consider following your mother into the medical profession?' enquired Alex.

'It did occur to me,' replied Renee, 'But to be honest I don't think I would be clever enough to qualify as a doctor. The prospect of so much studying did not appeal to me. I enjoyed the nightlife and I liked the young men. When I was in my early twenties I did settle down for a while… with Jean-Paul in Libreville and we produced a son, Pierre. Sadly, the relationship did not stand the test of time and we split up acrimoniously.'

'Where is Pierre now?' asked Alex.

'He went with his father,' replied Renee. 'They are both still living in Libreville. 'I came out here to get away from things.'

Alex was now beginning to feel uncomfortable in the tropical humidity and they turned back and retraced their steps. In the evening Alex missed Jean-Marc who was still away, but Renee produced an attractive meal made from ingredients she had acquired from a local village outside the Loango Park including exotic fruits and sea creatures Alex had never previously heard of. By the time they had finished dinner and spent time talking about their lives and their cares Renee suggested that they retire to her room where they continued their conversation. Alex found the humidity uncomfortable even late into the evening, but eventually gentle breezes began to blow in off the sea.

'You can stay with me tonight,' offered Renee. 'Jean-Marc is not due back until later tomorrow at the earliest.'

'Okay,' replied Alex, rather taken aback. 'If you'd like me to.'

Then Renee had turned out the lights and Alex found herself in Renee's bed with Renee lying on top of her, kissing her gently, at first.

'We are both lonely people,' said Renee, 'with much uncertainty in our lives. But still, we can help each other.'

Alex put her arms around Renee. She felt warm and comforting and neither of them were alone.

Chapter 11

Pirates!

'ETIENNE HAS GOT THINGS ARRANGED for us,' announced Jean Marc upon his return from Libreville.' We are to fly to Brazzaville on Saturday morning. Then the following day the wildlife service will provide us with a helicopter to take us out into the depths of the forests so that we can observe elephants and all kinds of other creatures. We might well be able to see some gorillas in their natural habitat.'

''That sounds fantastic,' enthused Alex. 'I can't wait to get out there.'

'In the meantime, we can just about fit in that trip to Sao Tome,' added Jean-Marc. 'The weather has settled down now. I suggest we set off early tomorrow morning. We may get to see some more whales and dolphins. I'll speak to Christophe, and he can make preparations.'

Jean-Marc busied himself conversing with Christophe and checking over La Croix du Sud. Alex assisted Renee with housework and general chores.

'Is there anything in particular I can help you with, Renee?' enquired Alex.

'I could benefit from some assistance cleaning the kitchen,' acknowledged Renee. 'People keep tramping in and out with their muddy feet especially after those storms.'

'I'm sorry. I am one of the culprits,' apologised Alex as she set to work scrubbing the floor.

Renee followed up with a mop and bucket and their efforts progressed to the utility room where leaves and all manner of debris had blown indoors.

'Look at the state of this place,' complained Renee. 'Will we ever get it sorted?'

Alex was not one to be defeated and was constantly bending over to pick up items of debris and litter. The effort caused her white shirt to lift above her waist.

'Oh, Alex, you know you have lovely legs,' praised Renee.

'Merci, Renee,' acknowledged Alex. 'You know I used to be a model when I was younger….in Paris and in Milan.'

'I should have guessed,' replied Renee. 'You could still work in modelling today. Did you know I worked for a while in the Moulin Rouge in Paris. It was good fun while it lasted. Hey… let's go to my room again.'

'But Jean-Marc will come back and find us together,' cautioned Alex.

'Don't worry… we'll hear him,' blustered Renee and took Alex by the hand.

Once in Renee's bedroom the two women wasted no time in pulling off their somewhat scanty clothing leaving it strewn untidily in disorder while Renee jumped on top of Alex kissing her lasciviously. Alex could feel Renee's lips move steadily downwards and opened her legs wide in eager anticipation. She was not disappointed and began sighing with pleasure feeling Renee's tongue exploring the most intimate folds between her moistened thighs. Eventually Alex cried out, but Renee kept going and Alex cried out again even more loudly and ecstatically. Suddenly the bedroom door was flung open and Janine, a new housemaid aged perhaps sixteen, came hurrying in.

'Quelle domage?' she asked anxiously.

'Don't worry, Janine,' replied Renee in French. 'I am just giving Alex a new treatment for backache.'

Janine appeared confused but retreated with some hesitation.

'Pardon pour l'intrusion,' she apologised.

Alex and Renee fell about laughing but then Alex said she thought she heard someone come in to the house.

'It might be Jean-Marc,' she cautioned.

'No… it'll just be Janine getting on with her chores,' replied Renee dismissively. 'Let's do sixty-nine.'

Alex knelt astride her female lover and carefully reversed her perfect behind, looking over her shoulder as though she was manoeuvring her Alfa Romeo back home, pausing while Renee kissed first the left cheek and then the right. Alex giggled but then the bedroom door opened once again. This time Jean-Marc stood in the doorway.

'And what is going on here?' he enquired.

'Renee has been looking after me,' explained Alex. 'She is just checking my private quarters as I felt a little soreness. It will be the humidity. You know how it is here in the tropics what with being practically on the equator.'

'Put some clothes on, both of you,' ordered Jean-Marc. 'Renee... get on with your housework. I will speak to you later. Alex, come with me.

Alex followed Jean-Marc in some trepidation to his room on the second floor. Was he going to give her a beating or throw her out?

'Christophe is ready to take us to Sao Tome,' announced Jean-Marc. 'You will need to pack a few things... a change of clothes and your toothbrush.'

With some relief Alex did as she was instructed and then boarded La Croix du Sud with Jean-Marc. Renee and Janine briefly came aboard with some provisions but then went back to the house. Christophe and Jean-Marc then ran through some checks with the boat and appeared satisfied that all appeared to be well. Jean-Marc also listened carefully once again to the up-to-date weather forecast for the Gulf of Guinea.

'High pressure,' announced Jean-Marc. 'We are in luck. The sun is going to shine.'

It was not long before they were out on the open water with a school of dolphins splashing and frolicking and providing their escort as the cruiser forged ahead into the calm and glassy sea.

'Keep a look out for whales,' warned Jean-Marc as he passed Alex a pair of binoculars. 'It wouldn't do them or us much good to have a collision.'

Alex kept a careful watch and eventually thought she had spotted something about a thousand metres off the starboard bow. Christophe reduced speed and altered course to take a closer look.

'It looks big, but it doesn't seem to be a whale,' reported Alex who was now standing on the roof of the boat.

'Could be a dead one,' replied Jean-Marc. 'We sometimes see them drifting about.'

As La Croix du Sud approached the object Alex said she believed it was some kind of vessel.

'Looks like a floating wreck,' observed Jean-Marc. 'They sometimes get carried into these waters on currents from out in the Gulf. I'd say it was a wreck from the Second World War... see those derricks and gantries breaking the surface... It looks like an American Liberty ship.'

Alex peered intently at the largely submerged vessel and thought of Eddie and his crew on the Aurora. Mobile phone reception was very poor out here and she had not spoken to her husband for a while.

'Christophe will warn the authorities,' commented Jean-Marc. 'A big wreck like that one drifting around is a danger to navigation. They will probably call out the Navy to sink it once and for all.'

Later in the afternoon when the weather was still hot and humid Alex and Jean-Marc retired down below and tuned into the BBC World service on the TV. It appeared that Liverpool had been the target of further Russian missiles of which more than one had been nuclear tipped. Casualties had been heavy, and much damage had been caused to the city and to the port infrastructure. Another issue had arisen since one of the missiles, which it was speculated probably dated from the Cold War era, had apparently overshot its intended target and struck the Republic of Ireland. The missile had come down on the small town of Carrickmacglen in County Cavan north-west of Dublin. A school had been set on fire and there were casualties amongst the schoolchildren and the townsfolk. Apart from the vehement protests of the Irish Government the effect upon public opinion in America was profound and was having an earth-shattering effect on the U S Presidential elections which were now in their final phase. All of a sudden Americans were clamouring for their government and armed forces to take the strongest possible action against the Russian aggressors. Jack McConnell was now powering ahead in the polls while Joe Valdez unexpectedly found his support weakening and slipping away.

'Perhaps at last we will get support from the Americans,' considered Alex. 'I think that calls for a tot in celebration. Mine's a pink gin.'

Jean-Marc opened the drinks cabinet and produced a bottle for them to share. It seemed to become empty all too soon and they adjourned to Jean-Marc's cabin and cast off their remaining clothes. Alex jumped on top of Jean-Marc and began kissing him fervently. Then she paused.

'I've been a bad girl. Aren't you going to spank me?'

'Perhaps later... after dinner,' replied Jean-Marc.

'I'd better do something about preparing our meal,' proposed Alex and went in search of the galley still in a state of undress. The cooking facilities were unfamiliar too her and relied upon butane gas. Alex switched on two of the rings and tried to strike some matches, but they were damp and useless. After rummaging around, she found another box and had a further attempt. This time the match lit up but almost resulted in a gas explosion as the rings had by now been turned on for some minutes. Alex yelled.

'Your damned cooker nearly blew my tits off!'

Jean-Marc came hurrying to the galley and Christophe was calling down from the wheelhouse to ask if everyone was alright.

'Yes, but no thanks to your damned cooker,' complained Alex.

'Sacre blue, Alex,' responded Jean-Marc. 'We can't leave you alone for a moment without you getting into some kind of trouble. What are you going to do in the jungles of the Congo?'

Jean-Marc checked over Alex before assisting with the culinary preparations.

'Your hair is very slightly singed at the front,' observed Jean-Marc.

'And my nipples feel a little sore,' added Alex.

'You will live,' concluded Jean-Marc. 'Pass me that packet of rice and those yams and breadfruits.'

Jean-Marc proceeded to take over cooking the evening meal and the end result was not bad. Alex had to concede that Jean-Marc made a decent chef.

'You're not just a pretty face,' she informed him.

'I do not know whether that is a compliment or an insult,' replied Jean-Marc.

Once they had finished their meal, they called Christophe to have his dinner while Jean-Marc took over the helm and Alex resumed whale watching duties. Regrettably, there were no whales in sight but the dolphins continued to provide an escort and there was a glorious sunset on the western skyline. During the night they took it in turns to steer the boat while those not on watch caught some sleep. The weather was warm and very humid, and Alex was happy to sleep out on deck where there were some light breezes. Christophe said he had seen the lights of several ships on the horizon, but he had kept well clear of them and no vessels had presented any danger. Dawn broke abruptly in these tropical latitudes. One moment it was still dark while minutes later there was broad daylight and clear blue skies. Alex welcomed the return of her dolphins while Christophe spotted the waterspouts of whales some way ahead and made a slight course correction to take a closer look. Once again Alex was enthralled by the sheer size of the immense Humpbacks as they broke surface, and Christophe eased the throttle keeping pace with the huge creatures. Then Christophe was pointing to the far horizon.

'Sao Tome,' he called out. 'There is land.'

Christophe then made a course alteration to take them towards the north up the eastern side of the island while mountains and other features became progressively distinguishable.

'That outcrop you can see there is Pico Cao Grande,' explained Jean-Marc. 'That means Great Dog Peak in English. It is more than two thousand feet high.'

Then La Croix du Sud was heading for a harbour on what Jean-Marc said was the northeast side of the island at a place called Ana Chaves Bay. There were a number of smaller vessels passing to and fro with several more riding at anchor. At the quayside was a single cruise ship, the Ocean Princess, apparently registered in the Bahamas. Jean-Marc decided that they would drop anchor in a more secluded area to the west side of the harbour.

'We can use the dinghy to get ashore and there are some good market stalls nearby,' advised Jean-Marc. 'Christophe can find something good for dinner. You and I can do a little exploring.'

Christophe duly ferried them to a small and somewhat rustic landing stage where they scrambled out with Alex and Jean-Marc hailing a taxi while Christophe headed for the market. Alex considered the island to be attractive with an old Portuguese colonial atmosphere. Leaving the harbour area, they passed farmland and cocoa plantations and then headed up into the hills where there was woodland and then rocky terrain with some quite spectacular waterfalls. It was another warm and humid afternoon and at one point Jean-Marc asked the driver to stop and gave Alex an opportunity to bathe in the cooling waters cascading down from the high ground. Then it was time to return to the harbour where Christophe was awaiting their arrival, and they were soon back aboard La Croix du Sud with dinner already prepared from fresh seafood purchased by Christophe from local fishermen earlier that day.

'You can't get fresher than that,' observed Jean-Marc.

Afterwards they sat in the stern of the cruiser as it swung gently at anchor and watched the sun set across the bay. The weather was still very warm, and Alex suggested to Jean-Marc that they take the opportunity to go for a swim while Christophe relaxed with his fishing rod and line. Later they sat in the saloon of La Croix du Sud and watched the BBC World Service on the television. It appeared that the Russian missile which had landed in Eire had been nuclear tipped creating justifiable fears that further casualties could result from the effects of radio activity and fallout. The Americans were furious and Jack McConnell was already making arrangements to fly to Ireland to meet the Irish Prime Minister, John Turner-Ward, to offer support and to have talks. The British Prime Minister, Robert Stuart, was also making similar arrangements. Meanwhile Jack McConnell's poll ratings were soaring to new highs.

Jean-Marc produced a bottle of Gin from his drinks cabinet and offers of glasses were willingly accepted by Alex and by Christophe who had by now caught several fish of species which Alex had not encountered previously.

'They will be tomorrow's lunch,' advised Christophe.

Not long afterwards a small boat came alongside with local people selling fresh caught fish and home-grown produce. Jean-Marc was reluctant to buy anything but the hawkers on the boat were very insistent and he did buy a few items partly because they could help with preparation of tomorrow's meals and partly to encourage the traders to be on their way. After about half an hour or so another small boat appeared. Some of the faces were different but

Jean-Marc thought he recognised one or two of the characters from the first boat. Christophe shouted at them to go away, and a scuffle briefly developed in which one of the African traders tried to climb aboard but was pushed into the water by Jean-Marc and Christophe. During the hours of darkness several small local craft remained in the immediate vicinity which Alex considered puzzling and somewhat sinister. Alex awoke early in the morning. One moment it was still dark, then all of a sudden it was broad daylight with clear blue skies and dazzling sunshine streaming in through the gaps in the curtains. Already some of the local fishermen were setting out in their boats but, frustratingly as far as Alex was concerned, Jean-Marc was still fast asleep and snoring loudly. Alex gave him a prod, but this produced no more than a grunt and still he slumbered. Then she tried jabbing him with the spear she had purchased from the market stall in Libreville. Finally, with not a little cursing, Jean-Marc surfaced to be greeted by Alex with her ankles drawn behind her ears or at least as near as she could achieve such a contortion.

'My head feels as though someone has been hitting it with a hammer,' complained Jean-Marc.

'Well, maybe they have,' retorted Alex. 'I thought you were just going to spend all morning asleep.'

Alex opened her legs apart and gave Jean-Marc a display of her not so private anatomy. At last he responded to Alex's efforts at arousal, his tongue beginning to probe her most intimate folds. Alex sighed gently with approval. Suddenly there was a tremendous jolt and the sound of breaking glass and crockery as the cruiser lurched almost on to its beam ends. Christophe was shouting at somebody or something.

'I had better go and find out what is going on,' said Jean-Marc as he grabbed a pair of shorts and hurriedly disappeared topside. Alex followed with some trepidation.

It is the pirates,' warned Christophe as he gesticulated towards a motor vessel which was lying perilously close and appeared to be preparing to ram La Croix du Sud. Christophe had already started the engines, and the anchor was being drawn up. A shot rang out from the other vessel and a bullet ricocheted off the corner of the wheelhouse structure followed by more shots.

'Get below… immediately!' Jean-Marc shouted to Alex.

Within a short while they were underway at a good speed dodging between several small fishing vessels and headed for the open sea. Alex glanced anxiously astern and saw that the motor vessel was giving chase.

'I think we may have sustained some damage,' warned Jean-Marc as he peered over the starboard side. I can see a crack and a hole in the fibre glass where they rammed us. I hope it does not extend below the waterline or we are in big trouble. Christophe pushed forward the throttles of the twin diesel engines of the fishing cruiser while Jean-Marc went below to make a further inspection of the damage. He came back up a few minutes later.

'The hole in our side extends down to just above the waterline but when we are moving at speed and throwing up a big bow wave we are taking in water,' reported Jean-Marc. 'I suggest we try to put as much distance between ourselves and the pirates but then we will have to slow down.'

'But then they will catch us,' replied Alex. Once again, she glanced astern and saw that the pirate vessel was still within sight.

For the time being Christophe was maintaining a good speed, but the pirate vessel kept apace. Jean-Marc turned on the radio as he was also concerned about some up-to-date meteorological reports.

'There are storms approaching from the west off the Atlantic,' he warned. 'With our damage it would be a bad thing if we were caught up in them.'

Alex looked out as the island of Sao Tome receded over the horizon. The sky was still clear but there was some high-level cloud to the west.

'What do they want… these pirates?' she asked.

'To be honest I think they would seek to capture us and take us hostage,' replied Jean-Marc. 'Then they would demand ransom monies. Someone has informed them who we are… who I am. They must be aware that I am from a wealthy family. '

Jean-Marc took over the helm and pushed La Croix du Sud to the limits of its maximum speed. After some time, Alex observed that the pirates were falling slightly behind but not so very far.

'They are clearly determined,' she said. 'I expect they are hoping to make a lot of money.'

Early in the afternoon Jean-Marc handed the helm back to Christophe so as to be able to go below and make a further inspection. Jean-Marc was not very pleased with the situation and travelling at this speed they were constantly taking in water through that hole in the starboard side. Jean-Marc returned to the wheelhouse and put out a request for assistance over the radio. The authorities on Sao Tome and Principe did eventually respond but said there was nothing they could do. A similar response was received from Equatorial Guinea. Jean-Marc urged Christophe to keep up the pace. The pirates were now on the horizon but still in visual range. Christophe made Jean-Marc aware that the temperature gauge was now showing that the diesel engines were beginning to run hot. Alex saw that they had been joined by a school of dolphins who splashed and cavorted off their bows but right now the playful creatures brought her no solace. Even the presence of a group of Humpback whales failed to attract her interest. Finally Jean-Marc managed to make radio contact with a French frigate, La Glassionere out on patrol and requested urgent assistance. Alex listened intently to the radio traffic with Jean-Marc pleading that his boat was already damaged and taking in water and under attack from armed pirates.

'Maintenant nous sommes soixante cinque kilometres au nord ouest du votre position,' the French radio operator informed them. 'Attention… attention!'

Meanwhile the temperature gauge was still rising, and Christophe had no option but to ease back the throttles and slow down. It was now a question of who would reach them first, the pirates or the French frigate. It was soon evident that the pirate vessel was gaining on them and closing the gap. Jean-Marc was on the radio once again to La Glassionerre exhorting them to hurry up.

'C'est une emergencie!' called Jean-Marc.

The radio operator on the frigate assured him that they were in the process of launching their helicopter and had gone to Action Stations with La Glassionerre accelerating to full power and maximum speed. The minutes passed and the pirate vessel was now close enough for Alex, using binoculars, to see figures out on deck on the vessel. More time passed, and Alex could see someone armed with a rocket launcher and someone else fixing a machine gun to a firing post. Then the gunner opened fire.

'They are shooting at us!' exclaimed Alex. Fortunately, the rounds fell short but all the time the pirates were closing the range.

In desperation Christophe pushed the throttles forward once more and La Croix du Sud accelerated just in time as the pirates fired a rocket.

'Tourner a droit!' shouted Jean-Marc. 'Immediatement!'

La Croix du Sud manoeuvred violently to port and starboard under full power and the rocket crashed into the sea off their starboard quarter. Jean-Marc was on the radio to the French frigate yet again informing them in the strongest terms that his vessel was under fire. Soon the pirates were shooting again. They had brought a second machine gun into action and Alex watched in trepidation as the bullets visibly whipped up the salt water in perilous proximity. Christophe continued to execute violent manoeuvres with the bullets raking the sea until finally they were hit and Jean-Marc shouted to Alex to get below and take cover in the forward cabin. Christophe then saw that the engine temperature gauge was way up and heading for the red danger zone and red warning lights were starting to flash on the control panel.

'We will have to slow down,' he warned Jean-Marc. 'At this speed the engines will catch fire and the bullet strikes may well have already caused us damage.'

Jean-Marc had no alternative but to agree to Christophe's request and La Croix du Sud began reducing speed with the pirates closing the range once more. More bullets smacked into the stern of the fishing cruiser as smoke began to emanate from her diesel engines and her speed reduced to a crawl. Visions of incarceration at the hands of West African pirates crossed Jean-Marc's mind. He did not care to contemplate what would happen to Alex. Taking cover behind the fibreglass wheelhouse structure he heard a rhythmic thumping sound which he took to be the engines of the pirate vessel as it bore down upon them. Then Christophe was shouting,

'Attention! Attention! ... Helicopter Navale Francais!'

Jean-Marc glanced up and saw with immense relief that a French naval helicopter had indeed arrived on the scene. An instant later, however, he was holding his breath as the pirate vessel fired a rocket at the helicopter. Fortunately, the pilot skilfully dodged the incoming missile and dived to sea level firing heavy machine guns and a salvo of rockets which struck the pirate vessel with a series of explosions. Jean-Marc could see the men operating the rocket launcher being literally blown to pieces with the limbless torso of one man rolling overboard into the sea while others were left sprawled across the deck either dead or dying. The helicopter, which the radio operator aboard La Glassionerre informed Jean-Marc was an NH-90, then came in for a second strafing pass and raked the now crippled and burning pirate vessel which then slowed to a standstill. The NH-90 then hovered above La Croix du Sud which was itself now crawling along at no more than five knots with damage to its engines. An NCO and two ratings abseiled down from the helicopter and came aboard the fishing cruiser carrying shoring timber and a small pump. Jean-Marc showed them the damage to the hull which the French sailors set about patching and making watertight. Attention then shifted to the engines which the Frenchmen spent some time examining and the NCO, Pierre Renaud, concluded with a shrug of his shoulders. It was clear to everyone that La Croix du Sud was not going to get home under her own power. Alex gave a sigh of relief when the frigate, La Glassionnere, appeared over the horizon and approached the scene of the recent combat. Initial priority was given to rescuing survivors from the pirate vessel which was on fire and sinking. Once this humanitarian task had been effected, the frigate hove alongside La Croix du Sud and Maitre Renaud spoke to someone aboard the frigate over the radio and a line was attached to the fishing cruiser. La Croix du Sud was duly taken in tow and the frigate, and her charge proceeded eastwards towards the African coast at a gentle ten knots. Fortunately, the sea remained calm with a glassy surface. Even the dolphins reappeared and provided a high-spirited entertainment. Someone aboard La Glassionnere informed Jean-Marc that they were making for Libreville where injured crew from the pirate vessel, which had been called the Jacob Banza, would be taken for medical treatment particularly those suffering from serious burns. Survivors who were unharmed would be handed over to the Gabonese authorities and doubtless end up in an African jail. La Croix du Sud would be put in the hands of a suitable repair facility. Later in the afternoon Alex received an invite to meet the crew of La Glassionnere and then to join the officers for dejeuner in the Officers' Mess. Jean-Marc grumbled that the invite had not been extended to himself. Alex gave him a kiss and promised to be on her best behaviour while being entertained by the Frenchmen.

Alex's arrival aboard La Glassionnere was greeted with cheers and whistles by the French sailors and morale amongst the crew was quite clearly raised notwithstanding the oppressive heat and humidity. Alex was then given a tour of the ship, and she concluded that she much preferred being out on deck to going down below to the Engine rooms with all their noise and discomfort. Early in the evening she joined the officers at their invitation in their air conditioned Mess and sat between Lieutenant de Vaisseau Xavier Dupont who explained to her that he was the ship's executive officer, and Lieutenant Remy Chapelon from the engineering department. Remy showed her photographs of his wife, Yvette, and his two children, Jean-Francois aged eleven and Marie aged six.

'We have a modest house overlooking the harbour at Toulon,' explained Remy. 'Yvette works at the naval base there in an administrative capacity. Jean-Francois is doing quite well at school. We hope that eventually he will go to university and perhaps he might join the navy and become an officer like his papa. Do you have children, Alex?'

'Unfortunately, not yet,' replied Alex wistfully. 'My husband is an officer in the British Royal Navy. He is captain of a frigate... the Aurora. But he seems to spend more and more time at sea.'

'My wife complains of exactly the same thing,' smiled Remy.

'We are hoping to be home by Christmas,' added Xavier Dupont. 'But I would not bet any money on it. I suppose we are fortunate to be despatched to this part of the world when things are rather hot closer to home but there is a feeling of isolation out here.'

'At present we are based principally at Dakar in Senegal,' explained Remy. 'It has its nightlife and other attractions, but it is a long way from Toulon.'

Alex welcomed the attentions of the French officers but expressed a wish to return to La Croix du Sud before nightfall.

'Before you go, we must exchange telephone numbers,' said Remy. 'Perhaps my wife and I and our children can call on you when we are in England. We come quite often to visit my wife's cousin, Katrine and her family. They live at Long Eaton in… how you say… Nottinghamshire. We have been to Sherwood Forest.'

'That sounds good fun,' replied Alex. 'I am sure your children would like to come to our farm in Norfolk sometime. We have horses, pigs, chickens, geese not to mention Myrtle the donkey.'

'Oh, les enfants adore tous les animaux!' exclaimed Remy.

'Alex… please let me have your number,' pleaded Lieutenant Pierre Bernier, the navigating officer.

'Alex… do not go so soon,' called someone else. 'We have so much more to show you.'

The sun was setting fast as Alex returned to La Croix du Sud and a tropical breeze was blowing in from the southwest off the Atlantic.

'I expect you enjoyed being entertained by the French sailors?' grumbled Jean-Marc. 'Presumably you will not be wanting dinner this evening.'

'I did my best to foster Anglo-French relations,' replied Alex. 'Who knows, some of them might even visit my farm in Norfolk.'

'I'm sure they have not forgotten that you British sank their fleet in 1940,' quipped Jean-Marc. 'More than a thousand French sailors lost their lives.'

'Oh, stop being so negative, Jean-Marc,' retorted Alex. 'Try to think of more pleasant things. Anyway, the French officers were all absolutely charming.'

Dawn was breaking when they finally arrived at the port area of Libreville and Jean-Marc gave instructions for La Croix du Sud to be moored alongside at the ship repair premises of Gulf Marine which he explained was where the vessel was overhauled. Then Alex was waving goodbye to the crew of La Glassionnerre. She recognised Pierre Bernier and Xavier Dupont, but Remy Chapelon was not present. She mused that presumably he would be down below tending to his engines and machinery. Not long afterwards a tremendous tropical storm blew up sending everyone running for cover from the lashing rain and near hurricane force winds.

'We are lucky not to have met this out in the Gulf,' called Jean-Marc. 'We would have been in danger of sinking what with that hole in our hull.'

Once Jean-Marc had made appropriate arrangements with the staff at Gulf Marine for repairs to be carried out to La Croix du Sud he and Alex returned to his house in Libreville where they made preparations for their next adventure.

Chapter 12

Into the Congo

ALEX WOKE AT AROUND 6AM with a painful crick in her neck and peered out of the small window of the twin-engine Fokker. A landscape of dense rain forest stretched endlessly to every horizon.

'We are about to cross the border with the Republic of the Congo,' advised Etienne Kasanga, the wildlife artist from whom she had purchased the painting of the elephants a couple of weeks ago in Libreville. 'Down there you can just about make out the town of Mbanda. Over there to the south is Manoko in the province of Niari.'

Although she was still feeling tired Alex peered intently and reflected that the inhabitants of these small, isolated towns would soon be stirring from their beds as the new day dawned, the sun appearing to almost explode with its powerful radiance on the eastern skyline. Alex also considered that down there in the forest lived an abundance of wildlife, the primary purpose of her visit to this remote country. There would be elephants, crocodiles, hippos, leopards and many other species. Gorillas and all kinds of other fauna.

'You know, many parts of the Congo region are still unexplored by mankind,' advised Etienne as though reading her mind. 'It is a wildlife paradise and many places are virtually inaccessible, but we still have big problems with poachers. They hunt the elephants for their ivory and the gorillas are under threat too. We are trying to establish a reserve up in Sangha Province south of the town called Ouesso. I will take you there during your visit to our country… Jean-Marc too… eh… Jean-Marc!'

'He is still sleepy,' whispered Alex. 'But I do wish to see as many of the animals as possible. It is clearly a wonderful place.'

Etienne proceeded to explain to Alex the efforts being made to conserve the creatures and their habitats until finally a large city appeared on the horizon to the south and the pilot began his descent.

'That is Brazzaville, our capital,' advised Etienne. 'You can just about make out the Congo River and Stanley Pool. That large urban area on the south bank of the river is Kinshasa, the capital of the Democratic Republic of the Congo. It is a totally separate country.'

'Why are there two different countries both called the Congo?' enquired Alex.

'It dates back to colonial times,' explained Etienne. 'Our own country was the French Congo. The Democratic Republic on the south bank used to be called Zaire and before that back in colonial days it was the Belgian Congo.'

'We are now preparing to land at Maya-Maya Airport announced the pilot. Fasten seatbelts everyone. Put away all food and drink and reading matter.'

Upon disembarking from the aeroplane Alex was met by the heat of the late morning and the high humidity. Fortunately, the formalities were not too daunting and she and Jean-Marc followed Etienne to his vehicle, a large Japanese manufactured SUV which was fortunately equipped with an effective air conditioning system. The drive from the airport took them through several squalid shanty towns with their inevitable open sewers and unpleasant smells, homes built from rubbish and rooves improvised from tarpaulins mounted on vertical poles for the luckier residents.

'At least they have a roof of sorts,' commented Etienne. 'These poor souls over to the right don't even have a tarpaulin to keep off the rain and the hot sun.'

Alex felt a lurch in her stomach as they passed a place where men and women were defecating into a filthy ditch. She hoped that Etienne's home was nowhere near this wretched place. Fortunately, they drove onwards and the traffic became heavier. At one point Alex looked out of the window to see a cow standing on a trailer being towed through Brazzaville in an adjoining traffic lane. The cow peered back at her lugubriously and remained in close proximity for some time as the city traffic ground to an inevitable standstill. Eventually Etienne was driving through an area of high-rise apartment blocks and they finally stopped at a building situated near to the river.

'Come with me,' said Etienne as once again Alex was met by a draft of hot equatorial air as she stepped out of the SUV.

Etienne exchanged pleasantries with the concierge and then he and his guests were clambering up numerous flights of stairs. The concierge had apologised that the lifts were out of order once again. Alex felt the sweat running off her as they reached the top floor. It felt like they were climbing to the top of the world but at least the views were panoramic with the great Congo River in the foreground and the city of Kinshasa visible on the south bank. Etienne's apartment had air conditioning which was no mere luxury in this baking hot climate. It had three bedrooms, one of which was allocated by Etienne to Alex and Jean-Marc. The other two bedrooms were full of all manner of clutter including paintings of wildlife and stacks of books some of which had been written by Etienne. The main living room had an impressive painting of elephants in a forest clearing. Another painting was of a group of lowland gorillas. There was a profusion of more traditional African art including tribal headdresses and masks, spears and firearms. The apartment had a separate dining room which contained a large table upon which several maps had been spread.

'When you have had a chance to get sorted out, we will study the maps,' said Etienne. 'In the meantime, you may wish to make use of the shower in your en-suite and then put your feet up for a little while after your journey.'

Both Alex and Jean-Marc were glad to accept his offer, taking a shower together after which they sat out on a balcony while the men had a couple of beers from the fridge and Alex had a white wine.

'This evening, I will take you both out to a restaurant on the riverside,' said Etienne. 'It is called Le Palais de Versailles, and it is really good. You can have French or local cuisine or… whatever you like… they will provide it for you.'

'That sounds very appealing,' acknowledged Alex who was beginning to feel rather hungry.

Later in the afternoon they watched the BBC World service on Etienne's TV. The processes were being put in place for Jack McConnell to be elected as the next president of the United States. There was footage of him in Ireland visiting people who had been injured in the Russian missile strike. These included Mrs Siobhain Flaherty, the head teacher of the school set ablaze by the warhead and her deputy, Mrs Kathleen Galway-Short, who together had heroically ensured that all the school children were evacuated from the burning building. Jack McConnell was shown visiting the two ladies in hospital in Dublin who were both being treated for serious burns. Afterwards he paid tribute to Father Padraig Connelly, another casualty of the missile, who died while visiting elderly and disabled people in Carrickmacglen. While in Ireland Jack McConnell took the opportunity to have talks with the Irish Prime Minister, John Turner-Ward, and they were due to be joined the following day by the British Prime minister, Robert Stewart.

After watching the news programmes Etienne was keen to show to his guests the maps which he had laid out. One of these showed the whole of the Congo region while the others covered the Cuvette and Sangha provinces of the country.

'Up here we are striving to establish a very large national park and game reserve,' explained Etienne. ''It is of vital importance to wildlife conservation. Here in the Congo, we are blessed with a great abundance of wild creatures but everywhere they are under threat. Poachers are constantly taking a huge toll of our precious animals. Thousands of elephants have been slaughtered for their ivory. If we do not act now most of our wild animals will be wiped out. This same problem is affecting all of Africa and the world in general.'

In the evening Etienne drove Alex and Jean-Marc to Le Palais de Versailles restaurant which was situated by the river with tantalising views across the Congo to Kinshasa with its city lights twinkling in the humid air at dusk. They were able to sit at a table outside in the restaurant gardens and Alex chose a mixed grill of locally caught fish. Etienne chose a vegetarian dish while conversely Jean-Marc opted for a very large steak.

'That looks like half a cow on your plate,' joked Alex.

'I am taking the opportunity to stoke up,' replied Jean-Marc. 'Soon before we know it we will be out in the wilderness. There will be no fancy restaurants out in the bush in Sangha province.'

'Tomorrow we will make preparations for our expedition,' explained Etienne. 'We must ensure we have enough food and medical supplies and suitable clothing. I have arranged for an aircraft to fly us out to Ouesso in two days' time. That does not give us long at all. Then there is the issue of firearms. I have a Remington repeater shotgun but the two of you will need your own guns.'

Alex and Jean-Marc glanced at each other anxiously.

'There are many dangers out there,' cautioned Etienne. 'Wild animals and poachers. Sadly, there have been a number of wars and civil conflicts in this region in past years so arms are plentiful and easy to obtain. Poachers and bandits carry them too. We do receive a lot of help from the French government. They have kindly agreed to fly us out into the bush in a helicopter once we have reached Ouesso. Our own government will also be providing assistance… and the World Wildlife Fund too.'

A smiling waiter named Joseph appeared and topped up everyone's' glasses from a cool bottle of Chablis which had been chilling in an ice bucket close to the table. Alex was beginning to wonder what she had let herself in for. Jean-Marc had similar misgivings but nobody had the nerve to let the side down and withdraw from the enterprise.

Alex was woken quite early in the morning by the bright sunshine and the sound of young boys playing football in the side street down below. Soon Etienne was knocking on the bedroom door and enquiring politely as to when people would be ready as he was anxious to get on with preparations for their expedition up country. Breakfast was limited to a couple of rather dry baguettes and some very strong black coffee. Then Etienne was ushering his guests into his SUV and driving into a district called Ouenze where they acquired camping equipment and a small stove. Tents and mosquito nets were also on their shopping list. Once all this equipment had been loaded into the back of the vehicle they were driving through squalid back streets with open sewers and, to Alex's dismay, children playing in the dirt and filth. The profusion of mangey stray dogs running loose everywhere was similarly distressing. Etienne parked the SUV in a narrow street near to a ramshackle two storey building whose frontage was almost totally obscured by bushes and undergrowth. Etienne beckoned to Alex and Jean-Marc to follow him inside where they were met initially by two heavily built African men one of whom had a bandolier of ammunition slung over his shoulder. Fortunately, they appeared to know Etienne and gave him a friendly greeting. The proprietor was duly called, and Etienne introduced a middle-aged Congolese man named Jacob Ilunga who smiled and shook their hands although Alex felt she would not wish to be the wrong side of any of these people. Etienne explained that they were shortly to embark on a mission up country to Sangha province to view the wildlife, particularly gorillas and also forest elephants.

'That is dangerous territory,' cautioned Jacob. 'The poachers in that region are more heavily armed than the soldiers in our army. They have AK-47s and the latest Russian and Western weaponry… Belgian FN rifles and machine guns.'

'We are aware of the dangers,' replied Etienne, ' but Alex here is particularly wishing to see the wild creatures at first hand. She has set her heart on it.'

'Surely you are not seriously thinking of taking this white woman into such a dangerous region?' queried Jacob. 'Do you know what the bandits and poachers will do to her if they catch her alive?'

'I understand the risks, but I am still determined to accompany my friends out there,' Alex retorted with firm resolution.

Jacob threw up his hands and appeared genuinely concerned.

'Come this way, please,' he said and led the way into the building passing through a heavy armoured door which was guarded by two armed men. The door was then closed behind Etienne's small group with a heavy thud and Alex found herself walking through a labyrinth of rooms and corridors with the most lethal looking firearms stacked everywhere.

Jacob paused and removed a weapon from its gun rack on the wall.

'Here, cheri,' he said to Alex, unexpectedly placing the gun in her hands. 'How does that feel? Belgian FN P90 sub machine gun. It has a good rate of fire, it is reliable and it is not too heavy. It could take out a poacher with an AK-47 or a Russian SKS.'

Alex glanced at Jean-Marc and at Etienne. This wildlife expedition was increasingly resembling a special forces mission, but she was not going to back out now.

'Fine. It'll do me okay,' she responded bravely.

The men selected a French HK416F assault rifle for Jean-Marc and a Finnish manufactured Sako TRG-42 sniper rifle which Jacob warned had a sharp recoil but was a very accurate weapon.

'Just mind your shoulder when you fire it,' warned Jacob.

The men then proceeded with negotiations to purchase the guns and quantities of ammunition and a total price was agreed which was split between Etienne and Jean-Marc.

'Look, I am very worried about you people venturing into bandit territory,' cautioned Jacob. 'How many of you are going?'

'Well, our party is just the three of us,' replied Etienne hesitantly, 'but the French Airforce is providing a helicopter to get us out into the bush… and the wildlife service is providing a boat to get us and our kit upriver to where we want to be.'

'They will vanish into thin air when things get tough,' scoffed Jacob.' I am prepared to send a team of four men to escort you wherever you go and whatever the conditions out there. They will be armed with Belgian FN machine guns… 7.62mm.'

'How much will that cost us?' enquired Jean-Marc.

'If you make it back we will agree a suitable figure,' replied Jacob.

'We are extremely grateful to you, Jacob,' Etienne thanked him and shook his hand with genuine gratitude.

Jacob then took his clients to an area of waste ground at the rear of the building and invited everyone to test the weapons on this makeshift firing range. Alex found the experience unnerving but successfully masked her fear. After all they were still in Brazzaville, the capital city. Jacob's men then assisted Etienne with loading the guns and ammunition into the SUV. By this time the heat of the afternoon was making everyone thirsty and on the way home Etienne stopped at a bar and bought ice creams for his guests and himself and chilled drinks with ice. Alex was glad of the refreshments. On the way back they passed the miserable looking shanty town they had driven through yesterday on their way from the airport. There were the inevitable unpleasant smells and the filthy ditch with people defecating into it in the open air. Suddenly Alex felt a lurch in her stomach.

'Oh dear,' she exclaimed. 'Etienne... stop the car... now!'

'What's the matter?' queried Jean-Marc as Etienne drew to a halt.

'It's my tummy,' responded Alex as she scrambled hurriedly out of the car and ran to join the people relieving themselves in the open sewer.

Alex pulled up her shirt and purged her bowels noisily into the stinking ditch. She was not accustomed to defecating in public but in this instance she had no option. An African woman aged perhaps about forty came and occupied the increasingly crowded edge of the open sewer next to Alex.

'Je ma fait mal,' remarked Alex to the woman.

'Au secours. Il est tres chaud aujourd'hui,' replied the woman. 'Je m'appelle Simone. Ici ma soeur, Renee et mon frere, Jacques.'

'Je suis Anglais,' Alex informed the smiling African people, making polite conversation in this somewhat unorthodox situation.

'Ah, Anglais!' exclaimed Jacques. 'Mes amis, Paul et Bernard... they are... how you say... trying to get to Angleterre. They had to get across the Sahara Desert. It is a long way, but they hope to find work in England... perhaps fixing cars or... selling cars. There is a man they know who says he can help them... for money.'

'Things are not at all good in England right now,' explained Alex. 'There is a war... with Russia... a big country that keeps firing missiles. Lots of people have been killed and injured. You are safer here in the Congo.'

'Alex... are you alright?' called Jean-Marc as he came hurrying from the car.

'Sorry,' apologised Alex. 'Just a bit of stomach ache, that's all.'

Jean-Marc and Etienne were keen to be off and bundled Alex back into the SUV. At Etienne's apartment she spent some time in the bathroom and Etienne cancelled that evening's reservation at the Palais de Versailles. It did not trouble him too much as it gave more time for preparations for the expedition up country.

Alex was still experiencing stomach ache when she was woken early by Etienne the following morning. He and Jean-Marc had already loaded up the SUV and they headed for the airport before 7am. The formalities there were minimal, and nobody appeared particularly concerned about the weaponry and the quantities of ammunition, but help was provided for loading the twin engine Islander aircraft which would be flying them up to Ouesso near the border with Cameroon. Alex noted that their fellow passengers comprised the four men promised by the arms dealer, Jacob Ilunga. By 9am they were in the air and heading north across a region known as Plateaux. Etienne pointed out a large town called Djambala, but Alex was still not feeling her best and tried to sleep. It was well into the afternoon before they landed at a place called Owando in the Cuvette region.

'It is just a refuelling stop,' advised Etienne. 'We will be here a short while to fill up the plane's fuel tanks. Then we can be on our way.'

Alex took the opportunity to visit the lavatory. Besides there was not much else to do at Owando airport which appeared to be situated in the back of beyond. Soon the plane was back in the air and flying over some very wild terrain. Etienne pointed out the Kouyou River and Alex was sufficiently animated to spot a herd of forest elephants in a clearing.

'To the left over there is the town of Makoua,' advised Etienne. 'That waterway you can see is the Likouala River.'

Their pilot then picked up the main highway far below running northwards from Owando and Makoua to Ouesso and crossed the Lengoue river.

'This is part of the area where we are trying to establish the game reserve,' advised Etienne. 'You can see it is very wild country with endless forests and swamps.'

Despite feeling tired Alex was fascinated by the primeval scenery and tried to spot the wildlife but they were still too high although eventually as they flew nearer to Ouesso and began their descent Etienne was able to point out another herd of forest elephants and then a family of lowland gorillas. Finally, as the sun began to set on the western horizon the plane landed, and Alex emerged into the humidity of this remote region close to the borders of Cameroon and the Central African Republic. Etienne had organised a pair of vehicles to transport their party and their kit to the Sangha Hotel where they were at least able to get some rest after their long and rather uncomfortable flight from Brazzaville.

Once again Alex found herself woken early in the morning and told to collect her belongings. Then they were boarding a truck and heading back to the airport along dusty roads lined with children making their way to school. At Ouesso airport they stowed their kit aboard a former French Airforce Puma helicopter which was now in the ownership of the wildlife protection organisation. They were soon joined by their small team of men provided by Jacob Ilunga along with their weaponry and ammunition and a local guide named Jacques Ngoy clad in his dark green game warden's uniform. The interior of the helicopter was soon becoming stifling as the sun rose higher in the morning skies and Alex was relieved when they finally took off and set course southwards along the Sangha river. The helicopter was flying at relatively low level, perhaps a couple of hundred feet or so and their passing disturbed many wild creatures including elephants and buffaloes. Jacques Ngoy pointed out a crocodile sunning themselves at the water's edge. Not far away they spotted a Bongo which had come down to the river for a drink and further downstream a colony of Chimpanzees was observed close to the river bank. Eventually the helicopter reached a location where there was an open area of what was clearly relatively firm ground and not far away two motor launches were awaiting their arrival. The pilot put the helicopter down as close to the boats as he and his observer considered prudent without undue risk of becoming bogged in marshy ground. Then everyone helped out with unloading the helicopter in the midday heat and humidity and the two motor launches were piled up with kit. Finally, the people found whatever space was left in the boats for themselves and set off southwards down river. In this hot equatorial environment Alex considered that the river was probably the best place to be and in many stretches of the waterway the jungle trees grew right up to the water's edge providing some sort of canopy against the blazing sun. In some strange sense the scene reminded her of sailing up the River Bure in

Norfolk. It seemed a world away and pangs of guilt caused her to reflect upon Longfleet Farm, Sandra and the animals who lived there. Indeed how was Eddie faring on the high seas? She resolved that once this present expedition was concluded she must return to England notwithstanding the missile attacks and obvious dangers. Alex was brought back to the present when Etienne called out and a crocodile emerged from the river bank and headed out into mid-stream. Not long afterwards hippos appeared both submerged in the river and standing on the mudflats. The helmsman of the launch gave these large and sometimes bad-tempered creatures a wide berth and Alex was reminded of what Renee had said about the African boy being bitten in half by one comparatively recently. The river now flowed through a heavily forested area and Etienne was peering into the surrounding jungle on both sides with the assistance of powerful binoculars. His efforts were eventually rewarded when he spotted a family of lowland gorillas basking under a stand of trees. He and Jacques Ngoy conferred together and half an hour later the boats slowed down and navigated cautiously through a narrow and somewhat overgrown channel off the main river. An area of grassland extended towards the endless forest.

'We will make our camp here,' announced Etienne.

The ground was firm, and the trees provided some shade from the fierce sun and shelter from the tropical storms prevalent in this isolated equatorial part of the world. Everyone was in agreement with Etienne and between them they unloaded such equipment and provisions as they would require at this juncture. By the time this task was completed it was early evening and Etienne decided that they should prepare a meal before he and Jacques Ngoy took Alex and Jean-Marc for an initial foray into the jungle before nightfall. Once they had eaten their dinner Jacob Ilunga's men were sent out to patrol the peripheries around the encampment and the others followed Jacques into the forest. Alex found it a very wild and primeval environment and it did not surprise her to be informed by her escorts that the depths of the jungle she was now entering were unexplored territory. There was birdlife everywhere and strange piercing howls and shrieks not to mention the ever-present biting and stinging insects. Jacques and Etienne were leading the small group, hacking their way through the jungle with machetes. Frequently they had to ford small streams and Jacques warned everyone to beware of leaches becoming attached to their skin. Eventually the sun began to set, and Jacques proposed that they pause at a small clearing where the ground was dry and they were able to rest a while. Alex was glad of the opportunity to sit down and drink from a water bottle. Aside from the buzzing of countless insects the place seemed quiet and peaceful until Alex heard a strange rumbling noise emanating from the undergrowth.

'My God... a leopard!' she exclaimed.

'Keep your voice down,' urged Jacques. 'Leave this to me.'

Jacques stood up and began walking slowly towards the source of the strange acoustics.

'Sabine,' he said calmly. 'Mathilde... Sabine.'

The silence of the forest was suddenly broken by the cracking of branches being crushed under heavy feet.

'Sabine,' said Jacques once again.

This time a huge shadow loomed over the place, but Jacques walked ahead showing no fear as finally the source of the sounds became apparent.

'Elephants!' called Alex. 'There must be a dozen or more.'

Jacques bid her once again to keep quiet as a very large pachyderm emerged from the dense forest and greeted him with a gentle wave of their trunk. Then he was speaking although no human could hear or understand what he was saying but once again Alex could detect the mysterious low rumbling sound. Then Jacques was motioning his small party to step forward cautiously and Alex found herself being introduced to Sabine.

'She is the Matriarch... the herd leader,' advised Jacques. 'Do not be afraid. I have explained to her that you are friends.'

'How wonderful,' whispered Alex as Sabine gripped her hand with her trunk and Alex felt herself being physically drawn towards the powerful animal.

Jacques said something to the elephant which appeared to mean something like,

'Put her down, Sabine,' and then he was introducing people to the second elephant standing to Sabine's right side.

'This is her deputy, Mathilde,' explained Jacques. 'She does not command as much authority as Sabine, but she assists Sabine with maintaining cohesion and discipline within the herd and she is in charge of the calves and youngsters and making sure no one gets lost or detached from the main body of the herd.'

'I 'm sure she has her work cut out for her in this forest wilderness,' responded Alex.

'This calf here is Bimbo,' said Jacques as he introduced a baby elephant about the size of a Shetland Pony. 'He is the son of Yvette who is standing just behind Mathilde.'

Alex reached out to Bimbo who came to her and wrapped his trunk around her wrist. Yvette and Mathilde were cautious and moved to usher Bimbo away.

'They are mindful that not all humans are friendly,' said Jacques. 'We have been having a lot of trouble with poaching gangs in this province recently. There are still many heavily armed renegade soldiers who have found the ivory trade very lucrative. Only last week I was about forty miles from here with a couple of my rangers and we found two whole herds wiped out by the gangs. The elephants had all been machine gunned... even the calves and youngsters. The poachers have no respect for these superb creatures... nor any mercy. The leader of the local band of brigands is Adolphus Banza. He has a price on his head, but he has always eluded us so far. As you can see for yourself, we have huge territories to defend. It is like how you say in English... trying to find a needle in a haystack.'

'In the morning when the light is better, I would like to paint this herd,' said Etienne. 'Let us hope it does not wander too far away.'

Alex was reluctant to leave these magnificent creatures but darkness was falling, and Jacques was anxious to return to the camp. Their guides had erected the tents which were protected by strong mosquito nets in an effort to keep at bay the ever-present insect life of the swamplands and marshes. Alex was nevertheless disturbed by all forms of creatures from biting insects to enormous water buffalo which came trampling around the encampment and sniffing questioningly at the occupants. More than once Etienne and Jacques had to shoo away the large lugubrious beasts.

Not long after first light Etienne was keen to be back with the elephants and urged everyone to make haste in finishing their breakfast. Alex felt she would have benefitted from more sleep. The weather was already very warm and humid and the clouds of mosquitoes were gathering for their mass attack. Indeed, she was glad she had taken Jean-Marc's advice to have those anti-malaria injections. After trudging for a couple of hours through the dense forest they finally came upon the herd who showed little intention of going anywhere in a hurry. A small sluggish river ran through that part of the jungle and the mature elephants imbibed considerable quantities of the green water while the youngsters splashed and cavorted and sprayed each other with their trunks. Eventually the elephants began to move on, and the leaders disappeared into the depths of the forest with the humans following behind. After some time Jacques Ngoy concluded that the big pachyderms were well ahead and although it was possible to follow their tracks from the large piles of dung and the broken branches of trees the sun was rising higher in the morning skies and everyone agreed, when they arrived at a small clearing, that this was a good place to pause. Alex was glad that they had brought with them adequate supplies of mineral water. There were pools of standing water nearby, but they were full of leaches and other unpleasant life forms. Jacques advised that on no account should they drink any of it. Jean-Marc took the opportunity to dose while Etienne Kasanga worked on his latest painting of forest elephants. There were the usual sounds of the jungle, but it was a peaceful place and Alex once again found herself thinking of home. Here she was out in the depths of the Congo in places where very few people had ever passed. She reckoned Jacques was right when he had said this was unexplored territory. No one else seemed to notice when a rather large animal appeared and began drinking from one of the stagnant pools. It looked in some ways like a giraffe, but it lacked a very long neck. It was quite clearly not a giraffe nor some kind of deer. Jacques leaned across to Alex and whispered,

'It is an Okapi. You are highly privileged. There are rarely seen.'

Etienne was so engrossed in his painting that he did not realise the Okapi was there. Jean-Marc was asleep and out for the count in the midday heat. The

Okapi began feeding on leaves and tropical fruits and was then joined by a second Okapi which was accompanied by a calf.

'Even better still,' whispered Jacques to Alex. 'Okapis are usually solitary creatures, but they do occasionally get together socially. You are extremely lucky to see three of them at once in the wild. We have established a centre for breeding them further down the river, but we had a big setback recently when it was attacked by poachers armed with automatic rifles. They killed sixteen Okapis as well as five of our rangers and several visitors. Unfortunately, this is bandit country.'

Alex observed her family group of these fascinating creatures for a while until they disappeared back into the forest, their striped camouflage blending with the sunlight breaking through the trees. Jacques explained that Okapis had not been discovered or known to mankind until the nineteen thirties.

Later in the afternoon Jacques led his small party further into the jungle until they came to a small shallow river. On the far side Alex spotted what she initially thought was a man of short stature until Etienne pointed out that it was a Chimpanzee and soon a whole colony of these intelligent apes became visible. This was the first time Alex had seen Chimps in their natural wild habitat and she was keen to move closer even though Jean-Marc urged caution. The Chimp whom Alex had first seen moved hesitantly towards the humans while Etienne proffered the creature a bread fruit which was duly snatched from his hands. Alex then offered a plantain to another Chimp who accepted the gift with better grace. Jacques was keen to move on deeper into the jungle and after about an hour bid everyone to be as silent as possible. Jacques then crept forward and invited his small party to follow him through a narrow gap in the trees. Soon Alex realised what it was that Jacques had brought them to see as she observed first one and as many as eight lowland gorillas relaxing in the hot equatorial afternoon. There was a big male with his wives and several offspring of different ages and stages of development. Alex was entranced and felt highly privileged to be able to see these superb creatures in their natural environment.

'The big male, the one in charge, we call Charles,' explained Jacques. 'His senior wife… the gorilla next to him to his right is Pauline. The female behind her is Helene.'

Alex became aware of a figure moving behind her but realised it could not be one of the men as they were all in close proximity. Suddenly she found herself face to face with a young gorilla, clearly not fully grown, who appeared as surprised as she was.

'Xavier… come to us,' said Jacques calmly and with quiet authority.

The adolescent gorilla hesitated and then edged towards the humans. Etienne offered the animal a bread fruit which gift was duly accepted. He was joined by another animal, not yet fully grown whom Jacques addressed as Marie-Claude.

'She is Xavier's sister,' whispered Jacques and proffered some food to the two youngsters.

Alex found herself sitting in a circle in a small clearing in the dense jungle with the men and two gorillas. She thought it was both surreal and wonderful. As the sun began to arc towards the west Jacques decided it was time for everyone to make a move and with some reluctance the humans began to make their way back to the encampment.

When they reached the base near the river everyone was hungry and glad that the native guides had dinner well advanced. Fortunately, the meal was almost consumed when the radio set crackled into life. Alex listened intently to a voice speaking French and gathered that the party were being warned of the presence of poachers who were advancing into this locality and more than one herd of forest elephants had already been massacred. Ominously the bandits, for that was what they were, had been reported to be armed with automatic rifles and even machine guns.

'They will be Adolphus Banza's men,' said Jacques when the messenger had finished. 'We need to do all we can to protect the elephants and the wildlife as a whole.'

Jacques wasted no time in organising a defensive perimeter around their small encampment with the very meagre group of people he could muster. Everyone was provided with a weapon including Alex who was handed the Belgian manufactured FN P90 sub machine gun and watches were organised so that some people would always be awake whatever the hour and even in the middle of the night. Every animal cry and every rustling in the undergrowth set peoples' nerves on edge. Alex really wondered whether she would be safer back home on her farm braving Mr Vatutin's missiles. Even before dawn Jacques was on the radio talking to the Wildlife service and he was clearly not happy with their latest reports.

'Banza's men are moving in closer,' he informed his group. 'The Wildlife service are sending us a helicopter with a team of soldiers, but it may be this evening before they can get to us. We are very isolated out here in the swamps. In the meantime, we will have to hold off the poachers as best we can.'

'We must all test our guns,' proposed Jean-Marc. 'In this kind of situation, we need to make sure they are all in good working order and each of us should know how to use their weapon effectively.'

One of Jacob Ilyunga's men, Sukeli Matetse, assisted Alex in stripping down and cleaning the FN sub machine gun. Then each person in turn test fired the weapons with which they had been allocated. Sukeli pointed to the branch of a tree which had broken off from somewhere and was drifting slowly down river. Alex aimed her firearm, but nothing happened.

'It must be jammed!' she exclaimed 'Always remember to turn off the safety catch,' smiled Sukeli.

This time when Alex squeezed the trigger a stream of lead burst forth from the potent weapon and sent splinters of wood flying in all directions around the target.

'She may be a mere woman but we will make a soldier of her yet,' laughed Sukeli.

After everyone had eaten some breakfast Jacob Ilyunga's small squad of just four men were sent off down river heading in the direction from which Banza's renegades were reported to be approaching. Alex felt even more afraid but helped to man a concealed defensive position on the edge of the forest with Jean-Marc and Etienne. Jacques was close by with several of his Congolese Rangers. Then they all waited while the sun rose higher in the clear skies and became blisteringly hot. The predations of the profusion of stinging and biting insects intensified. A large green snake slithered and hissed perilously close to Alex's legs. She stifled an urge to scream and wondered how long it would take to receive effective medical treatment if she or anyone else were bitten. Noon came and went. The heat and humidity grew even more oppressive. Then Jacques was urging people to listen.

'Ecout,' he whispered. 'That is automatic fire.'

Alex and Jean-Marc listened intently and then heard it themselves. Jean-Marc was armed with a PGM sniper rifle and peered into its powerful telescopic sight. Etienne was gathering brushwood to try and enhance their defensive position. Suddenly Alex was grabbing her weapon as the sound of trees and branches being crushed galvanised their attention.

'Behind us!' she yelled. 'They're attacking from behind!'

Alex was about to loose off a burst from the FN when Etienne called out,

'Don't shoot! It is Sabene and Mathilde with their herd.'

Alex breathed a sigh of relief, but Jean-Marc considered that the elephants would do better by taking themselves off to the most dense parts of the jungle.

'Allez! Allez!' urged Etienne as he tried to encourage the huge beasts to retreat back into the depths of the forest.

The elephants clearly wished to be sociable with their human visitors but clearly this was not the time particularly when Alex and her companions heard a shout from somewhere ahead followed by bursts of automatic gunfire. Bullets started to whizz and whine all around and Mathilde received one through her right ear. Trumpeting loudly in pain and protest she finally got the message that it was time to withdraw. Most of the other elephants in the herd also began retiring into the forest but Yvette was hit by a burst of fire from the poaching gang and collapsed in a badly wounded state. Jean-Marc spotted one of the attackers through the telescopic sights of his powerful sniper rifle and took a shot. He was gratified to see his target fall to the ground, but more poachers became visible and some of them could be seen to be armed with Kalashnikov assault rifles. At least one of Jacques Ngoy's men had been hit in the exchanges of fire and then Etienne took a bullet in his left shoulder and slumped to the ground, groaning in pain. Alex immediately put down her weapon and hurried to his assistance, administering morphine and whatever help she could give.

'I will be okay,' responded Etienne. 'Protect the elephants. Stop the poachers.'

Jacques Ngoy and his Rangers were also under intense pressure, and someone called out that Clarence Majuba, one of Jacques' right-hand men and a senior ranger had been killed. The elephant, Yvette, was just about still alive but lying moaning in pain close by with her calf, Bimbo, running around aimlessly in a traumatised state and making plaintiff distressed sounds. Suddenly several of the attackers broke through and ran into the small clearing where Jean-Marc and Alex were crouching. Jean-Marc shot one of the poachers who ran forward but then collapsed to the ground with a bullet through his head. Alex grabbed her FN sub machine gun and squeezed the trigger as three more bandits charged forward shouting some kind of war cry. Her gun remained silent, and she realised she had forgotten to undo the safety catch. Having done so the weapon spewed forth a torrent of lead and four attackers fell, one of them landing on top of Jean-Marc. Alex pulled the attacker aside and clubbed him angrily with her heavy gun. Two more ivory poachers burst through the undergrowth and Alex fired again as more poachers broke through the defensive perimeter. Jean-Marc reloaded his sniper rifle while Alex gave covering fire as bullets whined all around. Then her magazine was empty, but the bandits kept attacking.

'Don't shoot!' called Jacques Ngoy as he and Sukele Matetse pulled back to the clearing. 'We are having to retreat. They are too strong.'

'Come and help us here,' beckoned Jean-Marc as another poacher filled his sights. The recoil of the Finnish Army Sako rifle was powerful and his right shoulder was aching painfully, but Jean-Marc held his ground, and another poacher dropped to the ground.

In the meantime, Alex reloaded her sub-machine gun with a fresh magazine and was firing continuously, her weapon beginning to overheat with the combination of the hot equatorial weather and being in constant action and the paint was starting to run off the overheated barrel in strips. She had lost count of the number of men she had shot but she was well aware that it was a case of her or them. Dead and badly wounded poachers lay all around, some of them moaning in pain. Unexpectedly one of the bandits, a large and powerful man more than six feet tall with raging bloodshot eyes managed to scramble awkwardly to his feet and gathered sufficient strength to lunge towards Alex while she began turning her attention to Etienne. The assailant pulled out a fearsome looking knife with a blade more than ten inches long and Alex only just managed to scramble out of the way before the man tried to attack again. A shot rang out and the man's head disappeared in a greyish red mist of blood and brain matter, blasted apart at close range by Jean-Marc's lethal TRG-42 sniper rifle. Alex glanced around anxiously but none of the poachers in the vicinity appeared to be in any fit state to mount further attacks.

'Please pass me that water bottle,' asked Etienne weakly as Alex once more attempted to administer basic medical care. She felt giddy and sick and John-Marc was saying that the temperature this hot afternoon was higher than fifty degrees. They managed to ease Etienne into the shade and Alex made efforts to try to clean up his gunshot wound to his shoulder. Soon all manner of flies and stinging insects descended upon the clearing and the surrounding jungle, attracted by the dead and dying men and their profusion of wounds. Jacques Ngoy reappeared from the depths of the forest.

'I am sorry, but Yvette is dead,' he reported. 'But Sabine and Mathilde have survived. Mathilde took several bullet wounds, but she is a big elephant. I am sure she will survive.'

'Where is Bimbo?' asked Alex.

''He is alive and unharmed,' replied Jacques. 'He has lost his mother but the other elephants in the herd will rally round and look after him. Do not worry.'

Jacques began cautiously examining the poachers who lay strewn over the surrounding jungle. One man in particular caught his attention. Jacques prodded him with a sharp stick and the man groaned. Alex could see that he was a wiry individual aged perhaps about forty-five.

'This is Adolphus Banza,' called Jacques. 'He has a big price on his head as a wanted man. Who shot him?'

'I did,' replied Alex cautiously raising her hand.

'You will be entitled to a large reward from the government and the World

Wildlife Fund,' advised Jacques. 'He is a very bad man. Now, if he survives, we will be able to put him on trial and have him locked up in a Congolese jail where he will not be massacring God's creatures. Is that not right, Adolphus?' asked Jacques rhetorically as he jabbed Banza once again with the sharp stick.

The poachers who were clearly dead were left where they fell, at least for the time being but the wounded were carefully moved out towards the riverbank and examined while two of the surviving game reserve rangers kept them under armed guard. Several of the most badly wounded poachers soon died but Adolphus Banza drank some bottled mineral water and exhibited signs of regaining some strength. In the meantime, Sukele Matetse was talking to someone in French over the radio.

'The helicopter is on the way,' he reported, 'but it is likely to be a couple of hours before they reach us.'

'We should light a fire,' proposed Jacques. 'It will help to guide in the people flying the helicopter.'

He and Jean-Marc began to gather brushwood and used a can of petrol to set it alight. Alex moved closer to the fire. Although the weather was still hot and humid she began feeling cold and started to shiver. Frightful images of charging men filled her vision, she had lost count of the number of men she had shot and there was the big fellow who had attacked her with a knife. Much as she tried, she could not get him out of her mind, nor the spectacle of his head being blasted apart at close range by Jean-Marc's sniper rifle.

'I think you are suffering from PTSD,' commented Jacques Ngoy.

'Yes... put this round your shoulders,' said Jean-Marc as he proffered Alex his jacket. 'I am sorry, Alex. It was wrong of me to bring you out here into this dangerous jungle. It is all my fault.'

'Don't apologise,' replied Alex. 'I would not wish to have missed the experience for the world. It has opened my eyes.'

About an hour or so later the heavy rhythmic thumping sound of a large helicopter could be heard approaching from the north. Sukele fired a flare, and other men threw more combustible material on the open fire helping to build a tall column of smoke to help draw the attention of the crew. Then the machine was in sight and approaching the encampment. Once it had landed priority was given to getting Etienne Kasanga aboard where medics quickly examined his gunshot wound. Those poachers who had survived were also taken up on stretchers and more than one of them was put on a saline drip and given morphine. Alex made an effort to assist with this task and with loading up the weapons and supplies, but her knees buckled under her and she collapsed. Helping hands ensured that she was lifted safely aboard the helicopter and the pilot set course for Owando and hospital facilities. For Alex it was the culmination of several amazing weeks in West Africa but now it was time to return home.

Chapter 13

ON THE BRIDGE OF THE *Aurora* Commander Carlisle and Simon Barrington peered through binoculars at the Devon coastline until they found the entrance to the River Tamar where a tug, Roysterer, came to meet them to pilot them all the way into the Frigate Refit Complex in Devonport Dockyard. Even in the foggy murkiness of an autumnal morning it was clear that the town of Plymouth had taken a battering from Russian weaponry. Over to starboard a once tall building had collapsed into rubble while the Refit Complex itself was missing a sizeable portion of its roof. Batteries of lethal looking American manufactured SAM missiles had been positioned around the dockyard supported by heavy automatic guns. It seemed to Carlisle that no sooner had Aurora taken up her allocated berth, but Commodore Vincent appeared on board clearly intent on giving him his next orders. It was clear that this was to be no holiday. Carlisle invited the commodore to his cabin and offered him a chair while David Warwick brought them both mugs of strong black coffee and biscuits.

'I know you've seen quite a bit of action lately,' smiled the commodore, 'So while Aurora is catching up with that much needed refit and upgrade to her systems we've got you a desk job in Whitehall… Don't worry, it's just for a few months while Aurora is being worked on. You'll get your command back soon enough with most of the same crew. I know they're a good bunch and you and they work well together.'

'To be honest, sir, I'd much rather be back at sea right away,' responded Carlisle. 'Isn't there another ship available? You know I hate having to sit at a desk working in an office. It's not for me at all.'

'Fraid not,' replied Commodore Vincent. 'These orders come from on high. The thing is, we want you to help finalise the contracts with Darkforce. You have, of course worked closely with them already and tested one of their new systems in live combat scenarios. I think it's true to say that on more than one occasion the Darkforce systems saved your life and your ship and all its crew.'

'Yes, sir,' acknowledged Carlisle. 'I am sure that without the Darkforce technology I would not be sitting here talking to you this morning.'

'Well, that's splendid,' smiled Commodore Vincent. 'I've got you an office next to my own in Whitehall so we should be well able to keep in touch on a day-to-day basis. You'll need to get yourself fixed up with some digs… is it Suffolk where you live?'

'Norfolk, sir,' Carlisle corrected him.

'Well, that's rather a long way from Central London. Don't worry. My PA will let you have details of some suitable places in convenient travelling from your new office. Remember it's only for a while. But we really want you to get a contract drawn up particularly in relation to Darkforce's Project Schrodinger. It's quite incredible technology… far more advanced than anything else you or I have ever seen. It's an absolute war winner so you can understand we want to get it operational in our Service and the sooner the better.'

'Yes, I do understand that, sir,' conceded Carlisle.

The two officers discussed some points of detail and then Commodore Vincent was on his way. Carlisle busied himself making contact with the dockyard management in the hope that the refit could get started without delay. Later in the afternoon Carlisle attempted to phone Alex on her mobile but could not get an answer. He tried again early in the evening but similarly without success. When he tried later, he still could not get a reply and the landline at the farm would ring and ring and then just go to answerphone. In the morning, he made another attempt to contact Alex and finally managed to speak to a human being when a man answered the house phone.

'Is that Jack?' asked Carlisle upon hearing a man's voice.

'No, it's Gary. Jack's working on the *Moonbreeze* at the moment.'

'Is Alex around…? It's Eddie here and I'd like to speak to her if I may.'

'She's not here… gone on some sort of holiday,' replied Gary.

'Holiday?' queried Carlisle. 'Where has she gone?'

'Don't know,' replied Gary. Their conversation, such as it was, became interrupted briefly when a woman's voice called out,

'Who's that on the phone, Gary?'

'Eddie Carlisle,' replied Gary.

'Give me the phone... Sorry about that, Eddie,' apologised Sandra. 'I expect you're asking after Alex. She's taken herself off on a couple of weeks' holiday. She was worried about all those Russian missiles. We were all very frightened when the Russians attacked RAF Marham and other bases. It was really scary.'

'I can understand,' acknowledged Carlisle. 'Is she alright...? Are you and the others okay...? Where is Alex now? Has she gone far or what?'

'We're all okay,' Sandra assured him. 'I'm sure Alex will be back soon. I'm not sure where it is she was going... I'm not very good with these foreign place names. I don't usually go further than Cromer and Great Yarmouth.'

'Was it somewhere in the Mediterranean?' asked Carlisle.

'Yeah... somewhere like that,' responded Sandra vaguely.

Carlisle continued to ask questions of Sandra for several minutes but could not really glean much more information. He concluded that although he wanted to get things on the right track here at Devonport, he also needed to return to the farm as soon as possible. It sounded as though there was no one at the helm there and goodness knows what chaos might await him. David Warwick was, as always, very helpful and provided Carlisle with full details of train services up to London and onwards to Norwich. David even booked him a first class ticket for the 8-15am train from Plymouth the following morning. The journey home seemed to take forever, and this time Alex would not be there to greet him. Having got as far as Norwich Carlisle then took a local train which called at Wroxham. Jack Blofield had kindly offered to come out to collect him and his belongings. Jack was there to meet him driving his rather battered Landrover. The remaining part of the journey did not take long, and Jack was as tight lipped as everyone else as to where Alex was and what she was doing.

'I think she just felt a short holiday would do her good,' conceded Jack. 'I don't blame her what with them rockets landing too close for my liking. I think we was darned lucky nobody we knew got seriously harmed. Some poor bastards were not as fortunate.'

By the time they reached Longfleet Farm it had become dark but Carlisle was glad to be greeted by an array of pets including Elsa, Barley and Zara the Labradors and Bella, Carmen and Consuela the cats were also much in evidence. Once he had begun to get a little sorted out after his long journey, he took the opportunity to walk round to the stables to say 'hello' to the horses and bumped into Sandra in the process.

'Oh, Eddie... It's so good to see you again,' exclaimed Sandra. 'Are you keeping well?'

'Oh, mustn't complain,' replied Carlisle. His efforts to try to prise more information out of Sandra yielded no further results. Had Alex left him? Surely not. He was aware that she was not entirely happy being a naval officer's wife, but he had not considered things to be as bad as that.

In the morning he accompanied Jack in the *Moonbreeze*, sailing around Longfleet Broad and then quanting up the narrow dyke towards Neatishead. Some work had been carried out on the waterway, but it was still heavily overgrown and full of obstructions. After a couple of pints at a nearby hostelry they returned to the farm. Carlisle spent the next couple of days trying to sort out paperwork and bills and even to relax but he was worried about Alex and the place did not seem right without her. Later in the week he took the train to London followed by a taxi to his new office in Whitehall where he found Commodore Vincent.

'This is Naomi... your new PA,' the commodore introduced a dark-haired lady aged about thirty-five. 'She's very efficient and she's got everything set up for you. Even your temporary digs in London. She'll be able to fill you in on all the details.'

'I haven't put anything in your diary for today, sir,' explained Naomi to Carlisle, 'but you have a meeting tomorrow morning with the Malaysian Navy Minister and Dr Arnold Duvall from Darkforce. I'll let you have a browse through these files. They should give you some idea of the matters to be dealt with.'

The commodore returned to his office along the corridor in the Admiralty building and Naomi left him to read the files. Carlisle looked around at his new office. It was not unattractive being located in a Georgian building with a large fireplace albeit boarded up and no longer used. On the wall behind him were fitted bookshelves crammed with all manner of works on naval subjects including copies of Jane's Fighting Ships from the current edition and going back as far as the nineteen fifties. On the wall to his right was an impressive painting of the Battle of Camperdown fought in 1797 against the Dutch. Carlisle briefly examined the painting which appeared to be an original although he had not heard of the artist. He glanced through the windows opposite and saw that it was starting to rain. Then he sat down and began reading the files, but his thoughts kept turning to Alex. Would she be back by the weekend? Nobody seemed able to enlighten him one way or the other.

At 5-30pm Carlisle left the building and began to do battle with the Underground system. The first train to arrive at the platform was absolutely bursting with humanity and there was no possibility of getting on board. The next train was equally overcrowded, and he had to let several go before he was finally able to push his way in to a corner of one. Fortunately, it was not far to Camden, and he emerged back into the open air and made his way to North Western Mews where he found number 42, a decaying Edwardian edifice and clambered up the creaking staircase to the second floor. The paint on the wrought iron bannister was peeling. There was a lift, but it had a sign which said, 'out of order'. Carlisle guessed it had not worked for a long time. The property had clearly once been a fairly sizeable town house but was now subdivided into flats. His own flat was number 42c and he was initially let in by his new landlady, Mrs Petruska.

'Hello, my darlink,' Mrs Petruska greeted him as she unlocked the door to number 42c. 'This is your new home. I hope you find it comfortable.'

Carlisle observed that it was little more than a bedsitter and was told that he would be sharing the bathroom with the occupants of number 42a and 42b. Essentially number 42c was one draughty room with a curtained corner hiding a wash basin and an alcove containing two electric rings, a tiny fridge and a kitchen cupboard unit. There was a rather lumpy single bed of some age, a few bookshelves, an old wardrobe and a battered armchair. Mrs Petruska was clearly a lady of East European origin. Scents of her culinary efforts pervaded the whole building and Carlisle detected Carp and cabbage. It was not the most appealing cuisine and after briefly sorting himself out Carlisle walked up Camden High Street and found himself a rather small restaurant with not too many other diners. He ordered himself a steak and attempted to contact Alex on her mobile number but without success.

The following morning the meeting went quite well with the Malaysian Navy Minister, Juhar Haji Mahirattan, who confirmed his government's wish to become involved in a joint development and purchase with the UK of very high technology systems proposed by Darkforce Plc. They were joined by Commodore Vincent and Dr Arnold Duvall and it was agreed they would have further talks later that week when they would also be joined by Prince Faisal, who was now a director of Darkforce, and by the Pakistan Defence Minister who had already expressed his government's serious interest in joining the projects.

By Friday representatives of the governments of the UK, Malaysia, Pakistan and Saudi Arabia met together to sign preliminary contracts for the acquisition of systems developed under Project Ultra and the even more advanced Project Schrodinger. They were joined by Dr Samantha Langley and Professor Robert Finch from Darkforce who had, of course, both served aboard Aurora during combat operations. Carlisle was able to personally confirm the effectiveness of Project Ultra and how on more than one occasion it had saved his own skin and that of his crew when it had seemed almost certain that they would otherwise have been blown out of the water. By the end of the first week Carlisle felt he had at least achieved something, but he was increasingly worried about Alex and returned to Norfolk by train to spend the weekend at Longfleet Farm. There was still plenty of catching up to do on the administrative front even though the accountants had clearly called in to assist with these tasks in accordance with their instructions. However, when Carlisle tried to contact Alex he was unable to obtain a signal. The landline was no more successful. Sandra and Jack Blofield both tried to assist in this effort but to no avail. Carlisle returned to work in London on Monday morning more concerned than ever as to what had happened to Alex. Where on earth was she? If she had just gone to a resort in the Mediterranean, it is unlikely nowadays with up to date technology that she would be completely incommunicado. Matters were not made any easier for Carlisle when Commodore Vincent breezed cheerfully into his office.

'I have a small assignment for you this coming Thursday evening, Eddie,' he explained. 'The Yanks are very interested in Project Ultra and Project Schrodinger and want to know more about it. I felt you were the right chap to fill them in so I've arranged for you to attend a meeting at the new Anglo-American Staff College in Great Missenden. You'll meet the new U.S Ambassador, a chap called Robert Maddison, and some of the top brass from the States. I think General Weidenfeld will be there and General Petrowski. Oh, and just one thing... the American Ambassador will have his wife with him so you should take your wife too. The ladies will be able to chat to each other... you know the thing.'

Carlisle attempted to mutter some excuse but did not want to admit that he had absolutely no idea where his wife was at the moment.

'Very good, sir. I'll do my best.'

'Course you will... as always,' smiled the commodore and departed for his next port of call.

Carlisle spent the rest of the morning even more troubled than ever. He did not wish to mess things up with the Americans by breaching protocol. In the afternoon he had a meeting with Samantha Langley. Samantha was in a very ebullient frame of mind.

'Things are going really well for Darkforce,' she enthused. 'Everyone is wanting to buy our systems and invest in us... the British, the Saudis, the Malaysians... and now the United States are taking a serious interest too.'

'Well, that's splendid,' acknowledged Carlisle. 'But there are one or two things worrying me right now.'

'Which are?'

'Well, to start with, since I came home from our recent mission I haven't been able to contact Alex. She just isn't there and I can't get hold of her on her mobile phone. It's most strange. When I ask people around the farm they seem all buttoned up and just mutter something about her having gone on holiday.'

'Well... there you are,' responded Samantha. 'She clearly felt like taking a break. We all do sometimes.'

'And to cap it all,' added Carlisle, 'Commodore Vincent now wants me to attend some important function on Thursday evening at the Anglo-American Staff College and meet the American Ambassador and Top Brass... General Petrowski and General Weidenfeld. I'll expect there'll be admirals too.'

'I can't see what's wrong with that,' replied Samantha. 'It'll be a feather in your cap. Make the most of it. It's an opportunity.'

'The problem there is that I'm supposed to take my wife with me... it's protocol,' explained Carlisle.'

Samantha looked thoughtful and then broke into a smile.

'I'm sure most of these people have never met your wife and have no idea what she looks like. Why don't you take me along and I can fulfil that role. I can be Mrs Carlisle for one evening.'

'Sam, you're a genius!' enthused Carlisle. 'What would I do without you?'

'I can even drive you to the venue,' added Samantha. 'Where did you say it is?'

'Great Missenden... that's Buckinghamshire... to the west of London,' replied Carlisle. 'It's really not that far.'

'No problem at all,' acknowledged Samantha. 'I've got to attend an important Board meeting of Darkforce early this evening otherwise I'd take you out for dinner. In the meantime, we'd better discuss the finer points of the contract between Darkforce and the UK Government.'

At the end of the working day Carlisle did battle with the Underground system once again and made his way back to his digs in Camden. The weather was damp with a steady drizzle and the building still stank of stale fish and cabbage. Once again Carlisle decided to find a local restaurant and took the opportunity to try to phone Alex while waiting for his meal to arrive. Although he attempted to phone her a number of times during the evening it was to no avail.

The following morning Carlisle took a taxi to the Royal Courts in the Strand where he was attending on counsel in a dispute between HM Government and Tyne Shipbuilders over the cost of a new class of frigates being built for the Royal Navy.

'You know all about the problems with the Type 57s,' Commodore Vincent had declared breezily. 'You're just the man to explain to counsel the ins and outs of the issues involved.'

By lunchtime little progress had been made on the case and Carlisle was on the phone to Commodore Vincent and to more than one senior civil servant in the Ministry of Defence seeking further instructions. The proceedings resumed at 2pm and adjourned again during the afternoon for the parties to try to hammer out a deal. Counsel sent Carlisle to phone his superiors for clarification of a number of issues and what the Government's position would be. Somewhat to his surprise a female voice called out,

'Eddie... is that you?'

Carlisle turned round and recognised Emma, the younger half-sister of Alex's best friend, Lucy. Emma appeared very smart in her barrister's attire with her wig and gown.

'I didn't expect to meet you here,' she continued. 'Where is your ship? Shouldn't you be standing on the bridge somewhere out on the high seas?'

Carlisle explained that the Aurora was undergoing a refit and upgrades to her systems.

'I've been given command of a desk in Whitehall while the refit takes place. It's not really what I wanted but the decision was not mine. I can't wait to get back to sea but that may take a little time.'

'Look... I can't talk just now. I'm in the middle of a Big Money case,' explained Emma, 'but how are you fixed at about 5-30pm? I suggest we meet at the Royal George just across the road.'

'That sounds splendid,' agreed Carlisle. 'I'll see you there.'

Come the end of the afternoon Carlisle was glad to escape from the Frigate case and the Courts and made his way across the Strand. Many other people had clearly had the same idea, and the pub was very crowded, but he managed to spot Emma who waved to him in a welcoming manner from the bar.

'Let me buy you a drink,' proposed Emma. 'Then we can bag that table in that alcove just over there.'

Emma ordered a white wine for herself and a Scotch and soda for Carlisle. Then they sat down at the small table and brought each other up to date with their situations.

'So have you got somewhere to stay here in London?' enquired Emma. 'After all Norfolk is rather a long way to commute.'

'I have some digs in Camden which were chosen for me by the Ministry,' replied Carlisle. 'Actually, I hate them. The whole building is lousy. My flat is really just a bed sit and the whole place stinks of fish and cabbage.'

'Well, that sounds most unpleasant,' acknowledged Emma, 'But I live in Camden… my flat overlooks Camden Lock. It's really quite nice there. You ought to come and see it.'

'Yes, I'd love to,' said Carlisle as a waitress brought the steak and kidney pudding he had ordered.

Emma had ordered from the vegan menu and her dish seemed to involve nut cutlets and peppers. They spent an hour or so in the pub after which Emma was keen to show Carlisle her flat and they took a taxi up to Camden Lock. Although Emma's apartment was not very far from Carlisle's digs, he was of the firm opinion that Emma's property was in a much better neighbourhood, and this was clear even though it was now dark, and the inevitable drizzle had started again. Upon entering the flat they were greeted warmly by Emma's dog, Katie, a canine of uncertain parentage whom Emma had rescued a couple of years ago from Battersea Dogs' Home. Emma explained that Katie had some Labrador in her DNA and inevitably some Staffy. Emma also had two black cats named Paws and Pouncer who were brother and sister and had also been rescued from Battersea.

'Pouncer suffers quite a lot from kidney problems,' said Emma. 'I have to give her all sorts of medications. Try giving a pill to a cat!'

'No need to explain to me,' laughed Carlisle. 'Our farm has so many cats I can't remember all their names. Alex keeps acquiring more and more… Alex…' His visage turned anxious. 'Is it alright if I try to phone her? I really am quite worried.'

'Yes, go ahead, Eddie. I'm sure it'll be alright. She'll just have gone on holiday for a couple of weeks. Personally, I don't blame her what with missiles flying about. I'm sure she's safer wherever it is she's gone to.'

'That's a big part of the problem,' replied Carlisle. 'At the moment I have no idea where she is, and no one seems able to tell me.'

'Would you care for another Scotch?' enquired Emma. 'I just need to have a read through these papers for the case I'm doing tomorrow in Bristol. I won't give the names of the parties, but the Respondent husband is a drug dealer with Columbian connections. It's very difficult explaining to our client, the wife, that she can't expect the court to order the transfer to her of monies obtained by her husband from patently illegal activities.'

Emma put on her spectacles and sat reading her papers and documents in a corner of the living room. Carlisle reflected that she now looked very studious and professional. He sipped his glass of Scotch and Pouncer the cat decided he was the right sort of human and sat down in his lap. Carlisle tried phoning Alex on his mobile but again without an answer.

'No luck?' queried Emma. Carlisle shrugged. 'Be a darling and take Katie for a short walk, will you. Jenny calls in a couple of times a day to exercise Katie with half a dozen other dogs. I know it's not the ideal place for dogs here… but Katie is my main companion.'

Carlisle did as he was asked. Fortunately, the rain had stopped, and the sky was clearing to unfold a starlit night. He had not walked far when he saw an object he first mistook for a meteor flash overhead heading in a south westerly direction. After a few minutes there was a kind of muffled bang over the horizon. Then the air raid siren belatedly sounded. Shortly afterwards another of these objects, clearly missiles, streaked across the sky. Carlisle decided it was time to return Katie to her owner and headed back to Emma's flat.

'I think I ought to be heading back to my digs,' said Carlisle to Emma. 'It's getting a little late and Mrs Petruska will wonder where I've got to.' He began to gather up his papers.

'Oh, Eddie!' exclaimed Emma as she jumped up from her chair and blocked his path to the door. 'Please don't go.'

'What's the matter?' asked Carlisle.

'I'm frightened,' admitted Emma. 'I'm alone here apart from my dog and my cats. You can stay the night here. You've told me you hate your digs.'

'Er... well...' mumbled Carlisle. For once he was taken somewhat by surprise.

'You always make my knees turn to jelly. Please hold me and stop me from falling,' pleaded Emma.

Carlisle put his arms around her as Emma pressed hard against him and the two of them embraced. Then Carlisle found himself being pushed backwards on to a settee with Emma lying on top of him. She was not a lady of unusually substantial build, but Carlisle considered that resistance was futile as Emma kissed him fervently on the lips and on his chin. Carlisle ran his fingers through her dark and well-groomed hair.

'So, are you feeling less afraid now?' asked Carlisle.

'I do feel more reassured,' conceded Emma. 'I'm sure you've had to endure many dangerous situations recently.'

'You can say that again,' agreed Carlisle. 'There were quite a few occasions when I thought my number was up. Several times we were saved by our amazing new technology... but I'm not allowed to tell you about that. I did have some mind-blowing experiences. I'm still trying to work things out... without much success. Where's that titled husband of yours these days?'

'Charles and I went our own separate ways a while ago. I hardly ever see him now,' replied Emma. 'It was partly my fault. I'm a very independent person. But he was about fifteen years older than me. It was almost an arranged marriage... my parents were a driving force. They thought he was the right sort. I was never that sure. We're not actually divorced but the marriage is as good as dead except in name.'

'So, what's your full title?' enquired Carlisle.

'It's a bit of a mouthful,' responded Emma. 'It's Lady Emma Victoria Hamilton-Wallingford. '

'My... that sounds wonderfully posh,' smiled Carlisle. 'So, you have blue blood in your veins. Wallingford is clearly from Charles' side of the family?'

'That's right,' acknowledged Emma as she began to unbutton her white dress shirt with its lace fastenings. Soon it was cast aside. 'Here… give me a hand with my bra.'

Carlisle willingly obliged and the bra was unceremoniously tossed over the edge of the settee. Emma leaned forward, her eyes glinting in the soft lighting of the living room and allowed her impressive breasts to tumble freely.

'It always gives me pleasure to watch the expressions on the faces of guys when I do that,' admitted Emma. 'How do you rate them…? My tits, I mean. You can feel them… go on... you have my permission.'

'That's very decent of you. I'd say they're splendid,' praised Carlisle as he gently kissed each nipple. 'Let me assist you with that skirt. How does it undo?'

Emma soon divested herself of her dark skirt and placed it over the back of the settee. Carlisle caressed her soft warm body and returned her kisses with equal aplomb. The last line of defence of her modesty comprised a flimsy pair of black thong style briefs which matched her dark stockings and black high heels which were still on her feet. Emma assisted Carlisle's efforts to remove her briefs which found their way down her fine legs and were duly kicked unceremoniously from her feet.

'Why is it that whenever I'm in your company I seem to become separated from my underwear?' questioned Emma. 'Do you remember the Jacuzzi at Lucy's house in Belsize Park?'

'It's probably just coincidence,' replied Carlisle.

At that moment, the 'All Clear' sounded.

'Thank God for that,' sighed Emma. 'These rockets and missiles really do scare me. I have no wish to die. There's such a lot I still want to do.'

'It's fear of death which keeps us staying alive,' counselled Carlisle. 'There's nothing like it to keep us on our toes… talking of which… I really ought to be on my way.' He had not forgotten Alex and pangs of guilt came jabbing into his consciousness.

'Absolutely no way, Eddie!' retorted Emma as she stood up and barred his way to the door. 'I'm not letting you just slip through my fingers having got this far. I've got to be off early to Bristol in the morning… catching the 6-45am train from Paddington… to do a two-day ancillary relief hearing down there… so the quicker we get to bed the better. Who knows we might actually get some sleep.' Emma took Carlisle firmly by the hand and he realised that further resistance was futile. Besides Emma was indeed a very desirable lady and he admired her shapely profile as she led the way up a curving flight of stairs to her bedroom. Katie the dog and Paws and Pouncer the cats followed them at their heels and Carlisle considered that things were just a little overcrowded as he removed his clothing upon Emma's orders. Emma sat on her bed and touched up her makeup from an assortment of cosmetics at her bedside. Then she began to unfasten her suspenders and peeled off her dark stockings.

'It's ironic that I have the money to buy expensive underwear but usually there are no handsome guys to admire it,' considered Emma. 'But for once there is. Do you like it? It's from Bridewells of Bond Street.'

'Is it now. Absolutely first class,' enthused Carlisle as his pulse quickened in anticipation.

'Just the response I wanted,' replied Emma as she reached in her bedside drawer and produced a packet of twelve condoms. 'I keep them just in case I get lucky. Let's see how many of these we can get through. Do you want a hand with it?'

Carlisle accepted the assistance and with his impressive manhood appropriately sheathed Emma lay back on her spacious double bed with her legs drawn up and wide apart. Carlisle kissed the matt of dark curling hair in her groin.

'That's a pretty impressive bush you have. Lady Hamilton-Wallingford,' he complimented her before introducing his phallus gently but firmly into the moist chasm between her soft white thighs.

'I'm sorry I can't give you ostrich feathers,' apologised Emma. 'But I can give you a big hairy fanny. The thing is… I may be a member of the aristocracy… everybody keeps reminding me… but biologically I'm no different from Mrs Watkins, the cleaning lady.'

'Perhaps you have a point,' considered Carlisle. 'But I think you're sure to be a lot more desirable than Mrs Watkins even though I've never met her.'

'The reality is that I'm just a lonely girl living on my own in the Great

Metropolis,' sighed Emma, 'With just my dog and two cats as my companions.'

'It's the life you've chosen, Emma,' responded Carlisle. 'You could change direction if you wanted to.'

'I'll see how things go,' said Emma as the bed springs began to creak noisily. 'I was disappointed with how it turned out with Charles. Maybe I can turn things round and change course.'

As Carlisle thrust into her determinedly Emma stretched her arms behind her and gripped the bedhead. Eventually Katie jumped on to the bed followed by Paws and Pouncer. The bed had become somewhat overcrowded, but Carlisle did not know what time it was when he and Emma fell into an exhausted sleep. She rested her head on his chest, and he held her in a protective embrace.

It was still dark when Carlisle began to be aware that Emma was up and about, taking a shower and then putting on her clothes and packing a briefcase and a travel bag. The latter held a change of clothes and her wig and gown.

'I'm sorry but I'm going to have to catch that early train,' apologised Emma. 'If there are no unexpected hold ups it should get me into Temple Meads in sufficient time to get to the courts well before the hearing starts. I've put some muesli out for you on the kitchen table and some peanut butter. Be a darling and take Katie for a walk before you go to work. Pouncer needs to have her medication. Are you listening, dear?' She gave Carlisle a prod.

'The poop bags are under the kitchen sink. Pouncer has to have half a Benaze tablet mixed in with her breakfast and a sprinkling of Ipakadine powder.'

Carlisle grunted some sort of semi-incomprehensible reply.

'I expect I shall be in Bristol for the rest of this week,' added Emma. 'The case may even drag on into next week, so I'll have to love you and leave you.'

Emma gave him a kiss and then was gone. Carlisle then remembered that he was having to attend the function with the U.S. Ambassador that evening and Samantha Langley was driving him there and playing the part of his wife. Life was becoming somewhat complex but at least he only had one girl to entertain for the moment. Carlisle tried to remember the instructions which

Emma had given him and then headed for the Royal Courts in the Strand. Fortunately, the lawyers for Tyne Shipyards appeared a little more amenable and the basis for a settlement was reached before lunch. During the afternoon Carlisle returned to his Whitehall office and tidied up a few loose ends. At around 4pm the phone on his desk buzzed.

'There's a lady here to see you, sir. A Dr Langley,' announced his secretary.

'Show her in, please, Naomi,' replied Carlisle.

Samantha looked stunning in a dark blue velvet evening dress with a striking Egyptian style gold choker. For a moment Carlisle was speechless.

'I'm quite looking forward to this evening,' announced Samantha. 'After all there should be Americans present.'

'I am once again very grateful to you, Sam. You always save the day.' Carlisle spent a few minutes showing Samantha around his office and introducing him to one or two people. Then they were off on their way to Great Missenden in Samantha's red Ford Mustang.

'It's not new,' she explained as they picked their way through the busy Central London traffic. 'It's a classic car but listen to the roar of that V-8 engine. It's a real American muscle car.'

Samantha gave a demonstration of the car's acceleration as she took on all comers at the many junctions and sets of lights and beat them. With the help of the SatNav they reached the M40 and sped out into the countryside. Indeed, they arrived at the Manor sooner than Carlisle expected and he and Samantha had a little time in hand to stroll amongst the extensive grounds of the large country house. In due course they were shown to the high rooved and gilded dining hall by a young adjutant. Even Samantha, the cool American blonde, could not fail to be impressed by the Manor and by the company. The hall had been a ball room in the 17th and 18th centuries and in more recent times the ceiling had been painstakingly restored to show the original artwork with cherubs playing flutes and trumpets and dancing amongst the clouds. The huge dining table had been set as befitted a formal dinner with so many dignitaries present with silver candelabras and arrangements of roses and orchids. As Carlisle had expected he found himself seated directly opposite the American Ambassador, Robert Maddison, while Carlisle's 'wife' sat opposite the Ambassador's wife, Charlene. Carlisle found himself in serious discussion with the Ambassador regarding the war with Russia and the broader political situation. Carlisle was also introduced to Admiral Forrest Sherbrook who sat to his immediate right. The admiral explained that he had just been posted to the Command Centre at Northwood in London.

'I'd say I've been thrown in at the deep end,' smiled the admiral. 'But I understand you're an officer who has seen real combat very recently, so I want to pick your brains about the Russian Navy and their tactics and philosophies.'

'Yes, sir. I have seen a lot of the Russian Navy... and their air force,' replied Carlisle. 'Their surface forces tend to attract the limelight, but it is their submarine fleet which presents the most dangers and will be the hardest nut to crack.'

'I couldn't agree with you more,' said Admiral Sherbrook. 'We have in mind the creation of a series of hunter/ killer groups... highly mobile task forces to aggressively hunt down the enemy subs and destroy them. In that connection we are very interested in some new technology being developed by a company called Darkforce and their Project Schrodinger.'

'Well, you've certainly come to the right place this evening, sir,' responded Carlisle. 'My wife here is a director of Darkforce. I suggest you may want to arrange a meeting with her.'

Rather later into the evening the guests were given an opportunity to get some fresh air in the grounds. It was a rather chilly evening with a cool south easterly breeze and Samantha soon found herself collared by Admiral Sherbrook. Carlisle was not altogether concerned since he knew the admiral would be trying to quiz Samantha about the new Darkforce technology. The evening drew to a close with a toast to the King at midnight and the Ambassadors and high-ranking military commanders were hurriedly carried away in helicopters and stretched limousines amidst tight security. Carlisle climbed into the front passenger seat of Samantha's car as she set the SatNav for home which was somewhere in London's Dockland.

'I've had a wonderful evening!' enthused Samantha. 'Do you know... I've had an invite from Charlene, the American Ambassador's wife, to go shopping with her in the West End. Then… it gets even better. That American admiral… Sherbrook… says he wants his government to buy our Darkforce technology and he'll push for it as hard as he can. I think the U S Government will buy it… especially in present circumstances. We need to strike while the iron's hot.'

'I think you're on to a winner there,' concurred Carlisle.

Samantha came off the M40 to avoid the security and roadblocks as they headed for Central London and drove around various back roads and alleys where the traffic was light at this late hour.

'You don't want to go to those awful digs of yours in Camden, do you?' queried Samantha. 'I think I can honestly say that my place is better.'

Carlisle thought for a moment, weighing up the situation.

'I think you're right,' he nodded as Samantha pressed her foot down on the accelerator of the classic American muscle car and they sped through the darkened streets towards London's Docklands.

Carlisle felt tired but he kept awake in anticipation as they crossed the Thames showing their ID to security. He had experienced many adventures, and this was one more. There was the Shard and other prominent London landmarks. Then the tall skyscraper towers of the Canary Wharf development hove into view and Samantha was turning into a side alley and finally came to a halt opposite a row of garages. Pressing a button on the dashboard a door opened slowly, and Samantha drove forward. Then the door was closing behind them and Samantha was beckoning Carlisle to follow her into a lift which took them to the top floor and Samantha's luxury penthouse apartment.

'Welcome to my ivory tower,' announced Samantha. 'I think you'll find it more desirable than the flat provided for you by the Ministry.'

Even though it was now well into the small hours Carlisle could see that the apartment had spectacular views with the river snaking its way down towards Greenwich.

'Be a gentleman and unhook my dress, will you,' requested Samantha in her customary matter of fact style.

Carlisle politely obliged and the beautiful blue velvet evening dress dropped silently to the floor. Samantha then motioned to him to assist her in completing the process and casually cast her bra across the back of a convenient chair.

'This is my room, by the way,' Samantha informed him. 'We're up on the eighth floor here. You'll be able to see even more in the morning.'

Carlisle had no doubt of that as Samantha placed a comforting arm around his waist and somehow they drifted into bed with Samantha taking the initiative. Even in the dim light Carlisle was transfixed by Samantha's transcendently beautiful blue eyes and one dream merged into another until finally a new day dawned and Samantha was already up and about and telling him about her forthcoming meeting with the Saudi Defence Minister and her hopes of yet more success.

'Unfortunately, I've got to fly to Riyadh,' explained Samantha. 'So I won't be here over the weekend, but I'll call you early next week.'

'I hope you've packed your burka,' grunted Carlisle as the realities of his situation came back down to earth.

Carlisle spent another quiet weekend back at Longfleet Farm riding his horse and going sailing on the Broad with Jack Blofield. There was still no news from Alex and her continued absence caused him yet more anxiety. He did not know whether something dreadful had happened to her. After all it was a very dangerous world nowadays. Had she decided to leave him… perhaps to elope with another man? It was a possibility which he preferred not to dwell upon. Monday was damp and dreary and spent largely at the office in Whitehall while the evening was thoroughly wet and miserable and consisted largely of sitting in his bed sit in Camden watching television, his viewing being regularly disrupted by the people in the adjoining flat having a huge row with crockery and glassware being flung around. Tuesday morning was no better and Naomi dumped a huge stack of new files on his desk for his attention. Carlisle wished he was back at sea in command of the *Aurora*, but her refit was clearly going to take some time. He opened the file at the top of the heap which involved the compulsory purchase of land on the Devonshire coast for the purpose of creating new shipbuilding and ship repair facilities. He read through the correspondence and documentation, but it did not exactly fill him with inspiration. The boredom of sailing a desk was suddenly broken at around 12-30pm when his office phone buzzed. It was Naomi, his secretary,

'It's Lady Hamilton-Wallingford on the line,' she informed him.

'Hi Eddie. I've finished my case in Bristol,' enthused Emma. 'I think we got the best result we could in the circumstances. All the Respondent husband's properties which our instructing solicitors could find were transferred to our client. I'm sure the husband has lots of money stashed away in Columbia and in offshore tax havens but no one is likely to ever find it and it's most likely to be laundered drug money. We could hardly ask the court to order the transfer to our client of what would clearly have been the proceeds of crime.'

'Absolutely,' agreed Carlisle. 'I can clearly see your point.'

'By the way, I'll be back in Camden this evening,' added Emma. 'There's a new Portuguese restaurant just opened not far from my flat. I wondered if you might like to join me. It's called Reficos.'

'Of course I would,' replied Carlisle. 'What time should we meet up?'

'About 6-30pm,' suggested Emma. 'Not too late. I bought some new lingerie in Bristol which I'd like to show you. We can go back to my flat after dinner.'

'I think that sounds like a pretty good offer,' responded Carlisle. 'See you at this place... Reficos... at 6-30.'

During the afternoon Carlisle frequently glanced at his watch but at 4-45pm he put on his overcoat and made his way to the Underground and did battle with the thousands of other commuters all vying for their few feet of space on the overcrowded platforms and then being squashed into carriages like sardines in cans. Arriving in Camden to the usual drizzle it was at least a relief to find himself back in the open air and able to breathe. He soon found Reficos which was situated close to other eateries serving a variety of cuisine. He was rather early but peered tentatively inside and was pleased to see Emma in conversation with members of the restaurant staff.

'Ah, Eddie!' Emma greeted Carlisle warmly. 'This is Jaou. He's the manager.'

Carlisle was introduced to a dark-haired man of rather short stature but with a thick bushy moustache.

'Please, senor. Let me take your coat,' offered Jaou. 'Would you like to go to your table now?'

'Yes… that will be fine,' accepted Emma.

The diners duly seated themselves in a quiet corner of the restaurant at a table for two while someone came and lit the candles. Emma removed her glasses and put them away.

'Time to relax,' she smiled at Carlisle. 'The cases give me a buzz but sometimes it's good to be able to switch off.'

Jaou reappeared to take their orders for dinner. Carlisle was impressed by the menu which included a good selection of fish dishes. He finally settled upon a half lobster.

'A good choice, senor,' Jaou complimented Carlisle. 'And for you, madam?'

As usual Emma settled for a vegetarian option. Carlisle was invited to peer into a large aquarium on the far side of the dining room in which a variety of live crustaceans were housed.

'Please, senor… You may choose your lobster,' said Jaou and pointed to a large creature of somewhat fearsome appearance and large pincers. Carlisle accepted the recommendation and returned to his table. Two of the staff brought up a smaller tank of bubbling hot water.

'Oh no!' exclaimed Emma as she jumped up from the table. 'They're going to put your lobster in that vat of boiling water. No! No!'

After that the romantic meal out was somewhat truncated and Carlisle soon found himself at Emma's flat overlooking Camden Lock and being greeted enthusiastically by Katie the dog and a little more cautiously by Paws and Pouncer the cats. Carlisle helpfully assisted Emma in serving the pets with their meals and then the two of them took Katie for a short walk.

'I'm really very sorry about this evening,' apologised Emma. 'It's just that I can't bear seeing animals harmed.'

'It's me who should apologise,' replied Carlisle. 'I should have been more tactful in what I chose.'

The drizzle was by now turning to steady rain and they hastened back to Emma's flat where Emma rubbed down Katie's coat with a somewhat odorous dog towel. Emma and Carlisle then hung up their own damp coats and Emma offered her gentleman companion a glass of Scotch which offer was gratefully accepted.

'Well, at least the rest of the evening is ours,' smiled Emma. 'I read my Brief for tomorrow's case on the train coming back from Bristol, so work doesn't have to get in our way. Perhaps you might like to see some of the things I brought back.

'I certainly would,' enthused Carlisle as Emma proceeded to remove her working clothes including her white shirt and dark skirt. She then posed to show off her dark stockings and red suspender belt.

'How do you rate my briefs?' she asked. 'And I don't mean the briefs sent me by my instructing solicitors. '

Carlisle noted that Emma's new briefs were a matching red, but the front was made of a semi-transparent material while when Emma turned to show her behind the thong was effectively invisible.

'They're designed that way… to show off the bum,' explained Emma.

'Well, they certainly achieve that very well,' replied Carlisle as Emma joined him on the sofa.

'Help me unhook my bra,' requested Emma. 'I'm not one for wasting time, as you know already.'

Carlisle obliged and soon found Emma lying on top of him and removing his tie and unbuttoning his shirt.

'I fancy you,' Emma told him as she kissed him on the lips. 'Did you know that?'

'One doesn't wish to be presumptive,' replied Carlisle, 'But the feeling is mutual.'

'My God, what does that mean?' queried Emma. 'Be a gentleman and help me get these tight little briefs off. The truth is that they're rather uncomfortable… and dare I admit it… just a little damp.'

'I think I get you,' acknowledged Carlisle.

'You have that effect on me,' Emma informed him.

'What…? That I make you wet your knickers,' questioned Carlisle. 'Could it be that you find me frightening or repulsive?'

'I really don't think so,' Emma reassured him. Within a short time, she was leading him upstairs to her bedroom once again followed by the ever-present animals.

'Have you heard anything from Alex?' asked Emma as she and Carlisle made love in the dim light.

'No, I am becoming increasingly concerned that I've heard nothing at all,' responded Carlisle. 'I can't understand it.'

'I was talking to my sister, Lucy, over this last weekend,' said Emma. 'It was very interesting what she had to say.'

'Go on,' urged Carlisle.

'She went on holiday… as you know,' replied Emma somewhat guardedly.

'But where to?' asked Carlisle. 'I have no idea where she is.'

'To West Africa. The Republic of Gabon to be precise.'

'But why on earth has she gone there? We don't know anyone out there,' questioned Carlisle.

'I understand she met somebody who comes from that country,' explained Emma. 'Apparently, they decided to go on a holiday for several weeks to get away from the Russian missile attacks. It was getting really bad here. People have been fearing for their lives. Believe me.'

'Who is this person?' demanded Carlisle. 'Male or female? They're clearly not anyone I know.'

'He's a good looking young man,' responded Emma mischievously, 'But before you start casting judgement pause for breath and consider your own behaviour. What would Alex say if she saw you here now… in bed with me with our bottoms bouncing up and down.'

'I really don't know what to say,' sighed Carlisle. 'My mind is in a whirl. I had hoped she had not gone off with somebody else.'

'Don't feel so upset about it,' said Emma. 'You have me. I'm not going to let you just slip through my fingers.'

Emma entwined her legs tightly around Carlisle's torso and dug her fingernails into his back.

'Now you belong to me,' she informed him.

It was still dark when Emma prodded Carlisle in the ribs and reclined with her legs drawn back and well apart. Although he was still tired not to say shocked by the trauma of Emma's revelations Carlisle was nevertheless eager to satisfy his lover and kissed the matt of dark tangled hair between her thighs. Emma sighed appreciatively and then began to moan with pleasure. When she cried out, he did not stop but carried on until Emma cried out again and then again in a kind of chain reaction which was actually quite unnerving, but Carlisle was a man of the world and remained unperturbed. Suddenly Emma grabbed her bedside clock and scrambled out of bed.

'My God. It's nearly eight o'clock!' she exclaimed. 'I'm supposed to be having an early meeting in Chambers with my client and Instructing solicitors in less than half an hour.'

Emma dressed hurriedly and grabbed her papers. Then she was gone. At around lunchtime Carlisle received a text from Emma to say that she had been passed a Brief which involved a court hearing in Birmingham which would start tomorrow and go on for the rest of the week. For Carlisle it was back to work as usual followed by the battle with thousands of fellow commuters at 5-30pm and a dreary evening spent largely sitting watching television in his bedsit with the neighbours rowing and throwing crockery at each other. The following morning dawned unexpectedly fine and Carlisle arrived at work early where he met Commodore Vincent.

'Big day today,' announced the commodore. 'The Americans are due to sign the contract for the purchase and joint development of the Darkforce Schrodinger system. Their representatives should be joining us shortly.'

Half an hour later Samantha Langley appeared on behalf of Darkforce followed soon afterwards by U S Ambassador Robert Maddison and Admiral Sherbrook of the US Navy together with their entourage of assistants and people carrying files and brief cases. Everyone was ushered into a large boardroom and sat around an enormous oak table. Samantha made the introductions and summarised the Schrodinger technology. The Americans confirmed they were impressed by the system and wished to go ahead with buying it for their own armed forces. The parties then proceeded to sign official documents, and Carlisle was invited to take part in this process signing on behalf of HM Government. Samantha signed on behalf of Darkforce. By the end of the morning the task was complete, and the parties began to disperse. Samantha was on her mobile phone speaking to her boss, Carl Jaeger who was in New York and was pleased to inform him that the Americans had signed up for the Schrodinger system.

'I think that's worth a celebration' said Samantha to Carlisle when she had finished her call. She glanced at her wristwatch. 'I think it's time for a bite of lunch, don't you?'

Carlisle nodded in agreement as they headed out of the MOD building to a surprisingly bright and sunny day. Then Samantha's mobile phone rang, and Carl Jaeger was following up the earlier conversation. Suddenly Samantha gave a whoop of joy.

'Wow! I'm rich!' she exclaimed and began dancing around in the busy London street.

'Hey, be careful,' cautioned Carlisle as Samantha narrowly avoided being run over by a black taxi.

'Eddie, I'm rich!' called Samantha. 'Carl's just informed me that the Board of Darkforce have awarded me a bonus of two million dollars. That's on top of the million-dollar bonus for signing up the Malaysians and the Saudis… and the five hundred thousand Darkforce shares… the share price of the Company is powering through the roof right now!'

Samantha kissed Carlisle on his lips and on his chin. He found this display somewhat embarrassing.

'Well, you will be pleased,' replied Carlisle, his voice devoid of emotion or excitement.

'Oh, Eddie! You Englishmen are all the same. The Martians could land in St James's Park, and you'd just invite them to have a cup of tea!' Samantha admonished him frustratedly. 'You're all such stuffed shirts.'

'I was thinking of a good bottle of champagne at the Café Royal actually,' replied Carlisle as all of a sudden Samantha locked him in a tight embrace kissing him passionately.

'I love you!' Samantha told him and hurriedly unzipped and discarded the trousers of the dark pin striped business suit she was wearing, then resumed her tight embrace.

In the busy thoroughfare Carlisle was aware of a screech of brakes followed by several loud bangs and the tinkling of breaking glass. As he sought manfully to steer Samantha into the cover of a side alley off St James' Park and into a reassuringly dense thicket of bushes he heard a loud argument between a number of motorists.

'Can't you look where you're fucking going?' bemoaned the London taxi driver. 'Look at the state of my cab. I've just spent two thousand pounds having the bodywork done up after some other halfwit ran into the back of it in the Edgeware Road.'

'I'm terribly sorry,' replied the man who had clearly run into him. 'But I was distracted by the bare lady.'

'What bare lady?' retorted the taxi driver. They looked around but there was no such person to be seen. Another man, who had run into the man who hit the taxi, said he thought he had seen something but must have been mistaken.

In the meantime, Samantha shoved Carlisle unceremoniously behind a large and substantial laurel hedge which provided good cover and pulled him to her once again, kissing him lasciviously. Carlisle realised that his own trousers were round his ankles as he returned Samantha's kisses. Then they were on the ground with Samantha on top thrusting down upon him with passion. Carlisle found the ground damp and uncomfortable but lost sense of the passing of time until eventually they were prodded by a man with a stick or baton who said he was from 'Security' and told them to leave. Upon coming to her senses Samantha realised she was missing her trousers and did not know where they were. Cautiously Carlisle looked up and down the roadway where they had commenced their embraces. There was quite a lot of broken glass and debris but fortunately the damaged vehicles and their drivers appeared to have gone. Nevertheless, there was no sign of Samantha's missing trousers until he finally located them where they had blown against a tree near the side of the road. Samantha was relieved to be reunited with her clothing.

'Where to, now?' Carlisle asked her.

'My place,' replied Samantha. 'I don't think we'll be bothered by security men there.'

Carlisle was in full agreement, and they took a taxi, a different vehicle to the one in the accident. Before they entered the roadway where Samantha's penthouse apartment was situated Samantha called in at a chemist's apparently to get some medication for her hay fever.

'In November?' queried Carlisle.

Samantha winked and indeed within the twinkle of an eye they were in her bedroom hurriedly pulling off all their clothes and leaving them strewn untidily around the bedroom. Samantha handed Carlisle the pack of twenty-four condoms she had just purchased.

'Shall I give you a hand?' she suggested helpfully. Carlisle was pleased to accept the invitation.

Then Samantha was lying on her back with her fine legs drawn apart and Carlisle was glad to resume their love making begun in St James' Park.

The following day Samantha was flying off to Brazil to meet a delegation from several Latin American countries. Emma was away doing a trial in Stoke on Trent. Carlisle was feeling the anti-climax as it started to rain once more. Naomi brought a heavy stack of new files into his offices and deposited them unceremoniously upon his desk to join the stack of work which was already sitting there awaiting his attention. Then his mobile phone rang. It was an unfamiliar number which appeared foreign.

'Hello… Eddie,' announced the caller. 'It's Alex.'

Chapter 14

'EDDIE... I'M SORRY. IT DIDN'T turn out as I'd hoped,' apologised Alex. 'It was terrible. I ended up killing people. I was caught up in a gun battle.'

'What?' exclaimed Carlisle. 'Are you in serious trouble?'

'No... no... not at all,' replied Alex. 'On the contrary... I'm being given a reward... a big one. I was helping the authorities out there to combat ivory poachers.'

'I just don't know what to say. I am dumbfounded,' stammered Carlisle. For once he was lost for words.

Alex proceeded to tell Carlisle about her many adventures in West Africa including being chased and fired upon by pirates in the Gulf of Guinea.

'I would not have believed it possible,' responded Carlisle.

'Well... I'm on my way home now... If you'll still have me,' said Alex.

'Yes... I'll be very glad... and relieved to see you,' acknowledged Carlisle. 'But you could have kept in touch. I'll be back at the farm tomorrow evening. I think we have some catching up to do.'

For the rest of the day Carlisle's mind was in a state of turmoil. On the one hand he was relieved that Alex had at last contacted him and was on her way home. On the other hand, she would have a lot of explaining to do. In particular he would want to know about this young African man she had gone with. It sounded decidedly inappropriate.

The following evening Carlisle caught the 6-30pm train for Norwich from Liverpool Street. He had texted Alex to let her know and she had texted him in reply to confirm she would be at the station in Norwich to meet him. Alex was true to her word even though she had only just got home herself that afternoon and met him on the station concourse, greeting him with a big hug and kisses. At that point, the air raid alarm sounded with an ominous wail and people began hurrying for cover.

'Come on, let's get away from here,' urged Carlisle.

Alex had brought her white Alfa Romeo, and they were soon heading out of the city using Alex's knowledge of back routes and short cuts to circumvent the inevitable traffic jams and holdups. They had just left the town when there was a big explosion somewhere behind them in the city centre. Subsequently they heard further explosions and detonations, and Carlisle urged Alex to 'step on the gas.'

'Oh, those lovely historic buildings,' sighed Alex. 'This is why I escaped to Africa... if only for a short while. I'm afraid one might say it was a case of out of the frying pan into the fire.'

They managed to arrive back at the farm in one piece where they were greeted by assorted animals. Alex was still feeling very jet lagged after her flight not to mention her incredible experiences. By 9pm she was ready to turn in and it was not until the following morning when they switched on the radio that they learned that the main railway station in Norwich had been hit by Russian missiles. The cathedral had also been hit and damaged and there were more than three hundred casualties in the city. Even the mustard factory had been hit. Both of them knew how lucky they had been. Alex was glad that her husband was now in command of a desk in Whitehall. It was after all what she had wanted for a long time. Carlisle continued to be most concerned as to what Alex had been up to for the past few weeks, but he decided this was not the time to broach the subject. On Sunday morning he joined Jack Blofield to go sailing the *Lord Rodney*. They quanted the heavy craft up the still badly overgrown dyke and then out into open water on Barton Broad. At lunchtime they tied up at the staithe at Neatishead and adjourned to a convenient local hostelry.

'So, how's that wife of yours?' enquired Jack. 'I expect your glad she's finally returned safe and sound.'

'Well... certainly,' replied Carlisle, 'but I'm just dumbfounded as to the things she's been up to. Going off to West Africa with some Gabonese chap. Being chased and shot at by pirates and then to cap it all getting involved in some big gun battle with poachers up the jungle in the Congo.'

Jack sat thoughtfully for a short while and supped his pint of mild.

'You know there's a traditional way of dealing with a woman who's inclined to roam,' advised Jack with his air of wisdom. 'Give her a brace of brats to look after. Start a family. She'll be so busy she won't have time to go capering off to darkest Africa or anywhere else for that matter.'

'You know... I think you're right,' acknowledged Carlisle. 'I won't press her just now though. She needs time to get her bearings.'

'Oh, yes. Take yer time,' counselled Jack, 'but don't leave it too long, mind... otherwise she'll be gallivanting off again with that chap... or whoever.'

Monday morning found Carlisle back at his desk in London. The stack of files was still there and he did his best to work through them. At around 12 noon he was buzzed by Naomi who informed him that Lady Hamilton Wallingford was on the line.

'Eddie, darling. I've finished my trial in Stoke and I'll be back in London by this evening. I thought I might prepare a meal for the two of us at my place.'

Being too much of a gentleman to turn her down Carlisle politely accepted but then realised he was on a course which was bound to result in some form of collision. He would have to find a way of dealing with the situation while causing as little damage as possible. Throughout the afternoon he kept thinking of the lyrics of that song by the Kinks that went something along the lines 'that two girls are too many, threes a crowd and four your dead.' Come 5-30pm and he was off to the tube station to do battle with all the other hordes of commuters. Emma greeted him with hugs and kisses. Carlisle felt guilty. Sooner or later, he was going to have to tell her that Alex was home. Emma had clearly gone to some effort to prepare a romantic candlelit dinner for them both. There was Russian caviar for the starter.

'How did you manage to get hold of that?' asked Carlisle.

'I have my sources of supply,' replied Emma cagily. 'I have a younger cousin who works at Harrods. They kept something behind the counter for me.'

For the main course Emma provided Carlisle with venison while she had something which might have appeared similar, but she said was created from plant-based ingredients. Eventually they finished their meal and Emma said she wanted to show him some new underwear she had acquired in Stoke on Trent.

'I've been thinking,' said Emma as she began to undress. 'I know you hate your digs which the Ministry have provided. Why don't you move in with me? You can still go home sometimes at the weekends to check up on the farm. But it would make sense. The truth is... I wouldn't want to let you slip through my fingers.'

Carlisle was feeling guilty again, but he admired Emma's dark stockings and the transparent bodice which was laced up at the front.

'It comes with matching briefs, but I took them off earlier,' Emma informed him as Carlisle's mobile phone rang. He recognised the number instantly.

'Excuse me one moment,' he apologised to Emma. 'Private call... government business...'

Carlisle hurried into the next room. It was Alex on the line. Carlisle tried to speak to her in hushed tones. Alex was telling him about the various animals at the farm and how Myrtle the donkey had been very awkward that evening. They spoke for some time and discussed the Russian rocket attacks.

'You will take care won't you, darling,' Carlisle urged Alex. 'You know I love you.'

'Even after I've been a very naughty girl?' replied Alex. 'What I need is a good spanking... across your lap.'

'I'm looking forward to coming home on Friday. I'll give you a good spanking... for starters.'

Alex giggled in anticipation. Carlisle turned and saw Emma standing right behind him listening in to the phone conversation. There was a pause.

'Sorry, darling... must go now,' Carlisle apologised to Alex.

'I'm sorry, Emma. You may have gathered… Alex is back home. She arrived last Friday… Been to West Africa of all places.'

Emma not so much burst but exploded into floods of tears of rage and disappointment. Carlisle sought to calm her down and Katie the dog whimpered at her feet. This was not the situation Carlisle wanted. He tried to kiss her, but she turned away. Eventually he persuaded her to sit down with him on the settee.

'Emma… Alex is my wife. You know that. Nothing has changed… so why all these tears?'

'I thought you were mine,' sniffled Emma. 'I think I was unrealistic.'

'Look here, Emma. Dry your eyes. I'm likely to be here in London for some time to come. I hate my digs as you know. I'll be very glad to move in with you during the working week… if you'll have me. How does that sound?'

Emma managed a forced smile and Carlisle succeeded in giving her a kiss. Katie the dog rested her chin on Carlisle's knee and the cats emerged from wherever they had taken cover. Eventually Emma led them all upstairs to her room and Carlisle found himself in bed with Emma once again. She lay on top of him, and he could feel her tears upon his face in the darkness. Come the morning back at his desk Carlisle did his best to work through the mountain of files. They were all still there from last Friday. There was a text from Samantha on his mobile phone. She was now in Buenos Aires trying to interest the Argentinians in Darkforce systems. On Wednesday she was due to fly to Santiago to meet the Chileans. He mused that at least that would keep her busy for a while. Commodore Vincent breezed into his office, cheerful as ever notwithstanding the Russian missile strikes over the past weekend.

'Look, Eddie… We want you to nip down to Plymouth and check up on the Aurora's refit. We'd like to get her back in the water as soon as possible but realistically things are likely to take a while. You know how it is with contractors.'

'Don't I know it, sir,' acknowledged Carlisle.

'We're taking the opportunity to install launchers for the new Anglo-American Warhawk cruise missile and… this is very hush hush… incorporate the Darkforce Schrodinger system as well. When the job's finished Aurora will be one of the most heavily armed ships in our fleet... but not a word to anyone. You know what I mean.'

'That certainly sounds impressive, sir,' said Carlisle, 'But what about all this work here on my desk?'

'Oh, leave it until you get back,' replied the commodore dismissively. 'I suggest you stay in Plymouth until at least the end of the week. Pack a small suitcase or holdall. Don't forget your toothbrush and your shaver. The sooner you can get down there the better. Oh, by the way, the Japanese have a destroyer visiting that part of the world. I think you've met her captain... a chap called Takahashi.'

'Ah, yes,' acknowledged Carlisle. 'I met him not so long ago. He invited me for dinner on his destroyer... the *Yahagi*.'

'Well, keep them sweet as they say,' replied the commodore. 'We need all the friends and allies we can get nowadays.'

Carlisle took the train from Paddington and took due note of the gaping holes in the roof of the huge terminus, the result of some of Mr Vatutin's latest missile attacks. Fortunately, his journey down to Plymouth was largely uneventful until the train drew near the city and the naval base. Held up by adverse signals the train was at a standstill for more than two hours while a Russian attack was taking place. Carlisle observed explosions in both the built-up areas of Plymouth as well as the dockyard facilities. He did not see any missiles actually strike the Frigate Refit Complex but more than one landed perilously close. Great columns of smoke and dust rose literally hundreds of feet into the air. Eventually the train got on the move once more and arrived at the station where Carlisle was relieved to be met by Clive Robinson, the project manager from Babrock who was overseeing the Aurora's refit.

'We've moved Aurora out of the complex,' explained Clive. 'It was getting too hairy in there, so we've moved her out of the way to a place called Blackwater Creek. It's tucked away behind that headland you can see over there. Now the Ruskies can't see her, and she would be an almost impossible target because of the topography. '

They stopped at a jetty and took a lift in a small launch passing several other naval vessels on their way.

'There's Aurora's sister, or should I say brother, Achilles,' pointed out Clive. 'You can see the serious damage caused by a missile. That was last month.'

Carlisle could clearly see where the missile had struck the frigate amidships destroying the command-and-control centres.

'We didn't want the same thing to happen to Aurora,' explained Clive.

Finally, Carlisle was back aboard his ship although it was full of workmen and dockyard technicians and covered in tarpaulins. Two large barges, one on either side of the vessel supported a huge crane which was actually in the process of swinging a heavy piece of equipment into position forward of the bridge structure.

'That's the Type 58 launcher for the new Warhawk cruise missiles,' said Clive. 'It will greatly improve the firepower of your frigate. The missiles can be used either for land attack or against other ships.'

What is that installation behind the funnel?' enquired Carlisle.

'That's the new Japanese manufactured Sea Urchin gun system,' replied Clive. 'It has a rate of fire of four thousand rounds per minute and an effective range of eight thousand metres. It is highly effective against both air and surface targets.'

Carlisle reflected upon the many instances he had experienced when such a weapon would have been very useful. Clive proceeded to give him a full guided tour of the Aurora following which Carlisle retired to his private cabin. There were workmen everywhere and the noise was overwhelming, but Carlisle was pleasantly surprised to be greeted by his personal steward, David Warwick.

'I'm terribly sorry about all the mess, sir,' apologised David. 'I only arrived back on board yesterday afternoon. I know it resembles a construction site right now, but I'll do my best to create some kind of order out of chaos… at least in this bit of the ship.'

'Don't trouble yourself too much, David,' advised Carlisle. 'You'll be fighting a losing battle. I'm here until the end of the week. Then my wife will expect me back at the farm for the weekend.'

The following morning Carlisle woke early as the workmen and technicians arrived. They were clearly under pressure to get on with the refit as quickly as possible. David brought Carlisle a full English breakfast with plenty of bacon and hot buttered toast. He was just in the course of finishing his repast when the sound of a ship's hooter drew his attention. He looked out and was a little surprised to observe a destroyer flying the flag of the Japanese Navy with the rising sun emblem. The vessel was being assisted by two tugs and moored at a jetty on the far side of the creek. Later he managed to get a lift in a launch and was pleased to find that the destroyer was the *Yahagi,* and her captain was still Lieutenant Commander Chuichi Takahashi. It was a cold and murky day, but Carlisle continued to be impressed by the high standards of the Japanese crew. Showing his security pass Carlisle spoke to a Japanese Petty Officer who spoke some English and within a short time Carlisle was welcomed aboard and escorted to the bridge by Lieutenant Sendai. There he was able to resume his acquaintance with the captain.

'We are here to support the security agreement between our countries,' explained Takahashi. 'The first priority is to refuel and take on board live ammunition. Then we will be heading out to sea on exercises. You are very welcome to remain on board as our guest. It will be an honour.'

Carlisle remembered Commodore Vincent asking him to cultivate good relations, so he warmly accepted the captain's invitation. Before long, the red warning flags were flying as barges and lighters came alongside with their cargos of lethal shells and missiles. This task continued all day and into the night. It was not until dawn the next day that the *Yahagi* was able to set sail and, assisted by a tug, passed down through the River Tamar and out to sea. Before long she was joined by the British frigate, Arethusa, and Carlisle was able to occupy himself usefully as an unofficial liaison officer and translator. Eventually when they were about forty miles south of the Cornish coastline a petty officer in the *Yahagi's* Operations Room was reporting four aircraft approaching from the northeast and Takahashi called his ship to Action Stations. The planes were identified as being from RNAS Culdrose, but it was a good opportunity for the crew of the *Yahagi* to test their skills and procedures. Suddenly there was a roar of aero engines as the aircraft, which

Carlisle instantly recognised as very elderly Hawker Hunters now privately operated, came thundering in at wave top height and passed either side of the two naval ships at flashing speed and creating wakes on the surface of the sea .The crews of the *Yahagi* and the *Arethusa* were able to practice co-ordinated manoeuvres and working out defensive tactics. Before the flight of Hunters had finished their simulated attack radar operators on both warships were reporting small surface craft approaching at speed. This was clearly all part of the same exercise but as the small craft sped close to the larger warships, twisting and turning with considerable agility, Carlisle was reminded of his encounters with the Iranian Revolutionary Guards in the Persian Gulf and the Straits of Hormuz. Then all went quiet for some time with the Arethusa and the *Yah*agi steaming in close company. Eventually Lieutenant Commander Takahashi invited Carlisle to dinner with the picture of Admiral Yamamoto staring down at them sternly from the wall of the captain's quarters. Later Takahashi offered a glass of fine quality single malt Scotch whiskey which Carlisle was very pleased to accept. They did not turn in until around midnight and Carlisle was provided with an officer's cabin by a very polite steward. Carlisle did not know what time it was when the klaxons sounded, and the *Yah*agi was brought to Action Stations but outside it was still very dark and clearly the middle of the night. In a slightly disorientated state of mind Carlisle made his way to the Operations Room where he gathered that the Arethusa's Merlin helicopter had picked up a submarine contact. There was no IFF and no NATO or other friendly submarines were reported to be in the vicinity so the assumption had to be made that it was hostile. The *Yah*agi carried two American built anti-submarine helicopters and Takahashi gave orders for them both to be sent urgently to join the hunt. In the meantime, Carlisle found he was able to make himself particularly useful by acting as interpreter since no one in the Arethusa spoke Japanese. Fortuitously Carlisle had spent time on secondment to a Japanese officers' staff college in Yokahama as a young man so he had good knowledge of the language. As the crew of the Arethusa's Merlin helicopter sent information to the *Yahagi* on such matters as the location of the submarine and its course and speed Carlisle was able to pass on this data particularly to Takahashi and his First Officer,

Lieutenant Commander Raizo Yasuda. The pursuit continued and the first of the *Yahagi's* helicopters joined the Arethusa's Merlin. Both helicopters dropped sonar buoys providing further information which confirmed that the submarine was a Russian Delta IV rebuilt for carrying cruise missiles. The Merlin now dropped a homing torpedo and one of the Japanese helicopters did likewise with the weapons converging on the big submarine from opposite directions. The submarine was now reported to be diving to a greater depth and increasing speed. The second Japanese helicopter also joined the attack and dropped a torpedo. Then Chief Petty Officer Sakai in the Operations Room of the *Yahagi* was calling out that he had heard an explosion through his headphones in the immediate vicinity of where the submarine was located. At first it was thought that the submarine would be destroyed but then it became clear that it was still running. Then there was a second detonation and Sakai was reporting that the submarine was rising towards the surface.

'She has broken surface!' called Lieutenant Myoko from one of the *Yahagi's* helicopters. 'She is huge.'

The helicopters transmitted a stream of data to the parent ships which were still about thirty kilometres distant from the damaged Russian vessel. Suddenly Lieutenant Myoko reported that his machine was under fire as he overflew the submarine.

'Someone has fitted a machine gun in the top of the conning tower,' he called. 'We are hit.'

'We will be with you as soon as we can,' advised First Officer Yasuda. 'Can you make it back to the *Yahagi*? Keep out of range of enemy fire.'

'We will try to make it,' responded Lieutenant Myoko, 'But we are losing fuel. I don't know whether we will make it.'

Commander Bob Roxburgh in the Arethusa ordered maximum revolutions and full speed to the location of the Russian submarine.

'I want to try and capture the enemy vessel,' the Commander informed his Japanese companions by radio. 'It's something of an outside chance but it would be some coup if we succeeded.'

There was some discussion aboard the *Yahagi* and First Officer Yasuda expressed concern that the submarine would still be capable of using its weaponry. Both Carlisle and Lieutenant Commander Takahashi both had similar concerns, but Roxburgh had seniority and was in command of the small task group. After another half hour an RAF P-8 Poseidon Long Range Patrol Aircraft from St Mawgam in Cornwall approached the scene being guided by the Allied warships. Once again the submarine was reported to have opened fire with a machine gun. The aircraft radioed that the submarine appeared to be badly damaged and was down by the stern and listing about seven degrees to starboard.

'She may be too badly damaged to fire her torpedoes and missiles,' considered Carlisle.

'That could be a dangerous assumption,' warned Takahashi as both ships drew closer to the submarine which had now been identified by the P-8 aircraft as the Archangelsk and capable of carrying up to 36 cruise missiles as well as torpedoes for defence against surface ships and other submarines.

A few minutes later the *Yahagi*'s damaged helicopter signalled that it was leaking fuel and would soon have to ditch in the Atlantic. Takahashi sought permission from Commander Roxburgh to alter course to retrieve the crippled machine. In the meantime, a signal was received from the US Navy Destroyer, Thomas Kincaid, notifying them that it had set out from Cork accompanied by the Destroyer, Robert S. Gates, to assist in dealing with the damaged Russian submarine. Lieutenant Myoko signalled that he only had fuel remaining for a mere ten minutes of flying time. It was clearly going to be touch and go. Takahashi was worried about the possibility of losing the valuable helicopter. The RAF P-8 Poseidon signalled that the Archangelsk had reduced speed to just five knots and its list had increased to nine degrees.

'She is slowly sinking,' observed Takahashi and conferred with First Officer Yasuda. 'We had better start making preparations for rescuing survivors.'

Not long afterwards the crew of the *Yahagi* were glad to see their damaged helicopter hove into view and no time was lost in hauling the machine safely back on board and into the hanger. Lieutenant Myoko told them that for the past few minutes his fuel gauge had shown empty, and he and his navigator and winchman were seriously expecting to imminently end up in the grey wastes of the Ocean. Having safely retrieved their helicopter the crew of the

Yahagi sought to catch up with the Arethusa which was soon back in company and not long afterwards visual contact was made with the Archangelsk. Even at long range in the gathering gloom of the late afternoon it was clear that the submarine was in a bad state with its list to starboard clearly visible and its stern heavily awash. Commander Roxburgh sought to make radio contact with the Archangelsk and succeeded in speaking to the captain whose name was Mikhail Suvurov. Initially the Russian captain was warning the Allied units to keep away and that his missile launchers and torpedo tubes were still in action but as his vessel's list slowly increased and its stern settled lower in the water he clearly assessed the impossibility of his situation and began entering negotiations for his crew to be rescued and taken off. Commander Roxburgh still harboured a desire to capture the big submarine intact and to somehow get it to a friendly port. He conferred with Takahashi, making good use of Carlisle's skills as an interpreter, and then spoke by secure link with the captain of the Thomas Kincaid, Lieutenant Commander Brad Kingham. The American captain said he had not yet had an opportunity to assess the Russian vessel's condition but he thought there might be a chance of towing it to Bantry Bay in south west Ireland where there was a deep water harbour. Roxburgh responded that he thought this was the best option if it could be pulled off. The American and British commanders duly made contact with the appropriate authorities in Ireland and arrangements were made for an ocean going salvage tug to be despatched supported by the Irish naval patrol vessel, Maeve.

In the meantime the condition of the Archangelsk worsened but Commander Roxburgh succeeded in gaining permission for members of his crew to come aboard the submarine suitably equipped with pumps and shoring timbers when Captain Suvurov explained that twenty-four members of his crew including his senior engineering officer were trapped in the after compartments and several men had already drowned. Captain Suvurov also gave permission for some members of his crew to be taken off to safety aboard the Arethusa and the *Yahagi*. After about an hour, with the Allied warships also making use of their own pumps, the water level in the Archangelsk, while not reducing, was not rising so quickly. Nevertheless, both Carlisle and Takahashi were very doubtful of the chances of getting the submarine safely to an Irish port. There was also a forecast of bad weather coming in from the west which could certainly scupper any salvage effort. It was at about 8-30pm that the klaxons sounded the alarm and crewmen scrambled to their Action Stations on the Arethusa and the *Yahagi*. Carlisle joined Lieutenant Commander Takahashi and other officers in the Operations Room of the Japanese destroyer. A Russian Tupolev long range bomber had been detected by radar at a range of around sixty miles and when the range closed further Takahashi ordered the firing of a Standard missile. The Russian bomber now turned away and headed back north but not before it had launched two AS-38 anti-ship missiles towards the Allied vessels. Both the Arethusa and the *Yahagi* fired chaff rockets and one of the incoming missiles was decoyed away but the other one continued on its bearing. Once it had come within range Commander Roxburgh ordered the firing of a salvo of Aster 15 anti-aircraft missiles and the 5-inch guns of both Allied warships began blasting defiance. The pumps had to be detached from the Archangelsk to give the warships freedom to manoeuvre. Inevitably the water level in the submarine began rising again and its list increased. When the surviving Russian AS-38 missile was a mere five miles from the group centred around the crippled submarine Takahashi ordered the firing of another Standard missile while Roxburgh launched another salvo of Aster 15s. The AS-38 finally exploded when it was so close that fragments of the missile struck the Arethusa and the *Yahagi* and also the Archangelsk. Indeed, there was speculation aboard the Allied vessels that the Russian Navy was attempting to sink its own submarine to try to prevent it being taken to an Allied port. This line of thought was given further credence when with the coming of dawn the Russians launched another attack which began with a second Tupolev long range bomber shadowing the vessels at extreme range and then guiding in a force of six Backfire supersonic bombers. Roxburgh requested air cover from the UK and was informed that a pair of American F-15s had been scrambled from RAF Brawdy. Takahashi fired a Standard missile at long range at the shadowing Tupolev which turned away to the north. However, the Backfires were closing rapidly, and Takahashi ordered the despatch of two further SAMs. All eyes were now transfixed on the Air Warfare plot. The Backfires descended to low altitude making themselves difficult targets and even disappearing from the AW plot for a while which Carlisle found most worrisome. The F-15s were still a long way from making an intercept. Suddenly the Arethusa reported that the Russian bombers had reappeared on radar and were now only seven miles to the northwest. Three of the Backfires launched missiles and then turned away one hundred and eighty degrees. The other three bombers continued their attack at high speed and 'on the deck.' Roxburgh fired a salvo of Asters and two of the incoming anti-ship missiles were hit and exploded. Another incoming missile was decoyed away but the three bombers were now making their attack. Both the Arethusa and the *Yahagi* were firing their guns continuously creating palls of drifting cordite smoke. The leading bomber attacked the Arethusa with one bomb exploding in the sea fifty yards off the starboard quarter as the frigate twisted and turned under full power as it attempted to dodge the falling bombs. A second bomb hit the sea and bounced across the frigate's flight deck before ending up lodged in the helicopter hangar and starting fires in the adjoining galleys. The second Backfire attacked the *Yahagi* while the third aircraft targeted the Archangelsk. A heavy bomb exploded in the sea close to the port bow of the crippled submarine. However, as the aircraft slowed down to deliver the coup de grace it suddenly exploded in a fireball. The plane attacking the *Yahagi* was similarly taken out and cartwheeled into the sea scattering debris as it crashed at high speed. A signal from the Thomas Kincaid informed the Allied vessels that the American destroyer, recently refitted with the state of the art AEGIS 4000 system linked to the Valkyrie hypersonic missile, had successfully beaten off the Russian attack. The Archangelsk was now unable to move under its own power and most of its crew were taken off with the exception of Captain Suvurov and First Officer Yakovlev together with a handful of men including sailors from the Arethusa led by a Lieutenant Grenville. The submarine was then taken in tow by the *Yahagi* and dragged at five knots towards Bantry Bay. After several hours the salvage tug, Ocean Princess, arrived on the scene to assist with the towing of the severely damaged and waterlogged Archangelsk. Meanwhile the Thomas Kincaid and the Robert S. Gates stood by to repel any renewed Russian attacks. Carlisle and Takahashi were also concerned about the potential threat of a submarine attack and their fears proved well founded when a patrolling RAF P-8 Poseidon aircraft reported that it had dropped homing torpedoes in pursuit of a hostile submarine contact forty miles to the northeast. Commander Roxburgh sent his Merlin helicopter out to patrol the surrounding ocean and the aircraft was quickly joined by the *Yahagi*'s undamaged helicopter. The journey to Bantry Bay seemed to Carlisle to take forever but at dawn the following morning the Irish coast came within sight and the Irish naval patrol vessel, Maeve, also appeared to assist with the salvage work and to help guide the flotilla into the harbour. At this point, the alarms sounded once again as a pair of Russian Backfire bombers were reported approaching at speed from the northwest over the Atlantic. Carlisle felt they had come all this way to see their prize destroyed at the last hurdle but the crew of the Thomas Kincaid were on high alert and hypersonic Valkyrie missiles were fired at the incoming intruders which soon vanished from the Air Warfare plot.

With difficulty the Archangelsk was manoeuvred into a berth where there was some protection from the surrounding topography and the American destroyers remained on station to give missile protection against the expected continuing attacks. The Irish authorities were initially enthusiastic about the capture of the Russian submarine, but concerns began to grow that its presence made Bantry Bay with its oil terminal and storage facilities a target for the Russians. It was soon decided that the Archangelsk should be patched up as quickly as possible and moved to a location in the UK. During this drama Carlisle's mobile phone rang.

'Hi, Eddie,' called Alex. 'Will you be home this weekend?'

'I'll do my best,' replied Carlisle. 'I can't say where I am, of course, or what I am doing right now. I'll keep in touch.'

As it turned out the *Yahagi* was still required to help provide support for the repairs to the submarine, but Lieutenant Commander Takahashi thanked Carlisle for his valuable assistance and said he understood if Carlisle wished to return home on leave. Carlisle made his way to Shannon Airport where, by good fortune he was able to board a flight to Norwich on Saturday morning.

Chapter 15

CARLISLE PUT ON HIS DRESSING gown to give some protection from the early December chill and made his way downstairs followed by an entourage of dogs and cats who were all eager for sustenance. Alex was already outside with Sandra attending to the horses and other animals. He could clearly hear Myrtle the donkey braying in protest. His first priority was to feed the household menagerie. This task accomplished he switched on the radio and sat down at the kitchen table to listen to the news. In northern Norway there was fierce fighting between Russian and NATO forces and the Russians had taken Bodo airbase. The prospect of the Russians being just the other side of the North Sea was distinctly unappealing. In continental Europe, the Russians were also expanding their territorial gains, and Berlin was directly threatened by the Russian Army. Large tracts of Poland had also been overrun by the Russians and Warsaw was surrounded and under siege. The situation looked very bad indeed although there were some glimmers of hope. Jack McConnell had now become President of the United States and had immediately put his country on a war footing, increasing industrial production and taking steps to send large numbers of troops and military equipment to the European theatre. The 82nd Airborne Division had already arrived in Germany together with advanced elements of the 1st Armoured Division and these ground forces were being backed up by airpower. Breaking news was that the liner, *Queen of Sheba*, sailing in a huge troop convoy across the Atlantic had been hit overnight by a Russian missile and set on fire. She was carrying five thousand American soldiers previously based in Texas and efforts to rescue the people from the stricken liner were being severely hindered by bad weather. The news made Carlisle feel very frustrated and he wished he could be back at sea in command of the Aurora and taking revenge on the Russian forces. He continued listening to the reports of disasters and setbacks until his attention was interrupted by a knock on the front door. It was Tracey in her red Royal Mail van.

'One to sign for, Eddie,' called Tracey. 'Interesting postmark and stamp.' Carlisle obliged and hoped it was not from Robert Knighton's solicitors.

He noted it was addressed to Alex and the colourful stamp was from the Congo. Alex appeared coming from the stables.

'One for you, I think,' said Carlisle as he handed her the letter. 'It looks rather official.'

Alex accepted the letter and took it indoors to open it.

'What does it say?' asked Carlisle inquisitively peering over her shoulder.

'It's from the Wildlife Protection Department of the Congo,' replied Alex. 'They want me to attend an award ceremony in Brazzaville... for my part in helping to save their country's wildlife.'

'You're not going, of course,' said Carlisle dismissively.

'Well, actually I do want to attend it,' responded Alex. 'They'll be giving me a reward too... a lot of money... from the governments of France and the Congo... and the World Wildlife Fund as well.'

'How much money?' asked Carlisle.

'It could amount to more than fifty thousand pounds altogether. It's not to be dismissed just like that, Eddie,' explained Alex.

For once Carlisle felt confused. Having got Alex safely back from the jungles of West Africa he did not wish her to disappear in that direction yet again. There was also the danger from enemy action.

'There is a war on, you know,' he warned Alex.

Alex made no reply. She wished to avoid an enormous row. After breakfast they went sailing in the *Moonbreeze*, quanting up the dyke to Barton Broad and out onto the open water. Carlisle enjoyed this time of year when the holidaymakers had gone home, and Broadland was left to the wildlife. He looked up at the broad skies to observe a flock of wild geese in almost perfect v-formation honking to each other as they flew overhead on their way to wherever. After sailing the full length of Barton Broad, they navigated cautiously into a quiet corner hidden amongst the reed beds with just the wildlife for company. Alex found some stale bread which she broke into small pieces and distributed amongst some mallards who had decided it was already lunch time. Carlisle carefully eased the mud weight over the bows to anchor the *Moonbreeze* in place. Alex produced a plate of sandwiches for them both and a scotch egg for Carlisle and both of them sat down in the stern well. All seemed at peace. There was no sign of war or conflict.

'Auntie Isabella wants us to go over to Como for Christmas,' remarked Alex.

''I think that's a non-starter,' replied Carlisle. 'The national governments are requisitioning all the airliners as troop carriers. There won't be any civilian flights.'

'I guess you're right,' responded Alex disappointedly. 'I don't know how long it will take for peace and normality to return.'

'Don't get too despondent, Alex,' counselled Carlisle. 'I've been thinking… We shouldn't put off everything to some indeterminate time in the future. After all who knows what might happen tomorrow? I know you very much want to have a family… by which, of course, I don't just mean Auntie Isabella and Uncle Giovanni.'

'Children!' exclaimed Alex, her countenance brightening. 'Do you think I should stop taking the pill?'

'That's the gist of my drift,' acknowledged Carlisle as he handed a morsel of his scotch egg to a mallard drake who had alighted on the stern decking next to him.

'I've just finished my period,' commented Alex while eating a cucumber sandwich. 'As you say, Eddie, why put everything off until sometime later.'

'Come on,' she called. Carlisle stopped feeding the mallards and followed Alex into the cabin where she reclined on the bed. 'I'll keep my sweater on for now… and my woolly socks... It's cold,' said Alex shivering.

Carlisle willingly obliged without delay. They did not pause to close the curtains. There was no one else around to see their love making save for the wild fowl who were only interested in food. Alex gripped the bed head and presently began to moan with pleasure, softly at first but then louder until she cried out in a final crescendo which reverberated across the open marshes.

'One of our best efforts. I enjoyed that,' complimented Alex as they disentangled themselves 'Would you care for a cup of tea?' enquired Carlisle politely.

'Well, perhaps in a while once I'm the right way up,' replied Alex.

Later in the day once they were back at the Farm and Alex had attended to the animals, ably assisted by Sandra and Gaz, Alex prepared for Carlisle his favourite roast Pheasant. It was fortunate that they lived in the depths of the countryside, not only because they were not a priority target for Mr Vatutin's missiles but also because food remained largely plentiful notwithstanding the recent introduction of rationing. Carlisle referred to them as living off the land. Whatever happened people like Jack Blofield and his sons would be able to keep Alex and himself properly fed.

The following day Carlisle and Alex took the *Moonbreeze* out once again and after sailing up and down Barton Broad several times they tied up at the staithe at Neatishead and adjourned to the 'Fox & Hounds' for lunch. Carlisle was pleased that they were given a table by a window with attractive views across the Broad and furthermore he was able to choose Woodcock from the Specials Menu. Alex chose a vegetarian option.

'You know, we're fortunate to live out here in rural Norfolk,' commented Carlisle. 'If we were in a town or city I don't think the food would be anything like as good at the moment.'

For pudding Carlisle chose the landlady's home-made apple dumpling with lashings of hot custard. Alex opted for just a cup of coffee and began looking at her watch.

'No cause for us to hurry,' commented Carlisle.

'Shall we find our secret spot amongst the reeds again?'' asked Alex. 'I put a heater in the aft cabin.'

'Well done, Alex,' agreed Carlisle. 'It was really good yesterday. Even better than Doris Attleborough's apple dumplings…The only downside was that it felt cold in there. It's just the time of year.'

'You seafaring chaps are supposed to be used to a bit of cold weather,' quipped Alex.

They returned to the *Moonbreeze* and sailed across the open water of Barton Broad towards their secret location. As they approached the place the deep keel of the hundred-year-old yacht stuck firmly in the silt, and they ground to a standstill. Alex had to join Carlisle and the two of them pushed on the quant pole with all their strength. At first it appeared they were stranded well away from the navigation channel but finally the yacht was free, and they slowly manoeuvred the graceful craft into position. Here it was well secluded amongst the reeds, and they should be left in peace. Carlisle dropped the mud weight over the bows with a hefty splash. When he came back inside Alex had already dispensed with her trousers although she was still wearing a Parker over a thick sweater and was arranging the solar powered heater in the aft cabin.

'New technology,' commented Alex. 'It doesn't produce all that much warmth but it's better than nothing.'

It still felt cold in the *Moonbreeze* but Alex and Carlisle shrugged off the chill. With enthusiasm Alex assisted Carlisle in pulling off his trousers. He put up no resistance. Then she was backing towards him in a careful manoeuvre which reminded Carlisle of her reversing their Range Rover. She had taken off her Parker but still wore her big sweater. Carlisle had time only to kiss Alex briefly once on the left cheek and then on the right. Once again they had not closed the curtains because there was no one else there to see them. Carlisle was pleased to observe that Alex was making an effort to ensure that her shirt tails and sweater were kept above her waist Presently Alex began to moan with pleasure, gently at first and then with greater volume until her cries of ecstasy burst forth and reverberated around the surrounding wilderness. After a while they rolled over so that Carlisle was on top, and Alex entwined her fine legs possessively around his back.

'I'm not going to let you go,' Alex informed Carlisle. He was reminded of Geoffrey Chaucer's Knight's Tale and that what all women wanted more than anything else was sovereignty over men.

'Eventually Jack and Sandra and the lads might wonder where we are and come looking for us,' replied Carlisle.

'It might take them quite a long time to find us,' responded Alex. 'We'll be locked tightly together. They'll need crowbars to separate us.'

'Or possibly the fire brigade,' quipped Carlisle.

'Let's hope our efforts bring success,' considered Carlisle.

'We'll probably have to be patient,' cautioned Alex. 'I know of plenty of couples who've been trying for a baby for months... years even.

Alex continued to keep her long legs in the air for a while until they realised that the winter sun was losing its strength, and they needed to be back at the Farm before darkness fell. Carlisle pulled hard on the mud weight and the *Moonbreeze* began to drift as they set sail down Barton Broad. Alex took hold of the tiller as the graceful yacht gathered momentum with the sun beginning to set in a great panorama of red and gold with the sunbeams dancing on the rippled surface of the water. A light northerly wind hastened their progress but then brought a chill.

In the morning Alex drove Carlisle to the airport where he caught a flight down to Exeter followed by a train to Plymouth. He had just stepped out onto the platform at the port city when his mobile phone rang.

'Look, Eddie. Bit of a change of plan,' announced Commodore Vincent from his desk in London. 'You know Aurora's not going to be ready for a while yet. But there's a frigate, Galatea. She's been laid up in the Reserve Fleet for several years. You'll find her in the water just outside the Frigate Refit Complex. We need every ship we can get at the moment. There's already a party working on her under a Lieutenant Charles Dunbar and a Chief Petty Officer MacBride. Your orders are to take command and get her to sea... as quickly as you can. You'll receive further instructions very soon.'

Carlisle took a lift on a navy launch and arrived at a jetty where the Galatea was moored with several other vessels. Initially no one appeared to take much notice of him, but he spoke to a rating who called a petty officer whose name was Trevelyan.

'Welcome aboard, sir. I'll find Lieutenant Dunbar,' said Trevelyan, saluting. 'I believe he's with the Chief Engineering Officer attending to our engines. They're newly overhauled but there are always bugs needing to be ironed out.'

Lieutenant Dunbar appeared shortly afterwards looking slightly flustered with oil-stained overalls covering his uniform. Dunbar saluted. Carlisle noted that he was a young man aged perhaps about twenty-six and of medium height and build with a slight Scottish accent.

'Sorry I wasn't here initially to meet you, sir,' apologised Dunbar. 'We're still having some problems with that starboard turbine. The dockyard was supposed to have sorted it out but you know how it is. Let me take you to the Wardroom. I'll get one of the stewards to make you a coffee and some sandwiches. Have you come far?'

'Norfolk,' replied Carlisle. 'I was having a brief... all too brief... spot of leave at my farm with my wife.'

'I was looking forward to Christmas, with my wife,' remarked Dunbar. 'But things are getting pretty hot right now. The Russians are making advances in Norway. I'm not sure we'll make it home any time soon. The Admiralty have plenty of tasks lined up for us. It's my reckoning they'll put us on convoy escort work to start with. There are several big troop convoys crossing the Atlantic right now... and the liners carrying the men from America make fat targets for the Russians.'

'When do you estimate we'll be ready to put to sea?' asked Carlisle.

'We can pull out all the stops and be out tomorrow,' replied Dunbar, 'But I would caution that the starboard turbine could still give us some problems.'

'Hopefully, we'll have a chance to get such things sorted before we're sent into battle with Ivan, 'said Carlisle.

The following morning Carlisle stood on the port side bridge wing of the Galatea and was joined by Lieutenant Dunbar and with Chief Petty Officer MacBride at the helm. So far that starboard turbine was still running as the lines were cast off and Carlisle ordered revolutions for ten knots.

'Starboard fifteen... slow ahead both engines.'

Carlisle turned to Dunbar who was Officer of the Watch and keeping a sharp eye open for any difficulties or problems.

'We'll make a run past the Lizard and Land's End,' said the captain. 'Then we'll see how the old girl's doing. I want to test all the guns and make sure the radars and sensors are functioning as they should be.'

'Very good, sir,' acknowledged Dunbar.

Once they were safely out to sea and clear of other shipping the Galatea's 114mm main gun swung to port and fired five rounds without a hitch. The 20mm singles on the bridge wings and the .50 calibre machine guns were also tested. The surface search and air warning radars were in operation and appeared to be functioning satisfactorily. During the afternoon Carlisle took the opportunity to put the ship's Wildcat helicopter in the air piloted by Lieutenant James MacNamara and assisted by his Observer, Sub-Lieutenant Danny Morrison. They took the opportunity to use the dipping sonar and were relieved that this did not indicate any unexpected submarine contacts. Overnight the weather deteriorated with strong northerly winds and frequent snow showers, but Carlisle used these adverse conditions as an opportunity to put Galatea through her paces. By dawn they were passing to the south of Ireland when Carlisle's mobile phone rang.

'Any sign of getting that old tub out to sea?' questioned Commodore Vincent. 'There's a troop convoy under attack in mid-Atlantic and the escort is under heavy pressure.'

'Yes, sir. We're about 30 miles southeast of the Fastnet Rock heading west at 25 knots.'

'That's excellent!' complimented the commodore. 'We'll be sending you full information from Northwood on the position of the convoy and its course and speed.'

'Very good, sir,' acknowledged Carlisle.

He immediately ordered an increase in speed to 30 knots despite the rising seas. The engineering department were soon protesting.

'That starboard turbine is giving us cause for concern, sir,' reported Chief Petty Officer Howden. 'It's likely to break down any time soon.'

Carlisle was aware of the potential problems, but he needed to reach that convoy as quickly as possible. Reluctantly he ordered a small reduction in speed to 27 knots. As *Galatea* headed out into the Atlantic she was being pounded by forty foot waves and her ageing hull creaked and groaned under the constant battering. Some of the younger members of the crew began to feel decidedly unwell as the *Galatea* climbed a great wave and then plunged down into a trough 'shipping it green' over her bows. This unpleasant motion went on for hours without respite. Then *Galatea* was receiving signals from the convoy with vessels calling for urgent help.

'Urgent distress call from the troopship, Georgic,' advised Petty Officer MacBlane. 'She says she's carrying five thousand men from Fort Liberty, North Carolina to Europe and she's under attack by Russian bombers. This is her position, sir,' he added, handing a note to Carlisle.

'That puts her about eighty miles to the west of us,' considered Carlisle. 'Engine room, give me maximum revolutions. We've got to pull out all the stops now.'

Galatea dug her bows into the heaving seas with the water pouring over her foc'sle in torrents. Then came another distress call from the convoy.

'It's from the troopship, Princess Helena Victoria,' advised MacBlane. 'She's been hit and she's on fire with many casualties. These are the co-ordinates for her current position, sir.

'Thank you, MacBlane,' acknowledged Carlisle. 'That would put her close to the Georgic.'

At that point Galatea rode a mountainous wave, probably sixty feet high and as she plunged down the other side into a deep chasm she was pushed thirty degrees to starboard and began slowing to a standstill beam on to the heavy seas and rolling precariously. Able Seaman Alison Tregellis rushed to the guardrail and wretched violently. She was quickly pulled back to the bridge by Leading Seaman Gittens just moments before a huge wave swept over the deck and which would otherwise have carried her away to oblivion.

'Engine room, what's going on down there!?' called Carlisle over the internal Tannoy system.

'It was that last wave, sir,' replied Petty Officer Trevelyan. 'It knocked out all the power. We're doing our utmost to get it restored urgently.'

Carlisle cursed audibly but grabbed a handrail as another giant wave broke over the ship causing it to roll sickeningly almost on its beam ends. For more than half an hour the Galatea endured this pounding while unable to move or steer under her own power. Carlisle considered that the situation was as unnerving as being under attack from enemy forces. Finally Petty Officer Trevelyan was calling from the Engine room.

'We've managed to get the port turbine re-started, sir. We're still working on the others. Electrical power is being restored.'

Galatea finally began to head on a westerly course once again with the giant waves still battering her hull.

'What speed can we managed?' called Carlisle to the Engine room.

'Eighteen knots, sir,' replied Trevelyan. 'We're working on the two aft turbines. Give us another thirty minutes.'

'That's too slow,' barked Carlisle. 'We've got goodness knows how many poor bastards looking to us to save their lives. I don't want them to all drown because we were suffering from bloody engine trouble!'

'Very sorry, sir,' apologised Trevelyan, 'I hope to have good news to report although that starboard turbine is likely to still give us problems.'

'I'll give a case of eighteen-year-old single malt scotch to be shared amongst your department as soon as we get back to Plymouth if you can give us twenty-seven knots,' promised Carlisle.

'Don't worry, sir,' acknowledged Chief Petty Officer Howden, 'We'll give you twenty-seven knots… we'll get you twenty-eight.'

Howden was true to his word. Within forty minutes all the turbines were running. The gale began to abate slightly being replaced by heavy snowstorms and Galatea was making twenty-nine knots. It was now dark, and the distress calls kept coming in. Carlisle would have liked to have sent up the Wildcat to carry out a reconnaissance, but the conditions were too bad for flying. The sonar operators were glued to their consoles and searching hard for any sign of enemy submarine activity but fortunately there was no indication of this in Galatea's sector. At around midnight the Air Warfare team reported a large airborne contact about forty miles to the north flying at around ten thousand feet at four hundred knots.

'No IFF,' called Leading Seaman Bob Watson while listening intently through his headphones. 'Definitely unfriendly. It has the electronic signature of a Tupolev 114.' Watson gave details of the plane's course.

'She's clearly heading for the convoy,' acknowledged Carlisle.

Not more than thirty minutes later Bob Watson was reporting a second Russian Tupolev approaching from the northeast at five thousand feet and this one was taking an interest in the Galatea. Carlisle considered it prudent to call the ship to Action Stations with the klaxons blaring. Men and women jumped from their bunks and hurriedly donned protective clothing and body armour. The CWO (Air), Lieutenant Charles Wray, briefed Carlisle on the capabilities of the Galatea's ageing Seawolf anti-air missile system.

'The launcher on our foredeck is for the original GWS 25 system,' advised Wray. 'We have two Type 911 tracking radars, and the missiles have a maximum range of about five miles on a good day. It's certainly not a long-range weapon and has to be manually re-loaded.'

'We'll just have to do our best with what we've got,' responded Carlisle.

'That second Tupolev is making an attack run on us,' advised Bob Watson. 'They've launched an AS-32 missile in our direction. It's a supersonic terminal dive weapon.'

'Helmsman, alter course ninety degrees to starboard,' ordered Carlisle as he turned the Galatea to directly face her attacker.

Soon the Mk 8 114mm gun on the foredeck was blasting away creating bright yellow muzzle flashes which turned night into day. At the same time, the *Galatea* fired its chaff launchers to build up great clouds of the fine metal strips. Carlisle then ordered a reduction in speed to just eight knots. He had no doubt that the Engineering department would approve but his intention was to enable *Galatea* to hide amongst the chaff which would hopefully do its job of deflecting the incoming missile.

'The AS-32 is closing fast,' advised Bob Watson.

'Sea Wolf crew open fire as soon as we have the range,' ordered Lieutenant Wray.

'The AS-32 appears to have disappeared from the plot,' reported Bob Watson.

'Ours too,' called the Electronic Warfare Team.

'We must have hit it with the Mk8,' exclaimed Lieutenant Wray. 'Well done, everybody.'

'Keep your eyes and everything else peeled for a follow up attack,' warned Carlisle.

The Tupolev has come down to four hundred feet,' called Bob Watson.

'I'd guess she's making a bombing run. Range five thousand metres and closing fast.'

'Engine room, increase to maximum revolutions,' ordered Carlisle. 'Helmsman, alter course ninety degrees to port.'

As the Galatea swung to bring her onto her new bearing a Sea Wolf missile shot from the launcher on the fore deck but then exploded in a brilliant orange flash. A second missile quickly followed but this pursued an erratic course and seemed to end up in the sea. The Mk8 was still blasting away and the twin 30mm mounting abaft the funnel opened fire when the attacking aircraft came within range. The big Tupolev thundered overhead casting an ominous giant shadow and dropped several flares and then came round to attack from astern where the frigate's weaponry was weakest. Several heavy bombs were aimed at the *Galatea* with two crashing into the sea and exploding about fifty metres off the frigate's port side. Two more bombs fell about a hundred metres off the starboard side. Although the bombs did not hit the ship, they exploded in sufficiently close proximity to start leakages in the elderly warship's hull and to put sensitive electronic equipment out of action. The Russian bomber then headed away towards the north pursued by arcs of brightly coloured tracer ammunition. The crew of the Galatea quickly set about shoring up the leaks. The Engineering Department were worried that the outer port propeller shaft had sustained some damage and at least one gasket had been put out of alignment resulting in an ingress of water through the shaft. Carlisle was well aware that damage of that kind could really only be repaired in a dockyard.

'We'll just have to rely on the pumps for now,' he informed Petty Officer Howden.

'I'll keep you informed of the situation, sir,' acknowledged Howden.

Further distress calls from other vessels kept coming in. Carlisle conferred with Lieutenant Dunbar and the Officer of the Watch, Lieutenant David Penvennan, and as dawn arrived they scanned the horizon for signs of the nearest ship, the liner 'Georgic.' As the daylight improved slightly they were able to discern a large vessel about fifteen miles to the north west and altered course ten degrees to starboard to join it. During the ensuing minutes Carlisle spoke over the secure communications systems with the liner's captain who informed him that their close escort, an American destroyer, had been sunk by Russian missiles. Courageously the destroyer had sacrificed itself to save the liner which was carrying upwards of five thousand U S servicemen and women. As the Galatea approached the Georgic Carlisle brought the frigate round so that they were sailing on a parallel course to the liner at a speed of twenty-four knots. The *Galatea's* CWO (Air), Lieutenant Charles Wray, advised Carlisle to position the frigate about three hundred metres ahead of the Georgic so as to give the old GWS 25 Seawolf missile system with its short range a chance to effectively protect the big liner if the Russians renewed their attacks. Everyone expected that they would do. Carlisle glanced aft from the starboard bridge wing and gulped in a breath of the cold Atlantic air as the massive bulk of the Georgic loomed disconcertingly out of a squall. He understood from its captain that the vessel displaced in the region of one hundred and twenty thousand tons and prior to hostilities had been used primarily for taking wealthy passengers on cruises to the West Indies and Latin America. The captain also warned that he believed his ship was generally top heavy and that if it was hit by enemy weaponry would be in danger of capsizing. With all those people on board such an event would be totally catastrophic. Having taken the Georgic under their wing the crew of the Galatea continued to receive incoming distress calls from other ships from the convoy who were under attack or damaged. The liner, Princess Helena Victoria, was only six miles to the north, clearly visible under a tall column of fire and smoke which rose hundreds of feet into the angry overcast skies. Carlisle was minded to give her priority but first he despatched the *Galatea's* Wildcat helicopter to go and take a closer look and to report on the vessel's condition and the damage it had sustained. At about 10-30 am the klaxons blared again aboard the *Galatea* as Carlisle brought the frigate back to Action Stations. The Air Warfare team had identified another Russian Tupolev long range bomber approaching from the northeast at four hundred knots. Bob Watson reported that it had fired an AS-32 missile, and this was clearly targeting the *Galatea* and the Georgic. Carlisle ordered the helmsman to make some course adjustments to put the *Galatea* between the incoming missile and the Georgic. The 114mm opened fire as soon as the missile came within range and chaff rockets were launched. The electronic warfare team attempted to jam the missile's guidance system, but it kept on coming. Soon lookouts were reporting visual sightings of the incoming projectile. In desperation the CWO (Air) ordered the salvo launch of a series of Seawolf missiles from the launcher on the *Galatea's* foredeck. The first Seawolf exploded prematurely shortly after leaving the launcher. The second missile veered wildly off course and Carlisle was briefly concerned that it would hit either the Galatea or the Georgic. The third Seawolf appeared to be similarly off course as the Russian AS-32 homed in but suddenly a blinding flash told everyone that somehow the Seawolf had found its target. Cheers were short lived as Lieutenant Wray's anti-air warfare team warned that the Russian Tupolev was making a bombing run and heading in at an altitude of just 300 metres. The Galatea's 114 main gun shifted to this new target with the big Russian bomber being bracketed by the black smudges of exploding shells. The twin 30mm guns sited abaft the Galatea's funnel opened fire as soon as the aircraft came within range. Meanwhile as the Tupolev came thundering overhead the missile crew manning the Seawolf reloaded the ageing launcher by hand and the system fired automatically at the large airborne target. Once again the first missile veered off course and ended up in the ocean swell. However, the second missile, fired as the bomber was directly overhead, struck its target in the weapons bay causing a blinding flash and a massive explosion which blew the aircraft apart in a spectacular firework display. The whole starboard wing of the Tupolev with its contra-rotating propellers still turning, crashed into the sea perilously close to Galatea's port beam. Other parts of the destroyed aeroplane fell on and around both the frigate and the Georgic.

Carlisle now turned his attention to the Princess Helena Victoria which was steaming eastwards at nineteen knots. Her captain reported that she had been hit by a bomb and also a missile which they believed to have been fired by a Russian submarine operating out in the Atlantic. The bomb had penetrated through to one of the starboard Engine rooms and started fires which the ship was having difficulty bringing under control. The missile had struck near the liner's stern causing extensive damage to the ship and many casualties. Carlisle consulted his senior officers as well as the captain of the Georgic and made a decision to position the two liners so that they were steaming side by side with the Galatea close ahead of both vessels. Following refuelling the Galatea's Wildcat helicopter was sent out on anti-submarine patrol. The Georgic was carrying a number of helicopters of different types and two former swimming pools sited on the upper decks had been converted into helipads. Firefighting equipment was then transferred by helicopter from both the Georgic and the Galatea together with teams of men to tackle the fires and damage aboard the Princess Helena Victoria. The task was a difficult one and by nightfall the Engine room fires on the Princess Helena Victoria were still burning and her speed had reduced to fifteen knots. Carlisle was concerned that the fires would be visible for miles around and their slowing speed would mean spending longer out in the open ocean where they were extremely vulnerable to further attacks. Making use of the Georgic's helicopters arrangements were made to begin transferring personnel from the Princess Helena Victoria to the Georgic which was already overcrowded. By dawn the Engine room fires were just beginning to be brought under control, but the Galatea's Wildcat was investigating a submarine contact out to the northwest and by 9am it was evident that a Russian submarine was on the lookout for stragglers from the troop convoy. For the small crew of the Wildcat, it was like searching for a needle in a haystack, but it was with some relief that they were joined by a Merlin from the Dutch amphibious ship, Karel Doorman. The submarine was identified as a Russian Sierra class vessel with a very strong titanium hull enabling it to dive to great depths. Once the submarine realised she had been detected she made a number of manoeuvres to try to shake off her pursuers. These made it difficult for the NATO helicopters to get a precise fix, but they were joined by two more Merlins from the Karel Doorman and a homing torpedo was dropped forcing the submarine to dive deep. The Merlins then dropped a second homing torpedo and although no hits were claimed the Sierra class was kept fully occupied trying to survive instead of attacking the convoy.

Eventually the Wildcat had to return to the Galatea to refuel leaving the Dutch Merlins to continue their search. The sonar operators on the frigate were concerned that they had detected a possible submarine contact ahead of their small group of ships. No NATO submarines were known to be in the area. Carlisle ordered a course alteration thirty degrees to starboard and as soon as the Wildcat had refuelled it was sent up again to investigate this new contact. Meanwhile the fires had finally been extinguished aboard the Princess Helena Victoria and her speed had edged up slightly to 17 knots. She still had a list of seven degrees to port and had shipped two thousand tons of sea water. Damage control teams were being kept very busy and counter flooding of some starboard compartments was in progress to try to bring the huge ship back on to an even keel. Carlisle was still very worried about the danger of the liner capsizing and indeed about the extreme vulnerability of their situation. Sub-Lieutenant Danny Morrison, the Observer on the Galatea's Wildcat, reported that the submarine contact ahead was a Russian Kilo Class, diesel powered but quiet and manoeuvrable. She had clearly detected the Galatea's small group and was positioning herself to make an attack. Carlisle sought assistance from other NATO units in the area. Initially there were only the distress calls from other ships but finally the *Yahagi* answered and said she was making for their position at maximum speed. In the Operations Room of the Galatea Lieutenant Dunbar's team calculated that the *Yahagi* should approach the Kilo Class from behind and passed details of the submarine's course and speed to the Japanese destroyer. The *Yahagi* confirmed over the secure link that she was sending out her helicopter to assist with attacking the submarine. In the meantime, Carlisle ordered his force to make further course alterations first to port and then to starboard in an effort to spoil the submarine commander's own attack plan and firing solution. Sub-Lieutenant Morrison was continuing to gather information pinpointing the position of the submarine and a homing torpedo was dropped. The submarine promptly dived to four hundred metres and made a series of tight manoeuvres. Carlisle altered course again, zig zagging his small group. In the meantime, the *Yahagi*'s helicopter appeared on the scene and Morrison continued to pass information so that the Japanese helicopter was able to join in the attack and also dropped a homing torpedo. Initially it appeared that all this would achieve would be to keep the submariners' heads down for a while but then sonar operators on the Galatea reported an underwater explosion at a depth of nearly five hundred metres. Soon Petty Officer Inglefield from the sonar team announced,

'She's coming up.'

The helicopter crews excitedly reported that the submarine was breaking surface and the Galatea's machine dived above the Russian vessel intent on continuing the attack, dropping two large depth charges which exploded in the sea either side of the now surfaced and badly damaged submarine. The Officer of the Watch, Lieutenant Dunbar, reported from the starboard bridge wing of the Galatea that the submarine was now visible at a range of about ten thousand metres. Carlisle conferred briefly with Lieutenant Wray who then ordered that the frigate's 114mm main gun should open fire on the enemy vessel. The first round was a ranging shot and went over the target. The second round fell slightly short while the third round hit the submarine on the side of its conning tower. The fourth and fifth rounds struck the pressure hull and exploded, and further hits were quickly obtained. Carlisle was anxious to destroy the enemy submarine as quickly as possible because of the critical danger it posed to the ships under his protection and the thousands of people aboard them.

'She's going!' exclaimed Charles Dunbar. 'She's sinking stern first.'

'Should we stop to rescue survivors, sir?' enquired Petty Officer Alison Mullen.

'No,' replied the captain firmly, gritting his teeth. 'We need to get our people safely into Liverpool without delay. Signal the Karel Doorman and any other NATO ships in the area and ask if they can pick up the crew of the submarine.'

Carlisle conferred with Captain MacIntyre of the Princess Helena Victoria who said his engineering teams were working hard to repair the damage to his ship and they hoped to be able to increase speed shortly. In the meantime, he was emphatic in his agreement with Carlisle that they should keep going and not risk the lives of thousands of people on the Princess Helena Victoria and the Georgic by stopping to pick up survivors of the submarine which had been trying to sink them. With the coming of darkness Carlisle doubled the watch keepers. Another storm was brewing from the north west and Galatea's Wildcat was brought safely down and stowed in the hangar. Frequent snowstorms reduced visibility, sometimes to just a few metres, and Galatea was rolling and pitching disconcertingly. At 0100 hours Petty Officer Mullen advised Carlisle of a signal just received from Northwood warning of an approaching Russian Surface Action Group. Further signals were received in rapid succession and the SAG was reported to comprise a missile cruiser and two destroyers which were heading up from the south at 30 knots currently at a range of seventy miles.

'I expect they'll be operating from a base in West Africa,' remarked Carlisle to Charles Dunbar. 'No doubt looking for stragglers from the convoy. Ask Northwood if they can give us more info on the identity of these Russian warships and the armament they are carrying.'

'Aye aye, sir,' acknowledged Dunbar.

Carlisle then conferred with Lieutenant Commander Takahashi over the secure link, and they discussed tactics for combatting the Russian SAG. Galatea had launchers for eight Harpoon anti-ship missiles but only four missiles were loaded. The *Yahagi* had a full complement of Standard missiles which had a surface-to-surface capability. Carlisle ordered that the two Allied warships would attack together once the Russians were in range. At 0320 the Galatea and the *Yahagi* turned ninety degrees to starboard as the range closed.

'The enemy cruiser has fired two SSMs,' reported Lieutenant Wray. 'We are urgently seeking to identify them. The cruiser is the Admiral Makarov, and she is known to carry a battery of SS=N-38 cruise missiles with an anti-ship capability.'

Shortly afterwards Lieutenant Wray further reported that one of the destroyers had fired a salvo of four missiles.

'Engage the enemy cruiser with two Harpoons,' ordered Carlisle. Engage each destroyer with one Harpoon. Signal the *Yahagi* to open fire as soon as the Russians come within range.'

The salvo launch of anti-ship missiles by both Allied ships provided an impressive spectacle and briefly turned night into day. The firework display was short lived as Lieutenant Wray's team announced the fast approach of the

Admiral Makarov's cruise missiles at high subsonic speed. Both the Galatea and the *Yahagi* fired chaff rockets and attempted to jam the guidance systems of the incoming warheads. Once in range they opened fire with their main guns and one of the Russian weapons disappeared from the radar plots. The second cruise missile continued on its trajectory and Carlisle felt cold sweat running down his neck as Wray's team reported that it was targeting the Princess Helena Victoria.

'Port fifteen,' ordered Carlisle as the missile powered overhead at a height of less than one hundred metres streaming a fiery tail.

Finally, the Seawolf launcher on Galatea's foredeck swung into action and two missiles shot skywards into the darkness. The first missile disappeared and was not seen again. The second missile also missed but in seconds a third missile was fired and struck the Russian weapon, blasting it into a thousand fragments. Elation aboard the Allied vessels was short lived as Wray's team announced the fast approach of the salvo of what were now identified as SS-N-26 Strobile missiles fired by one of the destroyers. The missiles were now pursuing a sea skimming trajectory and made difficult targets for the *Yahagi*'s Standard missiles although one SS-N-26 was successfully engaged and disappeared from the radar plots. Galatea opened fire again with her 114mm main gun and hit a second missile. All this time the Galatea's electronic warfare team were working feverishly to try to jam the guidance systems of the incoming warheads or at least to divert them away from their intended targets. Carlisle could feel his heart pounding as Wray's team announced that the missiles were targeting the Princess Helena Victoria. At a range of four miles the Seawolf system engaged and fired five missiles in rapid succession. An explosion in the night sky indicated a hit but one of the Russian warheads continued on its trajectory heading for the big liner and its six thousand passengers. Captain MacIntyre ordered his helmsman to turn hard a'starboard but the Princess Helena Victoria was slow to manoeuvre and it appeared that an impact was inevitable. The seconds passed but time seemed to stand still. Carlisle steeled himself for the explosion, but none came.

'The thing shot straight between her two stacks!' exclaimed Charles Dunbar who was Officer of the Watch. 'It was that close.'

Lieutenant Wray's team then quickly turned their attention back to their own anti-ship missiles and were gratified to observe on the radar plot that the two Harpoons aimed at the Admiral Makarov had both hit their target. One of the destroyers was also hit by a Harpoon. The Admiral Makarov quickly burst into flames, the now burning ship clearly visible on the southern horizon. The destroyer, identified as the Yuri Andropov, also caught fire. The surviving destroyer quickly turned away to the south to make its escape. Meanwhile the Admiral Makarov was hit by a salvo of Standard missiles as it came within range of the *Yahagi* and suddenly blew up in a spectacular display of pyrotechnics. The Yuri Andropov was also hit by several of the *Yahagi*'s missiles and slowed to a standstill. Lieutenant Commander Takahashi then closed to gun range and opened fire with his 127mm scoring numerous hits. Carlisle would have welcomed the chance to deliver the coup de grace on the Russian destroyer, but he needed to closely escort his two troopships with their thousands of personnel. Enemy bombers and submarines were still out there presenting a constant threat. He was about to sound the alarm yet again when Wray announced the approach of two aircraft heading in fast from the northeast. The Air warfare team were glued to their consoles and radar plots, and it was a relief to everyone when they were identified as USAF F-15 Eagles operating from Shannon Airport in Eire. The F-15s were followed by an American Lockheed Poseidon patrol aircraft which had been sent out to search for stragglers. The big aircraft made contact with Galatea and reassuringly confirmed that it would remain on patrol in their sector for the next seven hours and would then be relieved by another plane. On board the ships the alarm was sounded when two Russian bombers were detected on radar but the F-15s were vectored to intercept them. One of the Russian planes, a Tupolev, was shot down while the other bomber wisely turned about and headed back north. There were further similar contacts during the night, but Carlisle's small convoy now had air cover as they skirted to the south of Ireland and into the St George's Channel. With the coming of dawn, the Poseidon aircraft was eventually relieved by an RAF plane of the same type operating from St Mawgam in Cornwall. Captain MacIntyre requested permission to bring his huge liner alongside the Galatea to salute her ship's company and to thank them for getting them safely through the Russian attacks. The massive one-hundred- and twenty-thousand-ton Princess Helena Victoria duly closed up on Galatea's port side while six thousand American servicemen and women lined the guardrails of the troopship causing it to list seven degrees to starboard with the weight of all those people. Such a tremendous cheer was raised that it could not be drowned out by the booming of the ships' sirens as they saluted each other. Carlisle gave permission for those of his crew who were not on duty at that moment to go on deck and cheer the liner. Subsequently the Georgic came up on Galatea's starboard side resulting in more cheering and the loud booming of ships' sirens. The *Yahagi* was also cheered until she was detached to escort other ships which had become detached from the convoy. Eventually the vessels steamed into Liverpool Bay and were greeted by huge crowds who had gathered to welcome them safely into the Port of Liverpool. Carlisle considered that his crew deserved a run ashore from their berth which was reassuringly protected by a battery of very lethal looking SAM missiles backed up by a battery of flak guns.

'I think the Engineering department deserve their case of 18-year-old scotch,' commented Carlisle to Lieutenant Dunbar. 'How about you, Charles? Care for a dram or two?'

'Well, the sun is over the yardarm, sir. Did I mention to you that my family own a small distillery in the Highlands?' replied Dunbar.

'Do they indeed,' smiled Carlisle as he poured out glasses for them both from his mahogany drinks cabinet. 'Cheers!'

There was a tentative knock on Carlisle's cabin door.

'Sorry to interrupt you, sir,' apologised Petty Officer Mullen, 'But there is a gentleman from the BBC with a film crew asking if they can come aboard. I think they wish to interview you. There's also an American lady from CBN News.'

Five minutes later Petty Officer Mullen was back.

'Captain MacIntyre of the Princess Helena Victoria and the Captain of the troopship, Georgic, also wish to see you, sir. I believe they want to thank you for saving their lives.'

'You're welcome to use the Officers' Wardroom, sir,' offered Charles Dunbar.

'I think we'll need it,' replied Carlisle.

Chapter 16

IT WAS STILL DARK WHEN Carlisle's mobile phone rang. He scrambled out of bed hurriedly and stubbed his toe in so doing. Cursing, he managed to answer it.

'The compliments of the season, Eddie,' announced Commodore Vincent cheerfully. I hope I didn't wake you too early but you're something of a celeb right now. The President of the United States is inviting you for tea at the White House. Did you know that?'

'Er, no, sir. I didn't. When do they want me to come?'

'Oh, I expect they'll sort something out,' replied Commodore Vincent. 'That's not all. The Americans want to award you the Medal of Honor... for saving thousands of American lives. I think they'll want to have some kind of ceremony over on their side of the Pond. But that won't trouble you, I'm sure. By the way, Aurora's refit is coming along well. She should be back in the water very soon.'

'That's a relief, sir,' acknowledged Carlise. 'I've been enjoying a spot of Christmas leave but what I really want is to be back at sea.' He glanced around the bedroom, but Alex was already outside helping Sandra with the animals.

'Good man,' replied Vincent. 'We'll be needing you. Make no mistake about that.'

They spoke for a while longer and then the commodore rang off and left Carlisle to enjoy his festive leave and to nurse his hangover. Later, when he was up and dressed, he spoke to Alex and Sandra and told them of his conversation earlier that morning with the commodore.

'Well, that's wonderful, Eddie!' exclaimed Alex. 'I expect you're very proud of yourself. It's a great honour.'

'I'd be absolutely terrified,' conceded Sandra. 'All those bombs and bullets would be bad enough but meeting the President and all them generals and top people would be really scary.'

Later that day various relatives descended upon Longfleet Farm including Alex's parents. Carlisle's parents were, of course, sadly both deceased but Carlisle recalled his recent meetings with members of his family when the Darkforce Ultra system had been in operation. Those encounters had been strikingly vivid, and he had been sceptical when people he had mentioned them to had dismissed them as mere hallucinations. He had no doubt that he would soon experience more side effects of the Ultra system and then there was also the even more advanced Project Schrodinger. He had heard from Samantha Langley and others that people had met copies of themselves from parallel realities. It was all totally mind blowing but perhaps it would help win this war with Russia or at least enable people to survive. The following morning Carlisle received another call on his mobile phone. This time it was Charles Dunbar with an invite to Carlisle and Alex to come up to Scotland and visit his family home and distillery on the Isle of Mull. Carlisle checked with Alex who said it sounded a great idea as long as it was after 2nd January when Lucy's New Year party was over.

During the afternoon, the weather brightened up and Carlisle and Alex took her parents and an elderly aunt and uncle sailing on Barton Broad in the *Moonbreeze*. The wind had dropped, and the yacht tacked to and fro across the broad expanse of open water. When Carlisle and Alex passed their secret place amongst the reed beds Alex gave Carlisle a wink and a nudge.

'Another time,' she whispered to him quietly.

On New Year's Eve they drove the relatively short distance to Lucy's country retreat near How Hill. There was now a bitingly cold northeast wind blowing and outbreaks of sleet and snow but Alex was relieved that Lucy and Jerome had a warm log fire burning in the grate of the main living room fireplace and the central heating was clearly working effectively as well. Lucy greeted them effusively with her usual,

'Darlings, how lovely to see you again!'

Kisses were exchanged but, of course, Lucy had a similar greeting for every guest. Lucy was, however, genuinely pleased when the Carlisles confirmed they had brought with them a haunch of venison in the back of the Range Rover together with several braces of pheasants and a variety of wild fowl. All these had been Christmas gifts from Jack Blofield and members of his family. A number of people assisted with unloading this very welcome game which was indeed central to the festivities and to Lucy's Party. Food rationing was now being strictly enforced and even such basics as bread and flour were becoming difficult to obtain. Carlisle felt gratified that he had been able to assist in this way, but he then felt decidedly uncomfortable when Lucy's sister, Emma, arrived having driven up from London. Alex had similar qualms when she saw Prince Faisal. Fortunately, he was a perfect gentleman and made no reference to his liaison with Alex when in Carlisle's company but invited them both to his country house at Hickling. You must come and see the progress I have been making,' he enthused. 'I have so many ideas. I already have more than fifty classic and vintage cars in the motor museum. My latest project is to establish a safari park for wild creatures. I have acquired another seventy acres of land. A lot of it is just marsh or even open water but my legal team are working on obtaining for me the necessary licences and permits.'

Alex proceeded to tell Prince Faisal about her recent adventures in West Africa and how she was caught up in a gun battle with ivory poachers while trying to help protect the forest elephants. Faisal was open mouthed when he heard the details of her encounter.

'I would love to have some elephants in my Wildlife Park,' enthused Faisal. 'I would also like to acquire and breed rhinoceroses. They are amazing creatures, but all the species are endangered.'

Inevitably Carlisle found himself in conversation with Emma Hamilton-Wallingford while in Alex's presence.

'I saw your name in the headlines,' remarked Emma to Carlisle. 'I must say I was impressed. But I expect you don't have very much time for family life what with the war and everything.'

'Actually, we've decided to try and have children,' responded Alex boldly. 'We've decided it's time for us to create a family,'

'I'm surprised you have the time,' commented Emma, 'Then there's your farm and all the animals... the sheep and pigs... oh and not forgetting the horses. Mind you, Alex, I would say that Eddie should be put to stud. When he's not being awarded medals or entertained at the White House, that is.'

Alex felt anger welling up and would probably have slapped Emma across the face, but Eddie drew her away in time. Jerome was in the Wine Tasting Room inviting the guests to try some of the vintages he had received for Christmas.

'Ah, just the people,' he greeted Eddie and Alex. 'We were just about to try this 1996 Margaux from the Rothschild cellars at Waddesdon Manor in Buckinghamshire. What do you think, everyone?'

The guests made approving noises. A number of people said it was very smooth and clearly a good vintage. Someone else said it had flavours of plums and blackberries. Another person said there was a hint of oranges and lemons. Carlisle said he thought it was a good bottle of wine and might Jerome be able to get him a case or two.

'Well, I'll see what I can do, Eddie,' replied Jerome. 'But you must understand that it is now a somewhat rare vintage... not the kind of thing you can just buy at the supermarket or from your local wine merchants.'

Later Carlisle discussed the economic fallout of the war with Jerome who had a few good investment tips and pieces of information.

'Right now oil stocks are doing very well,' advised Jerome, 'But it's the Defence sector you want to really weigh in on heavily.'

'Any company in particular?' asked Eddie.

'Well, there is a firm which is really flying at the moment,' replied Jerome. 'Darkforce... I think you're familiar with them... probably having their systems installed aboard your ship. There's an opportunity to make some money. Give me a ring and we'll fix up an appointment and you can come and see me at my office in the City. Perhaps have a bite of lunch or whatever.'

'That sounds a good idea,' acknowledged Eddie. 'Alex and I are due to have a few days up in Scotland shortly, but I'll give you a call when we're back.'

At dinner that evening people were doing their best to enjoy themselves and have a good time. However, Carlisle fielded more than a few questions about the war and what was likely to happen next.

'I think it will reach a climax shortly,' he told them. 'The arrival of the Americans into the conflict will certainly have a bearing on things but the Russians have now introduced conscription for men and women aged 18 to 40. They will raise a huge army. It's going to be tough.'

'Is it going to turn nuclear?' asked a middle-aged lady with dark hair sitting opposite him. The room fell into silence.

'I don't want to cause people unnecessary alarm,' replied Eddie guardedly. 'The Russians have used nuclear tipped weapons and some battlefield nuclear weapons already. It is a dangerous path to follow, and I think they understand that we have powerful nuclear weapons too. They will have factored into their calculations that if they overstep the mark it will result in terrible consequences for themselves.'

The lady sitting opposite him shuddered. Other people appeared white faced and anxious.

'Come on… eat up all of you,' urged Lucy. 'Look at all this lovely food. We have Eddie and Alex and their friends to thank.'

Jerome offered around some of his best vintages later followed by brandies and his finest Cognac together with cigars for the gentlemen. Carlisle considered that if they were to get hit now by one of Mr Vatutin's missiles at least they would die having a good time. Later in the evening the alcohol flowed even more freely, and the inevitable white powdery substance was passed around although Carlisle always strictly refused to partake. He did not know what time it was when Alex gave him a nudge.

'Clearly neither of us are in a fit state to drive home,' she said, 'so Lucy has kindly offered us a bed for the night.'

Carlisle saw that Lucy was guiding them upstairs to a large room which he had been shown on a previous occasion and which contained an enormous four poster bed decorated with ornate wooden carvings and surrounded by red velvet curtains. Once Lucy had gone Alex and Carlisle undressed hurriedly, their clothes strewn in untidy disarray. The room was dimly lit by candlelight.

'This is the bed that used to belong to a mistress of King Charles II,' Alex reminded Eddie. 'Are you my King and am I your mistress? It feels just like we're back in the 17th Century.'

Carlisle felt Alex lean upon him with her dark hair brushing his chest. Right now, at this late hour he was just a little worse for wear, but he placed his arms around Alex, and they embraced warmly. Clearly quite a number of people were staying overnight because there was still a general hubbub. At one point when Alex and Eddie were in the middle of making love the bedroom door suddenly opened.

'May I introduce Jean Francoise, Compte de Charente and his wife, Helene,' interrupted Emma Hamilton-Wallingford. 'Jean Francoise is a director of the National Bank of France. I have known them for quite a long time. Jean Francoise is attending an important conference in London at the moment.'

Emma was clearly somewhat the worse for alcohol and possibly even stronger substances. Alex sought to draw up the bed clothes to try to cover her bottom and Jean Francoise apologised for the intrusion.

'I think we must find another room,' he said as he retreated.

'Oh no,' retorted Emma. 'We must all be sociable. Look at the size of this enormous bed. There is plenty of room for all of us.'

Emma pulled back the sheets at which point Alex abruptly stood up naked and slapped Emma hard across the face. Lucy had heard the commotion and hurried to intervene.

'Come away, Emma,' she ordered her sister. 'You have had too much to drink. I'm sorry, everyone.'

With some assistance from Jean Francoise, Lucy managed to usher Emma to another part of the large house. Alex closed the bedroom door and locked it. In the morning Eddie and Alex did not stay for breakfast and drove back to Longfleet Farm. In the afternoon they went sailing in the *Moonbreeze* and found their secret place amongst the reed beds with only the wildfowl for company.

The following day they packed up some clothes and set off for their planned break in Scotland at the invite of Charles Dunbar, taking it in turns to share the driving on the long journey. At certain places they were held up by check points where all vehicles were thoroughly searched. Carlisle could understand the reason why this was deemed necessary, but it created long tailbacks of traffic and caused their journey to take all day even though they had set out early in the morning. Eventually they reached the isolated farmstead with superb panoramic views across Loch Lomond which was their initial stopover where they had booked to stay a couple of nights. It was getting late in the evening when they arrived but they were greeted by the old farmer, Mr Munro, who showed them into the former farm workers' cottage where they were staying.

'The place is called 'Shee More,' explained Mr Munro. 'It is built into the side of an Iron Age barrow known colloquially as a fairy hill because that is where the fairy folk live. Some archaeologists from St Andrews University have been carrying out a dig recently. I think some of the fairy folk may have been disturbed by their activities. They may make their presence known to you. I suggest putting one or two gifts in appropriate places to placate them.'

Mr Munro headed back to his own house which was about half a mile away down a rough trackway leaving Alex and Eddie to sort themselves out. They were tired after the day's travelling so after having an evening meal they retired to bed. For once they were too weary to make love but when it was about 11-30pm or thereabouts they both clearly heard the sound of footsteps coming down the hallway which ran the length of the old cottage. Carlisle immediately jumped out of bed and switched on the lights, opening the bedroom door to see who was responsible for the intrusion.

'There's no one there,' he remarked to Alex in surprise. The hallway was deserted.

Carlisle made a thorough search of the building. There was a second bedroom as well as the living room and kitchen and bathroom but there was no sign of anyone apart from themselves. He went back to bed and he and Alex tried to get to sleep in this decidedly creepy environment. Before long there were more sounds of footsteps, lighter ones this time, and in the gloom of the night Carlisle was sure he saw at least one small figure. Alex said she had seen something too. Their reaction was now to pull up the bedclothes and try to block out this strange activity. In the morning when they got out of bed they made sure to immediately switch on the lights of every room they entered. Fortunately, all seemed quiet and peaceful save for the bleating of sheep in a nearby field. After breakfast they went for a walk up the hillside behind the cottage and enjoyed the bracingly cold fresh air and the stunning views out across Loch Lomond. This gave them an appetite and they drove a few miles to a country pub where they had a bite of lunch. Eddie Carlisle chose haggis with neaps and tatties followed by clootie dumpling for pudding. Alex selected the vegetarian option. Later in the afternoon Alex bought some presents for people back home including some antique horse brasses for Sandra. In the evening, they had a light repast and then went to bed. Late at night there were more unexplained phenomena including footsteps in the hallway and small figures. Eddie plucked up courage to try to observe one of these properly, but it appeared somehow indistinct and disappeared out of reach.

In the morning, the couple packed up early and drove on towards Oban where they had a short period of time to look at the town before they boarded the car ferry to the Isle of Mull. They had insufficient time to climb up to MacCaig's Tower but one of the highlights was observing a seal swimming in the harbour. Eddie also took an interest in a Norwegian submarine which was tied up at the quay side. There was some air activity in the skies and the ferry was buzzed at low level by two planes but fortunately they were American F-18s carrying out a practice attack. It did not take long to reach Tobermory where they disembarked, and Alex did her best to navigate with the directions Charles Dunbar had given them. They passed the impressive Duart Castle and headed south along the west coast of the island noting several landmarks which Charles had mentioned. The scenery was stunning, a great wilderness stretching out for miles in every direction. In due course they came upon some higher ground upon which was situated a large house clearly built from locally quarried stone. Adjoining the house was a more modern structure which Eddie guessed was the distillery. There were also what appeared to be farm buildings no doubt housing domestic animals and machinery. To the west the place had panoramic views out to sea while to the south and east there were rows of hills and what Eddie guessed was Ben More, the highest mountain on the island. They were greeted by Charles Dunbar and his wife, Moira, who introduced the Carlisles to Charles' father, Hamish Dunbar and mother, Elizabeth. The Carlisles were given a brief tour of the large house and then shown to their room which had views out to sea. Elizabeth pointed out the isles of Coll and Tiree on the horizon. Once they had a chance to get themselves sorted out the Carlisles were given a tour of the distillery by Charles and his father.

'In the evening, we can sample the products properly, sir,' smiled Charles. 'I'd like you to try our 18-year-old single malt. I think you'll be impressed.'

'How long has the distillery been established?' asked Eddie.

'It was founded by my grandfather, Angus Dunbar, in the 1960s when he left the Navy,' explained Charles. 'He had to do something and making whisky is something people in the Highlands and Islands are generally good at.'

'The business has been quite successful,' added Hamish, 'but we have kept it a small family concern. We've avoided allowing it to become too commercialised.'

In the evening, dinner was served in the spacious dining room with views out towards the white sands of the nearby beach with the sea and other islands forming a backdrop. Elizabeth and Moira had prepared an attractive seafood starter. The main course was roast beef sourced from their own Highland cattle. Inevitably conversation centred upon the course of the war and what was likely to happen next.

'I'm concerned about Russian advances into Europe,' said Eddie. 'Berlin looks about to fall. Warsaw has been taken. Stockholm and Helsinki went last year… and Copenhagen. Oslo looks like the next domino.'

'It looks bad,' acknowledged Hamish. 'But at least the Americans are now committed. They should make a difference. Hopefully, things will start to turn around now.'

'Do you think the tide has turned?' asked Charles.

'Not yet,' replied Eddie. 'I think the situation will get worse before it gets better. There are going to be some ferocious battles ahead.'

'Is it going to turn nuclear?' asked Alex. It was the question on everyone's minds, the elephant in the room, but only Alex was bold enough to ask.

'It already has,' responded Hamish. 'The Russians have been using tactical nuclear weapons for a while.'

'And nuclear tipped missiles,' added Eddie. 'After all there was the attack on the airbases in Norfolk and elsewhere.'

'Don't I know it,' said Alex. 'I thought my number was up that time. It was far too close for comfort.'

'You know, if things get even hotter, you're welcome to come and stay with us here,' offered Hamish. 'We've plenty of room. It's a big house but I hardly think we'd be a prime target for Mr Vatutin's missiles.'

'That's very good of you,' replied Alex. 'It's lovely here. It would make a good bolt hole.'

'Thank you, Hamish,' added Eddie. 'It makes me feel just a little better about things that we have a safe haven if we need it.'

The following morning the sun was shining and promised a fine winter's day in the Western Isles. Charles suggested to the Carlisles that they take the boat out to explore some of the coastal waters and both Alex and Eddie agreed that this would be an excellent idea. Moira expressed a wish to come too and joined them on the boat which was called Maid of Lorn after the character created by Sir Walter Scott. The Maid of Lorn was a fairly modern craft and reminded Alex of the cruiser owned by Jean-Marc Moussavou although she hoped that on this occasion they would not be attacked by pirates. They were also joined by the Dunbar family Labradors, Bob and Madge, who sat in the bows of the craft with their ears streaming in the fresh breezes. Initially Charles steered for the island of Coll which was clearly visible from the Dunbar's house. On the way they were joined by dolphins who splashed and cavorted ahead of the boat and more than one seal raised its head above the surface of the sea. The abundance of marine life once again reminded her of her adventures in West Africa. Soon they had reached the eastern side of Coll and then cruised steadily northwards passed a remote location called Sonsdale and then steered round the north end of the island and began heading south westwards. Charles and Moira pointed out some attractive beaches with names such as Toriston and Fishing Gate and in due course Charles navigated the cruiser cautiously into a sheltered bay and approached a beautiful place called Cliad Beach with white sands and spectacular views. There was no one else around as Charles slowed the vessel to a crawl and dug the bows into soft sand. Eddie assisted with lowering the bow and stern anchors.

'Hardly any wind today,' smiled Charles. 'Not bad for early January, wouldn't you say?'

'You'd never guess there was a war,' responded Eddie.

'Don't remind us, dear,' Alex replied. 'It's lovely here. Can we stay for just a while?'

'Certainly,' acknowledged Charles. 'Moira and I come here regularly. It's one of our favourite spots. Just the place to get away from the problems of our lives. Let's have a look in the picnic basket.'

The basket contained sandwiches with a variety of fillings together with scotch eggs and fancy cakes while Charles produced a bottle of French white wine from the fridge.

'This is very civilised,' remarked Eddie. 'I'd rather be here than fighting Russians.' he added as he broke off pieces of his sandwiches to distribute between Bob and Madge, the Labradors.

'They'll be your friends for life,' Moira told him.

Once they had finished the picnic everyone was keen to take the dogs for some exercise along the deserted beach. Getting ashore presented one or two practical difficulties, but Alex said she wanted to feel that soft white sand under her feet. The cruiser had a stern well by which one could disembark and wade the few yards to the shore but the depth of water under the stern was about three to four feet.

'Either we get our clothes wet, or we have to take them off to get on to the beach,' considered Charles.

'What do you usually do?' asked Alex.

'Well, there's usually just Moira and I… so we just go in the buff,' replied Charles somewhat self-consciously. He was mindful of the presence of a senior officer.

'I propose we girls lead the way,' suggested Alex. 'You'll see what I mean in a minute or two.'

Moira and Alex retired briefly to a cabin and shut the door. Soon they reappeared having removed their boots and socks and their trousers. They were both still wearing thick sweaters. Moira was covering her modesty with a pair of clean white knickers. Alex on the other hand did not care for such underwear.

'Och, gentlemen! Close your eyes,' advised Moira.

'More a sight for sore eyes,' smiled Eddie as they assisted the girls into the water.

'Och, it's freezing!' exclaimed Moira as the cold water immersed her up to the waist. Her clean white knickers were thoroughly soaked.

Alex pulled up her sweater and just about managed to keep it out of the sea. Then they were ashore, and Alex was feeling that white sand between her toes. Eddie and Charles followed the girls' example, removing their clothing from the waist downwards and were soon ashore. The dogs had no hang ups and just splashed around in the sea. Their human companions scanned every horizon but there was no one else in sight for miles around apart from the occasional cottage inland but they were some distance away. Eddie felt somewhat strange being in the great outdoors without his trousers and the freezing water had done nothing to stimulate his manhood. Charles suggested they headed northwards where there were some more beaches. The sky was crystal clear and blue while the coastal waters were a beautiful aquamarine colour. Alex thought it reminded her of places she had known in the Mediterranean although they had generally been rather warmer.

'I think I'll wear my parker next time we come here,' she remarked.

Soon they arrived at another deserted beach and sat down amongst some dunes gaining a little warmth from the early afternoon sunshine. Charles was sure he spotted dolphins a short way out to sea while Eddie pointed out a whale spouting in the distance. Alex and Moira took the opportunity to go paddling even though the water was very cold but soon returned to join their husbands in the dunes. Moira was a young woman aged about 26 with mid length fair hair, about five feet six inches tall and attractive though of fairly competitive build. She was always most comfortable when in the saddle with her horses. Her ancestry was in farming in rural southwest Scotland. Her parents and grandparents were prosperous, and she was well cultivated having attended good schools.

'I must introduce you properly to Ellen and James,' proposed Moira to Alex. 'You have horses at home, don't you? Ellen is my white mare. She is beautiful and she has a good temperament. James has a nice nature too. It helps that he had his gentlemen's bits removed some time ago.'

'I hope you're not intending to remove my bits,' joked Charles.

'Don't worry, dear,' replied Moira. 'We need them intact. We're trying to start a family,' she informed the Carlisles.

'Us too,' replied Alex. 'But it doesn't help that Eddie has to spend so much time at sea.'

'I know exactly what you mean, Alex,' responded Moira. 'You and I are kindred spirits. We have exactly the same problem.'

Back at the Dunbar's home that evening Carlisle was relaxing while enjoying a glass of the family product with Charles and Hamish when his mobile phone unexpectedly rang.

'Sorry to interrupt whatever you're doing, Eddie,' apologised Commodore Vincent, 'But I thought you might like to know you've been nominated for a gong. As you are aware the Americans want to award you the Medal of Honor. Not to be outdone our powers that be intend to give you a Victoria Cross. How does that sound?'

For a moment Carlisle was stunned and lost for words. Then he managed,

'Sir, I'm… so grateful. I don't know what to say. Somehow, it's profoundly humbling. Our people all work together as a team. They have all done their duty magnificently. Nelson himself would have been proud of them. I could not have saved all those lives without them. If I am to be given a V.C. then all members of the crew of the Galatea should receive a gong as well. We all faced the same dangers together.'

'Well, I'll see what can be arranged,' replied the commodore. 'Your executive officer, Lieutenant Dunbar, is being recommended for a Distinguished Service Cross… and a well-earned promotion to Lieutenant Commander, I might add.'

'Sir, he's with me now,' said Carlisle. 'You might like to speak to him and give him the good news.'

Carlisle passed his mobile phone to Charles who was delighted with what the commodore informed him. Once they had finished speaking to Commodore Vincent, they were eager to tell their wives who were equally excited. Hamish opened a bottle of his best champagne and after dinner the gentlemen sampled whiskey which had been matured in oak casks for twenty-two years. They also lit up big Havana cigars which Hamish had retained for special occasions. Carlisle was not sure what time it was when he finally got to bed but it was after 2am.

In the morning, he was nursing a bad hangover as was Charles. Their wives decided to leave them to sleep it off while they went riding with Ellen and James. The weather was once again fine but rather cold and Alex was glad to have the opportunity to explore a little further inland on Mull. Ellen was indeed a fine white mare and was ridden by Moira. James was ridden by Alex who found him well behaved and an easy horse to manage. The women joked that if they had the choice of keeping their husbands or their horses they would probably choose the latter. Towards noon Moira pointed out a ring of standing stones not far to the southeast. These were not in the same league as Stonehenge but were interesting, nevertheless. Not far away Moira pointed out an Iron Age barrow and Alex told her about the experience she and Eddie recently had in the cottage overlooking Loch Lomond.

'There are quite a lot of these fairy hills in Scotland,' explained Moira. 'They are very much bound up with Celtic mythology and legend. In Ireland, of course, they talk of the 'little people'. Here in Scotland, we sometimes call them the 'Guid Folk'. That is really a rather weak attempt to placate the fairy folk. Not all of them are good. They are nature spirits… some say the spirits of dead people who have not yet been permitted to enter the next world and are currently held in a kind of purgatory.'

'That's fascinating,' responded Alex as they dismounted and began to explore the structures at close quarters.

'The fairy folk will be inside the fairy hill,' smiled Moira. 'I've brought along a loaf of bread. We'll leave it here for them as a gift. We want to keep in their good books… not get the wrong side.'

'Is there any way of getting inside the fairy hill?' asked Alex as she poked and prodded around some gorse and scrub.

'If you tried hard enough you might succeed,' advised Moira, 'But I wouldn't recommend it. There are tales of people doing just that in the past. They were never seen again.'

With dark clouds gathering to the northwest the two women rode back towards the Dunbar homestead. The men folk were slowly recovering from their sore heads and were assisting with culinary preparations.

The next day the weather had cleared and it was decided to take the Maid of Lorn to Tiree and Iona and then to come back via Coll. Alex stood in the bows with the dogs and was the first to spot a huge basking shark submerged in the clear waters. Not long afterwards they were joined by a pod of dolphins while Moira called out that she could see a whale spouting over to starboard. Charles steered the cruiser towards it and soon a second whale appeared. Soon they were passing Tiree and the Carlisles noted that it was slightly more populated than Coll but still a very attractive island. Charles was keen to push ahead to Iona which they reached around late morning and found a sheltered bay where they were able to step ashore without getting their feet wet and took the opportunity to visit Iona Abbey as well as St Oran's Chapel, the burial place of more than fifty Scottish kings. Bob and Madge, the Labradors were able to enjoy a run ashore until Charles decreed that everyone should be back aboard the Maid of Lorn to head north. They set course for Crossapol Bay on the southern shores of Coll with the wives preparing a light lunch which was served out to individuals while they were on the move. The Bay was relatively sheltered and once again Charles cautiously manoeuvred the cruiser so that it gently dug its bows into some soft sand and came to a standstill. Eddie assisted Charles in dropping the bow and stern anchors into the calm waters. The place was quiet and peaceful. There was no one around apart from their own small party. The dogs were keen to get another run ashore and jumped overboard with much splashing and barking. Charles assessed that they had about four feet of water under the stern and the rudder.

Alex was keen to enter the water but any clothing was likely to get soaked and although it was a fine day the seas were cold. She duly pulled off her attire save for her t-shirt which she was able to roll up and managed to keep relatively dry. Moira followed and this time dispensed with her white knickers while the gentlemen adopted a similar strategy. Charles and Eddie managed to bring ashore a windbreak which they duly erected in a sheltered location but with fine views out to sea. The dashboard of the cruiser indicated an outdoor temperature of 11 degrees and the wind was very light. Alex and Moira went paddling in the sea while the dogs were letting off steam.

'My family are from southwest Scotland,' Moira informed Alex. 'They still have quite a large farm there with about eight hundred acres. They do arable and keep beef cattle as well. When I was eleven, I was sent off to boarding school in Perthshire. I'm not sure why I was sent up there. I suppose it was considered the done thing. I missed our farm in Galloway... and my horse... but I love it up here in the Hebrides. On a fine day and when things are going well, I sometimes think it's the nearest to heaven that one can experience in this world.'

'I can understand what you mean,' agreed Alex. 'It's beautiful here... and so peaceful too.'

Eddie was now playing with the dogs and disputing possession of a stick with Bob. Alex and Moira came and sat down next to the windbreak admiring the views and enjoying the tranquillity.

'You've got a mole... or a birthmark on your bottom,' Moira remarked to Eddie.

'Oh yes, he's always had that,' advised Alex. 'On his left cheek. I understand he was born with it... but no need to worry. It doesn't bother him, does it, dear?' she sought to clarify with Eddie.

'What?' asked Eddie who was still embroiled in a tussle with Bob. They were joined by Charles who threw a stick for Madge which landed amongst the breakers.

'I should have brought my shades,' commented Alex. 'Not just for the sunshine. With shades you can look at the guys without them realising.'

'Lucky I brought mine,' acknowledged Moira.

The women enjoyed watching their men folk so engaged. Eventually Eddie came and sat down with them while Charles continued to throw brushwood for the dogs to retrieve.

'I think Bob got the better of me,' panted Eddie.

'You need a bit more exercise,' advised Alex.

'Soon we should go for a stroll,' proposed Moira. There's a tiny hamlet not far away called Ug. Before you get to it there's a lovely place called Breacachadh Beach. It's nice and sheltered and there's more white sand, Alex.'

Without any hurry they set off across some rugged ground with just the wildlife for company. There was not another human being in sight. Eventually they found a circle of prehistoric standing stones, the structures appearing shrouded in mystery in this very isolated location and Alex wondered about the people who placed them there long before the time of Christ.

'I believe they have magical powers… of healing… and fertility,' explained Moira.

'Well, fortunately I'm neither ill nor injured,' replied Alex, 'But fertility… that is of interest. How do we invoke these powers, Moira?'

'There are not enough of us to join hands around the whole circle,' considered Moira, 'So I suggest we form a ring around this stone, here. Everyone join hands… now we'll dance round it. I'll start the chanting… in Gaelic. The rest of you can pick up the words as we go along.'

Alex found herself dancing around naked in this mysterious and desolate place with her equally naked husband and companions chanting in a language she did not understand. After a while she observed that Eddie's manhood, while not unimpressive in normal conditions, appeared to have grown even larger still. Charles' genitalia seemed to have undergone a similar expansion while Alex felt her breasts, which while normally fulsome, had increased in size so that she could no longer see her feet. Moira appeared to have experienced an equivalent metamorphosis. The dancing and the chanting increased in intensity until suddenly the four of them tumbled together onto a small area of moss and grasses. Alex was aware of Eddie lying on top of her while she entwined her fine legs tightly around his torso. She was also conscious of Moira lying right next to her in a similar position with Charles making passionate love which continued until the sun began to descend in the broad clear skies and Charles recommended that they head back to the boat before darkness fell.

The following Monday found Carlisle back at his desk in London where the stack of work had grown to immense proportions. Outside the mixture of rain, sleet and snow was a total contrast to the glorious conditions in the Western Isles such a short time ago. There were so many e-mails he had no idea how he was going to read them all but eventually Commodore Vincent breezed into his office in his usual cheery manner.

'Good to see you back, Eddie. I hope you enjoyed your leave. I expect it finished all too soon, eh?'

'Unfortunately, yes, sir,' acknowledged Eddie. 'But I'm glad to be back doing my bit as they say.'

'Well, that's splendid,' replied Commodore Vincent. 'Now let me fill you in on one or two things. First, the Americans. The President wants you to attend a ceremony in Washington D C on 6th February. Apparently, a number of U. S. service people are receiving gongs at the same time, so you won't be on your own. We'll arrange to fly you over to America a day or two beforehand, so you have a chance to get settled in. Another thing… only US servicemen and women can be awarded the Medal of Honor. It's the highest military decoration they can receive… so you're to be made an honorary United States citizen. You'll be given further details over the next couple of weeks.'

'How's Aurora's refit coming along, sir?' enquired Eddie.

'Very well, I'm glad to say,' replied the commodore. 'As you know, she's having her radar and electronics fit fully upgraded and additional generator capacity. Her old Harpoon anti-ship missiles have been replaced with the new American Valkyrie system linked to AEGIS 4000. That's not all. She's also being equipped with the new Anglo-American Warhawk cruise missile. It can be used to hit targets up to two thousand miles away on land or up to fifteen hundred miles at sea using a satellite guidance system.'

'But how is all this additional kit going to fit into her hull?' asked Eddie. 'Won't she be too top heavy?'

'Don't worry. We've taken that properly into account,' responded Commodore Vincent. 'A new fifty metre section has been welded into her, so she'll be well capable of accommodating all this stuff. Essentially, you'll find her a much bigger ship than the one you commanded last year. Indeed, with all these powerful new systems she's being officially upgraded to a missile cruiser... a CG. It makes sense, of course. It's far quicker and cheaper than having to construct a new ship from scratch.'

'Yes, I see what you mean, sir,' agreed Eddie. 'I'm very much looking forward to her next commission.'

'Excellent,' acknowledged the commodore. 'One more thing. I appreciate it's a lot to take in at one go but there's a promotion in it for you as well... to Captain. It's fully appropriate now you'll be in command of a CG. It'll also give you a bit more clout dealing with the Americans and other NATO navies. Ah, yes... and just one more thing before I forget... The King wants to meet you at the Palace on 5th March. I think he wants to award you the Victoria Cross.'

''That's wonderful, sir,' managed Eddie. 'I'm walking six feet off the ground.'

Commodore Vincent saluted him, and Eddie responded in kind. At 5-30pm Carlisle joined battle with the thousands of fellow commuters. The tube seemed particularly overcrowded, and the weather was cold, wet and miserable but his mind was focussed on what Commodore Vincent had told him that morning. There was so much to take in. His digs in Camden were just as run down as ever. He was greeted by Mrs Petruska who handed him a pile of mail and an invoice for the forthcoming quarter's rent. He would pass it to the appropriate department at the MOD. During the evening he watched television which was dominated by news and current affairs programmes. In continental Europe, the critical battle for Berlin was reaching a climax and it was still not clear who would win. Dresden had fallen to the Russian forces and Leipzig was surrounded. In Scandinavia, the Russians were advancing in a pincer attack from both the north and from Sweden and Denmark. NATO were gathering their armies for a counterattack. Oslo was under bombardment from Russian planes and long-range artillery and missiles. There was discussion with politicians and the so-called 'experts' as to whether the conflict would turn nuclear. Carlisle considered that hopefully the Russians would keep mainly to conventional warfare as long as they believed it would win them the war. If the tide turned against them then the nuclear option could prove tempting. At around 9pm the air raid warning sirens sounded. Mrs Petruska called out that she was going down to the shelter. Carlisle thought about doing the same but then decided he would take his chances with Mr Vatutin's rockets. After a few minutes he heard a series of bangs and explosions in the distance but fortunately nothing appeared to fall on Camden.

The remainder of the week followed a rather similar pattern and on Friday evening Carlisle was glad to head for Norfolk and home. Alex met him at the railway station. There had been some delays with the train services due to enemy activity, but he was then glad to be back at Longfleet Farm where he was greeted by a profusion of dogs and cats and other creatures. Alex had cooked roast partridges for their dinner, the game provided by Jack Blofield. The meal was accompanied by a good burgundy and Carlisle praised Alex for the best dinner he had eaten all week. Subsequently Alex led him upstairs where their clothing was hastily discarded and left strewn untidily around the bedroom. Alex lay on her back and stretched out in anticipation.

'Would you say my tits are noticeably larger than they used to be?' she asked Eddie.

'Yes,' he replied. 'It has something to do with that mysterious stone circle, I'm sure. My gentleman's appendages have been larger than usual ever since. You may laugh but it can be damned uncomfortable when you have to spend the day sitting at a desk on a hard ministry swivel chair. My boxer shorts have been most constricting.'

'Well, you'll just have to do without them, won't you,' said Alex as Eddie leaned forwards and kissed both her nipples which were visibly expanding. Then Alex was entwining her fine legs around his back as Eddie eased his impressive manhood into the inviting chasm between her thighs.

'Moira did say the stone circle had powers of fertility,' mused Alex. 'Let's hope she was right.'

The following week Carlisle was back at his desk in Whitehall trying to wade through the mountain of work which no one else in his department appeared to have tackled while he was away. He was relieved when on Tuesday Commodore Vincent introduced a Lieutenant Embrey.

'This is John,' smiled the commodore affably. 'He's come to help you out with your workload here. Be a good chap and show him the ropes and all that.'

Carlisle was glad to have the assistance although it took Lieutenant Embrey a while to read through some of the files and initially he tended to be more of a hindrance than a help. Eddie was glad on Friday when the commodore informed him that on Monday he should travel down to Plymouth and start getting the Aurora into shape in readiness for her next commission.

'We need to have her operational again as quickly as possible,' said the commodore. 'Don't say a word to anyone but the Americans and NATO are planning a big attack in Norway. It'll involve amphibious landings and putting thousands of troops and all their kit ashore. *Aurora* will be invaluable with her state-of-the-art systems and her batteries of powerful missiles.'

Eddie beamed at the prospect. It was just what he wanted to hear. Early on Monday morning he took the train down to Plymouth and found Aurora outside the Refit complex moored in a location where the surrounding topography provided some cover from enemy attacks. Batteries of SAMs provided what he hoped would be effective air defence. Two floating cranes were positioned alongside the ship and were actively engaged in transferring equipment on board for installation. The Aurora was a hive of activity and to begin with few people seemed to notice Carlisle's arrival. However, before long he met Roy Stringer who called Lieutenant Commander Guy Hanson who was keen to show him the work in progress. The new Warhawk launchers for cruise missiles were positioned four on either side just aft of the bridge. Further aft was a giant radome mounted on a pyramid shaped mast which Guy explained related to the American AEGIS 4000 system.

'It controls the Valkyrie missiles, sir' advised Roy Stringer. 'The manufacturers claim it can shoot down a golf ball flying hypersonically at sixty thousand feet.'

'I'm not quite sure about that but I've seen them in action, and they were impressive,' replied Carlisle.

Walking further aft they came upon a second radome sited lower down on the upper deck.

'That relates to the Darkforce systems... Project Schrodinger,' explained Guy. 'Real futuristic high technology. I'm not sure where it leads us, but it might just save our lives one day.'

Carlisle observed the structure. It gave no indication of the incredible power of Schrodinger or of what it was capable of achieving. Atop the hangar was a new multi barrelled gun which appeared to have replaced the twin 30mm mounting.

'What's that?' asked Carlisle.

'That's the new Japanese Sea Urchin anti-aircraft / anti fast attack craft system. It has a rate of fire of 4000 rpm,' replied Guy. 'I'd wager it'll turn out to be a useful piece of kit.'

'I'm sure you're right,' agreed Carlisle. 'Are they intending to have a second mounting for'ard?'

'I'm not aware of one, sir,' said Guy.

'I'll speak to the powers that be and to Clive Robinson at Babrock. Do you know whether he's around at the moment?' enquired Carlisle.

Guy Hanson and Roy Stringer led the captain into the ship where they had to constantly step over all manner of cables and workmen. They found Clive in the Operations Room where he was overseeing the fitting of some new high-tech consoles. Carlisle told him he was most impressed by what he had seen so far.

'She's to all intents and purposes a new ship,' said Clive proudly. 'I think of her as my baby.'

At that point Carlisle bumped into Professor Finch from Darkforce. Behind him stood Dr Langley. The Operations Room had been significantly extended with a whole new area allocated to the Darkforce systems.

'Let us give you a brief demonstration of what Schro dinger is capable of,' proposed Professor Finch as he showed the captain an electronic map detailing a large area of the southwest coast of Britain as well as Southern Ireland. Carlisle observed the system rapidly springing to life.

'At the moment it is gathering information from the Multiverse,' explained

Finch. 'I'll guarantee that if there are any enemy units out there either on land or sea or in the air Schrodinger will find them and report them. Indeed, the system is so powerful and so valuable to our side that we have installed a data link directly from this ship's system to NATO Headquarters at Northwood in London, England.'

Carlisle watched the large map with its glowing lights marking the positions of friendly ships and aircraft. Then well out into the Atlantic to the west of Southern Ireland a red light started to flash.

'That's a submarine contact,' called Dr Arnold Duvall from his console. 'Hostile contact... identified by Schrodinger as a Russian Delta IV seventy miles south-west of the Fastnet Rock operating currently at a depth of one hundred metres... speed... eighteen knots.'

'That information is being passed immediately to Northwood over the secure link,' explained Professor Finch. 'We are also notifying NATO aircraft and ships in the area and the United States facilities at Shannon Airport and Bantry Bay.'

It did not take long for the operators on the Aurora to report that a Lockheed P-8 Poseidon patrol aircraft had been sent out from Shannon Airport and was being guided towards its quarry by Schrodinger. A Japanese destroyer, the *Yahagi*, which was out on patrol to the south of Ireland was also being homed in towards the hostile submarine contact. Carlisle watched in fascination as Allied units were vectored into position. The *Yahagi* sent up its helicopter and a second Poseidon aircraft took off from Shannon Airport. The British frigate, Arethusa, which had been on patrol in the St George's Channel was also diverted towards the reported contact. Time seemed to stand still but the first P-8 Poseidon patrol aircraft from Shannon Airport was quickly on the scene, initially dropping sonar buoys and then two homing torpedoes. The submarine sought to dive deeper to three hundred metres, but the big target was hit by one of the torpedoes and struggled to the surface where it was attacked by the P-8 with laser guided bombs and destroyed.

Two days later Carlisle was on his way to Washington DC in a USAF plane being wined and dined throughout the journey. There were just a handful of people aboard the aircraft including a General and several other senior officers and diplomats. At Washington Dulles Airport he was greeted by one of the President's aides, Brad Tierney, and driven to the hotel where he would be staying for the next five days. He was also introduced to John O'Connor from the President's personal staff who was to be his personal security officer during his stay in Washington and his driver, Leroy Johnson, also from the President's staff. John O'Connor was a big man, about six feet eight inches tall, who said he had previously been in the U S Marines and was an expert in martial arts. Leroy Johnson had also been in the Marines and was a heavily built man of African American ethnicity. Carlisle was duly checked in to the Hay Adams Hotel on National Mall with a room overlooking the White House. Security was tight everywhere, but Carlisle was assisted by his team of minders and bureaucracy and red tape were quickly overcome.

'We'll be in the rooms either side of the one directly opposite,' advised Brad Tierney. 'If there's anything you need just let us know.'

Carlisle was feeling tired after the long flight, but he was also hungry and managed to make it to the hotel restaurant for around 8pm where he ordered a rib eye steak of generous proportions. Brad Tierney joined him at the table and the other security men sat close by.

'The ceremony will take place at the White House the day after tomorrow,' Brad advised Carlisle. 'It'll give you a day's grace to start getting acclimatised. There will be some other service people attending who will also be given honours. Later in the afternoon you'll get to have tea with the President and his wife. Do you like dogs, sir?'

'Yes, I do,' replied Carlise. 'Our farmhouse back home in England is full of them. In fact, each time I go home on leave there seem to be more of them. My wife is a soft touch for a pooch in need of a roof over their head.'

'I know what you mean,' smiled Brad. He took out his mobile phone and showed Carlisle pictures of his wife, Erin, his son, Joe and daughter, Bridgette, and not forgetting his dog, Buster. 'He's a kind of bull terrier,' explained Brad. 'Do you have kids, sir?'

'Not as yet,' replied Carlisle slightly guardedly. 'But this is my wife, Alex,' he said showing Brad suitable pictures from his own mobile phone.

'She's a fine-looking lady,' remarked Brad. 'A real English rose. Say, do you and your wife have titles? Are you the lord of the manor, sir?'

'No…we're not from the aristocracy,' responded Carlisle. 'I have my rank in the British Royal Navy of Lieutenant Commander. I'm told I'm being promoted to captain although I may have to wait a few weeks before that's formally confirmed. I'm due to meet the King on 5th March.'

'Gee…! Are you meeting the King of England!? exclaimed Brad. 'That's awesome!'

By now Carlisle was feeling the effects of jet lag and retired to his room. He was aware that his security team were constantly keeping a close eye on him, but they were discrete and tried to stay out of the way.

In the morning after breakfast the security men offered to show him the sights of Washington DC and Leroy Johnson appeared at the front of the hotel with a big shiny black Cadillac from the pool of vehicles at the White House.

'We'll start off with Capitol Hill and the Library of Congress, sir,' advised Leroy Johnson as Carlisle buckled up and sat back in the comfort of the big limousine. 'Then we'll stop off at the Smithsonian Museum of Natural History. That's a very interesting place but after that we'll pay a visit to the National Air & Space Museum. That's one of my favourite places in Washington DC. Not so long ago I applied to NASA as they had one or two vacancies…. not to go to the Moon or Mars you understand! But they told me I was getting a little old. I'm sure I could have done a job servicing equipment or something like that.'

'You'd probably do a better job than some of the young people they employ,' contributed Brad Tierney.'

Carlisle enjoyed his guided tours of the museums but all too soon they were off to Old Town Alexandria and Mount Vernon but by then the jetlag was beginning to catch up with him again. Later in the afternoon his hosts took him to see the Arlington National Cemetery with its well-tended graves and memorials to famous Americans including John F. Kennedy. Before they deposited him back at his hotel Carlisle was given a tour of the National Mall which was particularly impressive being lit up as darkness fell. Carlisle warmly thanked his team for looking after him so well.

'I hope you enjoyed the day, sir,' proffered Brad as Carlisle left the Cadillac.

'I absolutely loved every minute of it,' replied Carlisle.

Brad joined him for dinner but once again Carlisle was feeling tired. He was well aware that tomorrow was an important day and accordingly he retired to his room early.

Although it was still dark Carlisle was awake at 6am and not long afterwards Brad was knocking lightly on his door.

'I thought you might benefit from a little help, sir,' offered Brad. 'But I'll give you longer if you need it.'

'That's very good of you, Brad,' replied Eddie. 'Actually, I could do with some assistance with my naval officer's dress uniform. Unfortunately, I wasn't able to bring my sword. I believe it would have caused a lot of trouble with security!'

Brad duly helped Eddie with putting on his uniform and soon they were joined by John O'Connor and went downstairs for a not insubstantial breakfast. Eddie chose his eggs sunny side up. Leroy was waiting outside with the Cadillac and soon they were driving the short distance to what Leroy announced as number 1600 Pennsylvania Avenue, Washington DC. Brad then led the way and dealt with White House security. They were then ushered to an ante room and met by another White House aide, Robert Bowater, who gave them some details of the day's itinerary.

'We'll begin by giving you a guided tour of the White House,' explained Robert. 'You'll have an opportunity to meet a few of the other service men and women who are here today to receive awards. This is Captain Howard Barmeitler of the 6th Armoured Division. He's being awarded the Medal of Honor, like you, for his bravery commanding a company of tanks in Germany last month. Although his tank was hit by the Russian forces and set on fire he stayed at his position in the tank and knocked out a whole column of enemy vehicles.'

'Pleased to meet you, Captain,' greeted Carlisle shaking the American officer's hand. He noted that Captain Barmeitler had sustained burns to his hands and face.

Carlisle was then introduced to Lieutenant Benjamin Rubenstein who also showed definite signs of burns and wounds sustained in combat.

'Lieutenant Rubenstein was an officer on the USS Frederick Sherman,' announced Robert. 'They were escorting an amphibious force towards the north German coast when his destroyer was hit by Russian missiles and set ablaze in a sinking condition. Without concern for his own safety Lieutenant Rubenstein stayed aboard the stricken destroyer until all the crew were rescued.'

Carlisle was pleased to shake the officer by the hand. They were clearly kindred spirits. Then Robert was taking them on the guided tour which lasted until lunchtime At this point President McConnell appeared and shook hands with the servicemen including Carlisle. The President praised each one for their courage and tenacity. Carlisle thought the President appeared tired and concerned and McConnell explained that he had just heard that Anchorage, Alaska and Seattle, Washington had just been hit by Russian missiles.

'Intelligence says the missiles fired at Anchorage were launched from Russian territory in Kamchatka, 'explained the President. 'I am told it may presage an amphibious attack on our country by Russian forces.'

'Don't worry, Mr President,' responded Captain Barmeitler. 'The Russians have a finite number of soldiers. We're pouring men into Europe right now and the Russians will have their hands full there.'

'I'm sure you're right,' replied Jack McConnell, 'But I don't know what effect it will have on public opinion in America. We're not used to the United States being attacked in its homelands by foreign powers. I'm going to address the nation at 5pm this afternoon. Captain Carlisle... could you assist by saying some words of support for our country... Perhaps some Churchillian speeches. Something to galvanise people and raise their spirits at this difficult time.'

'Yes, Mr President,' replied Carlisle without hesitation. 'I'll do whatever I can to help.'

After lunch Carlisle gave attention to what he was going to say. The President said that the address would be televised and broadcast across America. While Carlisle was engrossed in his task a hand patted him on the back and a female voice announced,

'Hi, Eddie. I thought it was you.'

'Samantha! What are you doing here?' asked Carlisle in surprise.

'I've been assisting Robert Finch with an exhibition here in Washington for the benefit of the President and the top brass,' explained Samantha. 'As you know the US military are buying our latest systems. The more they buy the better.'

'Yes, I understand,' acknowledged Carlisle. 'I'm here to receive my Medal of Honor.'

'That's great,' said Samantha. 'But isn't it only awarded to American service people?'

'That's right,' agreed Eddie. 'So they're making me an honorary US citizen.'

'Look, I've got to go and deliver a lecture,' interjected Samantha, 'But I'll meet up with you when it's finished. Give me a call on your phone and I'll take you out for dinner… Then perhaps we might adjourn to my hotel.'

Carlisle glanced up and smiled but Samantha was off and away.

'Friend of yours?' asked Lieutenant Rubenstein.

'Yes,' acknowledged Eddie. 'She's a very intelligent scientist. She has two university degrees and she's a director of a technology company.'

'Impressive,' replied Rubenstein.

During the afternoon Jack McConnell conferred with his aides and with Carlisle. They were joined by the President's wife, Bernadette, a dark-haired lady aged perhaps about forty-five who was accompanied by two of their dogs, Kujo and Nala. Kujo was introduced as a Bordeaux Mastiff while Nala was described as a Japanese Nikita. Both dogs appeared to instinctively head for Carlisle who surreptitiously fed them with tasty morsels as they sat either side of him at the tea table.

'Oh no!' exclaimed Bernadette. 'They're not supposed to eat between meals.'

'They'll be your friends for life,' smiled Jack McConnell. 'Anyway, to business. Father O'Brien will lead us with the Lord's Prayer and then announce the hymns. I think we should sing 'For those in peril on the sea,' Father O'Brien will announce other hymns of his choosing. Then I shall make an address to the American people after which we'll sing 'I'm proud to be an

American. Captain Carlisle… Can you then recite some famous Churchill speeches to inspire everyone at this difficult time?'

'Certainly, Mr President,' replied Carlisle who showed the President the texts of a number of Churchill's wartime speeches which Eddie had tapped out that afternoon on a laptop provided by Brad Tierney.

'They look great,' acknowledged the President. 'Then I'll deal with the awards for bravery and pronouncing Captain Carlisle an honorary US citizen.

The President's address had been due to be delivered around 5pm but there were technical hitches, and the ceremony did not begin until after 6pm being televised across the United States and indeed much of the world. Father O'Brien led with appropriate hymns and prayers. Then the President made his address to the nation.

'Earlier today the United States was hit my missiles fired by Russia causing the loss of American lives. I cannot put into words the anger which I feel at this outrage against the American people but whatever our response we must all stand firm and resolute. In these most difficult times, I am constantly reminded of the words of my great predecessor, Franklin D. Roosevelt…WE HAVE NOTHING TO FEAR EXCEPT FEAR ITSELF. Let us all now join together to sing *'I'm Proud to be an American.'*

'If tomorrow all the things were gone,
I worked for all my life…
God bless the U.S.A.'

The President proceeded to introduce Governor Donal MacAlaskey who joined him in his address to the nation,

'Joining me here on the rostrum is my good friend and ally, Governor Don MacAlaskey from New Hampshire. Don, do you have a message for the American people?'

'I sure do, Mr President,' replied Governor MacAlaskey. 'Our Motto in New Hampshire is: LIVE FREE OR DIE!'

The Governor had brought with him a strong contingent of political supporters and they cheered loudly and forcefully. The President then introduced Carlisle as a hero and saviour of the American people and explained that,

'Two troopships, the former passenger liners Georgic and Princess Helena Victoria, you may have sailed in them on your vacation sometime, were crossing the Atlantic Ocean bound for the war zones in Europe and packed full of many thousands of American servicemen and women. As you can imagine they were priority targets for the Russians and faced mass attacks by planes and submarines. Their close escort, a destroyer of the United States Navy, fought gallantly but was eventually overwhelmed by the Russian missiles and sank. But Captain Edmund Carlisle here of the British Royal Navy took over command of an elderly British frigate which might otherwise have been despatched to the breaker's yard and hurried to the rescue of the liners and successfully fought off attack after attack by planes and submarines and warships of the Russian forces. Thanks to Captain Carlisle and his crew more than eleven thousand personnel from the U.S. armed forces arrived safely in the port of Liverpool. Accordingly, it gives me great pleasure to bestow upon Captain Edmund Carlisle honorary citizenship of the United States of America. I understand Captain Carlisle would now like to address the American people.'

Carlisle walked up to the microphone and cleared his throat, considering the fact that many millions of people would be listening to his words.

'It is a great honour to have citizenship of this Great Nation bestowed upon me and to be able to call myself an American. You know, these difficult times in which we now find ourselves remind me very strongly of a previous conflict in the last century when Britain and America stood together against an evil power which was casting darkness across the world. President Roosevelt was a great friend and ally of the British people and of our British Prime Minister, Winston Churchill, whose mother, Jennie Jerome, was herself American and had lived in New York and Chicago. I would like to take this opportunity to read to you some of Winston Churchill's most well-known and inspiring speeches and trust that they will uplift your spirits and morale just as they did for people in the Free World in 1940.'

Carlisle spoke in what he hoped was his most Churchillian and authoritative voice. The assembled crowd including the President of the United States as well as governors and senators and top people in the U S military listened intently such that one could hear a proverbial pin drop.

'Hitler knows that he will have to break us in this island or lose the war.

If we can stand up to him all Europe may be free, and the life of the world may move forward into broad, sunlit uplands, but if we fail then the whole world, including the United States, and all that we have known and cared for, will sink into the abyss of a new dark age made more sinister, and perhaps more prolonged, by the lights of perverted science.'

Carlisle's words resounded across the White House and no doubt around the world. The situation was surreal, but he hoped he would lift the spirits of large numbers of people. He continued,

'Before I hand the microphone back to the President, I would like to read to you extracts from what is arguably Winston Churchill's most famous speech:

"Even though large tracts of Europe and many old and famous states have fallen or may fall into the grip of the Gestapo and all the odious apparatus of Nazi rule, we shall not flag or fail.

"We shall go on to the end, we shall fight in France, we shall fight on the seas and oceans, we shall fight with growing confidence and growing strength in the air, we shall defend our island, whatever the cost may be.

"We shall fight on the beaches, we shall fight on the landing grounds, we shall fight in the fields and in the streets, we shall fight in the hills, we shall never surrender, and even if, which I do not for a moment believe, this island or a larger part of it were subjugated and starving, then our Empire beyond the seas, armed and guarded by the British fleet, would carry on the struggle, until, in God's good time, the new world, with all its power and might, steps forth to the rescue and the liberation of the old".'

Carlisle received a standing ovation as he handed the stage back to the President. He had cause to be pleased. Glancing at Brad Tierney and Leroy Johnson he saw they had tears streaming down their faces as they stood to attention and saluted. Subsequently he was called forth along with brave Americans to be presented with the Medal of Honor, which was pinned to his chest by Admiral Chester Hamilton, commander of the U S First Fleet. After the ceremony Carlisle found himself collared by the Media including a representative from CBN News who wanted him to appear on their morning programme. Various newspaper reporters wanted him to give exclusive interviews and after making checks with the British Ministry of Defence and senior officers he was given permission to be interviewed by CBN News and by the New York Times, subject to many restrictions and to avoid saying anything controversial or politically embarrassing. Finally, when many people were departing from the White House to their various destinations Carlisle felt an arm around his shoulder.

'Hi, Mr Churchill,' said Samantha. 'How does it feel to be an American?'

Chapter 17

ALEX CARLISLE STEPPED OUT OF the small business jet which had brought her to Brazzaville and was immediately met by the Congolese Prime Minister, Jean Francoise Ndaye, the Minister of the Interior, Claude Vallaud and the intense heat and humidity of equatorial Africa. Alex was then chauffeur driven in a government limousine to her hotel near the city centre where she was reacquainted with Jean-Marc Moussavou and Etienne Kasanga. Claude Vallaud explained that the ceremony would be in two days' time to give her some opportunity to acclimatise. Both the Congolese Government and the French Government would be bestowing awards and rewards upon her and a representative from the World Wildlife Fund would also be attending. Later in the day Alex was given a tour of Brazzaville and had an opportunity to speak to a number of people involved with the conservation of the country's wildlife and then had dinner at her hotel before retiring early. In the morning after breakfast, she was again visited by Claude Vallaud who brought with him the Congolese Education Minister, Jean-Jacques Sassou-Rama. Both gentlemen were keen to give Alex an insight into the country's education system and Alex was taken to visit a number of schools around the city and to speak to the staff and the school children.

'There is so much we need to achieve,' explained Jean-Jacques, 'But money is always a problem. There is never enough of it.'

'I understand I am to receive rewards from several different sources,' responded Alex a little guardedly. 'But I believe that my involvement here is primarily in connection with conserving and protecting your wonderful wild creatures. Much of the Congo remains in its natural state but there are many threats. I know this first hand from my experience the last time I was here.'

'Certainly... certainly,' agreed Jean-Jacques. 'However, I would point out that in the Congo a little goes a long way. You find that you can make a difference in helping people who have nothing, and they will be forever grateful.'

'Might I make a suggestion. This is just a thought,' considered Alex. 'Hopefully, I may shortly be in a position to help establish a new game reserve in the northeast. Just possibly... and I am making no promises... I might be able to help establish a new school, perhaps in say Ouessou or another provincial town in that region. Realistically the Congolese Government would have to put up the lion's share of the resources.'

'Of course,' acknowledged Jean-Jacques. 'I am sure we can come to a suitable arrangement.'

'I can picture it already,' added Claude Vallaud, 'The Alex Carlisle Academy. Education is so important but given sufficient resources we can transform our country for the benefit of its people.'

The following day Alex was woken early by a call from Jean-Jacques Sassoo-Rama with details of the proposed arrangements for the ceremony which he explained would take place in a conference centre less than a mile from the hotel where Alex was staying. This was some relief to her as she was beginning to feel somewhat under the weather. The hotel was fortunately air conditioned but then Alex realised that she was late with her period. This was not altogether unusual for her metabolism and although she had felt unduly tired the previous day, she had put this down to the long journey from England. However, she had hardly any appetite for breakfast notwithstanding the delicious array of exotic tropical fruits laid out on a central table in the hotel dining room. At around 11am Jean-Jacques appeared with an Englishman who was introduced as David Blandforde-Speke, a senior official from the World Wildlife Fund. David congratulated Alex on her amazing efforts to assist the conservation of the wildlife of the region.

'You are clearly a very courageous lady,' praised David. 'We need people like yourself in this dangerous world.'

David went on to explain to Alex that the WWF were going to make an initial grant of £20,000 to her on condition that she utilised this money towards helping the relevant authorities in the Congo to develop a new Reserve in the northeast of the country.

'If you are able to achieve this then we would propose to make a further grant of a similar amount available and there is the prospect of additional monies being given in the future.'

Although she was not feeling at her best she thanked David for the generosity of his organisation. It did not take long to reach the conference centre where Alex was introduced to more officials including Jean-Paul Bretadeau from the French Government who also praised Alex for her courage and stamina.

'I can confirm that the Government of France is making a grant of 40,000 Euros available to you on condition that it is utilised towards development of secure game reserves in the Congo Republic,' explained Jean-Paul.

Claude Vallard added that his Government would be matching the award from the French but also that further sums would be made to Alex if she was successful with the wildlife conservation efforts and also that she assisted with developing educational establishments in the northern provinces. Once again Alex expressed her gratitude and said she would do all she could to help with these ventures.

The award ceremony began after a short break for refreshments. The Prime Minister, Jean Francois Ndaye introduced Alex to the gathering of officials and praised her for her courage and for her commitment to helping his country. The ceremony was conducted mainly in French, but Jean-Marc Moussavou kindly acted as interpreter for the benefit of Alex and others present whose first language was English. Alex was then presented with three cheques and made a fairly short speech thanking everyone for their generosity and emphasizing the importance of conservation and protecting the wildlife and the wilderness and habitats. Alex was well aware of the significance of all this but eventually had to make her apologies and retired to the lavatories feeling decidedly unwell. It was a relief for her when she was finally driven back to her hotel and found sanctuary alone in her room.

Several thousand miles to the north Carlisle had received confirmation of his promotion to Captain and had attended before the King at Buckingham Palace where he was awarded his Victoria Cross.

'Captain Carlisle, you have my undying admiration,' praised the King. 'I know you are very busy at this difficult time, but I wish you to come and join the Queen and myself for tea when things quieten down a little.'

'Your Majesty, I would be absolutely delighted to accept your kind invitation,' replied Carlisle.

'Well, that's splendid,' smiled the King. 'The Queen is very anxious to meet you as soon as possible. She would love you to tell us about your exploits on the high seas.'

'I certainly have a few tales to tell, sir,' replied Carlisle, 'But I have to concede that my crews are the real heroes and heroines. We always act as a team, and they have never failed to carry out their duty perfectly. Nelson himself would have been proud of them.'

The following morning Carlisle took the train down to Plymouth feeling on a high and metaphorically walking six feet off the ground. Boarding a launch, he was soon piped aboard the Aurora and met by several members of his crew including Simon Barrington and George McGlashan.

'May we start by congratulating you on your promotion, sir,' announced George. 'I would be grateful if you could come and join us for a wee dram in the Petty Officers' Mess once you have had an opportunity to get settled back in.'

'I will be very glad to accept your kind invitation, George,' replied Captain Carlisle. 'I always enjoy the excellent range of whiskeys you keep in the P.O.s mess, not to mention the rums.'

Simon Barrington was joined by Clive Robinson of Babrock Engineering who gave Carlisle a tour of the latest works which had been carried out on the Aurora. One of the floating cranes was still alongside but Clive assured the Captain that it would be moved out of the way within the next couple of days.

'We should then be in a position to begin sea trials,' said Simon Barrington. 'I'm keen to see what the Aurora is capable of. Essentially she's a new ship... completely rebuilt.'

Late in the evening Carlisle joined the Petty Officers in their Mess and enjoyed sampling their fine collection of top-quality single malt whiskies. He was not quite sure what time it was when he finally stumbled into bed, but it was certainly after 2am. The following evening, he was entertained by the Officers in their Mess. As well as being able to provide a first-class roast dinner whose delightful scents pervaded throughout the ship the Officers had an excellent collection of fine wines and Carlisle was pleased to be able to sample several of these. Despite nursing a sore head Carlisle was up early the following morning and Simon Barrington was reporting that the Aurora was now ready to commence sea trials. Those members of the crew who had been away on leave were now re-joining the ship. The civilian contingent from Darkforce were all present and eager to test their new technology while many of the contractors from Babrock remained on board for the time being to help ensure that the vessel's systems were operating properly and to iron out any bugs and glitches. The remaining floating crane was finally drawn out of the way and the ship's engines were started. By 1pm the Aurora was finally on the move with Carlisle giving the order for slow ahead navigating cautiously down the Tamar estuary with Sub-Lieutenant Gartmore acting in his capacity as Officer of the Watch. Simon Barrington and Mark Openshaw were also present on the bridge with George McGlashan at the helm. Carlisle noted that the estuary was becoming crowded with shipping, much of it from foreign navies and also vessels taken up from trade. Once out in the open sea he was able to order an increase in speed. Eventually as they approached Lulworth Cove Aurora was steaming at thirty knots and once within the zone of the firing range the order was given to test the ship's main 5-inch gun and the lighter calibre automatic weapons. From the Operations Room Roy Stringer, now promoted to Petty Officer, was reporting the approach of a flight of three Hawker Hunter jets from the civilian manned Fleet Requirements Unit.

'Crew to Action Stations… Crew to Action Stations!' called Carlisle over the Tannoy system as the klaxons sounded. 'This is a drill. Keep weapons tight.'

Despite their age the Hunters swept in fast and low creating the famous

Hawker Hunter blue note with their Rolls Royce Avon jet engines. Carlisle saw that the planes were right down skimming the surface of the sea and actually creating a wake. The *Aurora's* 5-inch was banging away continuously creating clouds of cordite smoke which quickly drifted astern. The opportunity was also taken to test the newly installed Japanese supplied Sea Urchin automatic gun system with its tremendous 4000 rpm rate of fire.

Having tested the gun systems Carlisle took Aurora further out to sea and ordered a further increase in speed.

'I want to see what she can do,' he informed the Engineering Department over the internal loop as they passed the Lizard.

Before long Engineering was reporting that they had attained 36 knots and as they headed further west the ship's speed rose further to 37 and then 38 knots. Carlisle was sure they could push Aurora even faster if the need arose, but darkness was now falling, and the shipping lanes were busy. Around 10pm Professor Finch of Darkforce appeared on the bridge and informed Carlisle that both the Ultra and Schrodinger systems were active. Carlisle remained on the bridge but sent Guy Hanson and Mark Openshaw to the Operations Room to oversee the working of these highly advanced systems. It was not long before they were reporting that Schrodinger had detected a submarine contact in the St George's Channel between Britain and Ireland. Soon this contact was identified as a Kilo class diesel powered submarine of the Russian Navy, and the information was immediately passed to Northwood and to the American base facility at Shannon Airport. A Lockheed P-8 Poseidon aircraft was quickly scrambled from Shannon while a Merlin helicopter was sent out from St Mawgam in Cornwall. In the meantime, Carlisle ordered a course alteration to intercept the enemy submarine. It was also an opportunity to test how fast the Aurora could now go.

'I want to get that submarine,' Carlisle informed Engineering. 'This one is ours.'

The Aurora's Engineering Department were similarly enthusiastic and did their utmost to oblige. By 5am the rebuilt frigate was powering ahead at 38 and then 39 knots. By 5-30am Carlisle took the opportunity to make use of the ship's new Goshawk helicopter piloted by Lieutenant Douglas Pentreath and assisted by his Observer, Sub-Lieutenant Kevin Farringdon. Roy Stringer was reporting that the USAF P-8 Poseidon from Shannon was nearing the position of the enemy vessel, but the Aurora was still 40 miles away. Their helicopter crew were given orders to make contact with the enemy with the utmost urgency. To add to the mounting tension a large convoy was heading eastwards bound for Liverpool at twenty knots. At 6-20am Roy Stringer informed the Captain that the USAF Poseidon aircraft was now making an attack on the Kilo Class vessel and had dropped sonar buoys and a homing torpedo. *Aurora's* Goshawk was still a few miles from the target submarine when the American aircraft signalled that it had hit and destroyed the Russian vessel. On board Aurora there was a combination of satisfaction but also anti-climax but within minutes the Darkforce Team were announcing that they had found a second submarine which had emerged from the cover of a submerged wreck and was now well positioned in the path of the approaching convoy. Aurora's helicopter was less than ten miles from this new contact and headed at full power to intercept. The P-8 from Shannon was still in the area and also headed towards the reported second submarine which was also identified as a Russian Kilo Class. When its captain realised they were under attack they dived the vessel to more than three hundred metres, rigging for silent running and shutting down as many systems as possible. The Aurora's Goshawk and the P-8 experienced difficulty in maintaining contact but the Darkforce operators soon relocated the submarine and guided in the attacking aircraft. Both the Goshawk and the P-8 dropped homing torpedoes. One of these struck the wreck which the submarine had been using for cover, but the torpedo dropped by Douglas Pentreath from the Goshawk was guided in by Schrodinger and no amount of clever cat and mouse tactics by the Russian captain could defeat the incredibly advanced technology of the Darkforce system. The crew of the helicopter and sonar operators aboard the Aurora were gratified to hear a thunderous trammel deep underwater sounding the destruction of their target.

The following day Carlisle received congratulations from Commodore Vincent and from Admiral Sir David Worcester who signalled,

'Many lives have been saved by your prompt and efficient action. Thanks to your efforts all the ships in the convoy to Liverpool arrived safely at their destination.'

Two days later Commodore Vincent came aboard Aurora accompanied by David Lloyd Carswell and were invited by Carlisle to the Captain's cabin. Both Commodore Vincent and Lloyd Carswell shook him firmly by the hand and took the opportunity to congratulate him once again on his successes. David Warwick knocked on the Captain's door and brought in three coffees.

'The top brass, led by the Americans, of course, are planning a major counter offensive against the Russian forces,' explained Lloyd Carswell. 'The main thrust will cross the north German plain... good tank country and I expect there will be an almighty battle. The naval forces will have an important role to guard the flanks of NATO and a major part of this will be to attack the Russians in Norway and Scandinavia and push them back. During the next few days, you will be ordered to attend a briefing in which the top commanders will set out their plans in more detail and no doubt they will tell you about your role in all this.'

'Who will be in overall command of our naval forces?' enquired Carlisle. 'Clearly they will be American.'

'The person in overall command will be Admiral Chester Hamilton USN, Commander of the U. S. First Fleet,' replied Commodore Vincent.

'I've met him,' said Carlisle. 'He pinned the Medal of Honor to my chest in Washington DC.'

'Well that's excellent,' responded the commodore. 'I expect he will have an important task for you to perform. I can tell you at this stage that you will be assigned to Task Force TF57 and one of your first roles will be to assist in landing special forces on enemy held shores. Aurora has, of course, the advantage of being equipped with the Darkforce Ultra system so you should be able to get in and out under the noses of the Russians hopefully without them seeing you or even knowing you are there.'

'Having performed this task another important role will be to knock out certain specified targets with your batteries of Warhawk cruise missiles,' explained Lloyd Carswell. 'It is likely that you will be part of a force of ships equipped with long range missiles. It is likely that these will be American, but the Japanese are also very generously providing a task group including at least two aircraft carriers and cruisers armed with long range cruise weapons. I believe they have also acquired the Warhawk system, and it is likely that you will be organised in the same task group. I understand you already have experience working with the Japanese Navy.'

'That's right,' acknowledged Carlisle. 'I have worked with the Japanese destroyer, *Yahagi*, and her commanding officer, Lieutenant Commander Chuichi Takahashi.'

'Good man,' smiled Commodore Vincent. 'This is clearly going to be very much a multi-national force.'

At that point Carlisle's mobile phone rang. He fumbled in his pocket.

'You'd better answer it,' advised the commodore. Carlisle did as instructed.

'Eddie, I'm sick,' announced a plaintiff voice.

'Alex? Where are you? What's the matter?' Carlisle was caught off balance.

'I'm not feeling well. I'm late with my period. The climate doesn't suit me. Eddie, I'm in hospital.'

'Hospital?' questioned Carlisle. 'Whereabouts? What's the matter? Presumably, you have some illness?'

'I'm in Brazzaville,' admitted Alex. 'In the Congo. You know... I received an invite from the Congolese Government to attend a ceremony, but I seem to have picked up some tropical illness. They're running some tests... Oh yes... and they think I may be pregnant... but it's early days.'

'Oh my God,' responded Carlisle. 'Is there a doctor or consultant there who I can speak to?'

Carlisle was put through to a young Congolese doctor, but they spoke only a few words of English and Carlisle found it difficult discussing tropical diseases in French.

'Let me speak to them,' interjected John Lloyd Carswell. Carlisle handed him his mobile phone and a conversation took place in French between Carswell and the doctor.

Carlisle considered the matter for a split second and then called Danielle

Sheldon who appeared at his cabin door. Carlisle gave her brief details of the problem.

'Don't worry, sir,' Danielle reassured him. 'As long as you're happy for me to do so I can make contact with the hospital in Brazzaville and the Congolese authorities. I expect the best thing would be to bring your wife home as soon as possible. Leave it to me.'

Two days later Carlisle was attending a briefing aboard the American cruiser, USS Leyte Gulf in Portsmouth. Admiral Hamilton in command of the US First Fleet chaired the meeting, and his subordinate officers included Rear Admiral Thomas Walton-Hague USN, Rear Admiral Charles Somerleyton RN and Captain Saburo Fuchida of the Japanese Navy. Admiral Hamilton explained that a major NATO Task Force was already being assembled for the purpose of launching an amphibious assault on the Norwegian coast.

'Our aim will be to drive out all Russian forces from Norway,' announced Admiral Hamilton. 'We have intelligence that the Russians have been planning an invasion of the British Isles using Norway as a springboard, so it is vitally important that our operation is a success. Rear Admiral Walton-Hague will be in command of Task Group 38.1 aboard the aircraft carrier USS Franklin D. Roosevelt. They will be accompanied by the carriers, USS Thomas Jefferson and USS John F. Kennedy as well as the Amphibious Carrier, USS America so you can see immediately that this will be a big enterprise. I can tell you that TG38.1 will head for the Kristiansund / Trondheim areas of the central Norwegian coastal region. Further north, an Anglo-Japanese Force known as Task Group 38.2 under Rear Admiral Somerleyton will head towards the Tromso region led by the British aircraft carrier, HMS Ark Royal and supported by the Carrier HMS Eagle and the Japanese Carriers, Shokaku and Zuikaku. Prior to their attacks Captain Carlisle here in command of HMS Aurora will land special forces in the Lofoten Islands and at certain specified points along the north Norwegian coast. Having achieved this task, he will re-join TG 38.2 where he will then partake in a long-range missile strike on vital Russian installations both in occupied Norway and on Russian territory including Murmansk. I understand that the Japanese missile cruisers Kinugasa and Haguro as well as the

American warships USS John S. McCain and USS Saratoga will also be part of this group. I would add that we will also have support from Strategic Air Command using B1 and B2 bombers to hit targets deep inside enemy territory.'

'May I ask, sir, when is this attack due to begin?' enquired Carlisle.

'As soon as possible,' replied Admiral Hamilton. 'Speed is of the essence. The Russians keep pouring their forces into Norway and Scandinavia. Can you get your ship to sea by the end of this week?'

Carlisle returned to the Aurora where every effort was made to get the ship ready for the planned operation. Dries van Riebeck came aboard with his special forces team and their electric boats. Samantha Langley also arrived at the Captain's quarters and asked Carlisle for permission to test the Ultra system as they would clearly be needing to make use of it. Carlisle conferred with Lieutenant Commander Takahashi and the Aurora, and the *Yahagi* slipped out before dawn on the Wednesday morning heading south-west towards the Bay of Biscay. Once they were well out to sea and away from land and the shipping lanes Carlisle authorised the Darkforce Team to activate Ultra. Initially the system was tested under low power and once again a greenish haze began to envelope the Aurora. Gradually the electromagnetic fields surrounding the ship were strengthened until the *Yahagi* reported that she was having difficulty maintaining both radar and visual contact. Samantha and her team then increased the power output further until the *Yahagi* signalled that she had lost contact. On board the Aurora crew members experienced the usual feelings of nausea and headaches when Ultra was activated and a handful even lost consciousness. Carlisle felt they had established that Ultra was functioning properly, and power output was steadily reduced with Aurora once again becoming visible both on radar and to the mark one eyeball.

Back in Plymouth the Aurora was moored in a quiet jetty. Red flags were flown, and ammunition was brought aboard including shells for the guns and Aster and Sea Venom missiles. Danielle Sheldon was able to report to Carlisle that she had communicated with the hospital in Brazzaville and had even spoken to Alex.

'They're still carrying out tests, sir,' Danielle informed the captain. 'They had been wondering about Schistosomiasis.'

'What's that?' queried Carlisle.

'Bilharzia,' added Danielle.

'Oh hell,' retorted Carlisle. 'That's very nasty, isn't it?'

'Yes, but apparently they don't think she's got it,' Danielle reassured him. 'The doctors think it's some kind of gastroenterological disorder. It's quite common out there. Probably some kind of water born infection possibly even carried by snails. Anyway, they're hoping to send her home to England soon.'

'Everything alright, sir?' enquired Simon Barrington.

'Not entirely,' responded the captain. 'It's Alex. It seems she can either succumb to some unpleasant tropical infection in the depths of the Congo or be sent home to England and take her chances with Mr Vatutin's missiles and bombs.'

'I'm sorry to hear that, sir, but I'm sure everything will be okay. At least I can report that we should be able to sail tomorrow night. Another oil barge is just coming alongside to top up our fuel tanks.'

'Well done, number one,' acknowledged Carlisle.

The following morning, he received a call from the hospital in Brazzaville with the assistance of the Aurora's advanced communications systems and was able to speak to Alex.

'How are you feeling?' he asked her with some trepidation.

'I am feeling a little better,' Alex assured him. 'They've established that I've not got Bilharzia, and they assess I'm well enough to be flown home this weekend. Will you be at home too?'

'I can't be specific,' replied Carlisle guardedly. He knew the enemy would be listening intently to all communications. 'I'll get home as soon as I can.'

'That's good,' acknowledged Alex. 'They have confirmed I'm pregnant. You're going to be a daddy.'

It was not just the Russians who were eavesdropping. For the rest of the day Carlisle kept receiving congratulations from members of his crew and even from the *Yahagi* and the USS John S. McCain which were moored close by. Then there was an encrypted signal from Rear Admiral Leighton,

Commander of the 9th Frigate Squadron which informed him curtly over the secure link,

'Operation Skua is active. Be ready to sail by 0200 hours.'

Carlisle knew exactly what this meant and final preparations were made. To help confuse any enemy agents or indeed spy satellites who might be observing them a large consignment of tropical equipment was brought on board and stowed prominently on the foredeck and on the helicopter pad at the stern. Finally, the Aurora slipped her moorings at 0130 hours with Carlisle and Simon Barrington standing on the bridge and George McGlashan at the helm. The ship was blacked out and moving almost silently. The watch keepers were doubled as the amount of shipping in the area was considerable and the risk of collision in the darkness was high. David Warwick was busily handing out mugs of hot black coffee and plates of sandwiches. By dawn they were entering the St George's Channel and heading northwards tucking in astern of a large Liberian registered freighter which was sailing independently at sixteen knots. Eventually the freighter headed towards Liverpool and Carlisle ordered an increase in speed to 25 knots and continued sailing northwards. Later in the day Carlisle called a meeting with his SAS and Royal Marine contingents. They had already been studying detailed maps of northern Norway including the Lofoten Islands and also the port of Narvik. The SAS were represented by Dreis van Reibeck and his sergeant, Henny Stein who confirmed that their task would initially be one of surveillance, keeping watch on enemy forces and installations. Once the main Allied landings were taking place the SAS would take on a more active role sabotaging Russian installations and attacking the enemy in his rear. The Marines were represented by Lieutenant John Cavanagh and Sergeant Campbell and Carlisle confirmed that, using the Ultra system, he would endeavour to get the Marines as close as possible to the port of Narvik. Like the SAS the Marines would initially be tasked with surveillance but would attack the enemy once the main Allied forces arrived. The meeting was also attended by an SBS contingent led by Lieutenant Simon Catesby and his second in command, Sergeant Liam King. The SBS team were tasked with landing near the airbase at Bodo and warning NATO forces particularly of sorties flown by the Russian Airforce. Later in the mission the SBS would also take part in sabotage and attacks on aircraft on the ground and even on planes landing and taking off. Carlisle conferred with Simon Catesby as to the best location for landing the SBS squad and a suitable site was chosen.

During the hours of darkness Aurora sailed further north beyond the Orkneys and Carlisle took a route between the Shetlands and the Faroes. During the middle of the day there were several alerts as Russian aircraft were detected on radar. The Ultra system was activated on moderate power to help cloak the ship in electro-magnetic fields and the consequent invisibility. Carlisle made a course alteration to take the ship further west into the North Atlantic and away from the Norwegian coast and its airbases. The following night Carlisle altered course to starboard and well before dawn the Aurora was moving into position to land the SBS team on the north shore of a large fjord where they would then climb to higher ground giving good visibility of the airfield at Bodo but at the same time providing cover for the special forces. The Aurora was enveloped in a green mist as she dropped anchor in the fjord and the SBS men were put silently ashore. There were several local fishing vessels located in the fjord and two small patrol boats but they all appeared to be unaware of the presence of the British warship. Once the special forces team had landed Carlisle was anxious to be away as quickly as possible. This time the Aurora was heading for a point about five miles from the small fishing village of Henningsvaer on the southern coast of the Lofoten Islands. The Ultra system was in constant use and although it was effective in concealing the position and indeed the existence of the Aurora there was at the same time a constant risk of collisions with other vessels. Fortunately Carlisle managed to land his SAS men apparently undetected by the enemy. Ultra had done its job well assisted by the foggy conditions in these high latitudes north of the Arctic Circle. Carlisle then conferred with Lieutenant John Cavanagh, the commander of the Aurora's temporarily expanded Marine detachment. Both men were concerned that dawn would be breaking by the time they navigated the network of fjords leading towards Narvik. Carefully studying maps of the area, it was clear that the wider Vestfjord narrowed into

Ofotfjord and Lieutenant Cavenagh requested Carlisle to put his Marines ashore on the south side of Ofotfjord probably in the vicinity of Ballangen or Skjomnes. The latter would be preferable as it was closer to the port, but Cavanagh was well aware of the difficulties and the dangers of being observed and discovered by the enemy.

Wasting no time Carlisle ordered course to be set for Vestfjord and for Engineering to give revolutions for 32 knots. Conditions were still dark and foggy, and radar was frequently warning of other vessels in the vicinity. A course alteration to starboard was necessary to avoid a large Ore carrier heading out towards the open sea and more than one Russian naval vessel patrolled the approaches. For Carlisle maintaining secrecy was essential and contact with all other shipping had to be avoided. As they headed into Vestfjord Carlisle ordered a reduction in speed to twenty knots and the lookouts were doubled. The Ultra system was operating on a moderate power outage and Aurora was enveloped in a thin green mist. Navigation was conducted largely with the use of radar and Carlisle was already aware that finding a suitable place to land the Marines was going to be difficult. John Cavanagh and Sergeant Turner arranged for several electric boats to be made ready and Carlisle confirmed he would bring Aurora to a standstill as close to Skjomnes as he dared so that the Marines could disembark. As they reduced speed to just sixteen knots upon entering Ofotfjord the Arctic fog suddenly cleared as the sun began to rise, and several vessels became visible including a Russian patrol boat. Carlisle ordered a small course alteration so as to gain some cover from a headland on the south shore. Speed was reduced still further until the Aurora drifted almost silently to a standstill. The electric boats were carefully lowered into the cold waters with a thin veil of mistiness rising from the fjord. Fortunately, the weather was still calm although an icy breeze funnelled up the valley. Then the Marines were quietly on their way heading for the shore and trying hard to keep out of human contact. Having performed his covert taxi service Carlisle ordered, 'Slow ahead,' and Aurora was heading west back up the confined waters of Ofotfjord. The Russian patrol vessel which they had spotted earlier appeared to be approaching from astern and travelling rather faster than the Aurora.

'He seems to be taking a look at us,' commented Sub-Lieutenant Gartmore. 'No doubt he's perplexed as to what we are.'

Carlisle conferred briefly with the Darkforce Team and power was temporarily increased. It was something of a dilemma because many of the crew were complaining of feeling unwell and several had already been taken sick. Then Roy Stringer was reporting another vessel dead ahead approximately where Ofotfjord joins into Vestfjord.

'He's slowing to a standstill,' reported Roy. There's another patrol boat astern of him.'

Carlisle had to react quickly to this dangerous situation. Secrecy was paramount but the Russians were clearly attempting to block them in.

'Engineering… Give me revolutions for 26 knots,' he ordered. 'Everyone brace for a collision.'

With her new engines Aurora picked up speed rapidly and two Russian vessels were clearly visible in the morning sunshine creating a barrier across the confined waters. George McGlashan was at the helm.

'BRACE!' called Carlisle over the internal Tannoy system. He was not sure what the outcome would be.

When it came the collision was something of an anti-climax. Sub-Lieutenant Gartmore, acting as Officer of the Watch, estimated that the Russian patrol vessel appeared to be a Matka Class and probably displaced around five hundred tons. Aurora on the other hand, in her rebuilt form, displaced nearer to ten thousand tons. As she increased speed her ice strengthened bows and hull sliced through the much smaller Russian vessel like a knife through butter. Able Seaman Frank Kerry who had been manning the twin 30mm mounting atop the hanger was surprised to see the two halves of the enemy patrol vessel pass either side of the Aurora, the bow section to port and the rapidly sinking stern section to starboard. This surreal scene was accompanied by the loud hissing of escaping superheated steam from ruptured pipework and water mains on the Russian ship and the cries of drowning men. The enemy had clearly been caught off balance. The second Russian patrol vessel stopped to rescue survivors, but Carlisle was well aware of the dangers of the situation for his own ship.

'We need to divert their attention from our Marine contingent,' said Carlisle to Simon Barrington and Mark Openshaw.

'Russian Nanuchka Class missile corvette approaching at twenty-seven knots from seaward,' advised Roy Stringer from the radar plot in the Operations Room.

Aurora was now entering Vestfjord but the waters were still confined with little room for manoeuvre.

'Chief Weapons Officer... Engage that enemy warship immediately with everything you have,' Carlisle ordered Mark Openshaw.

The *Aurora's* 5-inch main gun was already loaded and aiming at the target. Ten shells were fired in rapid succession. The first went over and exploded on the side of a mountain adjoining the fjord but the second and third shells hit the Nanuchka causing fires to break out. The fourth and fifth shells also struck their target which started to billow thick black smoke as the Russian vessel slewed to starboard with more projectiles slamming into its structure. Aurora kept firing as she passed less than a hundred metres from the stricken corvette. The 30mm and smaller calibre weapons mounted on the Aurora were now also pouring fire into the burning ship which was listing visibly to starboard and clearly sinking. Having dealt effectively with this threat Carlisle and his team had to make a quick course alteration to port to avoid a collision with a large Ore carrier heading into the fjord but finally they escaped the narrow confines of the fjords and headed around the southern tip of the Lofoten Islands. It was still broad daylight when the Anti-Air Warfare Team reported unidentified aircraft approaching from the south.

'Clearly from Bodo,' advised Mike Addison as members of his Team advised of the height and bearing of the incoming planes. 'Two waves of four aircraft each... a mix of Sukhoi Su-17s and SU-24s.'

Carlisle quickly conferred with the Darkforce Team and Dr Langley advised a temporary increase in the power output of the Ultra system. Once again Aurora disappeared in a thin green haze and Carlisle brought the ship close in towards land on the northerly side of the islands in an effort to gain additional cover. The leading flight of four Russian aircraft was now closing rapidly and clearly searching for their target. Carlisle was initially minded to shoot them down with his missiles but both Simon Barrington and Mike Addison believed this would help to give away their own position to the enemy. Accordingly, Carlisle gave the order to keep weapons tight. The Russian planes circled the area for more than an hour but eventually headed away to search the open ocean. Carlisle brought Aurora cautiously into a sheltered cove and, as darkness fell, dropped anchor and awaited further orders. For several hours, the mist and fog cleared. There were no further reports of enemy forces approaching the area and those members of the crew who were not on duty at the time were allowed to go out on deck to watch the spectacular Aurora Borealis, the Northern Lights. Even Carlisle allowed himself half an hour or so to observe this amazing phenomenon. Eventually by dawn the mist and fog returned to enwrap the large warship in a cold damp cloak. The surrounding topography also helped to conceal the ship from patrolling enemy vessels and aircraft, but Carlisle was becoming frustrated that there were no orders or signals from high command. Fortunately, although there were several reports of enemy air activity the planes were some distance away but Carlisle knew that the longer they sat tight the greater the chances of being detected by the enemy. Dusk fell and then nightfall, but the situation remained unchanged. Andrew Morton and his team listened in to the Russian radio traffic and signals, assisted considerably by Danielle Sheldon and her language skills. Finally at 23-40 hours Danielle reported receiving an encrypted message from Admiral Hamilton over the secure link giving Aurora orders as to where and when she was to rendezvous with the other ships in her allotted Task Group TG38.2 commanded by Rear Admiral Somerleyton flying his flag in the Royal Navy aircraft carrier, HMS Ark Royal.

Carlisle immediately gave orders for Aurora to weigh anchor and move slowly and silently away from the shelter of the cove and to head northwards into the Arctic Ocean. Well before dawn his teams were in communication with both Admiral Hamilton aboard the USS Franklin D. Roosevelt and with Admiral Somerleyton in the Ark Royal. Roy Stringer was reporting that the nearest elements of Task Group TG38.2 were only 50 miles to the west and similarly heading northwards. Not long after dawn planes from the two British carriers and also the Japanese Aircraft Carriers, Shokaku and Zuikaku, were launched. First to be flown off were a series of planes on reconnaissance missions while combat air patrols of fighters were sent aloft to give protection around the Task Group. A Russian Tupolev bomber which approached to within 40 miles of the Task Group was intercepted by British F-35 fighter aircraft from the Ark Royal and shot down. Carlisle knew that the Russians would now be aware that a powerful NATO force was approaching their territory and would be likely to launch their own attacks. It did not take long for the Russians to react and radar was soon reporting formations of enemy aircraft heading towards the Task Group. One group of six Sukhoi Su-24 bombers selected the Aurora and attacked from astern at low level. Mike Addison as PWO (Air) aboard the Aurora launched a salvo of Asters at the incoming jets. Two were shot down when still out of sight while a third was destroyed by a Japanese fighter from the Carrier, Zuikaku. The remaining three Russian aircraft continued their attack. Mike Addison fired a further salvo of Asters which shot down two more attacking planes while another was blasted out of the sky by the new Japanese manufactured Sea Urchin system firing shells at the rate of 4000 rounds per minute at the hostile aircraft. Mike and his anti-air warfare team had cause for jubilation, but Carlisle knew it would presage many more attacks by the Russians. Out to the west the Carrier Task Group was having to fight off multiple attacks by Tupolev long range bombers firing anti-ship missiles and by fast Migs and Sukhois carrying bombs and rockets. Later in the day Admiral Somerleyton issued orders for the ships in his Task Group to take up their allotted positions. Aurora remained on the eastern periphery of TG38.2 close to the American cruiser, USS Saratoga and the destroyer, USS John S. McCain. The Japanese missile cruisers, Kinugasa and Haguro, both equipped with the new Warhawk cruise missile, were also sailing in close proximity. Further to the west the aircraft carriers were stationed in the centre of the Group surrounded by their close escorts which included HMS Arethusa and also the British frigate HMS Galatea now commanded by Carlisle's good friend, Lieutenant Commander Charles Dunbar. Carlisle was reminded of that wonderful holiday he and Alex had spent in the Western Isles such a short time ago as guests of the Dunbar family. He was suddenly brought back down to earth by the blaring of klaxons and radar was reporting another formation of attacking Russian aircraft. Twelve Sukhois were leading the assault pursued by British and Japanese fighter planes which broke up the enemy formation and shot down five Sukhois. Three more Sukhois were destroyed by missiles and anti-aircraft fire from the warships but four managed to get through the defences and hit the Japanese Helicopter Carrier, Hyuga, with several bombs. The Hyuga was set on fire and the billowing clouds of black smoke towered into the Arctic skies, visible for miles around. This attack was followed up by three big Tupolev bombers carrying long range anti-ship missiles. One of the Tupolevs was shot down by F-35 fighters when still fifty miles from the Task Group but two others managed to launch their missiles before they themselves were destroyed. As two of the missiles approached the Task Group at supersonic speed one was shot down by the Aurora's Asters while the USS Thomas Kinkaid shot down two further missiles with the new Valkyrie system.

Once this latest attack had been repulsed Rear-Admiral Somerleyton was anxious to launch the salvoes of Warhawk cruise missiles carried by a number of the ships under his command. On the Aurora the Chief Weapons Officer, Mark Openshaw, had already been supplied with the co-ordinates for his allotted targets. At 20-30 hours the order was given to fire the first salvo of four Warhawk long range cruise missiles at the Russian military base near Tromso. Even in these high latitudes darkness was falling and the sight of the four missiles being blasted from their launchers and streaking away at supersonic speed towards the eastern horizon was spectacular. Carlisle then made a course alteration to enable the Warhawks carried in the missile batteries on the port side to be fired. Once again the missiles blasted from their launchers, targeted on the Russian base and port facilities in Murmansk several hundred miles away. This firing was quickly followed up by missiles launched from the Japanese cruisers, Haguro and Kinugasa. The Haguro was targeting Russian held airfields at Bodo and Tromso while the Kinugasa attacked Russian troop concentrations in northern Norway and Arctic Russia. Cruise missiles were also fired by the USS Saratoga and the USS John S. McCain as well as the Destroyer, USS Thomas Kincaid. These attacks were followed up by bombing raids by USAF B1 and B2 strategic bombers flying directly from their bases in America, which focused upon strikes against Russian ports and infrastructure. Aircraft from the Carriers in Task Group 38.2 interdicted roads and railways and bombed Russian troop concentrations and armour. Enemy missile and radar sites as well as command centres were priority targets which were also hit.

It was still dark when the escorting frigates, HMS Arethusa and HMS Galatea, reported submarine contacts to the north. Both frigates sent out their Wildcat helicopters to seek out these new targets. At dawn Carlisle sent the Aurora's new Goshawk to join the search while the Ark Royal launched two of her new Sea Eagle tilt rotor aircraft which were configured primarily as anti-submarine platforms. Inevitably there were more air raid alarms, but Rear Admiral Somerleyton congratulated the Aurora and other ships in the Task Group for the accurate shooting of their cruise missiles and the damage caused to their allotted targets. Later in the morning came confirmation that two Russian submarines which had been stalking the Task Group had been sunk. By the evening Admiral Chester Hamilton was feeling sufficiently confident to bring forward Task Force 39 which was the NATO amphibious assault. Task Group 39.1 would follow TG38.1 to land the advanced elements of the Anglo-American Army on the Norwegian coast near Kristiansund. Task Group 39.2 would rendezvous with TG38.1 prior to landing NATO and Japanese troops near Tromso in northern Norway. There was still a strong element of risk, but it was felt that the best option was to hit the Russians while they were off balance after the latest bombing and cruise missile strikes. Meanwhile the missions flown by the American B1 and B2 bombers intensified and sorties flown by planes from the Carriers increased. After dark, the leading elements of Task Group 39.2 joined TG38.2 and Carlisle was pleased that the *Yahagi* was amongst them, commanded by his good friend, Chuichi Takahashi, escorting the Japanese Helicopter Carrier, Ise, which had been hurried up north as a replacement for the badly damaged Hyuga. The latter had been towed out of the immediate combat zone having sustained heavy casualties with ninety-three men dead and more than two hundred wounded. Both Admiral Hamilton and Rear Admiral Somerleyton were anxious to get the lead elements of the amphibious force ashore as quickly as possible. Just before dawn the landings began preceded by air drops of paratroopers who seized vital bridges and other important facilities. The airbase at Bodo was taken together with other smaller airfields and significantly the port of Narvik was also captured. Carlisle was able to make contact with his Marines who informed him that the Russians had been driven out after sustaining heavy casualties. With Narvik in NATO hands the task of landing troops and supplies was made much more straightforward. Rear Admiral Somerleyton ordered TG38.2 to head towards the Norwegian coast to give covering fire to the landings. During the morning Russian positions on land were engaged and faced a barrage of shell fire from the assembled warships as well as bombing attacks from NATO aircraft. On more than one occasion where Russian troops were offering strong resistance particularly amongst the mountains and fjords the USAF flew large transport aircraft dropping enormous fuel air bombs on the enemy positions. These were non-nuclear weapons but created a massive blast effect similar to that of a tactical nuclear weapon which could devastate a swathe of territory and kill everyone within it. In the otherwise sparsely populated regions of northern Norway where the danger of harming civilians was minimal such weapons were most efficient at clearing paths ahead of advancing NATO troops. Once again the NATO commanders were anxious to make progress as quickly as possible and to avoid their forces becoming bogged down.

Carlisle was very satisfied with the progress being made and reports were received of similar advances further south where TG38.1 was achieving its objectives. Importantly the NATO armies on the North German Plain were also moving forward and making gains. Everywhere the Russians were now in retreat. During the night, the Aurora was ordered to join other ships in TG38.2 in bombarding Russian troops further north who were being sent southwards as reinforcements for their beleaguered comrades. Before dawn Aurora had fired two hundred 5-inch shells mostly at Russian land forces. Two Russian Nanuchka Class missile corvettes which had attempted to attack the NATO ships were sunk and a Russian Tupolev bomber had been shot down. In the morning once the mist and fog had cleared the weather was cold, but the skies were azure blue. Carlisle stood on the bridge of the

Aurora and considered that for once things were heading in the right direction. He had managed to speak to Alex on his mobile phone and she had confirmed that she was now back at Longfleet Farm being ably assisted by Sandra and members of Sandra's family. Out on the starboard beam Carlisle could just about discern figures clad in warm Arctic clothing standing on the bridge wing of HMS Galatea and he felt reassured that his friend, Charles Dunbar, was amongst them. On the port quarter, the Japanese destroyer, *Yahagi*, was keeping station both with *Aurora* and with the big cruiser, Kinugasa. He was brought down to earth when Danielle Sheldon passed him a signal from the flagship ordering the vessels in TG38.2 to advance northwards towards the Barents Sea. The USS Thomas Kincaid and the USS Saratoga with their AEGIS 4000 systems formed an outer screen while the vulnerable aircraft carriers were held back to try to keep them out of harm's way. By the afternoon advanced elements of TG38.2 were passing the North Cape and an American Fast Combat Support Ship, the 40,000-ton USS Jefferson City, was brought up to re-supply the warships which were running low on supplies and ammunition. At 19-30 hours the Jefferson City came alongside the Aurora and the two ships sailed side by side at fifteen knots with George McGlashan at the helm of the British vessel. The replenishment at sea took several hours and soon after it was completed the USS Thomas Kincaid was reporting enemy air activity with Russian aircraft approaching from the southeast. Two Tupolev bombers were shot down at a range of more than fifty miles by the Kincaid's Valkyrie missiles. Simultaneously helicopters from the NATO and Japanese warships out on anti-submarine patrol reported several submarine contacts. Sonar operators on the NATO warships reported an underwater explosion to the east of the Task Group marking the destruction of a Russian vessel. Another enemy submarine, a Victor III, was blown to the surface in a badly damaged condition. Its crew managed to scuttle their vessel before it was captured by NATO forces. TG38.2 continued its advance into hostile seas, brushing aside opposition until a warning was received from the flagship.

'Salvo launch of SS-N-44 missiles reported from location thirty miles north of Murmansk. These weapons are believed to carry nuclear warheads and are capable of hypersonic velocity. Adopt immediate procedure for dealing with NBC attack.'

On board the Aurora the klaxons were blaring a cacophony of noise which was in itself unnerving,

'BARGGH! BARGGH! BARGGH! Incoming tactical nuclear bombs,' announced the inhuman electronic voice.

The USS Thomas Kincaid and the USS Saratoga both announced that they had succeeded in shooting down two of these missiles, but a further salvo was fired by the Russians.

'Captain, we need to ramp up the Ultra power output,' urged Dr Langley. Professor Finch also made clear his support for this move.

Carlisle conferred with his senior officers, but he was of two minds as to the correct course of action in these circumstances.

'If we power up the Ultra system now we will be leaving the other ships in the Task Group to their fate,' he argued.

'I know what you mean, sir, but there's probably little we can do right now other than try to save our own skins,' responded Simon Barrington.

Seconds later Mike Addison and his team were reporting that they were engaging two of the incoming nuclear warheads. Shortly afterwards they were able to announce that they had hit and destroyed one of the SS-N-44s while another was shot down by the Saratoga. In the meantime the Russians launched air attacks with Sukhois supported by Tupolevs firing long range anti-ship missiles.

'Sir, we've just received a distress call from the *Yahagi*,' announced Danielle Sheldon. 'She says she's been hit by a missile and has sustained severe damage and many casualties.'

Carlisle immediately made a course alteration to head to the assistance of the *Yahagi*. He greatly hoped that his good friend, Chuichi Takahashi, was unharmed. The *Aurora's* 5-inch gun was blasting away continuously at enemy planes and missiles and Mike Addison, and his team were firing salvoes of Asters and making good use of the Sea Urchin system. The battle raged as Aurora drew alongside the crippled *Yahagi*. The Japanese destroyer's helicopter was fortunately undamaged and began ferrying men across to the

Aurora. Carlisle recalled his ship's own Goshawk helicopter from patrol, and this too joined in the rescue effort together with helicopters from the Japanese Carrier, Ise, which was close by. The *Yahagi* had been hit amidships by a Russian anti-ship missile and was on fire with thick black smoke billowing a thousand feet into the Arctic sky. Crewmen from the Japanese destroyer assembled in the ship's hangar awaiting rescue while others attempted to fight the fires. Priority was given to wounded men and these included the Captain, Chuichi Takahashi, who was suffering from severe burns. First Officer Yasuda had temporarily taken command of the *Yahagi*.

While this drama was taking place the electronic warning was blaring out again aboard the Aurora.

'Incoming tactical nuclear weapons approaching. Prepare ship for immediate NBC attack!'

Initially Carlisle thought the blinding flash of light was a magazine exploding on the *Yahagi*. It was followed by a tremendous blast which knocked everyone off their feet. Petty Officer Roy Stringer was calling from his console,

'All communication is lost, sir. I can't make contact with any of the ships or planes in the TG.'

From below the Engineering Department were also announcing that all power had been lost.

'Steering's gone, sir,' called George McGlashan. 'She won't respond to the helm.'

Carlisle picked himself up off the deck and carried on issuing orders as if this was a normal situation.

'Switch to auxiliary power,' he instructed the Engineering Department while using his best efforts to maintain a cool countenance. Whatever the pressures he now faced he was mindful that he was one of that very small band of Victoria Cross holders and he was compelled to behave accordingly particularly in front of his crew.

Emergency lighting came on and Engineering were able to confirm they had restored limited power but then came a second blinding flash and a huge atomic mushroom cloud which towered thousands of feet into the sky. All around the sea was boiling at unimaginably high temperatures and worst of all the Officer of the Watch was shouting that a huge wall of water more than a hundred feet high was rapidly approaching the Task Group and had already engulfed ships positioned further ahead in the column. Carlisle had but a short time to issue a warning to his crew over the internal communications loop as the giant tsunami swept upon them, a massive tidal wave caused by the explosion of one or possibly two tactical nuclear weapons. Fires had begun to break out around the Aurora but many of these were quickly extinguished by the sudden inrush of thousands of tons of sea water. As Carlisle, and indeed everyone else, gripped hold tightly to whatever was to hand he thought of Alex and of his farm and its animals and of his as yet unborn child. Then all was darkness. This was the end.

'Good night, Alex.'

Chapter 18

AT LONGFLEET FARM ALEX AND Sandra were constantly listening to the news broadcasts on the radio and television. Every time the fighting was mentioned they held their breath, terrified of bad tidings. Sometimes Alex was physically sick. They were aware of the recent NATO successes but also that the Russians had resorted in desperation to their powerful nuclear arsenal. Alex did not know where her husband was since this was classified information, but she had heard that the Russians had used tactical nuclear weapons against NATO forces in Norway as well as in other sectors. She and Sandra were listening to one such broadcast when Gaz appeared hesitantly at the kitchen door.

'I think someone has just arrived in the courtyard,' he said. 'There's a black car outside.'

Alex and Sandra glanced worriedly at each other. Alex's heart missed a beat. She knew what was coming. A distinguished looking man aged in his forties in full naval officer's uniform appeared at the front door accompanied by another man, slightly older and smartly dressed in a dark suit.

'Come this way, please,' said Gaz.

Alex turned as white as a sheet when the two men entered the farmhouse.

'Please forgive our intrusion,' apologised the man in naval uniform. 'I am Commodore Charles Vincent. This gentleman here is Mr John Lloyd Carswell, a senior civil servant in the Ministry of Defence. I'm afraid we have some very bad news.'

'It's Eddie, isn't it?' stammered Alex. 'I knew something dreadful had happened. Somehow, I've been awaiting this moment.' Alex felt her world suddenly disappear down a dark hole in the ground.

'I'm not permitted to say very much,' continued the commodore, 'But your husband and his frigate were engaged in operations against the enemy in Arctic waters. They and NATO forces as a whole were achieving many successes but eventually the Russians took to using their nuclear weapons. The Task Force in which your husband and his ship were sailing was attacked with nuclear missiles. You can understand the consequences of that.'

'Was his ship sunk?' asked Sandra.

'Eyewitness reports say the Aurora was lost with all hands. There were no survivors,' replied the commodore. 'At the time they were attacked your husband, and his crew were rescuing survivors from another Allied ship which was also sunk.'

'Eddie can't be dead. They'll find him,' gasped Alex. 'Tell me he'll be alright.'

'My dear, I really am most dreadfully sorry,' responded Commodore Vincent. 'Your husband was a most remarkable man, my best officer and a personal friend. His loss is a grave loss to us all.'

'But what am I going to do!?' pleaded Alex as the reality of her situation sank in. 'How am I going to run this farm? I'm having a baby. What on earth am I going to do? Alex collapsed under the pressure of this terrible news and Sandra managed to sit her in an arm chair where a number of dogs and cats came to offer her consolation.

'Would you gentlemen care for a cup of tea?' enquired Gaz who was joined in the kitchen by Jack Blofield.

'It's Eddie,' whispered Gaz to Jack.

Jack nodded an acknowledgement. He knew the smartly dressed men were clearly bearers of bad news. By this time Alex was in floods of tears and being comforted by Sandra. Commodore Vincent and John Lloyd Carswell bid their sad farewells. As they headed across the gravelled courtyard to their car and their waiting driver Carswell asked the commodore,

'Where to next?'

'I think after that I need a stiff drink,' replied the commodore. 'Driver, could you find us a quiet country pub.'

Two days later Alex and Sandra were watching the news on television when there was reference to very heavy fighting in Norway and the Aurora was specifically referred to as being amongst several Allied ships which had been sunk when Russian forces counter attacked with nuclear weapons. Several military 'experts' were interviewed and expressed the view that this was a very dangerous escalation of the conflict. However, the Prime Minister, Robert Stewart, counselled everyone not to panic and that NATO and its Allies were now winning.

As people became aware of what had happened Alex received messages of support from relatives and friends. Her parents soon arrived to assist and Auntie Isabella in northern Italy said she would come as soon as she could travel to England and in the meantime, she and Alex's uncle, the Count of Cavoura, would provide Alex with whatever amount of money she needed. The Ministry of Defence were in touch to advise Alex that she would soon start to receive a widow's pension. They also made reference to a forthcoming ceremony probably to be held in Central London to honour the British and Allied service people who had died in the fighting. Alex did her best to cope with this tragic situation and to keep running the farm. After all she had been having to do this since long before Eddie lost his life.

There was a small glimmer of good news when reports came through on the TV News and the radio that the Russians were being pushed out of Oslo and that Hamburg, which had been under siege from Russian forces was now clear of the enemy. Bad news came later when it was reported that the Russians were using battlefield tactical nuclear weapons against NATO forces on land. President MacConnell and Prime Minister Robert Stewart presented a united front when they threatened nuclear retaliation against Russia and that included Russian cities. President Vatutin quickly broadcast counter threats and backed these with nuclear attacks on the Norwegian town of Trondheim and the British town of Sunderland causing very heavy casualties amongst the people there and widespread destruction. Hamburg, which by now was full of NATO forces including many American troops, was also the target of a

Russian nuclear missile. Once again there was very heavy loss of life particularly as the German city had been crammed full of refugees who had been fleeing from the Russian Army advancing from the east. In response to these massive outrages the Americans and the British gave warning to the Russians that the nuclear forces of those western countries were now at the highest state of alert. Vatutin responded by launching nuclear tipped missiles against the British bases at Fairford in Gloucestershire and Lossiemouth in Scotland as well as against Shannon Airport in Ireland. As the world held its breath American and British nuclear submarines fired Trident ballistic missiles against Murmansk and Archangelsk in northern Russia causing massive damage to the Russian fleet and the port facilities there as well as very considerable casualties.

In Norfolk Alex received an invite from Moira Dunbar to come and stay with her on the Isle of Mull. Moira said that Charles was in hospital in Iceland having been airlifted there when HMS Galatea had been sunk in the same battle in which the Aurora was lost. Alex replied that she would love to take up Moira's invite once she was feeling a little better. At present she did not know which way to turn, and her life was one big disaster area. Furthermore, she felt she had a duty to oversee the running of Longfleet Farm at this extremely difficult time. In the meantime, Lucy came to offer assistance. She was very concerned about the international situation and particularly about her husband working in London.

'Will that be the next target for Vatutin's nuclear missiles?' questioned Lucy. 'I keep telling Jerome to come and work from home here in Norfolk. He says he is making arrangements but I'm still waiting. Every morning when I wake up I worry that it will be my last.'

As if to heighten her fears the TV and radio news broadcasts kept speculating as to where the next Russian nuclear warheads would strike. London was now considered to be near the top of the list as well as Birmingham and Glasgow. The following day Newcastle upon Tyne and Liverpool were hit. The missiles were not entirely accurate with the weapon aimed at Newcastle landing on South Shields while the warhead intended for Liverpool landed on Runcorn. In the meantime, reports arrived of American cities being struck by nuclear weapons. Portland, Maine and Buffalo, New York State were both devastated with many thousands of casualties which totally swamped the medical facilities in those parts of the world. Nuclear missiles were also fired at fixed missile silos in Montana where several American weapons were destroyed although the US authorities maintained that the majority of their own missiles remained undamaged and in support of this contention weapons were fired at known Russian missile installations and bomber bases. As the war escalated rapidly out of control panic set in amongst civilian populations with the inhabitants of towns and cities in Europe and America as well as in Russia fleeing en masse into the countryside. In rural Norfolk, England, local residents including Alex and Lucy found themselves assailed by crowds of frightened people who had fled from Norwich and from London. Barns and outbuildings were being forcibly occupied by refugees and when they attempted to break into the main farmhouse at Longfleet Farm, Jack Blofield and his sons had to assist Alex in trying to keep them out. On more than one occasion the residents had to fire shots into the air. It was clear that law and order was breaking down and calls to the Police for assistance went unanswered apart from an answerphone messaging service. News came in of more towns and cities being hit both in Europe and America. In Germany Berlin was hit by a Russian nuclear warhead resulting in many thousands of people killed and seriously injured. Once again the medical services were completely overwhelmed and transport systems put out of action causing widespread gridlock. Ambulances and fire engines were unable to get through streets blocked with mountains of rubble from collapsed buildings. In America Miami, Atlanta and Jacksonville became the next victims while Trenton, New Jersey was also hit. It was suspected that the Russian missile aimed at Trenton had really been aimed at New York. The President, Jack MacConnell, was under pressure to 'Nuke Moscow' and this became a rallying cry amongst right wingers in America. These threats led to reports that thousands of Muscovites were leaving the Russian capital including the Government and heading south and east. Speculation was rife that the temporary seat of the Russian Government was to be Novosibirsk or possibly Krasnoyarsk in Siberia. As if to drive home the urgent need for this move the Russian enclave of Kaliningrad in the Baltic was devastated by a nuclear attack. It was not clear whether the missiles had been fired by US or British forces but the Americans subsequently targeted Voronezh and Kursk as reprisals for American cities devastated by Russian nuclear weapons. In the Far East, the Russian port city of Vladivostok was hit by a Trident missile fired from an American nuclear submarine and Russian military installations in Kamchatka were also targeted by a salvo of nuclear missiles. The Americans intended to destroy this threat to the United States from Russian bases and missile sites in the Far East.

At Longfleet Farm Alex now slept with a loaded 12 bore shotgun under her bed. The dogs were permanently on edge and kept barking furiously. With the assistance of Jack Blofield and his friends and relations they had managed with difficulty to clear most of the barns and outbuildings of unauthorised persons, but it was necessary to be constantly vigilant. Frequently Alex would be disturbed during the night. On one particular occasion she was unable to get to sleep and heard the sound of voices at the back of the house. Taking hold of her shotgun she moved cautiously from her bed when a large shadow loomed at her bedroom window and a figure broke a pane of glass and was in the process of attempting to open the window when Alex fired both barrels. There was a shout from the figure who fell backwards to the ground below. Clearly, they were not alone and Alex caught glimpses of others dragging the wounded person to safety. In the morning Jack Blofield and Gaz assisted Alex in repairing the broken window. There was no sign of the intruders save for a trail of blood which began on the gravel below Alex's bedroom and continued for some distance into some bushes beyond the boatsheds. A search was made but no persons or bodies were found.

'See these tyre tracks,' pointed out Jack. 'They'll 'ave made off in a car or truck. Judging by the amount of blood I'd say they was in a bad way. Them twelve bores are deadly at close range.'

Alex felt that things could hardly get any worse. Her husband was dead. Death and destruction could come hurtling out of the sky at any time or some person or persons with evil intent could break into her own home and attack her. Moira's offer for her to come and stay with her on Mull was tempting but

Alex felt that at this time of crisis she needed to take care of the farm and all the animals. Her spirits were lifted very slightly when Lucy came over to the farm with Jerome. They were not the most practical of people, but their presence was welcome, and Lucy was able to be of some assistance feeding the animals and grooming the horses. At lunchtime they all sat avidly watching the news programmes on television. Breaking news was that some kind of coup d'etat was taking place in Russia. Konstantin Vatutin had left Moscow with his Government travelling east on the Trans-Siberian Railway but latest reports were that the trains they were travelling in had been attacked en route by Russian forces loyal to a General Pavel Kuznetsov. It appeared that the general's men had taken control of Moscow Radio and other media outlets including the TV networks. Konstantin Vatutin was reported to have been killed in a violent gun battle between his praetorian guard and soldiers loyal to Kuznetsov. To many people in the West it was good news but the political and military 'experts' warned that General Kuznetsov was even further to the 'Right' politically than Vatutin had been and these latest events certainly did not necessarily presage the end of hostilities.

A couple of days later Jerome and Lucy took Alex to a medical appointment in Norwich where she was given an examination and scans. Despite the traumas which Alex had endured recently the pregnancy was considered to be fairly trouble free so far. However, when the Congolese authorities were in touch with Alex trying to encourage her to return to West Africa within the next fortnight to help establish the new Game reserves and schools up country both Sandra and Lucy were emphatic that she should stay at home and try and get some rest. Alex said she would do so, but her main concern was to look after the farm. In the meantime she would arrange a bank transfer of appropriate resources to the relevant authorities in the Congo.

In the meantime the British nuclear submarine, HMS Dreadnought, which was on patrol near the southern edge of the Arctic ice sheet received orders to investigate an unidentified vessel which appeared to be stranded in pack ice to the north of Svalbard. The precise location of the ship had been difficult to establish with any accuracy. The Dreadnought proceeded under the ice towards the last reported position of this mystery vessel and after two days sonar operators on the submarine thought they detected a ship about forty miles to the north-west. Then sonar contact was lost for several hours but then regained.

'She must be practically on top of us,' commented Lieutenant Keith Baxter from the control room of the Dreadnought.

At that point, the sonar team reported a stationary ship only about five hundred metres to the west and the captain, Commander Douglas MacIntyre, ordered the submarine to surface through the ice. A party of men led by Lieutenant Baxter was then sent topside to make an initial visual inspection. They reported that the weather was clear with bright sunshine but the ship, which was British, was surrounded by a kind of green mist and difficult to discern. The reconnaissance party was duly sent off across the ice sheet. As they approached the mystery ship they experienced a strange buzzing noise and the vessel almost disappeared from sight. Briefly it vanished leaving just a big hole in the ice which it had occupied. Then the ship reappeared but still shrouded in the green mist and some members of the party reported headaches and nausea. Nevertheless, they managed to clamber aboard via the stern. Indeed, there were scramble nets draped over the sides and stern of the ship which facilitated boarding. In the helicopter hangar they found a large number of men who were either wounded or appeared unwell. Many of them were of Far Eastern ethnicity and a British sailor managed to explain that these people were survivors from a Japanese destroyer which had been hit by Russian missiles and then their Task Group had come under nuclear attack. Lieutenant Baxter and his men made their way forward and entered the Operations Room where once again they found many people alive but either wounded or ill. Baxter radioed the Dreadnought, reporting the situation on board and requesting urgent medical assistance. This was soon forthcoming, and they succeeded in resuscitating Lieutenant Commander Guy Hanson and a civilian who said her name was Dr Samantha Langley from a company called Darkforce which had supplied some of the high technology installed aboard this ship which was the frigate, Aurora. Lieutenant Baxter was well aware that the Aurora had been reported sunk a couple of weeks ago. Dr Langley explained that the Russians had detonated two or more nuclear hypersonic missiles over the Task Group and the Aurora was in the process of being overwhelmed and would most likely have been destroyed had she not programmed the Ultra system. This is how they ended up effectively entombed in the ice many hundreds of miles from the location of the Russian nuclear attack.

'It's difficult to explain,' said Dr Langley. 'But the Ultra system can not only make a ship invisible to both radar and the mark one eyeball, but it can also in effect teleport an object as big as a ship from one place to another.'

'That's just mind-blowing stuff,' replied Lieutenant Baxter. 'So that's how you got to be here stuck in the middle of the Arctic ice field.'

He proceeded to send a detailed report to Commander MacIntyre on the Dreadnought requesting icebreakers.

'Somehow we need to get aircraft up here… but that's going to be problematic,' explained Baxter. 'We have literally hundreds of sick and wounded people. Many of them need urgent hospital treatment. I understand the Aurora's captain is unconscious….in some kind of coma, it seems. Many other crew members are in a similar comatose state. I am told that the nuclear attack knocked out the Aurora's electrical systems and left her disabled apart from Ultra. A further problem to compound matters is that the Aurora has on board more than a hundred survivors from the Japanese destroyer, *Yahagi*, and many of these crewmen are in a bad state, suffering from severe burns and other injuries. There are also the effects of radiation.'

The crew of the Dreadnought did what they could to help but their medical facilities were very limited. It was to some extent a morale boost when two planes arrived fitted with skis and took away some of the most badly wounded crewmen. It was understood that they would first be flown to Greenland and then transferred to military transport aircraft and taken to hospital in Reykjavic, Iceland. After a delay more ski fitted planes arrived to take away a few more of the wounded and the Dreadnought was informed that an American nuclear powered icebreaker, the USS Arctic Challenger, was on the way to assist in clearing a passage through the ice. In the meantime the crew of HMS Dreadnought and those few members of the Aurora's crew who were capable, assisted in trying to get some systems operational aboard the frigate.

Gradually some limited power was restored with priority being given to medical facilities and weaponry. Repairs were carried out to the ship's engines and although the Aurora was initially unable to move due to being trapped in the ice the arrival of the Arctic Challenger changed the situation. With painful slowness a channel began to be cleared through thick pack ice and the Aurora followed the Arctic Challenger at little more than walking pace heading south west.

Following the Russian nuclear attack Eddie Carlisle experienced passing through a long dark tunnel during which his thoughts were dominated by home and Alex as well as his parents and other family members and friends. In his own country and in America and much of the Western World he was now regarded as a hero and highly praised. Regrettably that life appeared to have come to a premature end, and he had no idea what lay ahead, perhaps just eternal night or nothing at all. It was by any stretch of the imagination a disconcerting prospect made worse as demons began to appear before him firing guns and missiles. He reminded himself of the award of his Victoria Cross, for valour. In a logical way it also occurred to him that if he was already dead then no one should be able to cause him any further harm. Accordingly, he did his best to ignore the demons but he was still being carried down the tunnel which seemed unending. Finally, the darkness opened out into bright sunshine and he found himself in a huge port or naval base full of every kind of ship or vessel, both ancient and modern. As he stared around him in amazement, he saw battleships and aircraft carriers, frigates and destroyers and submarines as well as vessels from an earlier era altogether, Ships of the Line which would have been familiar to Nelson. Cautiously Carlisle walked forward and approached a Nelsonian era man o'war which was in the process of taking on stores and clearly being prepared to set sail and put to sea.

'I am Captain Edmund Carlisle,' explained Eddie to a Master at Arms who duly saluted. 'It is somehow difficult to explain but my ship was hit in combat with enemy forces and I suddenly found myself here. Please tell me where I am.' Carlisle duly returned the man's salute.

'Don't worry, sir,' the Master at Arms reassured him. 'The admiral is just on his way from his quarters. We've been expecting you. Here he comes now.'

Carlisle observed that the Master at Arms was wearing clothing more suited to the 18th or early 19th Centuries. The admiral smiled affably as he greeted Carlisle on the quayside and shook him warmly by the hand.

'Captain Carlisle, how good to meet you at last. I am Admiral Lord Godwinson. This fine vessel you see here is my flagship, HMS Royal Sovereign. She has one hundred guns, and her stout hull is sheathed with copper. She can outrun the fastest French Ship of the Line… but that's not really necessary nowadays. We are all at peace and that is how it should remain. Come aboard my flagship and I'll show you round and give you a guided tour.'

Carlisle did as he was instructed aware that he was being watched by many eyes of sailors from a bygone age. Some of them were busily engaged in mending and hoisting sails while others were scrubbing the wooden decks. One man was playing the flute while others sat round and listened, not so the ship's monkey who was eager to join sailors scrambling up rat lines and to help them unfurl the sails.

'Forgive me but you must be tired,' observed Admiral Godwinson when they had finished their tour of the ship. 'Come and join me for a glass of port in my quarters.'

Carlisle was glad to be able to sit in a very comfortable and well upholstered armchair while the admiral handed him a generously full glass.

'The sun's over the yardarm,' smiled Admiral Godwinson, 'so cheers.'

Carlisle cautiously took a sip of his drink and thought it was the best port he had ever tasted.

'I know it's a big change of environment, but you'll soon get used to it here,' said the admiral reassuringly. 'You'll find it very peaceful. The skies are always blue and the sunshine and fresh air are divine.'

'That sounds good,' acknowledged Carlisle, 'but when am I being sent home, sir?'

'Oh, you're not going home,' responded Admiral Godwinson.

'Not going home, sir? Why not?' questioned Eddie.

'Because you're dead,' replied the admiral.

Carlisle dropped his glass of port in shock and astonishment. Only then did he realise that his uniform and indeed he himself were covered in burns and scorch marks.

'I'm sorry to be so blunt,' apologised Admiral Godwinson, 'but you're an intelligent fellow. You were a serving naval officer in the middle of a war zone. The Russians succeeded in detonating two nuclear warheads over your task group. I'm afraid you're toast.'

'But my wife, sir. Poor Alex. What is she going to do now? She's pregnant and she has the Farm to manage and all those animals to care for.'

'I am well aware of all of this,' replied the admiral. 'I know all about you. Alex will find a way of sorting things out and she has many friends and relations... from local people to wealthy friends and her aunt and uncle in Italy have already taken steps to assist her financially.'

'I just don't know what to say or do,' responded Carlisle. 'Alex didn't deserve this... and my unborn child. I will never be able to see them... ever.'

The Master at Arms was calling that the Royal Sovereign was ready to put to sea and Admiral Godwinson apologised to Carlisle but said he had to be on hand to oversee the ship's departure. Carlisle followed him to the Quarter deck and was amazed to observe the array of warships from different eras and of different nationalities. There were French and Spanish Ships of the Line from the 18th Century, British and German Battleships, cruisers and destroyers from the World War 1 era and American and Japanese aircraft carriers, battleships and cruisers from the 1940s.

'What is this place, sir?' asked Carlisle.

'Port Valhalla,' replied the admiral as the huge white sails of the Royal Sovereign billowed outwards in the freshening breeze. 'A place fit for heroes... and you are one of them. You arrived here straight from the combat zone without having to face the Court of Divine Judgement.'

'Bow lines cast off!' someone called from for'ard.

'Stern lines cast off!' called someone else as the Royal Sovereign slowly began to move. With her huge white sails unfurled Carlisle considered the ship to be one of the most beautiful creations made by man.

The Royal Sovereign was now sailing cautiously past the packed rows of moored vessels and in some instances Carlisle was able to read their names… Indefatigable… Invincible… both lost at Jutland in 1916.

'Look… he's saluting you,' remarked Admiral Godwinson to Carlisle as the officers recognised Rear Admiral Sir Horace Hood standing by the guard rails on the Quarter deck of the Battlecruiser, Invincible, former flagship of the 3rd Battle cruiser squadron at Jutland.

Carlisle returned the salute and then saw that the whole crew of the Invincible were lining the rails cheering him and on every ship they passed he was welcomed by rousing cheers. It was the same on the Barham and the Royal Oak while on the Battleship, Prince of Wales, Carlisle could clearly make out Captain Jack Leach and Admiral Tom Philips. The Royal Sovereign was now gaining a little speed in the fresh breezes and Carlisle read the names of HM Ships Aboukir, Crecy and Hogue. Moored to a buoy at the edge of the navigation channel Carlisle was astonished to see the famous Battlecruiser, HMS Hood. The fine ship shone brightly with an ethereal brilliance in the reflected sunlight and on her port bridge wing stood Vice Admiral Holland with his distinctive white hair. All the other members of the crew were lining the rails. Eventually the Royal Sovereign cleared the vast port area and headed out into the open sea.

'Where are we going?' enquired Carlisle. 'What is our mission?'

'We are heading north,' replied Admiral Godwinson. 'Our mission is to rescue the souls of drowned sailors.'

Later the admiral invited Carlisle to join him for dinner in his quarters. Carlisle politely accepted the invite although he was not feeling at all hungry.

'I wish more than anything else that I could return to my wife and the world I have apparently left behind,' explained Carlisle.

'How many men have expressed such sentiments,' replied the admiral as he offered Carlisle another slice of tender roast beef and refilled his glass. 'Let me explain that the universe is really a very different place to the way it appears in the world you have so recently departed. Do you know, for example, that every moment which has ever occurred still exists. The problem lies in trying to access events in the past… and indeed those still to come in the future. What is more there are thousands upon thousands of parallel realities… parallel worlds with each one being a little different from the next. I think you have some awareness of this through the Darkforce Project Schrodinger system you carried on the Aurora. One aspect of the universe is the way that new realities keep branching out from the main trunk. It is like this with your own existence and everyone else's and one result of all this is that there are many copies of yourself all living in their own branches of the multiverse.'

'It is all positively mind blowing,' responded Carlisle, 'but it does not get me back to Alex and living my former life.'

The admiral smiled and offered him another glass of Port. Subsequently the admiral's personal steward, Peter, appeared with a large plum pudding which he proceeded to divide between the two officers. Admiral Godwinson rubbed his hands together and began to tuck in. Carlisle ate sufficient to be polite but by now he was feeling over tired and was glad when he was able to return to his comfortable armchair where he soon drifted off to sleep. During the night he surfaced more than once and was vaguely aware of people cleaning him up and attending to his burns and wounds. When he woke up the following morning he found himself in bed being tended by the ship's surgeon and his assistants who told him to rest and to remain where he was for the time being. Carlisle noted amongst many things that the air was feeling distinctly colder, and someone mentioned that when they had been up on deck that morning they had seen huge icebergs drifting southwards and the helmsman and the Officer of the Watch had been having to keep a sharp lookout. It was not until the following day that Carlisle was allowed to get out of bed and clad in many coats as well as heavy boots was eventually able, with assistance from sailors and medical orderlies, to go up on deck. Carlisle found a freezing environment with the Royal Sovereign's stout hull punching and crunching its way through the pack ice. Then someone was calling out,

'Ship ahoy! Over to starboard on the horizon.'

Someone passed Carlisle a telescope of a design which Nelson would have found familiar. Carlisle took a good look at the distant vessel and as the range closed he realised it was a ship of some size, perhaps twenty thousand tons.

Then, behind this unidentified vessel he discerned a second ship trailing the first which was clearly punching a channel through the ice. This second vessel was difficult to identify as it was frequently disappearing into banks of mist and fog, but Carlisle became aware that it had a familiar silhouette. Carlisle glanced around and realised that Admiral Godwinson was standing just behind him.

'I can't be sure, sir, but I think the second ship may be the Aurora,' observed Carlisle. 'It's not easy to tell because she keeps vanishing into mist and fog.'

'If you are right then we have found your ship,' responded the admiral. 'But it is not simply a matter of putting you in a long boat and rowing you across. As far as the people on those ships are concerned you are deceased and so are the rest of us. They probably can't see us at all. We are occupying a different region of space-time.'

'Then what are we to do, sir? We seem to be so close,' queried Carlisle who was now feeling extremely cold in the Arctic chill.

'I have an idea,' said Admiral Godwinson. 'But I want to speak to the ship's surgeon first. You are in a gravely weakened state after your ordeal and I want his opinion on the risks involved.'

Surgeon Commander Thomas Stafford was duly summoned from his work in the surgery and he and the admiral conferred earnestly on the technical problems and the possibility of things going badly wrong.

'He could end up trapped between two different realities,' warned Admiral Godwinson. 'I'm not sure how we'd get him out if that happened.'

'On the other hand, the fact is that he's dead already,' considered Thomas Stafford. 'I'm sorry to be blunt but in my view we have to take a leap in the dark so to speak.'

'Very well,' acknowledged the admiral. 'Captain Carlisle… are you prepared to take the risk?'

'Yes, sir. I am desperate to return to my wife and my world.'

Carlisle was helped down below decks and found himself in a dimly lit chamber deep within the bowels of the ship which contained technology of a highly advanced nature which one would certainly not expect to find in an eighteenth-century Ship of the Line. Then he was invited to lie on his back on a flat surface while he was connected up to equipment of an unknown nature. Power was applied, at first on low intensity but steadily increasing until he found himself being drawn at ever increasing speed down a black hole in the fabric of space-time. The strain placed upon him became unbearable until it felt as though his whole being including his soul were being violently torn apart. Still the power of the unknown system was increased until Carlisle felt his mind would be destroyed. He wished he had not elected to follow this route. However, the hellish experience in the dark tunnel finally eased away. He was in a lot of pain, and someone said,

'These people over here have had it, I'm afraid... Line them up in the hangar and we'll just have to bury them at sea.'

Carlisle realised he was one of those being referred to and he tried to call out but was unable to do so let alone move his limbs or his body. There was nothing he could do. The bodies of other sailors were being carried away as a prelude to being consigned to the freezing ocean.

'This one's the captain of the Aurora... Edmund Carlisle,' someone remarked. 'A big hero but he looks a sorry state now. Put him with the others.'

Carlisle felt his body being lifted and he attempted to struggle and to shout out that he was still alive and conscious. Finally, he heard a woman's voice saying,

'No... we can't just throw him in the sea. Not after all he achieved. We must try to get his body back to England.'

Carlisle recognised that it was Samantha Langley. He was aware that she was observing him closely and he made a special effort to call out.

'Hey! Wait a minute,' intervened Samantha. 'He's trying to say something. He's not dead after all.'

Other members of the crews were initially sceptical but one by one began to agree with Dr Langley and Lieutenant Baxter from the Arctic Challenger was called over. By this time Carlisle was able to murmur a few words and to gently touch Samantha's hand.

'We need to get him to proper medical facilities urgently,' announced

Lieutenant Baxter. 'Make arrangements with the Arctic Challenger to have him flown out.'

As the helicopter arrived Samantha kissed Carlisle who managed to thank her for saving his life once again. Then Carlisle was aware of being carried away until he drifted back into unconsciousness. When he finally woke up he found himself in a hospital ward with a number of other survivors from Allied warships including sailors from the *Yahagi*. He was told that he was in Reykjavik and was introduced to his consultant, Ragnar Ragnarsson, who explained to him the extent of his injuries and the initial treatment which would be prescribed. After several days Carlisle was able to sit up in bed and to begin taking a little food and water although he was still feeling generally nauseous which the medical people informed him was radiation sickness. In particular he was anxious to phone Alex to let her know he was safe in hospital and indeed he was wanting to hear that Alex herself was alright.

Back at Longfleet Farm Jack Blofield and his family rallied round to support Alex and give her all the help possible. Alex was grateful for their efforts, but she was still living a nightmare and there was no getting away from the fact that Eddie was dead. He was never coming back, and she would have to manage the farm single handedly. It was around 11am one Tuesday morning when the landline telephone rang at the farm and was answered initially by Gaz.

'Who is it, Gaz?' called Alex from the kitchen.

'It's Eddie,' replied Gaz sounding somewhat perplexed and confused.

'What?' questioned Alex and grabbed the handset from Gaz. 'Who is this?' demanded Alex. 'Are you some kind of scammer? My husband is dead and I'm in no state of mind to be fucked about at the moment. Please go away.'

Alex slammed down the handset, but the phone rang again a short while later and a Nordic voice explained,

'This is Dr Hofi Karlsdottir from the Reykjavik General Hospital. We have your husband, Captain Edmund Carlisle here. He is lucky to be alive, but I can assure you he is safe in our hands. Let me pass you over to him.'

For a moment Alex was in shock and completely lost for words. Then she managed,

'Eddie... is that really you?'

Carlisle's voice was still weak but was nevertheless recognisable to Alex.

'Yes, it is me. I have had one or two adventures which I can tell you all about when I am home. I am likely to be here in hospital in Iceland for a couple of weeks and then I think the idea is that I will be transferred to a hospital probably in London for further treatment. Tell me... are you okay? Nowhere is safe these days.'

Alex assured him that everything was as well as could be expected at Longfleet Farm and they spoke for a few minutes until Dr Karlsdottir intervened and said it was time for Eddie to rest. Indeed he remained in hospital in Iceland for five weeks until he was deemed strong enough to be sent on to England, initially to London, and subsequently to the Norwich City Hospital where Alex and others found it relatively easy to visit him. As his health slowly improved Carlisle became more impatient to be discharged from medical treatment and to be able to return to the farm and, importantly to him, to go back to sea. Commodore Vincent came to see him and to keep him updated.

'Aurora took a mighty battering,' explained the commodore. 'She'll have to be thoroughly rebuilt. Expect her to be in dock for at least a year. Realistically I'd say longer than that.'

'I'm sure I could be given a different command, sir,' grumbled Carlisle. 'What about those three frigates we've just acquired from the Brazilians? Crews will have to be found for them.'

'That's someone else's problem,' replied Commodore Vincent. 'You need to get a well-earned rest. I've already spoken to the consultant in charge of your treatment. He says you should be discharged next month. Then I shall make sure you get a decent spot of leave. You'll need to go home to your farm and help your wife to run the place. I know she's been through a lot recently and she'll need to have you around. Once you're well enough we'll fix you up with another desk job in Whitehall. I'll fix it so that you can have your old office back, next to mine.'

Carlisle sighed audibly. He wanted to throw some heavy object at the commodore but had sufficient self-control not to do anything of the sort.

'Oh, by the way,' added Commodore Vincent. 'Has it occurred to you that there have been far fewer missile attacks by the Russians during the past few weeks. I am told by reliable sources that there is a reason for this.'

'I know they've had a coup d'etat, sir,' replied Carlisle. 'No doubt they're putting more energy into fighting each other.'

'You may have a point there,' continued the commodore. 'But more specifically, when Konstantin Vatutin was deposed and killed, the firing codes for the Russian arsenal of nuclear warheads went missing and have still not been located by the new regime. Their conventional forces are now on the back foot, and they are unable to fall back on their nuclear stockpiles. I'll keep you updated as soon as I hear anything more. In the meantime, our people and the CIA are in contact with groups in Russia and the old Soviet Union who are wanting to end the war and who, in some instances, are pro-Western and even backed by the West financially.'

A nurse appeared and advised the commodore that Captain Carlisle needed to rest. Charles Vincent smiled and headed back to London. Carlisle received more visits from Alex and from friends and family. He was now counting off the days before he was due to be discharged but one morning there seemed to be a buzz in the air and security appeared tighter than usual. When he enquired of the medical staff in his ward they were noticeably tight lipped. His queries were answered at around 11-30am when the King and Queen suddenly appeared surrounded by equerries and security men as well as senior hospital consultants and staff. The King and Queen made directly for Carlisle and were most anxious to learn of his condition. They were relieved to be told that he expected to be discharged shortly to continue his convalescence at home. The Queen was emphatic that Carlisle should come over for tea at the Palace as soon as he was feeling sufficiently well enough to do so. The King went further,

'Once you're feeling a little better you must come over to Sandringham with your good wife and spend some time convalescing there. After all it's not that far from where you live. You can just hop over when the time's right.'

'Sir, I am delighted to accept your most generous invitation,' replied Carlisle, 'And I know Alex will be too. She's had a lot to contend with in the past few months as I'm sure you can understand… and of course she's pregnant with our child. I understand it's to be a boy.'

'That's wonderful news,' exclaimed the Queen. 'I'm sure he'll grow up to be a national hero like his father.'

In due course the King and Queen went on their way. For the first time in months Carlisle was metaphorically walking six feet off the ground. Time now appeared to pass quickly and before he knew it he was back at Longfleet Farm with Alex and his horse and his dogs and cats. It was summer and for once the weather was fine and warm. Jack Blofield and his sons took Eddie and Alex out sailing in the *Lord Rodney* with inevitable visits to local hostelries although Eddie had to be careful not to allow imbibing of alcohol to detrimentally affect his medication. He was still suffering some symptoms of radiation sickness although fortunately the burns were healing up well. The medical specialists had done their work effectively. As the days and weeks passed Eddie continued to make a recovery and to regain his strength. He and Alex were even able to take the *Moonbreeze* sailing on Barton Broad and to reacquaint themselves with their secret place amongst the reed beds and the wildlife. As they lay together in the aft cabin of the vintage yacht Alex considered,

'Not long ago I thought I was on my own now and I believed I would never see you again. I can't explain how bad it felt. Everyone was very helpful and rallied round but there was always a dark cloud hanging over me. When Gaz said you were on the phone that time I thought it was just some ne'r do well trying to pull a scam or just messing about.'

'Well, I came back to you,' replied Eddie. 'They don't get rid of me that easily.'

Alex rolled carefully on top of him and looked into his face, kissing him gently.

'A funny thing is, you know,' she commented, 'But you always used to have blue eyes. Now they are green.'

'I expect it's just an effect of the radiation,' replied Eddie. 'Anyway, as far as I can recall I've always had green eyes except when I was a small child, that is.'

'And another thing,' commented Alex. 'There's a very small scar behind your left ear… It's been there for years….but it's now behind your right ear.'

'I shouldn't worry,' Eddie reassured her. 'I think I got it from fencing classes at Dartmouth College.'

'You used to say it was an injury from playing Rugby,' responded Alex.

'Whatever,' shrugged Eddie. 'I'm afraid I'm rather battered and bruised these days.'

Several weeks later Carlisle found himself at Buckingham Palace as the honoured guest of the King and Queen. They were very keen to learn all about his exploits first hand but when it came to it he found difficulty talking about what he had experienced and the many people who had died. Nevertheless, he managed to maintain their interest and there were discussions about the forthcoming invitation to Sandringham.

'Alex was over the Moon when I told her,' enthused Eddie. 'It's just what she needs, and she can take a little time off from running the Farm.'

'Don't you worry, Captain Carlisle,' the Queen assured him. 'I shall take personal charge, and I will make sure she takes things easy.'

'Thank you, ma'am,' acknowledged Carlisle. 'If we're not careful she'll be off to West Africa again setting up schools and game reserves. She does that, you know.'

'That's absolutely wonderful!' enthused the Queen. 'Once she's had the baby and when this dreadful War is over I would love to arrange a royal visit out there so that I can give my direct support.'

Later that summer Eddie and Alex received their formal invitation to stay at Sandringham. The weather was fine and warm, and they enjoyed relaxing in the grounds and playing with the royal dogs. They were also introduced to some of the horses including a beautiful white mare, belonging to the Queen, called Calpurnia who had a very mild and gentle temperament such that Alex was sometimes permitted to ride her subject to suitable assistance being readily to hand bearing in mind Alex's pregnancy. Eddie rode the King's horse, Sunstar, a fine stallion but also possessing an easy-going temperament and being straightforward to control. Eddie also made the acquaintance of Ramises who occupied the next stable to Sunstar and another horse, Sun Chariot, who had won a number of races in his time and was a fine thoroughbred. Eddie expressed a strong wish to ride Sun Chariot although the King was reluctant on the ground that Eddie was still convalescing and weakened by his injuries and the effects of radiation sickness. Nevertheless, Eddie continued to plead his case and the King finally relented subject to Eddie being accompanied by several members of staff from the royal stables.

Alex and Eddie both greatly enjoyed their stay at Sandringham, and it was something of an anti-climax when they returned to normal life at Longfleet Farm although they were glad to be home amongst their own animals. They would spend a lot of time listening to radio and TV news broadcasts and Russia appeared to be descending into a state of civil war with various factions fighting each other within the country. One of these was called the Young Russians Movement which called for a pro-Western stance and even for Russia to join the EU and NATO. As well as being backed by the Western powers they received much support from a pro-Western faction in Belarus called the Front for the Freedom of Belarus which quickly took the opportunity to seize power in that country. The Western powers were now able to channel military aid through Belarus and directly into Russia.

In August Eddie and Alex were very pleased to accept an invitation from Charles and Moira Dunbar on the Isle of Mull. Charles was still recovering from his own injuries and having to take things easy, and Alex believed that Mull was the perfect place for Eddie to convalesce. This time they brought Eddie's dog, Sam, and the Labradors, Elsa, Zara and Barley in the back of the Range Rover. Eddie found the long drive up to the Western Isles tiring and they spent the first couple of days of their visit mainly just relaxing at the Dunbar's farmstead. However, Charles eventually suggested they take the Maid of Lorn to visit some of the neighbouring islands. The weather was glorious, and the Hebrides were seen at their very best. The Carlisle family dogs joined Bob and Madge out on deck sniffing the bracing fresh air and there was much barking when a pod of dolphins appeared and proceeded to splash and cavort playfully around the fishing cruiser. Alex was fascinated when a huge basking shark became visible just below the surface in the clear waters. By around noon they had reached the Isle of Coll and found the sheltered bay with its fine white sands which Alex and Eddie had experienced on their first visit. Charles gently dug the bows of the Maid of Lorn into the soft sand while Carlisle put an anchor over the stern. All the dogs were keen to jump into the cooling sea before heading up the beach. The humans followed at a more sedate pace and succeeded in finding the perfect spot which was both sheltered from the winds but where they were also able to bask in the warm sunshine. There was no one else around. The beach was deserted apart from themselves, and the women were able to sunbathe naked while Charles and Eddie played with the dogs. Time seemed to stand still and Alex considered how lucky she was to be here, with Eddie, and to have survived everything they had both endured during the past year. At length Moira remarked,

'There's just one thing… Eddie had a mole on the left cheek of his behind. Now it's on his right cheek. How does one explain that?'

'I expect it's one of the effects of the nuclear explosion,' replied Alex. 'He suffered many burns to his skin, and he's had to have a lot of medical treatment including skin grafts.'

'It's been the same for Charles,' acknowledged Moira. 'We're just glad to have them back more or less in one piece.'

The holiday in the Western Isles was over all too soon and Alex and Eddie returned to Longfleet Farm. As September turned into October the weather deteriorated and became wet. Carlisle felt he had regained sufficient strength to return to work on a part time basis three days per week in his former office in Whitehall next door to Commodore Vincent. He found it dull and uninspiring, but he had no illusions that he was lucky to still be alive. Alex would soon be giving birth to their son. This prospect had been one of the main driving forces maintaining his will to survive. On one particularly damp and miserable Monday morning Carlisle's desk telephone rang. It was his secretary, Naomi,

'Dr Langley is here to see you, sir.'

Samantha appeared in the office dressed in expensive but tasteful clothing. Her hair was finely coiffured, and her makeup was similarly of top quality.

'You look a million dollars,' praised Eddie as Samantha embraced him tightly. When she released her grip Carlisle saw that her eyes were wet.

'It's good to have you back,' said Samantha quietly. 'Have you got time for a bite of lunch? I've got my new car outside. I'll take you for a spin.'

Carlisle glanced at his watch and noted it was nearly 12-45pm.

'I don't have any other appointments or engagements this afternoon,' he responded. 'Just this great heap of files... but what the hell. I'm glad to accept your invite.'

Within minutes they were speeding through the streets of Central London in Samantha's 'new' car, a classic black 1976 Dodge. Eddie thought the car was very appropriate as they weaved in and out of the heavy traffic and more than once Samantha went through a red light. Amazingly they arrived in one piece at the Savoy. Inside they were greeted by the charming head waiter,

'Ah, Doctor Langley. I have your usual table available,' he announced.

Samantha introduced Captain Edmund Carlisle.

'I am proud to have this opportunity to shake your hand,' smiled the head waiter as he guided them to their seats and menus were handed out.

Despite the stringencies and the rationing Carlisle was able to choose a large fillet steak while Samantha opted for Scottish smoked salmon. Once they had finished their main course a waiter produced what he called a visitors' book and invited both Carlisle and Samantha to sign it.

'Do you have to go back to work today?' Samantha enquired of Eddie. 'You had that enormous stack of files on your desk.'

'They can wait,' replied Carlisle dismissively. 'Besides... I'm just easing back into work one step at a time. I think it'll be a while before I get my command back... and poor old Aurora needs a full rebuild after the battering she took.'

'We all took a battering,' responded Samantha. 'It's incredible that we've come back. Eddie... you know they gave you up as lost. You had no pulse. You were no longer breathing, and they were going to chuck you overboard. Don't take this the wrong way, Eddie, but you were dead. I don't know how you managed it but you're here... very much alive.'

'I have Admiral Lord Godwinson to thank... and Surgeon Commander

Stafford and his team,' explained Carlisle. 'Without them I would just have been thrown to the fishes.'

'Who are those people?' questioned Samantha as a waiter brought their desserts.

'You might well ask,' smiled Eddie. 'I'd say they were not of this world... not the one we are familiar with.'

'You know, the real world is not as we generally perceive it,' considered Samantha as she stirred her coffee thoughtfully. 'Have you read Irwin Schrodinger...? The concept that a cat in a box could be alive or dead at the same time?'

'Yes, I did read it a few years ago and the concept of many worlds,' replied Eddie. 'I know what you mean about the universe... or multiverse... being hard to fathom. I'm still trying hard to work it out and it remains a mystery.'

'Have I shown you my luxury apartment I've just bought in Eton Square?' asked Samantha, changing the subject. 'It's cost me a mere £7 million.'

'I'd love to see it,' said Eddie.

In a very short time Samantha drove them round to Eton Square and parked the Dodge in an underground private car park. The apartment was decorated in a Georgian style with high ceilings and Chippendale furniture. The main living room was spacious although Carlisle guessed it might feel cold in the winter. There was a library with oak panelling and shelves filled from floor to ceiling with books on many subjects. Carlisle liked the Wine Tasting room and Samantha explained that she had a large cellar full of bottles of wine as well as brandy some of them being of unusual vintages. Inevitably they arrived at the master bedroom. There were six other bedrooms, but this one was the largest and contained a four poster bed of generous dimensions. Knowing Samantha well it was not a surprise to Eddie when she embraced him tightly and he found himself propelled into the four- poster with Samantha lying on top of him and removing his clothing as well as her own. Eddie then thought of Alex and expressed his concerns. Samantha continued to make passionate love. Eventually she felt temporarily replete and lay naked beside Eddie running her well-manicured fingers through the hairs on his chest.

'Eddie, I've been thinking,' began Samantha cautiously. 'I'm not getting any younger but as you know I'm a very independent kind of person. I enjoy the jet setting lifestyle without family ties. I have all the things that money can buy. Notwithstanding those factors I think it would be a shame to remain childless.'

'Well, you'd need a daddy,' considered Eddie. 'If you're thinking of making babies. Perhaps you have someone in mind who would fulfil that role?'

'Actually… yes. Don't get me wrong, Eddie. After procreation you wouldn't have to do anything,' stammered Samantha. 'I have all the money I need, and I'd be able to hire a nanny to look after the child while I was away on business or at sea.'

'Samantha, you know I can't agree to that,' retorted Eddie. 'Alex is due to have her baby soon and my loyalty has to be to her.'

'I promise you… Alex would not have to know about what I'm suggesting,' argued Samantha. 'But you owe me, Eddie. I've saved your life so many times.'

'Samantha, I will never forget that. I think about it every day, but I don't know what is for the best. Give me time... and what about your own health? We both need to get over the effects of radiation sickness.'

'I guess we do,' replied Samantha reluctantly.

For a while Eddie fell asleep until sometime later he surfaced and heard the rain rattling against the bedroom windows. Samantha was strumming her big guitar sitting naked at the foot of the large bed with the curtains open. When she saw that Eddie was awake she performed a good rendition of 'Monday, Monday' by the Mamas and the Papas followed by 'California Dreaming'.

'My Daddy bought me this guitar the Christmas before he left home,' explained Samantha. 'At least it gives me something to remind me of him. I met him again recently, you know. I don't think it was in this world. He died of a heart attack a while back. It was after we got nuked that I saw him again. I think I was dead, but he told me to go back… my time had not yet come and there was much that I still had to do.'

Samantha continued to play her big guitar. The rain was getting worse as she sang *'Look Through my Window'*:-

'... And the rain beats on my roof...

Look through my window...'

Samantha continued to play her guitar and sing until Eddie drew her to him and they made love once more.

In early December Alex gave birth to a son whom she and Eddie christened Samuel Charles, the first name being inspired by Eddie's illustrious ancestor. Both Eddie and Alex were thrilled when the King and Queen visited the hospital in Norwich and the Queen cradled new born Samuel in her arms. The Queen said she would love the Carlisles to pay a further visit to Sandringham and arrangements could be made in due course. Once home to Longfleet Farm, Samuel immediately became the centre of everyone's attention. Alex was very glad to have the benefit of Sandra's practical assistance saying that the new arrival came without an instruction manual. Inevitably there were many sleepless nights, but Eddie found much pleasure in watching his son grow and develop and he would hurry home early on the train from London on Fridays to be with his family. Sometimes when he was not snowed under with work or with his family responsibilities and the farm, he would reflect upon how fortunate he had been to survive at all. He was mindful of what Samantha Langley had told him that at one point he had been given up for dead. Indeed, he recalled his experience aboard the Royal Sovereign and the considerable help given to him by Admiral Lord Godwinson and Surgeon Commander Stafford and his team. He had much to be grateful for. Somehow, they had succeeded in bringing him back to life. There was a point he could recall when his very body and soul felt as though they were being prised apart by some unknown force. In a dream or vision which he had experienced he had not survived in this world. On the Aurora his body had been consigned to the icy waters of the Arctic Ocean and what was presumably his soul had been taken back to Port Valhalla. Admiral Godwinson and Surgeon Commander Stafford explained to him that unfortunately he was still dead in the context of the world he had recently left but they had managed to transfer a copy of him back there who was alive and able to return to normal life.

'I'm afraid it is rather complex,' explained Admiral Godwinson. 'You are both dead and alive at the same time but as far as Alex is concerned she has got you back. You are Schrodinger's cat... both alive and dead at the same time. Albert Einstein said that God does not play dice. Well... he had a point but not in the way he meant it. We managed to resuscitate a significant part of your being by prising it away from the main trunk of your existence so that you are now on a branch in a separate world or reality. There are many other alternate versions of you living in their own independent worlds. This is so for every human being. The universe... or multiverse, I should say...is a vast and complex structure.'

'Will I be able to return to my original reality?' asked Carlisle as he contemplated a world without Alex and indeed without his child.

'To be absolutely frank and honest for all intents and purposes you are stuck here,' replied Admiral Godwinson. 'Alex will join you when it is her time. But do not lose heart. Your family have arranged a grand homecoming for you. Look over there.'

Carlisle saw the golden cornfields stretching out towards the sea, the white painted windmill with its sails turning slowly in the gentle breeze and there was the Carlisle family home with his parents and a large gathering of aunts and uncles and grandparents and people from earlier generations. He quickly recognised Great Uncle Samuel. There was also his Great Grandfather James who had served with distinction in the Navy in the Second World War.

'John Lennon maintained that, 'Nothing is real', remarked Admiral Godwinson who was still standing at his side. 'But you are not a ghost. Everything is real. One could say that this world which you now occupy is more real than the one you have recently left.'

'We knew you were coming,' smiled Eddie's father. 'Your Mother is over the moon. Come with me. There are so many people who want to see you and congratulate you.'

'Go with him,' instructed Admiral Godwinson. 'This is your day. You are the hero... the celebrity.'

Everyone welcomed Eddie with open arms. All these people felt very solid and real. Then there was a great banquet spread out in the dining room with lobster and other seafood dishes, venison and other kinds of game, roasts and sumptuous puddings and desserts. Eddie considered that the food was delicious, and he complimented his hosts effusively. There was no rationing or shortages here. It was very much a land of plenty. Eddie's father, Charles Carlisle, was similarly generous in opening his best vintages of wines and champagnes followed by brandies and fine single malt whiskies. Eventually Eddie felt his head beginning to spin somewhat and he sat down in a comfortable armchair whereupon several cats vied to sit in his lap. He was their hero too. Half asleep, Eddie began to relax and listened to the background music. Someone had been playing a compilation of hits from the Sixties and Seventies and the song by John Lennon entitled *'Nobody Told Me'* appeared particularly appropriate in this situation in which he found himself:

    'Nobody told me there'd be days like these....'

At this point Eddie was roused from his slumber when a number of honoured guests arrived at the party including Admiral Nelson with Lady Hamilton. They were introduced to Eddie by Great Uncle Samuel and Eddie noticed immediately that Nelson was physically complete having both eyes and both arms. Nevertheless, he was still a man of small and light stature. Admiral *Lord Rodney* also appeared, having arrived in the same carriage as Nelson. Not long afterwards Winston Churchill also arrived at the party complete with big cigar and his wife, Clementine. Eddie's Great Grandfather, James Carlisle, also introduced Admiral Sir James Somerville and Vice Admiral Lancelot Holland. They all shook Eddie warmly by the hand and all seemed very solid and real. A little while later George Harrison and John Lennon arrived at the large country house in a white chauffeur driven Rolls Royce. They created quite a stir and Admiral Godwinson was a little concerned that Eddie should not be upstaged on his special day.

'Hi, man, nothing is real,' John Lennon greeted Eddie as they shook hands.

'I beg to differ,' interrupted Lord Godwinson brusquely. 'Everything is real. God has spoken.'